Silvern

Silvern

CHRISTINA FARLEY

SKYSCAPE

SKYSCAPE

Published by Skyscape, New York

www.apub.com

ISBN-13: 9781477820353 (hardcover)
ISBN-10: 1477820353 (hardcover)
ISBN-13: 9781477820346 (paperback)
ISBN-10: 1477820345 (paperback)

Library of Congress Control Number: 2014902141

Cover illustration by Cliff Nielsen

Printed in the United States of America

For Mom and Dad,
who showed me not only the beauty of language,
but also love.

CHAPTER 1

Sometimes winning *is* everything.

My Tae Kwon Do instructor says my obsession with winning isn't healthy. But he hasn't seen his skin shrivel before his eyes. Hasn't breathed his last breath. Hasn't seen his grip loosen from his loved ones as they are carried off by dragons.

But I have. These memories are branded into my mind, a nightmare on instant replay.

Winning for me has become the difference between life and death.

Just thinking of that final fight with Haemosu, the Korean demigod obsessed with kidnapping me, and of the creepy tomb where he kept the souls of my ancestors in jars, makes my throat pinch. Sweat trickles down my back underneath my *dobok*.

I squeeze my eyes shut. *Focus*, I tell myself. *Focus on this fight. Nothing else.*

I sit cross-legged on the edge of the mat, waiting for my turn to spar. This is just a belt test, but Kukkiwon's three-story arena is packed. The stands can hold three thousand people and surround all four sides of the mat. This afternoon they are nearly full. Each section is color coded, and behind the rows of plastic seats, wide windows overlook the city. Flags of different countries and organizations stare down at me from the ceiling, and the powerful lights streaming onto the mat make everything appear glitzy and glamorous.

I have to take the final test here at the headquarters in order to get my second-degree black belt. It's mandatory for all the *dojangs* in Seoul. Otherwise I'd skip all the drama and hype. Ever since I found out about my family's curse, crowds and noise have made me jittery. Nervous. I'm always glancing over my shoulder.

But I need to be here. It's my stand against the insanity that ruled my life three months ago. It's my way to tell the ones I love that I'm stronger because of everything that happened.

Even if most days I don't believe it.

The anticipation of performing for the judges and my need to win this match send my pulse into overdrive. I inhale deep breaths. Around me, students sit calmly, waiting for their names to be called, while my muscles grow tense, prepared to spring at the slightest provocation. My best friend, Michelle, always says I'm too paranoid. Marc, my boyfriend, says it's totally normal after what I've been through. I don't want to admit to Marc that I feel the Spirit World tugging at me, calling to me in my dreams. That I'm terrified my life will never be the same.

How could it? I mean, how many girls have an ancestor who escaped being kidnapped by a Korean demigod, leaving the oldest daughter of every future generation cursed with Haemosu's rage?

That is, until three months ago, when I beat the crap out of him and then killed him with a magical arrow. Remembering his death still brings a smile to my lips.

I search the sea of faces above for Marc and Michelle until I spot them halfway up the bleachers, waving. My heart warms, knowing they're here to support me. Marc is one of the few white kids in the arena, so he sticks out in the crowd. He's wearing a black henley-style shirt and dark jeans, his brown hair wild and sexy as usual. Even this far away, his green eyes seem to sparkle when he looks at me, as if I'm the most amazing thing on the planet. I touch my mouth, where the good-luck kiss he brushed against my lips still lingers.

Michelle is beside him, looking sophisticated in her black dress, which she said was in honor of my black belt status. Her long dark hair is combed straight to perfection and pinned back with two silver butterfly clips. She must be wearing heels, too, because she's almost as tall as Marc. I chuckle as I adjust my shin guards. Only Michelle would come to a Tae Kwon Do belt test looking as if she were headed to the opera.

My eyes pass over the empty seat next to them. The one they saved for Dad. He's not here. Again.

He's never around. He's busier and more distant than ever. Sure, he made it to my last belt test, but that was back in Malibu before we moved to Seoul. Before my world was turned upside down.

My thoughts are interrupted when my name is called. I stride to my quadrant of the giant mat, but before I bow and face the judges, I glance back up at Marc. He shoots me a smile, but there's worry hidden beneath those eyes of his, and I know he remembers. This won't be the first time he's seen me fight. Just the first time it's not to the death.

My opponent meets me in the center of our section of the mat and nods to the judges. They frown at his lack of proper etiquette. He'll probably get a point off for it. Sizing him up, I see he's ethnic Korean like me, with long hair pulled back in a ponytail, and a trace of a mustache and beard. His *dobok* is almost shimmering. He looks like he's from another time.

His gaze finds mine and I gasp. His eyes are dark pools, so black I can't tell where his irises meet his pupils. We bow to each other, and a thread of unease curls through my belly.

"Seijak!" our instructor yells out, signaling the beginning of the fight.

I spring to the ready stance, bouncing on the balls of my feet. He comes at me with a quick front-kick. I retaliate by stepping to the side and giving a twisting-kick, smacking him in the side of his arm.

Leaping to the right, he side-kicks into my shoulder, so swift I don't even see it coming. I stumble, shocked at his power. In a blur, he's already in front of me again, kicking me in the chest.

My body flies backward and lands hard on the mat. Stunned, I gasp for air. Maybe I've lost my touch. This guy isn't even breathing heavily, and his expression hasn't once changed.

A shimmering dome rises from the floor and circles the two of us like some kind of shield, muffling the sounds of the stadium.

My heart rams against my rib cage as I sit and frantically crane my neck. Outside this strange wall, the crowd looks intently on the match while the judges bury their chins in their hands, eyes glazed as if they couldn't be more bored. No one seems to notice anything.

I stagger to my feet and scan the room for Marc. I need to see him. I need to look into his eyes and know everything is going to be okay.

Finally, I spot him moving in slow motion. He's slowly, so slowly, standing, reaching out to me, mouth opened as if screaming. The shield has somehow altered time. I can see the whites of his eyes despite our distance.

My heart stops. Ever since Marc was struck in the eyes by Haemosu, he's been able to see the supernatural.

And the terror in his face tells me everything.

This man with empty eyes before me isn't from our world. He's from the Spirit World. It's as if I've stopped breathing. This shouldn't be happening.

I killed Haemosu. I'm supposed to be free of the curse.

I sprint toward the exit. I don't care that I'll lose. My black belt is no longer important. But I smack into the shimmery barrier. It bends slightly to my body weight as if made of a clear, rubbery substance, but it keeps me inside, trapped. I run its entire perimeter, pushing against it and hoping for a weakness.

There isn't one.

My opponent cocks his head to the side, unfazed or perhaps amused as I scramble around like a mouse caught by the tail. I'm imprisoned with a guy whose empty eyes mirror death. I should feel strong, unstoppable with the memory of defeating Haemosu. But I don't. Fear grips me as images of pain and suffering numb my muscles.

My attacker breaks into a run with unbelievable speed, attacking me with a roundhouse-kick. Somehow my body unfreezes. I sidestep and duck, twisting around and giving a back-kick. Reeling, he recovers and jabs a front-punch. I jump higher than I'd thought humanly possible and spin in a double roundhouse, nailing him in the forehead. He staggers backward, his expression unchanging.

I race at him before he can recover. As I lift my leg in a front-kick, he grabs my foot, twisting it, and I crash to the ground. Pain shoots up my leg. In a normal world, I'd be writhing in agony. But whatever shield this lunatic has put around us, it must be connected to the Spirit World. Its power floods my body.

I'm invincible.

He bounces to his feet and slices the air with his fist. I block it, then rotate into a wheel-kick, causing him to lurch. Leaping up, I snap out a jump-kick, and he drops to the mat.

A half glance at the judges' bored faces tell me they see none of this. I don't know what they see, but it's definitely not me fighting for my life. I'm on my own.

I kick the guy again. Again and again until I know he won't stand back up. Then I punch him. Pain shatters through my fist, but I don't care. I shove every bit of leftover anger at Haemosu into each blow.

This is my life, and I claim it as my own.

I step back, heaving from my endless pounding. I stare down at my hands. They are bloody, shaking. A rush flows through me. I've defeated him. The triumph of winning energizes me.

A rush of wind whips around the two of us, sucking up the man at my feet.

And then a voice echoes through the dome. "Most impressive, Jae Hwa, descendant of the water god. I will be watching you."

The man vanishes, along with the shimmery dome, and I'm left alone on the mat. I face the judges, waiting for them to exclaim in shock, but they just write something down and wave me off the mat.

Numbly, I turn to see Marc leaping over the barrier between the audience and the competitors' area. Looking at his face, I know he saw the entire fight. I slip off my helmet, letting it drop to the floor. My long braid tumbles over my shoulder, and I stagger to him. When he reaches me, he draws me into his arms, clutching me so fiercely I think I might suffocate.

"Oh my God," Marc says. "I couldn't get to you!"

I shudder, burying my face into his chest, drinking in the smell of him.

"What the hell was that?" he says. "I thought this Spirit World stuff was over."

"So did I." I bite back tears. Here I thought I'd left my worries over the Spirit World behind when I killed Haemosu. But it's happening all over again.

I knead my fingers over my temples. I can't live like this, knowing for the rest of my life I'll be haunted and tortured by immortals trying to kill me.

This has to stop. Because it's only a matter of time before I lose.

CHAPTER 2

"I think you were in a time warp," Marc says into my ear. "I tried to help you, but I couldn't get there fast enough."

His arms tighten around me, and I sag against him, listening to the thump of his heartbeat.

One of the instructors runs over to us. "You two must get off the mat. They can't start the match until you leave."

"Let's get out of here," I mumble.

After I take off the rest of my protective gear, we head out into the main hallway. His arm drapes over my shoulders, but his muscles are tense. Before we leave, Marc gives the arena one final glance.

"Anything?" I ask, afraid of what he might see.

"Nothing."

Michelle comes running up to us, teetering a little in her heels and holding my backpack in her hand. "Guys, where are you going?" she asks, and then her eyes focus on my hands. "Girl. Your hands. They're bleeding. You should get them wrapped."

"There isn't time." Marc pushes me into the hallway. "We've got to get out of here."

"Thanks for grabbing my bag," I tell Michelle, flashing her a half smile. "She's right. I can't go in public in my uniform with bloody hands."

Marc groans, running his hands through his hair as I hurry into the bathroom. The blood washes off, snaking down the drain like a tail of a dragon. I slip on my jeans, T-shirt, and sneakers. Just as I'm pulling my long hair into a twist-bun, Michelle peeks inside.

"You okay in here?" Michelle asks.

"I'm fine," I lie.

"Marc says I'm supposed to check on you." She lets the door slam behind her and slides next to me at the sink counter.

I hope she won't insist I get medical help or something drastic. Every time I enter the Spirit World, my wounds heal at an insanely accelerated pace. I'm hoping the same thing will happen this time, since that shield was somehow connected to the Spirit World.

Still, a lump of guilt wedges against my chest. Michelle is my best friend, but I never told her what I went through when Haemosu hunted me down to capture my soul.

She pulls out a tube of lipstick and slathers it on. "Sometimes Marc acts stalkerish, don't you think? It's like he can't let you out of his sight."

"He just gets worried about me." I try to smile. It doesn't work. Marc has reasons for his paranoia.

"I guess so." She shrugs. "There are all kinds of crazy out there."

"No kidding." I splash water over my face and pick up my pack. "I've got to get out of here."

"You can't just leave." Michelle's heels echo on the tile floor as she follows me out of the bathroom. "What about your second-degree belt? Don't you need to stay to get it?"

"I just want to go home," I say.

Marc's on the phone talking to—I'd bet a million bucks—my grandfather. He hangs up when he sees me. I already know he won't tell me what the conversation was about, and I can't stop that twist of annoyance in my chest.

"But I thought you said this was important to you." Michelle rushes after us to the front doors.

"Not really," I say and bite my lip, hating how vague I'm being. If anyone has the right to know what's going on, it's Michelle, and my guilt only grows with each lie.

"Who were you talking to?" I ask Marc.

"Your grandfather," he says. "Left a message."

"You didn't tell him what just happened." I know it's not fair to be angry at Marc, but sometimes I want to be the one calling the shots here and not have him calling up my grandfather over every little incident.

"No, but I told him we had a code red." He crosses his arms and glares at me. "Don't look at me like that. If you were in my shoes, you'd be doing the same thing. I'm not about to let you get hurt again. Not if I have any way to stop it from happening first."

We burst outside, the sky as gray as the building we just left. The air is damp and smells of spring. It'll probably rain soon. Marc turns right and sets a fast, clipped pace toward the

Gangnam subway station. It's a fifteen-minute walk, but I need the fresh air to think through what just happened.

The small, two-lane road is canopied with trees and lined with cars. We exit the Kukkiwon grounds by passing under the blue-tiled roof-gate and out onto the busy road.

"Something's wrong," Michelle says, "and somebody better tell me what's going on, right now."

I stop and cross my arms as I watch the black and silver cars speed by us. "The guy I just fought was trying to hurt me," I finally admit.

Marc's pointed look warns me to be quiet.

"But didn't you beat the crap out of him?" Michelle asks. "He should be worried about you. You may look tiny, but from what I saw back there, you throw a mean kick."

I stare at her, wondering what everyone else in the stadium actually saw. I'm about to ask, but decide saying nothing is a better choice. "It's a little more complicated than that," I say.

We continue on in silence. I try to focus on the normal around me, like the chestnut seller we pass, steam from the cooker curling into the air, carrying its sharp scent. Or the first hints of cherry blossoms giving the sky above a burst of color. Or the way the women have replaced their winter boots with the latest wedges. I'm always amazed at the sharp contrasts of Seoul's post–Korean War buildings of flat concrete blocks, plastered with faded signs and advertisements, mixed in with modern architectural works that could almost belong in a futuristic world. There are buildings that remind me of ocean waves and others resembling Lego creations.

Even though it's only mid-afternoon, the sidewalks are already crowded. Gangnam is a popular hot spot for people to shop and eat. We weave through the throngs of pedestrians who are out enjoying this Saturday afternoon before the rain hits.

I dare to glance over at Michelle; her face is tight, lips pressed together. I decide to tell her the truth. At least, the watered-down version.

"Remember when we went on the junior class ski trip? Well, there was this guy who was, um . . . stalking me. So after that whole incident, I kind of freak out easily."

"You had a stalker?" Michelle grabs my shoulders and stops me in the middle of the sidewalk, completely interrupting the flow of pedestrian traffic. "Why didn't you tell me this earlier?"

I shrug, thinking maybe it's good I'm not telling her the whole truth. When I was hunting Haemosu, he kidnapped my aunt, Marc, and my grandfather, knowing they were my weaknesses. I was able to save Marc and Grandfather, but my aunt is still lying in a coma in the hospital. I don't want to put anyone else in danger, especially Michelle.

"He's been taken care of, though," Marc adds, but his words don't come out as confident as I'd like them to be. "We should get going."

He's worried, I realize. His eyes keep shifting as if searching for something, and I wonder if there's something he hasn't told me. I hate keeping secrets, and after everything Marc and I have been through, I certainly don't want us having secrets from each other.

The sidewalk is lined with vendors selling massive plump strawberries, *dak-gangjeong*, shoes, and handbags. I contemplate stopping at the *dak-gangjeong* stall, because I love that sweet-and-sour fried chicken. But when Michelle doesn't even attempt to stop at the shoe cart, I know she's thinking. Hard. That troubles me.

We finally arrive at the subway entrance, which looks like a glass beehive tunneling underground. We head down the concrete steps of the subway station, and Michelle hooks her arm around my elbow and squeezes me.

"I'm glad everything is okay," she says. "You can tell me about this stuff, you know."

"Thanks," I say, knowing I can't. Not completely. But it still warms me that she's here.

We cross the lobby and scan our subway cards before heading down another flight of stairs. It's midday, so the platform is relatively empty. I can't help but feel a little paranoid in the subway after running into a *dokkaebi* in the train tunnels. I shudder, remembering the giant troll's ugly red skin and bulging eyes. But there are no monsters here.

"You okay?" Marc asks as we step inside the train.

I stiffen. I appreciate Marc always trying to be there for me, but sometimes he gets a little overprotective. Maybe Michelle's right.

"You don't have to ask me every second if I'm okay," I snap. "I can handle a few bumps along the way."

Marc's eyebrows rise. "That was more than just a bump back there. You don't have to act all brave for me."

"Yeah, I know." I can't look at either of them. "I'm fine. Just bad memories. That's all."

"You should see a therapist." Michelle sways with the movement of the train. "Otherwise you'll be scarred for life."

Too late for that. Besides, if I told a therapist, she'd be scheduling me appointments for a decade.

The train roars down the tunnel. Why did that guy come for me in the middle of my belt test? Who was he? Who will be watching me? I lean against the pole and rub my head, remembering the jars filled with my ancestor's ashes. Pouring Komo's remains over the magical orb. Komo swirling back to life. I grip the steel pole until my knuckles are red.

"I'm transferring to the green line," I announce.

Marc's eyebrows knit together. "Why?"

"I know this sounds stupid, but I need to see Komo. Make sure she's okay."

"How is your aunt doing?" Michelle says.

I shrug. "No change."

When I rescued Komo from Haemosu's tomb, I used the power of one of the magical orbs of Korea to bring her back to life. But no matter what we do, she remains in a coma. It's been months since she entered the hospital. No signs of recovery.

"I'll go with you." Marc lightly touches my arm.

"I'll be fine. You saw me back there. I kicked his butt." But when I see that worry creep across his face, I say, "If you want to."

"Then I'm coming, too," Michelle announces, straightening her designer rain jacket. "Afterward, we'll go out and do something wild and crazy and forget about creepy stalkers."

"That sounds great," I say, almost believing it.

The doors swoosh open, and the three of us get off to switch to the green line. Soon we arrive at the Yonsei station, near the university. Posters for the Seoul Arts Festival and the latest k-dramas plaster the walls. The subway corridors are packed with college students wearing tight spring jackets and scarves. With my nerves on hyperactive mode, I find it all stifling. I rush up the stairs, focusing on breathing in and out and trying to keep my panic at bay.

Rainwater has made the ground slick and puddle heavy, but we've avoided the shower. The three of us walk along the uneven sidewalk of Sinchon, ducking in and out of the crowds. A flower cart catches my eye—stacks and stacks of perfect roses arranged by color. I buy a half dozen on a whim. Even though I've visited Komo only in the winter, I remember the thorny rosebushes lining her house. Maybe she'll recognize the smell of these roses.

The ground rises the closer we get to Yonsei University, which is at the base of Ansan Mountain.

Michelle huffs beside me. "Do we have to sprint there?" she says.

"Sorry." I slow down, but it pains me to do so. I blink away images of Komo's bed being empty. Or her bloody body being dragged away by Haemosu's wild boar, just like before.

He's gone, I tell myself. *He can't hurt us anymore.*

I clench my fists, desperate to believe those words.

The air quiets as we leave the bustle of Sinchon's crowds, distance muting the traffic and the cries of the street vendors. Ivy clings to the university's stone buildings, and the maze gardens remind me of Europe.

"Are your parents working today?" I ask Marc, trying to focus on something else. Both his parents are professors of religious studies here on the campus.

"Not on Saturdays. They're probably planning their big trip to China."

"Didn't they just get back from Norway or something?" I say.

Marc laughs. "Yeah, and I'm still mad at them for not taking me. I'm guilt-tripping them into bringing me to Xi'an, though."

We veer right from the main drag and head to the hospital, our shoes crunching on the gravel path. My heart rate speeds up and my muscles tense. Every bush seems to come to life. Marc pauses to let Michelle catch up, but I notice how his eyes stray to the forest and the alleys between the buildings.

"I don't notice anything unusual," Marc says.

"Good," I say, selfishly glad he can see the nonhuman creatures. "I need to get over my paranoia."

"You have every reason to be paranoid," Marc says. "Paranoia has kept you alive."

When we enter Severance Hospital, the air has the familiar scent of antiseptic. The entire front entrance and the ceiling are glass, which allows sunlight to stream inside, creating a perfect environment for the gardens scattered about the lobby, where a string quartet is playing classical music. We skirt past the chrome columns and duck inside the glass elevator.

"I know they're trying to make this place all pretty and nice," Michelle says, pinning her hair into place, "but hospitals creep me out."

"I guess I'm used to it now," I say. "I try to come every week at least."

After I check in with the nurse, I turn to Marc and Michelle. "If you guys don't mind, I'd like to see Komo alone."

"Of course." Michelle perches on one of the chairs lining the wall and pulls out her phone. "We'll wait here."

"If you need anything, let me know," Marc says, but his brow is furrowed, and he's got that brooding expression on his face. It must be taking every inch of his willpower to not demand to follow me. But he pulls out his phone and settles next to Michelle.

I give them a half wave with my bouquet and proceed down the hallway, my sneakers squeaking on the freshly cleaned floor. But when I reach Komo's door, I hesitate, my hand on the cold knob. I swallow hard, hoping I'm wrong and Komo's perfectly safe. I step inside, and my eyes dart to her bed.

She's there, buried under a pile of blankets. Her head rests on a tumble of pillows, and her eyes are closed. The soft rising of her chest tells me she's alive, and I let a long breath of relief. Gently, I close the door, and as I do my emotions almost come rolling out of me. Tears creep to the corners of my eyes, and the room swirls for a moment. I realize how panicked I'd become thinking they'd come after her.

I hover by the door until I pull myself together.

"Komo," I say, knowing she can't respond, but hoping somehow she can hear me. "It's me. Your niece, Jae Hwa."

Quietly, I fill a cup with water and arrange the roses on the nightstand next to her bed. They fill the room with a sweet scent. I pick up her brush and slowly comb her black hair, sprinkled with gray, until it fans out perfectly on her pillow. Then I press down her blankets, crisp and tight, and sit next to her.

This has become our routine these past few months. The tightness in my chest releases with the familiarity.

"Today was my belt test." I finger the corner of the sheet. "A guy showed up. I think he was from the Spirit World."

Before she had been taken by Haemosu, her eyes would light at those words, and a plan of action would spin through her mind. But she doesn't move. Her face keeps its peaceful lines.

"I'm scared," I admit, and curl my fingers around her hand. "I thought I'd left all that behind when I killed Haemosu. I don't understand why someone would want to hurt me. He wanted to *kill* me, Komo. I need you to tell me what to do. I need your help, Komo."

Something rattles behind me. I stiffen and jerk to face the noise. The room remains unchanged. With only a bed and nightstand, its sparseness could qualify for a convent. Grandfather and Dad insisted she get a private room, but now, sitting here, jumping at every rustle and creak, I'm not sure if that was the best idea.

Slowly, I edge off the bed and tiptoe my way to the bathroom. Maybe what I heard was just an orderly pushing a trolley?

Or a tray falling in the next room?

I slip my hand around the wall and flick on the switch. Nothing here but a toilet and sink. I shake my head at my paranoia.

But then, out of the corner of my eye, a flicker of black catches my attention. I squint at the mirror. I shuffle closer.

It isn't my face staring back at me, but a dark-clothed figure.

I scream.

"Jae Hwa," lips whisper, blanketed in darkness. "Come. We must talk."

I push off the sink to escape but slip and fall across the floor. I scramble to my knees and crawl out of the bathroom. A cold pressure clamps around my ankle, dragging me backward. I throw myself against the pull, clawing at the ground with one hand while the other grabs for the doorframe. My leg throbs as if it's being yanked out of its socket.

I'm hauled across the floor, back into the bathroom, toward the sink.

"Marc!" I can't stop screaming. Someone *must* hear me.

Terror explodes through every inch of my body as I'm dragged upward and sucked into the mirror.

CHAPTER 3

Darkness rolls around me in thick tendrils. I'm lying on my belly, and the cold stone floor stings my palms. I sit and take in my surroundings. A domed glass ceiling hangs over the large circular room, revealing a midnight sky. The stone walls are the color of onyx, with silver engravings etched into them. A quick glance tells me they're actually pictures forming a narrative, one after the next.

Hundreds of candles are suspended from the ceiling, hanging upside down. Their flames dangle beneath their holders, reminiscent of snakes' tongues snapping out at their prey. Black mist drifts across the floor, moving as if alive, seeking to consume anything in its path.

My attention is drawn to the dark-clothed figure standing on a dais in the dome's center. His features are obscured in black except for two piercing silver eyes. They stare at me, cutting through the darkness like knives.

"I have been so eager to meet you," the figure says in a deep, vibrating voice.

"Who are you?" My voice is a whisper. "Where am I?"

"Ah, you do not recognize me?" The figure glides around the room. "The ruler of the darkness? The dweller of the night? The keeper of evil?"

"Kud," I say. Standing before me is the god of darkness. The god Haemosu was working for. My heart sinks.

"Indeed." Kud sounds pleased with my knowledge of his existence. I don't like him happy. Not one bit. "The Spirit World speaks of your greatness. Your power."

I swallow the lump in my throat and stand on shaking legs. "I've no idea what you're talking about."

"Do not mistake me for a fool. Of course, you know what I speak of. Your land awaits you, its ruler."

"I think you've got me confused with someone else." I scan the room for a way to escape. "Why am I here?"

"You've ruined everything," he spits harshly.

I'm glad I ruined whatever hell-bent plan he had connived. I know I must tread carefully, but still, I want him angry.

"I don't know what you're talking about," I say, trying to sound carefree, flippant even. Anything but let him see the fear racing through me.

And then, far, far away, I hear a voice.

Marc?

"Haemosu and I were going to change everything," Kud continues, raising his fist in emphasis. "Joined as one, we would no longer be limited to night or day. Our power would be limitless, and not even Palk would be able to stop us. But you went and killed Haemosu."

"Yes, I did." I lift my chin. "He had my ancestors' souls. He deserved the fate he got."

Kud shakes his head and clucks his tongue. "Foolish child. To think you could stand against me."

I know I should've learned not to anger these immortals, but they make it so freaking hard. Then the room begins to spin. What's happening? The pictures on the walls glow to life, moving and interacting as if they're mini-TVs. Each one has its own story playing before my eyes.

"We are running out of time," Kud snaps. "Where is the orb?"

I blink, confused. According to my grandfather, there were six orbs sent from the heavens to create Korea. But over time, nearly all the orbs were lost or put into hiding by the Guardians of Shinshi. The only orb I've ever seen was the blue one Haemosu had stolen.

"I gave Haemosu's orb to Palk," I say. "It's now where it belongs."

Kud growls. His growl amplifies until it shakes the room. The floor quakes, and I stumble and fall to the ground. "No!" he shrieks. "Now Palk's power will only increase!"

Seeing Kud's reaction, I'm even more glad—gleeful, even—that I gave Palk the orb. Kud paces the room, the tentacles of his cape swirling around him in a storm.

"All is not lost. There are two left that haven't been found," Kud says. "Bring them to me."

As if I'm actually going to help him. I press my hands to my sides to keep them from shaking. "I'll pass." I scowl. "A job like that really calls for an expert. You understand. Where's the exit to this forsaken place?"

"Oh, my dear. How wrong you are. It was you who defeated Haemosu. It was you who killed my most prized assassin today. I underestimated you. But now I see how perfect you are for what I need."

I stiffen. Kud sent his assassin to kill me? And now he wants me to do his dirty work? Crap. I swivel, searching the walls. There has to be a way out of here.

"I know what ails your aunt," he said.

"You do?" I bite my lip, wishing I hadn't shown any interest. He'll only use it against me. Stupid, stupid.

"She is lost. The White Tiger orb is the only thing that can find her. It seeks the lost and awakens courage in the weak. Bring me this orb, and I will help you find her."

Marc's voice rings across the room again, calling my name over and over. His voice sounds forever away, as if he's at the end of a distant tunnel. Then I notice one of the moving pictures has me in it. I watch as my own life plays before my eyes.

Me blowing out my birthday candles, hugging my mom, riding in the subway, sitting in class. How is this possible?

And then Marc's in the picture, his eyes blazing green, his fingers reaching for mine. The pictures spin around and around the room. I break into a run, chasing after the mural with the scenes of my life flashing through it. This has to be the way out. My escape from this monster.

"I cannot let you leave until you agree to help me," Kud says from his dais. "We could be great together, you and I."

I race in an endless circle around Kud. The room sways, and I stagger from dizziness. I'm gasping, heaving for air. My legs ache, and I realize I'll never catch up to the picture with Marc. It's a merry-go-round that can never be caught.

I stop, bend over, and glance up at Kud. The mist contorting around me, I realize, is actually pieces of his cloak snaking around my legs, pythons ready to strike.

I glare at him. "I will never work with you."

"Your aunt does not have much more time. Are you willing to risk her life for your stubbornness? But perhaps it is your grandfather's and father's lives that you find more valuable. I am sure you could be coaxed into an agreement."

I gape at him in horror. And then, just as my story picture comes careening back around, I leap and dive into the picture. I reach for Marc's hand, praying and hoping that it's a portal and not a wall.

My body slides through the picture. The stone surface stretches and bends around my body as if I'm diving through thick sludge. Marc's palm clasps hold of mine, and his fingers wrap and squeeze my hand, sending tingles through me like electricity.

For a moment, we're lost in time. Between worlds. For a breath, it's only Marc and me, caught in forever and never. Our eyes meet, and I know, I *know*, he would go to the end of the world and die right there for me.

The thought shatters as something seizes my ankle. I glance over my shoulder. It's one of the black tentacles, dragging me back. My skin is stretched, my muscles pulled, and my hip bones snap one by one. My body screams in agony. Marc's fingers start to slip from mine.

I can't let him go. I cry out in frustration and pain. Then, through a watery mirage, I see Michelle race up next to Marc, something in her hand. Tiny scissors. How will she get into this space between worlds?

Undaunted, she reaches out and starts cutting at the misty tentacle wrapped around my ankle. The grip loosens.

Then I'm free and tumbling into Marc's arms. Back in the world where I belong.

CHAPTER 4

"What in freaking heaven's name was that?" Michelle asks, her voice a half screech, half quiver.

I press my fingers over my eyes, wishing I could erase those last few moments. I'd thought that after killing Haemosu and telling Palk I didn't want a part in the Spirit World, my connection to that world would whisk away, and I could be normal again.

I was so wrong. It was foolish of me to even think that.

Marc rubs my arms and pulls me up and out of the bathroom just as a nurse hurries into the room. The nurse's face is bunched up in worry lines.

"Neo gwaenchanh ni?" she asks us.

"Everything is fine," Marc tells her in Korean. "She just slipped in the bathroom."

"Okay." The nurse nods, eying us all curiously before leaving. "But if your noise continues, I will call security."

"Normally I'd be saying how weird it is that you speak better Korean than me," Michelle tells Marc as she paces the room, "but what happened just a minute ago was beyond bizarre."

Marc leads me to Komo's bed, and I perch on its edge.

"I shouldn't have left you," he says, his jaw ticking.

"I thought I'd never have to go back to the Spirit World," I say numbly. "But there I was. All over again."

"It doesn't make sense." Marc begins pacing the room. "This is supposed to be over. Haemosu is gone. What happened? What was that place?"

I shrug. "Kud's hangout, I guess. I don't even know. I don't want to know."

"Kud?" Marc swears under his breath.

"Who's Kud?" Michelle practically yells, throwing her arms up. "What was that back there? You were *in* a mirror, but it wasn't a mirror. It was like a window or something."

"Shh." Marc looks pointedly at the door. "We don't need to get kicked out of here."

"They call him the dark god," I say. "He was supposedly plotting some scheme with Haemosu, and since I ruined that, he sent his assassin to kill me." I turn to Marc. "Apparently that guy I killed back at the Kukkiwon headquarters was his assassin."

"So he's ticked," Marc says.

"You killed someone?" Michelle gawks at me.

"Yes and yes." I bury my face in my hands. "I can't deal with all of this right now."

"Okay," Michelle says. "I get why Marc's all stalkerish now."

"Stalkerish?" Marc says. "I am *not* stalkerish."

"Um . . . you are," Michelle says.

"Will everyone stop the nonsense," I practically yell, "and focus on our problem?"

"Listen," Marc tells Michelle. "I'll explain everything later. Right now we need to figure out what to do next."

"I need to talk to Haraboji." I pull out my phone to call my grandfather. "He'll know what to do."

"You know your grandfather will call the whole Council, especially with two hits in one day." Marc runs his hands through his hair. "It means you'll have to get involved."

"I'm way past getting involved." I take Komo's warm hand in mine and squeeze it. Somehow I need to find a way to get out of this situation. Kud's warning vibrates through my mind. He'll hunt them all down. Every one of my family members, because a god like that won't be satisfied with killing just my dad and grandfather. Nothing will stop him unless I work with him.

Haraboji doesn't answer the phone. *Figures.*

"Sitting around isn't going to solve anything," Michelle says. "I propose we get some food. I can never think clearly on an empty stomach. Besides, Jae is about to pass out, and Marc, you look like the walking dead."

The three of us head down the hill into Sinchon for *kalbi*. Normally my mouth would be watering just thinking about Korean barbecue and steamed rice, but right now it's chalk-dry and my stomach won't stop rolling. When we step into the restaurant, it's swarming with college students. I put my name in for the next open table, practically yelling at the hostess since the restaurant is so loud.

This place is a popular hangout, with floor-to-ceiling glass walls and round, candy-colored paper lanterns hanging from above. Small rectangular tables rest low to the ground in traditional Korean style with built-in stoves in their centers. Seeing all of this reminds me of the last time Marc and I were here. We'd come after the APAC basketball tournament, secretly, since Dad still wasn't thrilled about me dating Marc. I'll never forget that feeling of pure happiness. No demanding calls from Grandfather or Komo, just the two of us daring each other to eat the most—or endure the spiciest bite. No strange creatures chasing us down.

That was just a facade, I now realize. I had been living in an imaginary world.

While we wait for a table to open up, I try to call Grandfather again. If anyone would know what to do with this mess, he'd know. But he doesn't answer. I could kill him. This isn't the time to decide to go phoneless.

"Haraboji!" I yell into his answering service, probably too loud, but really, he needs to start using his phone. "Call me back. ASAP. This is *important*."

"You think your grandfather can help you?" Michelle asks. A white sheen still covers her face, and her hands shake. I hope she'll be able to recover after seeing what she saw today.

"Yes." I try to use my most confident voice. "He's an expert in this kind of stuff."

Finally, we get a table, and my stomach starts growling. Maybe because I skipped breakfast this morning. After I order us a meal to feed ten, Michelle wags a finger at me.

"No more secrets," she says. "There's something going on. Something big, and I want to know what it is. I'm tired of all your riddles and half explanations."

Marc rubs the side of his jaw and looks at me. I shrug and take a sip of my Coke.

"She did see it with her own eyes," I tell Marc. "Who knows what kind of trouble we'd be in if she hadn't intervened?"

"Think of the Spirit World and our world as parallel lines." Marc turns the meat over on the griddle in the table's center. "Each world is separate, but they move at different speeds. And in some places, they touch each other."

"If the worlds touch," I add, picking two straws from our Cokes and bending them so one part touches, but the other parts of the straws don't, "they can enter our world and we can enter theirs. It seems there are specific places that are more likely to connect. Especially if they have a spiritual connection either through an object or a historical place. Does that make sense?"

"No, not at all." Michelle taps her chopsticks on the table. "We need to talk to Kumar and Lily about this. This is huge. Kumar's so smart, he'll know what to do. We've got to find somebody who can help you."

"No!" Marc and I yell at the same time.

I scan the restaurant. The dishes clank in the kitchen. A group in the corner laughs and then raises their glasses in a toast. The couple next to us glances our way, but resume talking. I let out a short breath. Thank God for noisy college hangouts.

"You can't tell anyone about this," I say, quieter this time. "As a punishment for being sent to jail, the dean has me seeing the counselor, and Dad's already considering therapy to stop me from 'seeing things.'"

"Girl, after seeing what I saw, I might need therapy. There's nothing wrong with that."

"Dad takes things to the extreme," I say. "I can't risk it."

"There's a council that I'm a part of," Marc explains to Michelle. "They are the best suited for this. In fact, this kind of thing is exactly what the Council was created for."

My phone rings. It's Grandfather. "Haraboji?" I say. "What took you so long to call back? Why aren't you answering your phone?"

"The Council has called an emergency meeting," Grandfather says, totally ignoring my comment. "We have already assembled and discussed a plan. They want you to come."

My head reels. I hadn't expected this. "Me? But I'm not a member. I didn't think I was allowed at your secret meetings."

"Things have changed," he says in his brisk, deep voice. "Marc will be getting a call shortly. He'll escort you there."

Escort? I rub my forehead. Sometimes Grandfather acts like he's from the last century. "Okay."

"Until then, *annyeong kyeseyo*." And he hangs up.

I set my phone down just as Marc's rings. His eyes find mine as he listens to the person on the other line. I suddenly notice his ring. It's no longer a simple gold band. It has the symbol of the Tiger of Shinshi engraved on it. Things have just gone from complicated to impossibly complicated.

"We've got to go," Marc tells me as he puts his phone away. "They're already assembling."

"Your ring," I say. "It has a tiger on it now."

"They inducted me last night." Marc stares at the ring and then back at me. He lets out a long breath. "I wanted to tell you in person over dinner, after your belt test."

It's finally happened. He's now an official Guardian of Shinshi. I should be thrilled for him. This is something he's wanted for a long time. The truth is I don't want him a part of any of this. My chest pricks knowing that as one of the Guardians of Shinshi, he'll be sent on secret missions as a defender and protector of Korea's heritage. Without me.

He'll be putting himself in danger every time. He could get hurt, killed even.

It's bad enough that my grandfather is all cloak-and-dagger, since he's a member of the Council. But to have my boyfriend be a part of it all, too? It's not settling in so well.

"Don't look at me like that," Marc says, his eyes pleading. "You know what this means to me."

"Congratulations." Guilt tugs at me, and I force a smile. "We'll have to celebrate."

"Yes." He rolls the ring around his finger. "After we make sure you're safe." Worry flicks across his features. He tosses some *won* on the table. "We should go."

I pick up my chopsticks and stuff my mouth with rice. "Not until I eat something. I'm starved."

"They don't like to be kept waiting." Marc jams his hands into his pockets.

"And I really don't like being told what to do."

"Leave her alone," Michelle says. "She should eat. Especially after going through such a traumatic situation."

I check the steak, and seeing it's cooked enough, blow on it and pop it into my mouth. "Listen, I know it's not your fault that the Council of Shinshi is insanely obsessed with protocol, but they can wait two minutes, so I can shovel some food down my throat."

Michelle ticks the ends of her perfectly manicured nails on the table. "These council people need to chill. Personally, I don't like any of it. Jae, you really should stop and think about this. Do you have to go? Maybe if you just ignore this crazy Kud guy, he'll leave you alone."

Marc snorts and crosses his arms, but he doesn't say anything, so I've got to give him some credit.

"He's the one pursuing me," I say, not caring that my mouth is full. "He seems to think I have some special ability or something that can help him. Which is ridiculous, but whatever."

I rip out tiny square napkins from the table dispenser, stacking them into a pile. Then I load them with meat strips. Grease spills onto the table, but it will do.

"Thanks, girl, for saving me back there," I say.

She stands. "I'm coming with you."

My heart twists, seeing her panicked expression.

"Afraid I can't let you," Marc says. "The Council doesn't allow outsiders. Jae Hwa will be the first exception. Ever."

"Well," Michelle huffs. "Who made you her boss?"

"Not boss," Marc says. "Protector. And the Council did."

I roll my eyes at Marc's nonsense. "Just humor him, Michelle," I say. "We both know *I'm* the real protector. Besides, I can't let you get hurt. It's too dangerous."

"I'm not an idiot." She crosses her arms, glaring. "Sure it's dangerous, but if I hadn't been back there, snipping away, who knows what would've happened. You need me. Ever think about that?"

I take her hand. "You have to promise you won't try to get involved. I could never forgive myself if anything happened to you."

"And you don't think I feel the same way?" she huffs. "Fine. But call me when you get home, so I know you're okay." Then to Marc, "And you now have my approval to stalk her."

"See you at school tomorrow." I give her a hug.

Marc puts his hand on the small of my back as we exit the restaurant. "So back to the protector thing," he says. "Who was it that found you when you were stuck fighting Haemosu or when you got lost in Kud's creepy room?"

"We'll call it a team effort, since you paid for dinner."

"If you insist." He smiles.

I can't resist that smile, and I kiss the dimple on his cheek. "I do."

There's something about Marc that one kiss doesn't satisfy. Maybe it's the feel of his body pressed against mine or the way his lips kiss me back softly and desperately all at the same time. But here I am again, wrapping my free hand behind his neck and pulling him in for more. It's not until a group of students pushes past us that I'm dragged back to reality.

We step away from each other, but I hold on to his fingers, not wanting to let the moment go.

"That was an avoidance tactic," Marc says. "You know how to make a guy forget everything. Including secret meetings."

"Where are we going?" I ask, popping the last of the steak into my mouth and wiping my hands down with a wet wipe.

"Yonsei," Marc says.

I freeze. The wipe grows cold in my palms. "The Council meets at the university?"

"Shh. It's supposed to be a secret."

We duck into the now jam-packed sidewalks where university students are browsing the stalls that line the road. The sidewalk is so full that we have to squeeze ourselves into the throng. It also doesn't help that almost everyone is going down into Sinchon, while we are going up to the university.

The neon lights illuminate the night, and the steam from the pushcart vendors curls into the sky. We pass by an *odaeng* cart, the fish skewers all neatly arranged in stacked rows, and another cart selling fresh juices. People are laughing and shoving themselves into coffee shops, and I can't help but think how every night feels like a festival in Sinchon. I grab Marc's hand, wishing we were ducking into one of the karaoke rooms along the street rather than heading to meet the Council.

It doesn't take long to make our way back under the pillared entrance and onto the Yonsei University campus. Now that it's dark, the campus has sunk into a stillness it doesn't know during the day. The shadows stretch in twisted angles, and the buildings have become looming giants.

I eye the bushes lining the path, knowing they are perfect hideouts for creatures to lurk. I jump at every noise and shadow as we cut across the diagonal of a garden maze near the back of the main campus.

We come to a small courtyard flanked by the back of Underwood Hall. The ivy growing along its stone walls reminds me of snakes crawling up its side. I shiver in the cool night air.

Marc wraps his arm around me and suggests we sit on the bench for a while.

"Why are we sitting here?" I ask, trying not to laugh. "What happened to your desperate hurry to get there? Don't tell me you want to stop for a quick make-out session?"

Marc's face leans close to mine. "Tempting, but I think we're being followed."

I peek over my shoulder and spy a shadow before it blends in with the lamppost. "Perfect. What are we going to do? Sit here all night?"

Marc runs his other hand through his hair until it looks even wilder than before. "Good question. You could beat the guy up."

"Funny," I say dryly. "Why don't we just run for it? Then we'll be too obvious for him to follow us."

In the end, we decide to backtrack and take a new route. We choose a wooded dirt path that follows a low stone wall bordering the university. It runs along the edge of a pine grove. The damp air clings to my clothes and skin. I can't stop myself from continually glancing over my shoulder, waiting for dark shadows to leap out.

I stop and squint in the dark, trying to figure out where we are. If we were to turn right, we'd end up hiking all the way to the top of Ansan Mountain. I know the back side of our school butts against Yonsei University, but I've never been so close to this side of the wall before. Here I thought school was so removed from all of this Spirit World insanity, but in fact, I'd been right in the middle of it all along.

We continue along the path, the ground uneven and root infested, and pass through a small cemetery. The cold stones glint silvery under the moonlight. I pause and study this forgotten nook of the forest. It's rare to find a cemetery in Korea, since most people are cremated, and it's even stranger to find one tucked away on top of a hill.

"An old missionary and founder cemetery," Marc says. "Most people don't even know it exists."

Once we round back down to the main buildings on the Yonsei campus, Marc hesitates, concealing himself behind the bushes and giving the area a swooping glance. Then, dragging me along, he bolts up the stone steps to the back door of the building in front of us.

Just as he reaches for the handle, the blast of a motorcycle's engine shatters the night.

CHAPTER 5

Headlights flare in the gloom around us, and I cover my eyes from the blinding brightness. The rider cuts off his engine and slides off the bike. Wearing all black leather, he practically blends in with the darkness except for the lines of silver criss-crossing his helmet. I try to push past Marc to get inside, but he doesn't budge.

"We can't let anyone see us enter," Marc whispers.

I stiffen and hold my breath.

The rider lifts his helmet and tucks it into a compartment in the back of his bike. Then, after a salute of his gloved hand, he strides to where we're standing. Marc stiffens and clears his throat.

"Kang-dae," Marc says. "I see you received the summons, too."

"Indeed," Kang-dae says with a slight British accent. Then seeing me, he smiles. *"Annyeong haseyo. Eereumee muhyehyo?"*

I don't know how to respond. Am I allowed to tell him my name? Who is this guy? And why do I feel my face burning under his intense gaze? I'd be blind to not notice how hot Kang-dae looks. Chiseled high cheekbones, piercing dark eyes, thick eyebrows, and perfect gel-styled black hair. I can already imagine Michelle and Lily swooning.

"We should get inside," Marc says. "You're supposed to be discreet, not blast up in a motorcycle."

I hurry after Marc, Kang-dae trailing behind us with easy long strides.

"Discreet?" Kang-dae laughs. "Your ridiculous slinking about in the bushes was hardly discreet. You both screamed secret mission."

Marc scowls at Kang-dae as we enter an elevator. The doors clamp shut, and Kang-dae slips a thin key into a small panel under the elevator buttons. He's wearing the same ring Marc and Grandfather wear—a gold band with the imprint of the Tiger of Shinshi on the top. When the panel flips open, Kang-dae presses his ring into the small circle in the center. The elevator jerks and begins descending.

"You still haven't told me who our guest is." Kang-dae leans against the back of the elevator, arms crossed. "I do hope you're not breaking protocol. It'd be unfortunate to lose you as a fellow brother."

"This is Jae Hwa," Marc says. "She's the one who defeated Haemosu."

"Ah." Kang-dae's eyebrows rise and he grins. "A descendant of the gods. How does that feel?"

"It pretty much sucks," I say as I focus on the numbers above the elevator doors, wishing they would move faster. But the numbers are stuck on number one. "Are we even moving?"

"The Council meets in the ancient caves," Marc explains. "It's approximately four stories below ground level."

"And this elevator is about as ancient as those caves," Kang-dae adds.

Finally, a bell rings, but the elevator still doesn't open. It's hot and stuffy in this small space even without the stifling tension between the two guys. We're all supposed to be on the same team, but from the tense conversation and the lack of eye contact, I know there must be something else going on. I decide to ask Marc about it later.

A panel slides open just above the elevator's numbers. A remote eye pops out and moves, making a quick scan of the elevator as it washes everything in its path with a crimson red.

"Wow," I say. "That's high tech."

"We can hardly have just anyone strolling into our headquarters, can we?" Kang-dae asks. "Even someone as gorgeous as you."

Marc's scowl deepens, if that's even possible. Thank God the doors groan open. I rush out of the claustrophobic elevator, which was becoming more cramped by the second. But when I step outside, I stop in surprise. We're in some type of cavern, empty except for a metal bridge that leads to a single wooden door. Spotlights illuminate the stone walls. Bands of lights glow from inside the bridge as if leading the way to the other side. I peer over the edge of the bridge's railing. The bottom is lost in emptiness.

With a swoop of his hand, Kang-dae motions for me to go ahead. "It probably won't break," he says. "But just in case, you go first."

"If you're trying to scare her," Marc says, grabbing my hand and leading me to the far door, "you're wasting your time."

"Ah yes," Kang-dae says from behind us. "She is fearless, then. Intimidated by nothing."

I frown at both of the boys. "You two give me too much credit," I say. "I'm neither. I'm just me. Nothing special."

"Obviously." Kang-dae's mouth quirks.

We reach the wooden door, which is carved with the picture of the Tiger of Shinshi. Its eyes stare down at me, and the memory of meeting him as he guarded the golden thread between the worlds tumbles back through my mind. The Tiger of Shinshi had warned me that the only way to win my battle with Haemosu was through sacrifice. I hadn't believed him until that time came.

Carved into the stone next to each corner of the door are the four immortal guardians of Korea: the Blue Dragon of the east in the bottom right corner, the White Tiger of the west in the top left corner, the Red Phoenix of the south in the bottom left corner, and the Black Turtle of the north in the top right corner.

Marc punches another code into a keypad and the door creaks open.

We enter another room; this one is square and not much bigger than my bedroom. The walls are carved out of the stone, and wooden beams in the traditional Korean colors of green, red, and yellow crisscross the ceiling. A man—a guard wearing a black robe with a massive sword hanging by his side—greets us by pressing his palms against his sides and bowing. A jagged scar runs across his forehead, and his hair is cropped in a buzz cut. From the width of his shoulders and bulk of his chest, I can tell he works out. He's not the kind of guy I'd want to encounter in an alleyway. Still, I refuse to let him intimidate me. I lift my chin higher and snap a tight nod. A sliver of a smile crosses his face, but his eyebrows rise as if he's still not sure of me.

"She's exactly how you described her," Buzz Guy tells Marc in Korean.

I glance at Marc. What has he been telling everyone about me? But Marc just gives me a mischievous grin. "Jae, this is Jung. He's my trainer."

We nod to each other as Marc grabs one of the black cloaks hanging on a peg on the stone wall and drapes it over his shoulders. As Kang-dae follows suit, I take in my surroundings and breathe in the stale, musty air. What is this place? Who carries swords around these days?

An eerie chill crawls over my arms as we head through a narrow corridor, also carved out of the rock. Candles are set into notches in the walls along the floor to light the way, but their light casts harsh shapes along the walls, which are full of paintings of Korean battle scenes, scenery, and animals. All I can think about is how much this is like something from a horror movie.

"This place is creepy," I say. "You're not going to sacrifice me or anything, right?"

"Of course not!" Marc says in a loud whisper.

"Tempting," Kang-dae says.

At the rounded archway, my steps falter. This is all so strange and new, and yet seeing Marc's confident strides, it strikes me that Marc has been here many times now. There's a whole part of Marc's life that I don't really know. A whole part of him I've never seen.

The room before me curves in an oval. Soft lights line the bare walls. A mural depicting the origins of Korea spreads above us on the ceiling. Mountains, tigers, bears, kings.

On the far side of the room rests a massive hourglass, larger than me. Black sand trickles down its center while pairs of pewter dragons stretch up the sides of the glass, as if they're counting the grains themselves.

A ring of maybe thirty emerald-colored cushions is arranged around a low wooden table inlaid with mother-of-pearl designs around its perimeter.

As we stride down the stone steps, a robed man moves toward us. I recognize him.

"Haraboji!" Relief floods me. When I first moved to Seoul, I thought Grandfather was crazy, because his stories about Haemosu seemed impossible. But now I know better. He'd do anything for me.

"Jae Hwa," he says, patting my hand. "You are safe. When I received the messages from you and Marc, I was deeply concerned. The Council agreed it was time we met with you and came to the root of the problem."

Other robed figures, most dressed in brown robes, are scattered about the room, speaking in hushed voices. They notice us and settle onto the cushions. I don't recognize any of them except Marc's dad. He sticks out like a bamboo tree among pines as the only non-Korean here besides Marc.

"Those dressed in brown are the Council members," Marc whispers in my ear. "The thin, shorter guy is Mr. Han. He's the head of the Council. The others wearing black like me are Guardians."

I make a quick count. Only five Guardians. "What's the difference between the two?" I ask.

"The Council members once were Guardians," Marc explains, "but they have retired from the battles and missions. Now they mainly focus on the decision making. The Guardians do all the grunt work."

Marc flashes me a smile and squeezes my arm, making me feel a little less overwhelmed. Meanwhile, Grandfather indicates for me to stand next to him.

"Greetings, you who are dedicated to the preservation of Korea," Grandfather begins, speaking in Korean. "At our last gathering, we came to you with wonderful news. Haemosu was defeated by Jae Hwa, who today stands before you. The third orb of six was returned to its rightful place in the Heavenly Chest."

A murmur of approval rushes through the room, and I stare straight ahead, trying my best to appear unfazed by all of the attention.

"We thought our worries had ended with Haemosu's demise," Grandfather continues. "Apparently we could not have been more wrong." Grandfather motions to me to take his place. "Tell the Council what happened today."

I rub my sweaty hands down my jeans. The weight of today's events sinks deep into my shoulders. It's only a matter of time before I buckle under the strain of it.

"Annyeong haseyo." I bow and then tell them what happened.

I wait for the Council to respond, but instead, the group sits in an agonizingly long silence. Oddly, it's Marc who speaks first.

"Can't you all see that Jae's in danger?" he asks. "*Again*, I might add. We need to find a way to protect her, because what we're doing isn't working. Who knows if Kud will let her free next time? He's only allowing her to live because he thinks she's valuable. What if he one day decides she isn't useful any longer?"

"If the dark god thinks Jae Hwa is useful," one of the robed figures says, "we should take notice. She could be beneficial to us."

"She's not yours to control," Marc snaps, clenching the sides of his robe.

I resist throwing glares at the robed ones. They act as if I'm some weapon they can use on a whim.

"Jae Hwa," the thin man says, standing. He gathers his robes and positions himself before the group. His face is lined and heavy; dark circles ring his eyes as if he hasn't slept in years. "I am Mr. Han, head of the Council. It is my role to keep Korea safe, and I do not take that lightly. You are a descendant of Princess Yuhwa. Whether you like it or not, you have powers in the Spirit World and you can use them."

"Your powers are a burden you must face, but I will not allow you to face this alone," Grandfather tells me, and then he stares accusingly at the group. "Nor will I allow you to become a pawn of anyone."

"So does this mean I really need to leave the country this time to be safe?"

"That is an option." Grandfather sighs. "It is one I suggested long ago."

"If she leaves," Kang-dae says, "we have no chance of retrieving this orb. She's our best hope."

Grandfather shoots him a sharp look. "You are too young to understand. She is not a Guardian. This is not her battle. We cannot put this burden on her."

"It is the only way," Mr. Han says. "Tell her our plan."

Jung rushes to Mr. Han's side, takes the offered remote, and holds it to the ceiling. The lights along the walls dim, and a three-dimensional hologram springs to life before us: six orbs as planets orbiting the sun.

"There were six heavenly artifacts, or orbs, brought to Korea at the beginning of time," Jung begins. "Each orb gave the land power. There was a time when the land was peaceful and the artifacts were safe among the people. Until Kud, the dark god, captured the Red Phoenix orb for himself. The wielder of this artifact is gifted with great power when engulfed in anger. Thrilled with this newfound control, Kud began to seek the other orbs. This is why the Guardians of Shinshi were formed: to search for the orbs and prevent them from falling into the wrong hands."

An amber orb radiates and enlarges above us in the hologram. "The Samjoko orb was the first to be secured safely in the Heavenly Chest, due to the help of Mr. Grayson here."

I glance over at Marc's dad, who nods gravely. Then the jade orb is enlarged before us. "The Chollima's artifact, known for giving its wielder the power of flight, also has been returned to the Heavenly Chest."

"Next we have the Blue Dragon's artifact," Jung says as the blue orb grows larger, swirling with cobalt bands. "It was discovered by Lee Jae Hwa after she defeated Haemosu. It, too, has been returned to the Heavenly Chest."

"Finally, the two remaining artifacts we've yet to discover. There is the Black Turtle orb, which gives its owner the ability to stop time. Some believe it has been lost to us forever; we have yet to find any written record of it since the first century. And then there is the one that has been brought into question today. The White Tiger orb."

The hologram focuses on the final orb. It is silky white, shimmering as a star on a winter night.

"No Guardian has ever laid eyes on the White Tiger orb," he says. "But the ancient manuscripts have drawings and descriptions of it. The White Tiger orb can seek objects, including the other orbs. If Kud gains possession of this orb, then he can find the location of the Heavenly Chest, and Korea is doomed."

"But it isn't just about Korea," Marc's dad says. "Each orb gives its wielder strength, so if a deity were to hold all six orbs, that immortal would have unlimited power. With that kind of power, one could rule the world. Our agreement with the other guardian sects around the globe has stood firm ever since World War II. We must not allow matters to get out of hand again."

"If the Triads or Illuminati were to hear of our perilous situation," Mr. Han says, "they would be at our doorstep this minute, which is the last thing we need."

"There are other guardian groups around the world?" I whisper to Marc.

He leans in close. "I'm just learning a little at a time. But each country has a group bound to keep the mythological creatures within their country in check."

"My bones ache, telling me that this is our time of action," Mr. Han says with a clap of his hands, catching my attention.

"Our order has waited a millennium to retrieve the White Tiger orb and bring it to the Heavenly Chest. Never have we had someone with us who is skilled in our world, but also has power in the Spirit World."

Fantastic. They've signed me up before I've even had the chance to refuse.

"I say it's the perfect time," Kang-dae says, his face glowing under the red hologram. "I am willing to assist in any way needed."

"This task is too great for my granddaughter to take on," Grandfather says. "She has suffered already. I cannot ask more of her."

My heart swells as I watch Grandfather argue on my behalf. Yet at the same time, I can't stop that flutter inside me reminding me of Kud's threats. I need more time to figure out a way around his demands. And hadn't Mr. Han said I was the Guardians' best chance to find this artifact? He had a point. I'm the only one who can easily travel between worlds, and I have the power to shape-shift and fight in the Spirit World. Still, all of this sounds exactly like what Kud would want me to do, and I don't like the idea of pleasing him—or of falling into a trap.

"I need a little clarification." I interrupt the group when I stand, terribly disrespectful, but I am beyond caring at this point. "Are you asking me to actually do what Kud suggests? Don't you find that awfully convenient? What if he follows me? He's got these magical TVs that can see snapshots of all of our lives. He probably knows I'm here in your underground location right now."

In fact, the more I think about Kud, the more unsettled I get. I drop back to my cushion, clenching my fists, wishing for my punching bag to release some of this nervous energy.

"Jae is right. Why seek trouble?" Marc's dad asks. "We should wait until we must take action. Let's not rush into anything."

"Besides," Marc says. "We have no idea where this orb might be."

"That is not *completely* accurate. We have an inkling of its location." Mr. Han nods to a heavier-set Council member. "Ms. Byun, it is time to show them our plan."

Ms. Byun never sat down with the rest of us, I realize, but has been standing off in the shadows holding a long tube in her hands. At Mr. Han's nod, she steps into the light and slips out a sheet of rice paper. As she unfurls the paper on the table, I realize it's an ancient painting. The paper is yellowed and its colors are muted, with the ends shredded along the sides.

Ms. Byun leans back after securing the ends to the table beneath the projector. The painting's image is cast onto the screen behind Mr. Han. It's a mural of endless mountains.

"I don't understand," Marc says. "What is this painting's significance?"

"I know this mountain range," Kang-dae says. "It's Kumgangsan."

Marc's face blanches. "North Korea."

"Now you understand," Grandfather mutters.

"And this"—Ms. Byun points to an egg-like shape, tucked inside the mountains with lines shooting out from it like a starburst—"we believe is an orb."

I take a deep breath, trying to process what these Council members are saying. "You want me to go to North Korea?"

The room remains silent.

Mr. Han draws back his hood, revealing his full features. His hairline has receded but is still black, probably dyed. His cheeks are sunken from age, but he has a strong jawline and his shrewd eyes stare back, challenging me. "We cannot let fear dissuade us. The time is now."

His eyes turn and focus on the hourglass. The sand trills down in a steady stream. I'm not sure what the hourglass means, but the top half has decidedly less sand than the bottom half. There's something about the hourglass that sends a trickle of fear through me, and the ache of loss.

"I am still against sending teenagers into that forsaken land," Ms. Byun says, leaning closer to the map. "It is irresponsible."

"You dare speak to me of responsibility?" Mr. Han's voice vibrates through the cavern. "The safety of Korea, perhaps of our entire world, rests on obtaining this orb before Kud does. To ignore this would be irresponsible."

"Kumgangsan is a very large area." Ms. Byun waves her hands over the map. "How can we even know where to begin? Besides, if we know this information, then Kud must, too."

"But he hasn't found it," Marc's dad says. "Otherwise he wouldn't be asking for Jae Hwa's help. You give him too much credit."

"True," Grandfather says. "We must not forget that like all immortals, Kud's powers are limited in our world. This inhibits him and has been our one advantage thus far."

"And yet you do not give Jae Hwa and Marc Grayson enough credit." Mr. Han strolls the perimeter of the group. "She has fought immortals and walked away victorious. Marc has time and again proven his ability to protect her with his unusual sight. Do not let their age deceive you."

I can't help feeling inspired by this strange, thin Councilman. He doesn't snub me for my age or look at it as a handicap. Instead, he is assessing me by my ability.

The argument continues, round and round. I watch them go from a perfectly calm group to a heated one. Some wanting the orb to be found, others willing to leave it be and hope Kud doesn't find it first. I don't know what the best way is, but if Kud can't get me to find the orb for him, he'll kill my family and then find someone else to do it. I am just one human of many.

But Komo lingers in the back of my mind, her limp hand in mine, her spirit lost, wandering aimlessly. I press my fingers over my eyelids to shut out the visions. I've already lost Mom. If it's in my power to save Komo, I need to try.

I stand, decided. "I will go." As I utter the words, the Council falls into silence. "I can't guarantee I can find anything, but if you can send me to this Kumgangsan area, I'll do my best to help however I can. All I ask is that I don't go alone."

The group stares at me, as if considering my offer. I shift uncomfortably in the utter silence. Why doesn't anyone say anything?

"I offer my services as well," Kang-dae says, stepping forward. "This is a mission that must not fail. I have more experience than Marc and can be an asset to the team."

"There's no way she's going without me," Marc says, bristling and glaring at Kang-dae as he comes to stand at my side.

I flash him a grateful smile. His obsession with protecting me can get annoying sometimes, but I can't deny I kind of like it, too.

Finally, Grandfather says, "I cannot approve of this, Jae Hwa." His face looks pained as he speaks. "I nearly lost you last time. But if you will go into the heart of the enemy's territory, I will be at your side."

"You know I hate to send your granddaughter into the face of danger again," Mr. Han says. "But she is our best option. Not only is she a strong fighter, she has the advantage of having fought and defeated immortals before."

As if on cue, Jung strides back to the front of the room and clicks his remote, showing us the border station of North and South Korea: the DMZ line. My stomach sinks as he doles out our instructions. "You will travel in a group. In the past, we've worked in solitude to maintain secrecy, but the risk is too great to do so. Your mission must look like anything but a mission. It must appear normal. Ordinary. This will be your greatest challenge."

"Kud may be powerful, but he is hardly omniscient," Mr. Han says.

Grandfather scoffs. "So what is your plan?"

"North Korean authorities are known to give out tourist visas to humanitarian groups. Jae Hwa and the three of you as representative Guardians will go into North Korea under the guise of a medical relief team. We propose you get the National Honors Society to organize a medical volunteer trip to North Korea. We will make sure you have all the necessary documents."

"Kud will be suspicious," I say.

"Then make sure he is not." Mr. Han leans down and raises his thin eyebrows at me. "It will be your job to give the world the idea that this is a school-funded humanitarian trip."

The Council starts talking again as if a decision has been made. I'm going. Now they must decide how it will unfold. I rub my hands up and down my jeans, wondering what kind of insanity I've gotten myself into.

CHAPTER 6

The next day as I ride in the car with Dad driving down the highway toward his favorite golf course, Sky 72, I know I'm not much company. My mind can't stop trying to dissect everything that happened at the meeting last night.

Dad is explaining his latest work with Netlife in providing food and supplies to impoverished areas. I try to focus on what he's saying, but I keep thinking about the Council and how Marc is a full-fledged Guardian. I bite my lip, trying to decide if Marc's involvement is a good thing or not.

Tomorrow at our NHS meeting, Marc and I will invent a reason for us as NHS students to visit North Korea. Meanwhile, the Council will work on procuring our visas to enter the country.

"How is school going?" Dad asks as he pulls into the parking lot. He's dressed in khakis and a navy collared polo shirt. He appears relaxed today without his usual shirt and tie, and the navy brings out the color in his skin. "Are you keeping up with your grades? I don't want you slipping behind again."

"That was only because of the whole Haemosu fiasco," I say.

He turns the key, shutting off the ignition. His lips press together, and he leans back in his seat. "I thought we'd agreed that was over."

It irks me that he won't look at me. He doesn't ever look at me when we're talking about what happened with Haemosu, or, according to him, what *didn't* happen. The silence eats the space between us.

He sighs, rubbing his hands over his face. "I'm sorry I missed your black belt test. I should've been there. It was for your second degree, wasn't it?"

Nodding, I finger the edge of my bag, wondering if I should tell him I was attacked.

"I know you did great," he says, and reaches out, patting me on the shoulder. "You always do."

"I didn't pass," I blurt out. I know he can't read my thoughts and he can't possibly understand what I'm going through, but isn't that partly his fault? If he would only be more open to believing me, he might understand me better.

"Well." Dad's eyes widen in surprise. "That's okay. I'm still proud of you. And I'm sure Master Park will give you another chance."

"Thanks, Dad," I mumble. I know he means well, but I hate how my secrets widen the gap between us. I just want to tell him about the Spirit World and everything I'm going through and for him to believe me.

"I have something for you." Dad fumbles with his pocket and pulls out a blue piece of paper. "There's a lady at work who says origami creation helps relieve stress. I thought I'd give it a go." He laughs and hands me a paper fish. "It's kind of trivial, I guess, thinking about it now. The fish is supposed to represent happiness, determination, and strength. All of these are needed for the fish to swim upstream."

I hold the fish in my hand, tracing the rice paper swirls with my finger. "It's perfect."

"Good. Well." Dad taps the steering wheel and gets out of the car, signaling the end of our awkward conversation. And yet this awkwardness is our way of slowly finding each other. A beginning.

My steps are light as we stroll up to the clubhouse. The front is all glass; it looks like a swanky modern hotel. We step into the clean, sparse lobby, and I breathe in its sandalwood scent. Flat-screen TVs line the walls, tuned to golf channels. I'm tempted by the leather couches scattered throughout the area. For a moment, I imagine coming here on a date with Marc, just the two of us. No crazy mythological creatures. No choices or destinies or hunts for orbs.

I push that treacherous thought aside as I trail after Dad across the slate floor toward the onyx-colored marble reception counter. After Dad checks us in, the receptionist gives Dad a starting time, and we head to the lockers.

As soon as I step through the door, an attendant rushes to assist me.

"I'm fine," I tell her, and strip off my jeans and gray T-shirt, replacing them with the golf shorts and matching shirt that Dad bought me, insistent that I wear these particular brands. Here in Korea, it really doesn't matter if I'm a good golfer, just as long as I look the part. But I've gotten good at that, I realize. Playing the part.

After I slip on my spikes and a disgusting pink visor, I deposit my street clothes in a wooden locker and head outside to meet Dad. He's waiting for me at the starter desk downstairs. His dark hair is perfectly styled, and the pleats in his pants still look crisp and pressed despite our drive here. We find our golf bags, and I pull a nine iron while Dad gets his driver.

Of course, he has to get the biggest club in his bag. I smile. The mood and the atmosphere are finally seeping into my pores, and my muscles are just starting to relax when Dad has to go ruin it all.

"Had any more of those hallucinations lately?" He swings a practice shot.

I frown. "Why?"

"It's not something you should be ashamed of. Your grandfather used to get them after Sun, your aunt, was killed," Dad says. "You should keep me informed if you experience anything unusual."

"And then what happens? You medicate me like you wanted Grandfather to be medicated?"

The starter interrupts us, calling Dad's name. I stomp toward our cart. Meanwhile, Dad's face is resolute. We are both stubborn as mules.

"I'm trying to help." Dad's brow furrows with worry. "I know I'm not the expert at this, but you have to know I have good intentions."

I sigh and touch his arm. "You're right. I shouldn't have lost it there. Let's just have fun today and forget about anything related to crazy."

Dad laughs at that. "Sounds like a plan. It's about time I get a day off to enjoy being with my daughter."

He's right. We rarely get these moments. We deposit our bags in the back and clamber into the cart. Dad pushes the gas pedal, and the cart automatically drives down the path, following the GPS, toward the first tee box.

We wait in the cart as the group in front of us finishes. They stand perfectly still. Their entire focus is set on the current player.

"They look as if they really know what they're doing." I point to the golfers in front of us. "They won't kick me off the course for being an idiot, will they?"

"Sometimes it's not how well you golf, but how well you look the part." Dad chuckles. "If only that were the way of things in real life. Looking good won't get you anywhere. It's what you do that counts."

I think about the pressure the Council is putting on me to find this orb before Kud does. They are so desperate that they're willing to send us to North Korea. I don't even want to think about how Dad will react to the news. I want to do things that count and make our world a better place. Why does it have to be so freaking hard?

When it's our turn, Dad goes first, hitting a straight shot down the green. He twirls his club lightly in his hand, grinning. "Not bad, huh?"

"Good one, Dad." I position the ball on the ground, moving it slightly to the right, then slightly to the left. No matter where I put the ball, it seems out of place. As if it doesn't have a *right* place.

Kind of like me.

"Don't forget to bend your knees," Dad says. "And your feet should be shoulder width apart."

I shift, trying to follow all of Dad's directions.

"Pull back more," he adds. "Your grip is slightly off."

"It's too much, Dad!" I blow out a long breath, my shoulders knotted and tense. "Just let me hit it!"

Thankfully, Dad steps back. I swing and *bam!* The ball sails through the air. Right into the woods. My mouth gapes open.

"Nice hit, except you hit it in the OB area," Dad says with a snort. At my questioning look, he explains. "'Out-of-bounds' markers."

"So I'll just hit another ball." I move to grab another ball from our basket.

Muttering under his breath, Dad stalks to the cart. "Get in," he says. "We'll go get it."

"You can't be serious."

"That's one of my lucky balls," he explains, "and I don't want to lose it."

"Why are we even golfing with those balls? They should be on a shelf somewhere."

I groan as Dad turns off the GPS and veers the cart toward the wooded area. Once we get out of the cart, I hesitate at the white wooden block stuck in the ground, marking the area we aren't allowed to pass.

"Won't we get into trouble?" I scrutinize the greens for any security carts that might see us.

But Dad marches across the marker, jaw tight and eyes scanning the ground for my white ball. Sure enough, it doesn't take long for security to show up.

"We need you to vacate this area," the security officer says into his megaphone. "This is a restricted space."

Dad purposely ignores the man and tromps deeper into the forest. I push past the security guard to follow Dad.

We are so going to get kicked out of here.

"Where do you think you hit it?" Dad asks me.

"This is ridiculous, Dad!" I stumble over a log trying to catch up to him. "Forget about the ball. It's just a ball. Who cares?"

"Your mother gave that set of balls to me," he says. "I wanted our day to have a little of her in it."

I let out a long breath, everything becoming clear. This is the first big thing other than moving to Korea that Dad and I've done, just the two of us. Without Mom. It's been four years since she passed away, and yet we've stuck strictly to our routine. School—work. School—work. No vacations where it was just us. No special trips. No fun outings.

Dad stops to bend over and dig through the dirt. Carefully, he lifts out a white ball buried beneath a pile of leaves. "I can't lose them. Not now."

I stare at him, catching that desperate look in his eyes. He moves toward me, and taking my hand, he presses the smooth sphere into my palm. I study the ball. It has the initials "J&H" on it. My parents' initials.

"I know you think I've lost my mind," he says, his jaw tight. "But I won't lose you either. You can call me crazy, ridiculous even, but I'll do anything to make sure that doesn't happen."

There's something scary about his expression because I know that look.

I see it in my own face whenever I stare into the mirror.

CHAPTER 7

The next day at school, I blow my hair out of my eyes as I stare at my locker. No matter what I do, I have to prepare myself every time I open it. Sure, it was three months ago, but seriously, after getting sucked into the Spirit World through this same locker and nearly being ripped to shreds, I can't stop the major anxiety attacks every time I open it.

You can do this, I tell myself as I spin the combination. *Five, four, three, two, one.*

It has become my tradition. I count down and then open it. It's cheesy, but I have to open it on one or I'm not sure if I'll ever open it. If I don't, it means I'm scared. It means I'm weak. And that's something I can't handle either.

Because I must stay strong. If I'm strong, I can survive.

I pop open the door.

"Hey, girl!" Michelle bops up to stand next to my locker. She's wearing a sparkly pink shirt, jeans, and a cropped black jacket. Her hair is pulled into a low ponytail, and her lip gloss even matches her shirt. "You coming to NHS?"

A twinge of guilt tugs at me. Once again I'm keeping secrets from Michelle. But the less Michelle knows, the better. I don't want to drag anyone into this life of mine more than I have to.

"I'm planning on it," I tell her as I toss my books into my locker and take out the ones I'll need for the rest of the day. I suck in a deep breath, trying to remember how Mr. Han suggested I broach the topic. "I have a great idea for our next NHS project."

"Excellent. I want to hear every detail," Michelle says as we head to the cafeteria to pick up lunch. "But first, how are you doing? After everything that happened in your aunt's bathroom on Saturday, I can hardly sleep."

"Tell me about it," I mutter as I pick my usual, *kimbap* and bottled water. "My only consolation is that Komo is okay. She's had no change, good or bad. The doctors said they'll call me right away if there are irregularities."

Sunlight streams through the tall glass walls as we weave our way through the tables and head outside to the veranda, where the NHS is meeting today. The concrete-floored balcony is on the second floor of this five-story building. Since the school is halfway up Ansan Mountain, there's a great view of the neighborhood, Yonhi-Dong, below. People say that Seoul's really just a big city full of small neighborhoods. Yonhi-Dong is tucked full of tile-roofed houses and tiny alleys that have turned into tight roads.

"I have a confession to make," Michelle says.

I stop midstride. "What is it?"

"I followed you. To Yonsei University."

"What?"

I think about when Marc and I stopped because he realized someone was following us. It must have been Michelle. I'm just glad we lost her in the woods. It would have made things far more complicated if she had found the actual entrance. I rub my forehead, unsure what to do with this information.

"I know this supposed secret council meets at the Yonsei campus." She's whispering now. "And I know that whatever you're planning with the NHS is about these mythological creatures."

I open my mouth to ask how, but she bats her hand through the air. "It's not like you to wake up and announce that you want to organize an event. Girl, I'm not *that* moronic. Whatever you are planning, I'm *in*." Then she bats her eyelashes and says in a mocking tone, "And if you say no, then I'm going to the police with a fun little story about the Council's secret location."

"You're blackmailing me?" I press my hand to my chest, pretending to be shocked. "My best friend?"

"If that's what it takes to help, you got that damn straight."

"I don't—I can't," I moan, and close my eyes, because we can joke around about it, but it's not a game. Not for a second. "Michelle, I told you to stay out of this. It's not safe. Trust me."

"I don't care. Because whatever you are doing, you need me, even if it's just as your personal psychologist. So I'm in, and there's nothing that's going to stop you from saying yes."

I don't know what to say, so I spin on my heels and head out onto the balcony. A light breeze brushes across my face, full of the first hints of spring, whipping my hair over my eyes. It smells of fresh-cut grass and cherry blossoms. I breathe it in, soaking in the freeness of the moment. It's in these moments that I feel truly alive. I'm breathing and soaking in the sun, and I wish it was enough. That I could abandon the Council's plan to sneak into North Korea in search of the orb.

I want to believe that there is no such thing as magic and powerful creatures that are trying to control my life and threaten my family. But that would be a lie, and the last time I tried to pretend it all away, it didn't work out so well. In fact, I ended up with a nice little golden trinket on my wrist.

My toe rams into something on the ground and I stumble. My tray slides out of my hands, my food and water bottle scattering across the ground. A hand swoops down and pulls me up. It's Marc, of course. My hero. Sporting dark jeans and a black T-shirt, looking way too adorable.

"Your water, my lady," Marc says with a twinkle in his eyes, handing me my bottle.

"Thanks." I take the bottle, its surface cool against my palm. "I was remembering a certain somebody and wasn't paying attention to where I was going."

He wraps his hands behind my neck and kisses me on the forehead. "He's gone," Marc whispers into my ear. "I remember you kicking his butt. Vividly."

"Hey, you two." Michelle bats me on the shoulder with her chopsticks. "Enough. Come and sit. We only have twenty-two minutes left of lunch."

"We'll talk later," Marc says.

"Talk?" I flash Marc a mischievous grin.

He laughs as he sits next to me. Most of the NHS students have already gathered at the concrete tables, so after we settle in, Mrs. Freeman gets right to business.

She starts off the meeting with a quick reminder of what we've been doing as a group. "We have one final project that we want to do before the end of the year. Any thoughts?"

"Lily has this great idea of doing a Dano mask party," Kumar says.

"I posted the details on the wiki," Lily adds, tucking her long blond hair behind her ears. She's biting her lips as if she's nervous. From her tense posture and wide blue eyes, I can tell this Dano mask party means a lot to her. I cringe, knowing I'm about to shove her idea aside as if it's not important. I flip open my tablet and log in to the NHS wiki. I scroll down until I find our brainstorming thread.

"I also posted an idea on the wiki last night," I tell the group.

"Jae Hwa," Mrs. Freeman says, smiling and bobbing her head vigorously. "I'm so pleased you're starting to contribute to our group."

I want to sink under the table. I don't deserve her praise. My motives are far more complicated than I could possibly explain. Instead, I plunge in. "I'd like to raise money to buy medical supplies for North Korean TB patients. And then deliver them."

Everyone stares at me, gaping mouths and saucer eyes.

"Dude," Yuuki says. "That's crazy talk."

"A death wish," Myung-Hee says, nodding. "But it's a heroic way to go down."

"I thought North Korea wasn't allowing tourists into the country," Kumar says in his usual practical voice. "Not that anyone would after that last missile launch test."

Everyone starts sharing the most horrific North Korean story they can remember. I look over at Marc, seeking his support, but he's sketching a picture in his notebook of two people lying on the beach under an umbrella. He labels it "Bora-Bora" and then shoots me a wicked grin.

"There's still time to back out," he whispers. "Think of all the fun we'd have there."

"You're not helping," I whisper. Still, a smile creeps over my face.

"What an admirable endeavor," Mrs. Freeman says, a smile plastered to her face. One that appears to be painful, as if she's trying not to grimace. "But I doubt Dr. Baker would approve."

She's right. Our principal will nix this faster than I can eat *kimbap*. My mind scrambles for a convincing argument. Honestly, it feels as if this mission is doomed before it's even begun.

"True, but I was doing some research," I say, even though it was Jung who did the research. "They do allow relief and medical aid workers in. And it's something the North Korean government encourages for their supposed reunification image."

"The Keck School of Medicine has recently started a program for their students to volunteer at a medical facility near the North Korean-Chinese border," Marc says. "If our school could provide a similar program on this southern border, think how great it would look on our college transcripts. And it'd be great media coverage for the school."

"Or bad media coverage"—Mrs. Freeman frowns—"if my students don't return."

I kick Marc under the table. "Don't mention *media*," I say under my breath.

"North Korea is currently in need of TB medicine," Marc says hurriedly. "All we need to do is raise the money and send a small group to deliver it."

"Plan on me *not* being in that small delivery group," Yuuki says.

"Hear, hear," Myung-Hee says, laughing, along with a couple of others.

"Well, we'll add this to our list of ideas," Mrs. Freeman says, and then clears her throat. "Any other proposals?"

"Jae's idea sounds fabulous." Michelle taps her manicured nails on the table. *Crap.* She's got that look in her eyes. I can already see the schemes churning through her head. "What if we use Lily's idea of doing a Dano mask party to raise money for this? We could combine both of your ideas."

"I'm game for anything," I say. To be honest, I don't care how we raise the money. If it means we're going to bring medicine to TB patients in North Korea while searching for the orb, it's a complete win in my book.

"Students, we should focus our efforts on real, tangible projects," Mrs. Freeman says, checking her watch. "We don't even know if the North Korean authorities have opened the border. Didn't they close it a few years back?"

"Actually, the entry point from Goseong has been open for six months," Marc says.

"Just realize that before any decisions are finalized," Mrs. Freeman says, "we must get approval from Dr. Baker *and* the school board." She picks up her notebook and flips the page. "Lily, do you wish to share your ideas on the Dano Festival?"

Lily stands and her long blond hair flutters in the breeze. She shoves her hands behind her back and then clasps them in front of her before clearing her throat a couple of times. "For those of you who don't know what the Dano Festival is, it's a traditional Korean holiday that falls in the fifth month after Lunar New Year. Some people call it the festival of love." Lily blushes at this, glancing over at Kumar, who is all smiles.

"Anyway," she continues, "I thought we could decorate the cafeteria with paper cherry blossoms and lanterns. Everyone would come wearing a mask, and we'd serve rice cakes and cherry punch."

"That sounds fun and expensive," Yuuki says. "How will this raise money?"

"We could charge a cover fee," Kumar suggests.

"What if we have everyone make a wishing lantern?" Lily says. "I could check out their prices over at the Namdaemun Market. People could buy the lanterns from us, write their wishes on them, and we could release them to the sky."

"That sounds great." I give Lily a high five.

"Love it." Michelle types furiously. "I say we vote, and I vote yes."

She raises her hand, daring anyone in the group to say no to her. The truth is, she runs the show. I lean back in my chair after Mrs. Freeman approves Lily's fund-raiser.

"So what are we going to use this money for?" I say.

"For your TB medicine drive," Michelle says. Mrs. Freeman raises her eyebrows. "After it's approved, of course. Jae and I can work on the proposal for the school board together. How many college applicants to Harvard organize relief aid to North

Korea? Zilch. If you ask me, it's a one-way ticket to Ivy League heaven."

"Or a one-way ticket to the morgue," Yuuki says, shrugging.

"And who wants to risk it to deliver the supplies?" Kumar asks.

I glance over at Marc. He crosses his arms and looks away. I know he's not happy about me going to investigate this orb, but the Council is right. I have the ability to fight, and Marc can spot any creature from the Spirit World in seconds. Still, the whole idea scares the heck out of me. And I haven't even broached the subject with Dad yet.

"My parents travel nearly every month to remote areas," Marc finally says. "They are always getting visas and could help us out."

"Fabulous," Michelle says. "And I will be going, too. My parents won't care. Dad is on another business trip to Shanghai together and Mom is too busy planning her journalism trip to Tokyo."

"Yeah," Marc says. "I don't think that's a good idea."

"It's the *only* option." Michelle flashes him a steely smile. "Ask Jae."

I glower at her. "She goes," I mutter.

"There," Michelle says. "It's all settled. Let's schedule our next meeting for Friday. Lily, Jae, and I can try to meet at my house one night before then and organize the details."

"Keep me informed at all times," Mrs. Freeman says, her forehead knit together. "I suppose if this plan works, this group will be making history."

"Yep," Marc mutters under his breath. "History in the making."

CHAPTER 8

In the media center after school, Michelle and I draft up the medical relief proposal for the principal and the school board. We use the Keck medical school program as our model and make our list of arguments. It helps that Michelle has a knack for making something horrible sound wonderful.

"Are you sure this is something you have to do?" Michelle asks me.

"Yes, but you don't," I say. "You're being helpful already just by helping me write this."

"Listen. Whatever you are involved in is way bigger than my latest calculus class. I'm in this with you 100 percent. I just don't understand why you suddenly have to go to North Korea."

"We think there is a group there that can help heal Komo," I say. "But with North Korea being so closed off, there isn't any way to get in touch with them."

"Seems like a lot of effort for something you don't even know will work." Michelle pulls out her ruler and starts creating a chart. "But if this is what you want, I'll do what I can to make it happen."

After Michelle and I turn in our proposal, I text Marc and make plans to stop by his house tonight so we can research the Kumgangsan area and brainstorm where the orb could be hidden.

Since I missed the school bus, I take the city bus home. It's a long, bumpy ride, but I pull out my phone and begin to read about traveling to North Korea. Yet as I wave to the doorman and ride up the long elevator to the ninth floor of my apartment building, my stomach twists.

I hate going home. It feels too quiet and still. Ever since Mom died of cancer four years ago, Dad's been an insane workaholic. And I've been alone.

As I press my finger into the scanner to unlock the door, I wish I'd agreed to head home with Marc or Michelle rather than deal with this huge empty lump in my stomach. The door beeps after I punch in the code, and the lock unsnaps. I slide my shoes off and shrug out of my leather jacket, letting it drop to the ground. As if anyone would notice. The black counter in the kitchen practically shines, the granite free of fingerprints, evidence of my dad's and my lack of cooking ability.

I grab a water bottle from the fridge and try to block out the memory of our home back in California, stuffed with books and old furniture. Such a contrast to this apartment. The silence overwhelms me, ringing in my ears. I need to get out of this place. It's practically a funeral home.

I spot a note from Dad on the counter. Sitting next to it is a paper butterfly.

Jae,

I won't be able to make it home until after nine tonight since I've got a meeting in Busan. Your haraboji wants to meet us for brunch on Saturday so make sure you keep your schedule free. We'll catch up soon.
~Dad

I set the note aside, already knowing the reason for the brunch, and my heart sinks thinking about it. What if Dad says no to the North Korea trip? It could ruin everything.

In my bedroom, I tape the butterfly next to the fish on the top of my laptop, tracing my finger around the paper edges. Then I pull out my horn bow case, get the bare essentials that I'll need for an afternoon of target shooting, and stuff them into my backpack. Dad got me a membership at the Pavilion of the Yellow Stork after we got complaints about me shooting in the basement, but it's been over a week since I practiced my bow-and-arrow shooting.

Before I leave the apartment, I check the balcony one more time. The rope I have coiled up and tied to the pole is neatly hidden beneath the porch chair. After having to climb down like I did last time, I like having a better option. I double-check the knots, because one thing I have learned along the way: it's good to be prepared.

Since the archery center is located near downtown Gwanghwamun, it's a short city bus ride and then a hike up the hill. There's something so real and alive about springtime in Seoul. Winter is harsh and bitter, but spring breathes hope and possibilities.

The archery center is located halfway up the mountain, in a traditional wooden building that overlooks the forest below. You'd never know we were in the center of a city of over ten million people.

I bow to Master Ahn as I enter the main building of the Pavilion of the Yellow Stork. After I slide off my shoes, I set my case on the floor and pull out my bow. I run my fingers along the dragon image carved into the handle. Grandfather gave me this bow. I have no idea how old it must be, but it's lasted centuries. It even survived the massive fire in Grandfather's cave. This is the weapon that helped me defeat Haemosu.

"Miss Lee," Master Ahn says. "Will you practice here or on the hillside?"

I start at his voice and find my face burning. "Um, outside."

"Do you wish to bend your bow?" he asks.

Most people come here to work their bows under the fire. It's the traditional method for keeping wooden bows in proper working order. I wonder if I should tell him that my bow never needs correction. It never needs new strings either, because magic runs through its sinews.

No, telling him would be a very bad idea. I smile. "I already did it at home. I have my own burner."

"Of course." He nods and gives my bow a quick glance before he attends to some Japanese tourists coming in loaded with cameras and questions.

I tie my *goong dae* to my waist, fill it with five arrows, and snap my case closed before heading outside. It's a short stroll to the top of the hill where the large archery range is located. Cherry trees line the road. Their petals spin and swirl around me like snowflakes. I lift my hand and catch one. It settles into my palm.

Lily says if you catch a cherry blossom and make a wish as you blow it away, it'll come true. But what to wish for? My heart feels torn. Do I wish for Komo's health? For Kud to be out of my life and everything from the Spirit World to forget about my existence? For Marc and me never to be separated? To be closer to Dad? To hold Mom's hand in mine one more time and feel her warmth?

I clench the petal into my fist and hurry up the road. From the corner of my eye, I notice, at the top of the hill next to the pagoda, the light almost shimmers, wavering like a mirage in a desert. I blink and it's gone. A couple of people are shooting, their packs lying on the table in the pagoda. I let my pack slide off my shoulders, rest it on the table, and set my bow on top of it.

Slowly, I inch closer to the waving light, studying it. The scene through the trees looks totally different from where I'm standing. Wide, open fields roll out before me like a desert. The grass is brown, and the trees scattered about the hills lie barren, stark and lifeless. Two jagged peaks rise up in the distance, with clouds curling through them.

Sweat beads up on my forehead and my heart skips a beat. Even with its stark barrenness, I know this place.

The Spirit World.

There's an odd tug at my insides, and I'm irresistibly compelled to take a step closer. A part of me wonders if I can find Komo there. Glancing around me, I see no one is watching. I tell myself I'll only be gone for a moment. That I need to go and find answers.

I inch closer and allow a gust of wind to curl around me until it drags me through the wavering light. The force yanks and pulls at my skin and muscles. Darkness and stars swirl around me in a kaleidoscope. Then I'm tumbling through a second wavering wall.

Into another world.

CHAPTER 9

The moment my boots sink into the crisp, brunet grass, I know I've entered the Spirit World. Everything appears sharper. The air almost tastes thicker.

Marc told me that the worlds are connected by shared histories, and that places where the Spirit World has crossed into ours will always maintain a stronger connection. I'm still not clear how the two worlds piece together, but obviously they do, because here I am, standing in the misty gray of a lifeless world. It isn't hard to figure out where I am, either. The winding dusty path, the barren forest, the bone-filled stream, the dilapidated queen's palace. This is Haemosu's world. It's entrenched in my memory forever.

My heart slams against my chest as the memories clatter through my mind like a *kkwaenggwari* gong. Haemosu's screams vibrate around me; my knees buckle and I sink to the ground. I remember how the burning flames of his fire monster singed my skin, and how his claws ripped me to shreds after he transformed into a tiger.

I squeeze my fists tight and crack open my eyes. He is no longer here. I have to believe that. Even still, he lived in this place for too long, destroying it slowly in his quest for power. He craved power so much that he sucked the life force out of the trees, the water, even the buildings.

Despite the barrenness, the air drips rich as honey. I stand, realizing there's something about this place that feels different. With each breath I take, the power of the land soaks into me. My body buzzes with energy. I've never felt so alive.

I should turn back. I eye the wavering wall where I stumbled out of reality. This must be the portal. I step back toward it, fear clawing my mind as past memories continue to ricochet through me. Yet somehow a greater need makes me plant my feet. There's something about this place that feels right. Like I belong. Perhaps this place has the answers I seek.

A blast of hot air slices across my back. I spin around to face three golden dragons.

Oryonggeo.

These three must be part of the group of five dragons that drove Haemosu's golden chariot. They're stunning: sleek bodies glistening in the dull air, finely sculpted necks and faces, smoke puffing from their noses as they study me from ruby eyes, which are the same color as the five dragon gems that ringed the bracelet Haemosu gilded me with. These are the same dragons that clawed through Komo's house, and the same ones that snatched Grandfather off the boat. I'd been powerless to stop them then.

I swivel to retreat, but one of the dragons snakes out a claw and catches my shirt.

Why do you return? they speak in my mind.

Despite the grimy grayness around me, their scales glint as if covered in a thousand shimmering coins. If I were anywhere but here, I would have thought them beautiful, but my memories are too strong for those thoughts.

"Quite the welcoming committee," I say.

You should not have come.

No kidding. I struggle against their hold. "Don't sweat it. I'm leaving."

A tail swoops from behind, swiping my feet from beneath me. I fall to the ground and land on my bottom. A rumble shudders over them. I think they're laughing at me.

But since you are here, they say, *we cannot allow you to leave.*

"Are you always this cordial?" I ask, standing.

You killed the master and left. Now the land falls to ruin. We are dying with it. This is your fault.

There is no warning, no preparation for the attack. An explosion bursts in the air, creating a golden glow, blinding me. I raise my arm to shield my eyes and four claws slash across my cheek. Pain races through me like fire. I scream in shock.

On my other side, a tail smacks me in the side. I fly through the air, and the ground shakes with the impact of my fall. I moan into the dirt.

Being tossed like that back on earth would break every bone in my body. Not here. This world has its own set of rules. I grunt and spit out the chunk of dirt that managed to get into my mouth. The dragons blink their chilling red eyes and glare at me. I wonder if they're secretly doing that mind talk to each other but leaving me out of the conversation.

I cringe as I struggle to stand, trying to bear the agony of bones popped out of their sockets, maybe even broken. I snap my neck into place and then straighten, adjusting my ribs. There's something disconcerting about having your bones dislocated and yet still being able to walk. The last time I was here, I healed at impossible speeds. Today is no different.

"None of this is my fault," I say, but anger rises up. "You blame me for Haemosu's actions?" My vision blurs, I'm so ticked. I'm still paying the price for Haemosu. He's long dead, yet even now I'm dealing with his crap.

I clench my fists and take off running. Toward them. I pump my arms, willing the pain to fade away as I charge at them. One dragon cocks its head, still not moving, while another flies away. The third screeches at me in a bloodcurdling cry, its razor-tooth-filled jaw open so wide I could run right into it. I'm kicking myself for leaving my bow on the table.

Once I'm close enough to the screeching dragon, I leap into the air and snap out a side-kick into his belly. Airborne, I twist and kick the dragon again with my other foot as I descend.

My feet touch the earth and I tumble into a series of backflips, using my momentum for extra impact when I kick the other dragon. My kick is far more powerful than I could have imagined. The dragon stumbles backward, surprise flashing across its jeweled face, and snarls. Waves of water burst from its mouth this time. There's no escape from the flood. I hold out my hand to stop it, ducking my face behind my outstretched arm.

The blast hits my palm, but instead of drowning me, I somehow redirect the water, hitting the dragon in turn and smacking it onto the ground.

Evil thing! The dragon chokes and wallows on the ground, trying to escape the pool of water. *What has it done?*

I study my hand, shocked. How *did* I do that?

"Serves you right for attacking me out of nowhere," I say, but my words sound more like a question than the confidence I wish to exude.

The other dragon slides over to where I stand, studying me with its huge red eyeball. *Perhaps it has the power,* it says.

"I am not an *it,*" I say. "My name is Jae Hwa. Not that it matters because I'm leaving. This place is too horrific to stay another minute."

No! the three dragons say at once.

If it has the power, the bigger dragon says, *it can heal the land.*

"I suggest next time someone like me comes along, don't try to burn them with fire or cannonball them across the field. No one wants to be treated like that. Or be called an *it,* for that matter."

The sound of wingbeats fills the air. The two missing dragons swoop above my head and let out a long screech. Wind swirls around me like a tornado, so strong I can hardly stand. I push my hands out as if to hold the winds at bay, but it's useless. I'm trapped in their funnel.

Look what has arrived! the dragon next to me cries. *It changed the land.*

I look where the dragon points. A path of green grass, vibrant as emeralds, spreads before us. The winds die just as abruptly as they came, leaving us with absolute silence.

"Where did that come from?" I say.

You, the dragons say as one.

I gape at them, unsure what they could mean.

It is the master, one dragon says.

This pretty one? another asks. *It's too young.*

Too small.

It can heal the land, the first dragon says. *It has been given the power.*

"Listen." I hold up my hands. "You've got me confused with someone else. I'm not any master."

The three dragons in the air sail down to where we stand. I'm sure all five of them are going to attack as one and incinerate me into wisps of ash, drown me, or do something else even more horrible. There's no way I can stand against them. But they do the exact opposite. They bow before me.

It's the master, they say. *We are here to serve you.*

Unbelievable. First they try to break every bone in my body, next they attempt to burn me to a crisp, and now they want to call me their master.

"Um." I try to smile. "Thanks. I think."

I touch the grass that has turned green. It's soft and tickles my skin. With tentative fingers, I reach out and touch the brown grass next to it. I watch as the blade sparks to life beneath my fingers. Color blooms over its blade, spreading to the tip.

I jerk back my hand, shocked, and glance over at the dragons. They nod gravely, as if this is some formal event, and settle to the ground, waiting. I've no idea what they are waiting for.

"I'm not like Haemosu," I say. "I'm not the next ruler."

Only the master has the power here, they say.

I really need to get out of here, but I can't help but be curious. Did something happen to me when I killed Haemosu? Palk had offered me Haemosu's lands, but I'd rejected the offer. Perhaps, even though I rejected it, the offer had never left. Regardless, the surge of power is invigorating. I take off running toward a line of bamboo trees. Once there, I slowly turn to face the truth. A path of bright-green trails from where I stand to the wavering wall of light. The dragons were right. I created that path.

I reach out and touch the bamboo tree next to me. As if by magic, the tree shimmers. The trunk brightens from a dead gray into a golden brown, the colors snaking up the tree until they reach the leaves in a burst of green.

I jerk my hand away, tucking it to my chest. An edge of fear scrapes against my nerves. I don't like the thought of being tied to this world. It brings too many horrors with it. Too many nightmares. But what if they are right? What if I can undo all the destruction Haemosu created?

This place is completely flipping me out. Of course, when hasn't it? When Haemosu ruled this land, he had his own bag of tricks to play on me. But now everything is different. I start running along the line of bamboo trees until I reach the thick evergreen forest. Whatever I touch sparks to life. My chest explodes with a million emotions.

I have power here.

I can do the impossible.

I am the impossible.

But if I have power, what does that mean? My heart slows with dread. Does this mean I can't return to my world? Does this mean I'm not mortal anymore?

My eyes seek the wall of wavering light in the center of the field. The portal. It's still there, but that doesn't necessarily mean anything. Haemosu could come and go between his world and our world as he pleased, but he never belonged in our world and could never stay for long.

Where do I belong?

CHAPTER 10

Warmth shines over my head and shoulders. I lift my gaze, following the bright sunlight to the mountain above. A pagoda rests on top, and there I spot a figure, glistening white through the gray. My breath catches. Palk, the god of light and goodness.

"Come, Jae Hwa," he says. He sounds as if he's speaking next to me, rather than on the cliff top. "We must talk."

So I'm not alone, after all. I need to talk to him. If anyone has answers, he does.

I take off running down the path that curls into the woods, hoping it will lead me up the rocks to the pagoda. After pushing through leafless brambles and shrubs that spring to life as I touch them, I'm blockaded by a massive cliff that climbs straight up the mountain. There's no way I can climb that cliff, but then I remember soaring even higher than that once before.

It was during one of my fights with Haemosu. He morphed into a bird, so to defend myself, I did the same. Could I transform again? It's been months since I shape-shifted, and I'm not even sure I can still do it. But I'm desperate for help.

Closing my eyes, I visualize myself.

Feathered, beaked, clawed.

A hawk.

A rush of fire sizzles through me. I double over in pain. It has been so long since I shape-shifted that my body resists the transformation. My fingers twitch, tingling, and my vision sharpens. I watch in horror as my fingers alter into claws. Soft brown feathers cover my arms. My vision tunnels, and the world around me crystallizes.

My throat tightens, because even though I've done this before, the sensations are overwhelming, and there's always the lingering terror that I won't be able to make the shift back to my human self. I flutter about on the ground, unsure what to do with my wings. It had seemed so natural when I faced Haemosu, when panic caused my inner reflexes to take over.

I sit still and redirect my thoughts to focus on the cliff top. I take a deep breath, flap my wings, and lift.

And I'm flying, the wind whooshing through my feathers. The ground falls forever away as I beat my wings and rise. My heart catapults a few times, but I release my control, allowing instinct to take over. It's terrifying and liberating all at once as I stretch out on the breath of the wind.

I swoop over the trees, barely missing their outstretched limbs. Then I propel myself higher, loving the feeling of sunlight trickling over my wings and the wind gusting around me. I call out to the sky, a high, piercing cry. Then dive, allowing gravity to pull me. I plummet toward the ground, waiting until the last second, when I pull up, flapping my wings furiously. This is the feeling I try to capture every time I half leap down the stairs at my apartment building, but that doesn't even come close to this rush.

Finally, I reach the pagoda and land on the edge of the wooden railing. Palk stands there, hands behind his back, waiting with patient golden eyes.

"Jae Hwa." He nods solemnly. "Good of you to come."

I release the image of myself as a bird, refocusing on my humanity. It happens too quickly, and I find myself perched on the railing precariously close to the edge of the cliff. My balance is thrown off, and I fall backward toward the edge. Palk reaches out and yanks me back into the pagoda.

"Watch yourself." His lips twitch.

I drag the hair out of my eyes, trying to pull myself together. It would help if I could be a little more graceful. The world around me still feels off-kilter. I bend at the knees, my stomach churning, and clamp my eyes closed, refusing to puke in front of the god of light. I've only morphed a few times, but it usually took a few moments to recover. If I'd fallen, I wouldn't have had the strength or orientation to shape-shift back into a bird. My body heals quickly here, but I'm not sure I would have survived a fall like that.

"The more often you transform"—Palk pats my shoulder—"the easier your body adjusts."

Palk's touch soothes my skin, and my stomach stops rolling.

"Thanks for that." I straighten.

"It is an honor," he says. His eyes are kind, and I look away, disarmed.

"I suppose it's been a while." I wipe the trail of sweat trickling down the side of my face. "I'm not really sure why I'm here. Or that I should be."

I sound like a complete blathering idiot. Why can't I be more articulate, like Michelle?

"This was once Haemosu's land," Palk says, obviously skipping the small talk. "He destroyed it until it became a barren wasteland."

Palk motions for me to stand next to him at the edge of the railing. The wind cuts against our faces, cool and sharp. From high up on these peaks, the land stretches out to the sea, rolling in patchy brown hills. Skeletal trees are remnants of what I imagine were once lush pine forests. In the distance, the ocean's waves rake along slate-colored beaches.

"It's pretty depressing," I say. "Haemosu at least knew how to make it look good if he wanted to."

"Lies only deepen the wounds of the weak until they are left gaping and seeping in filth."

"That's one way to look at it." I study Palk. His white robes shimmer like a thousand stars. It almost hurts to look at him. "You opened the portal at my archery center, didn't you?"

"This land you see belongs to you now," Palk says, completely avoiding my question. "It beckons your healing touch."

I resist laughing, tempting as it is. "I'm usually the girl you call when you need someone to beat up your enemy."

Palk sighs. "You see that streak of green below. Just your presence here awakens the land. It takes on the power within you."

I bite my lip. I hate how he's always right. "Isn't it the other way around?" I ask. "Doesn't the land give power to me?"

"The land brings you, its rightful ruler, power," Palk says. "You determine how the power will be used: to heal, to morph. Haemosu collected it to increase his power in the human world."

"Will it help me find Komo? Her spirit is lost. She's been in a coma."

"Perhaps."

"Perhaps? That's all you have to say? She spent her life training in battle and studying Haemosu and his tactics all so that she could save me. Me, the niece she never met. I can't leave her alone in a coma. I have to help her."

"And so you shall. The time will come, and the decision will be set before you."

"Coming here was a waste of time, then, if I'm supposed to sit around and wait for the perfect time. I can't do that. I need answers, and if you can't give them to me, I'll find someone who can. I'm supposed to meet Marc soon, and he'd be upset if he knew I was here."

"The Spirit World needs you." Palk's face focuses on me, grim and far too serious for my taste. "Haemosu has left us with an imbalance perilous to both the human and spirit worlds. Kud's power grows, and yet we here in the Spirit World cannot reach him."

"Kud." I clench my fists. "He threatened me. Said he would kill my family if I didn't find the White Tiger orb for him."

"His threats are not to be taken lightly," Palk says. "If you agree to join us and rule this land, he would leave you alone. Without that special ability to enter your world and ours and still hold power in both, you would no longer be valuable to him."

I gape at Palk, shaking my head. "I can't leave my family and friends. They mean too much to me."

"Of course. And yet, this may be to our advantage. As a mortal, you have access to places we immortals do not. If the orb were returned to the Heavenly Chest, it would make us stronger on this side, give us the upper hand against Kud's power. It is the risk that worries me."

Deep down I know he's right. I was the one who defeated Haemosu when none of my other ancestors could achieve this. Moments ago, I touched the trees and they burst green. But no one can seem to understand that I don't want this. I never wanted any of this. I wanted a normal life, hanging out with Marc, my family, and my friends.

"What do you mean by 'this side'? Isn't Kud in the Spirit World, too?"

Palk waves his hand and the world shudders. I grip the railing as the ground races before us as if flying away at an impossible speed. Yet Palk and I remain, standing on the pagoda.

Seas and islands and snowcapped mountains sail beneath us.

"The Spirit World," I whisper.

"Yes." Palk draws his hand into a fist, and we come to a screeching stop. "It needs you."

I back away. This is way too complicated. Why can't everything be simple? Like, *Hey, you did a great job with Haemosu, so we're going to leave you alone to live happily ever after.*

I'm about to turn away when he takes my hand. After my experiences with Haemosu, this freaks me out. But before I can break into a roundhouse, a sense of peace wraps over me. A glow emanates over our hands and grows until we're completely surrounded in a ball of glittery light. A blast erupts, and the light explodes like fireworks around us. Everything around us vanishes, and the light trickles away into a million stars.

We're hanging in the center of darkness, the stars swirling around us. My whole body shakes from the shock of what has just happened, is still happening. I've seen a lot over the last three months, but this is taking things to a new dimension.

"Look into the distance," Palk says.

I follow his gaze. There at the edge of the nothing lies a red river, snaking through the emptiness like a sea of blood. It bubbles, and steam curls into the nothingness. We float closer until it's as if we're standing at the edge of the starry sky. A blast of air hits us, sending my long hair whipping around my face. Deep within my chest, a mixture of anger and fear and terror swirls inside me.

"Do you feel it?" Palk asks.

I nod, too overwhelmed to speak.

"Kud has stolen the Red Phoenix orb and is using it to build his own empire in the north. He has caused a rift in the Spirit World, dividing Korea. We have no access to his lands, and because our powers are weak in the human world, we cannot enter his portals from there either. His land is slowly stretching deeper and deeper into darkness and isolation. He feeds off the darkness that grows within North Korea. Even I am powerless to stop him unless I use the two orbs from the Heavenly Chest to break the seal of the divide. But the toll it would take on your world would be catastrophic. It would mean war."

"So *you* are asking me to find the White Tiger orb?" I stare at him in horror at how much bigger this is than I'd thought. "But what if I fail?"

He smiles. "Princess Yuhwa's blood still runs through you. And though that is true of all your ancestors, you were the one brave enough to stand up to Haemosu. You were the only one to be successful after centuries of bondage. You still have power in both worlds. At least for now."

"I don't understand." But that's a lie. I know exactly what he means. "There's got to be someone else. I might be good at fighting, but this is way beyond what I can do."

"I have tried." He sighs, stroking his pointed white beard. "No one has entered Kud's lands and lived to speak of it. Until you. He forced you into his land without asking. And you found your way out."

Yay for me. I get dragged through a mirror into Kud's sick world, get terrorized, and this is how I'm rewarded. "He let me go. That's the only way to explain it."

"Yes, interesting, is it not?"

I can't believe I'm getting drawn back into the Spirit World's problems. Why won't everybody leave me alone?

As if reading my thoughts, Palk says, "This is not something to be taken lightly."

"I don't take it lightly." How could I after all I've been through? "I've agreed to help the Council of Shinshi search for the White Tiger orb. They're worried that Kud will find it first, and since it's a seeker orb, he'll then find the others."

"You plan to enter the northern lands?"

"I'll look for the orb. If we find it, I'll bring it back to you. But I can't save Haemosu's lands. I can't give up my family for this."

"A great light shines in the Cave of the Nine Dragons." Palk looks at me. "Our powers are not strong enough to travel long in the human lands, and the northern lands are all under the power of Kud. Perhaps this cave will give you the answers you seek."

The Cave of the Nine Dragons. I haven't the faintest idea where this is, but I'm certain Marc will know.

"If Kud gains possession of another orb, his power will only increase," Palk says. "This is the risk you take in seeking out this artifact. He has been looking for all the orbs for endless ages. They have been well hidden. It is hard to foresee if this is the best step."

"I'm not certain of anything. I just get this feeling that he's closer to the orb than we realize, and that worries me."

Palk stares hard at the blood-red river, serving as a boundary between the two lands. Crimson reflects against his face, and his forehead wrinkles. "You are right to worry." He turns and claps both hands on my shoulders. "This is the path that has been set before you. Take it and use your powers with wisdom and strength. Both will be needed for success."

His form seems to be pulling away from me. I watch him growing farther and farther away, as if we're in an endless tunnel. I reach out, already missing that feeling of strength that I realize I was drawing from him.

"Seek also your *komo*," Palk's voice calls from the distance. "She holds a key that must not die with her."

His words hit hard. Does he believe she's dying? What does she hold? Why must everything be so cryptic with him?

Before I can fully wrap my head around everything Palk said, I'm tumbling into the soft grass of the archery center. *Fantastic.* I'm back in Seoul and feeling more clueless than when I left. People are glancing over at me, muttering to each other, but I don't care what they think. I find my bow, and I wrap my fingers around its smooth wooden surface, and I draw it close. A tingle skitters through my body, making me smile. It's as if my bow understands what I'm going through.

Even if I can't.

CHAPTER 11

It's a quick taxi ride from the archery center to Marc's house in Sungbuk-Dong. This neighborhood of Seoul sits on the hill right behind the Blue House where the president lives. Most of the houses are similar in style to Marc's family's home, two stories high and cream colored.

I ring the doorbell, my bow strapped to my back and a bag of Marc's favorite food—Indian—tucked against my chest. His house is an eclectic mix of modern and traditional, with slick contemporary rooflines yet windows with Korean-style geometric wooden panes. A low stone wall surrounds the house, and an iron gate opens out to a courtyard.

As I wait, I study the view from the stoop. Pruned bushes border the walls, and a pebbled pathway leads to a stone fountain. Two cherry trees are planted on either side of the house like sentinels. Beyond the courtyard, the view of downtown Seoul sweeps before me. The high-rises glisten in the setting sun, reflecting pumpkin- and scarlet-colored streaks of light.

I blow the loose strands from my face and rap on the door.

Then it swings open. "Well, well," Marc says. "What do we have here?"

I take in the sight of him: wild brown hair, that right dimple that shows up every time he smiles. The casual look he tries to wear with his faded jeans and gray archeaology shirt is such a sharp contrast to the intensity in his green eyes.

But it's more than all of that. It's his presence that fills the space between us. It's the way his eyes drink in the sight of me as if he doesn't ever want to forget who I am.

He blocks the entrance with his arms extended as if holding up the doorframe. The muscles on his arms are stretched taut, and I wonder if he's been working out.

"What can I do for you, ma'am?" he asks, eyebrows rising and face deadpan.

I huff and roll my eyes, but a smile still creeps across my face. "Just let me in, you silly boy. I'm starving." I hold up the bag. "I brought chicken marsala and naan. Your favorite."

"Tempting." He snatches the bag from me and peers inside.

I move to duck under his arm, but he slides his body to block me.

"Not so fast, Fighter Girl. As enticing as this food is, it gains you no entrance here." He cups my chin with his hand. "It'll have to be something more lasting than that."

Then his lips are on mine, and the bag of food slips to the floor, forgotten. I drink in his kiss, long and soft. He pulls me closer and kisses my forehead, as if he doesn't want to ever let me go.

"I missed you," he whispers into my ear.

When we finally part, every muscle in me aches to cling to him. His skin feels warm against mine, chilled from the evening air. He trails his finger from my ear to my chin, and his breath tickles my forehead. I can barely think straight when he looks at me like I'm the moon and stars all wrapped into one.

I drag my palms over his chest and shoulders. His muscles are harder and more sculpted than I remember.

"You've been working out?" I ask.

He grins and taps his finger against my lips. "Nothing gets past my Fighter Girl. Jung has been giving me sword-fighting lessons every Saturday. A requirement for all Guardians."

"I didn't realize it was every weekend." I straighten the collar of his shirt.

He kisses me again, harder this time. Almost as if he's worried it will be his last.

"I wouldn't complain if we did this all night," Marc says huskily, finally breaking away.

"I take it your parents aren't home." I finger the edge of his shirt, not quite wanting to let him go.

"They're at a Yonsei event. You'll have to enter at your own risk. There's no one here to keep me in check."

I lightly smack him on his chest as he lets me inside.

I'm always shocked when I enter Marc's house. It's such an odd contrast to my dad's and mine, which is stark, clean, and modern. After I kick off my shoes, I trail after Marc, ascending up the stairs.

The photographs and medals awarded to his family members climb up the wall like perfect soldiers all the way to the top of the staircase. I wonder if his dad is proud of him now that he's made Guardian status, and if that alone would be enough to contribute to their family legacy.

"Too bad the Guardians are so secretive," I say. "Otherwise your parents could place a plaque here in your honor."

Marc pauses midstride and glances at the wall. A pained look slips over his face, but it's gone so quickly I wonder if I imagined it.

At the top of the stairs, we enter the living room. There are wooden crates everywhere, some opened. Scattered around the crates are pots that reach my hips, wooden statues, painted urns, silk paintings. The place smells like a library, a mix of old books and wood.

"What is all this?" I ask.

"Junk my parents picked up on their last trip to Norway."

"I didn't think they had room for anything new."

"Not new." Marc chuckles, squeezing past a large wooden crate. "Old. Very old."

I follow him to the kitchen, weaving past a miniature Viking ship, several wooden warriors, and a giant bronze shield. I cross my fingers with every step, terrified I'm going to break something, since I'm so good at that sort of thing.

"The Norwegians actually let your parents leave the country with this stuff?"

My leg knocks against a stack of books. I dive, grasping for the tower to keep the teetering stack from falling. As I straighten them, dust cakes my palms. These look so old I bet if they'd fallen, they would've turned to dust.

"Unfortunately." Marc sets the bag on the counter and starts pulling out plates. "They're actually replicas for my parents to study. Dad wanted to put the warriors on top of the bookshelf, but they're too tall. So now they get to guard the door until he can find a different place for them. I have to admit, I'm jealous. They should've taken me."

"You guys need another house to put all this stuff in," I say as I rip off a piece of naan and pop it into my mouth. It's still warm and soft.

"No way. And whatever you do, don't give them that idea. It'll mean more space for them to gather more junk."

We load our plates with rice, chicken, and naan. I sit on a bench at what looks like a replica of a Nordic farmhouse table. Marc slides aside the pile of books and unrolled maps and sits across from me. They're maps of North Korea.

"You've been busy!" I say.

He nods and points out where our entry point will be and where we'll be delivering the supplies.

"Other than that," he says, "I'm not sure where we should look for the orb. According to this legend, there is reference to a magical artifact near Kunsong in 1231, after the Mongol invasion. A stone helped repel the Mongols and gave the Koreans a victory. But those are just stories. Who knows what parts are real or not."

"You've already found all of this?" I say. "That's really good research."

"What can I say? Research is my thing." He shakes his head as he scoops a chunk of chicken up with his naan. "It's no wonder Korea gets its butt kicked over and over. The orbs, which are supposed to be its protection, have been lost."

I swirl my naan through the sauce, wondering how I'm going to bring up the cave. He'll want to know how I found out about it.

Should I tell him the truth? That I went to the Spirit World?

"What is it? You're not telling me something."

"Have you ever heard of the Cave of the Nine Dragons?"

"Of course. I've read the myths." Marc drops his bread and gives me a wary look. "Why?"

"I was thinking that might be a good place to start. It's a sacred area, isn't it?"

He frowns. "Who have you been talking to?"

Now it's my turn to frown. I set my fork down and lean back. "What's that supposed to mean?"

"You've been to the Spirit World, haven't you?"

I sit taller, hating his tone, as if he's accusing me. "Yes, I have. You make it sound like I've done something wrong."

"That's not it." Marc sighs. "I swear, I wish you would stay away from that place. One of these days you're going to go there and never come back."

"That's not going to happen."

"There's something else. I've been doing some research."

"Enough with the research. We can't even have a meal together without *the research*."

I rest my head in my hands. Tears threaten to burst out. I hate crying. It's a sign of weakness, and after everything Haemosu did to my family, I promised myself I'd be strong. I'd be the one who would fight to the end. I would be standing tall, no groveling.

Marc moves to my side of the table and pulls me to him. I don't push him away, because the reality is I need him. Sure, I'd never actually admit it, but his arm reassures me he'll always be there for me.

"You're right, Jae," Marc says, finally breaking the silence. "We need at least one night where we're not in the middle of insanity. I'm paranoid I'm going to lose you. Every time we're together, I wonder if it'll be our last. After watching you fight Haemosu at his palace—"

He stops and drags in a deep breath. "His claws tore you to shreds, Jae."

I look into Marc's face. His eyes are wide with fear, and his jaw is set.

"Does this have anything to do with your training with Jung?"

"I watched you age a hundred years right before my eyes. Those memories haunt me every day. Every night. I will do everything I can to not let you get hurt like that again. That's why I have to be prepared and train. If there is anything in my power to save you, I will do it."

"I know. A hundred times over, I know. I totally lost it there." I I trace his jawline and then kiss his neck, breathing in his smell. "You're right. We need to research. We don't have much time, and knowledge is power. Tell me what you were going to say about your research. I want to know."

Marc picks up a book at the end of the table and cracks it open. "It's all here."

It's a myth about Bari under the subheading *mythological beings.*

Princess Bari

Princess Bari crossed twelve mountains, each full of ghosts. When she came to the river only the dead could cross, she showed them magical flowers she had been given. Seeing these, the guards of the river allowed her to cross and enter the Underworld.

There she found a fortress built of iron thorns. She used the flowers to melt the fortress and free the prisoners. She became a heroine.

But time and again she was asked to return to the Underworld to save loved ones. After each time she entered, she took on a silvern sheen in the real world. Finally, when she entered the Underworld to rescue her parents, she lost all her humanity. She had only a silvery ghostlike form in the real world.

From that day forward, she never returned to her people, but remained in the Spirit World for all of eternity as the one who guides the dead into the Underworld.

"Wow." I reread it again to make sure I didn't misunderstand anything. "I don't think I've ever read this myth. So you think she lost her humanity because she spent so much time in the Spirit World?"

The thought of being stuck in Haemosu's land terrifies me. I don't want to lose my life here, even if it did mean immortality.

"It might be nothing," Marc says. "But since all these other myths have become reality in some way, I'm worried that there is some truth to it."

I face Marc. "Do you think I have this silvern look?"

"No." Marc rubs his eyes and then studies me again, his forehead knitting together. "I don't know. Maybe I'm completely paranoid, but tonight you look a little different. More sparkly?"

"Sparkly?" I laugh. When he doesn't join in, I take his hands in mine. "Listen, Marc. I love you. More than anything. But you've got to let me live my life. And I need to be able to tell you stuff, but if you're going to flip out every time something happens, I can't handle that."

"I know. I'll try." His mouth curves into a smile, and he shakes his head. "We are either perfect for each other or we'll drive each other crazy."

I laugh again, harder this time. Marc drags out his tablet and types in "nine dragons" to search on the web. He scrolls through some articles until he clicks on one, his eyes lighting up. He mutters something under his breath.

"What did you say?"

"Kuryong." He slaps his forehead. "Why didn't I think of it before? This makes perfect sense." He drums his fingers on the table as he reads. "Kuryong is located in Kumgangsan, North Korea. Translated into English, it's the Diamond Mountains. According to the myths, once upon a time nine dragons defended Kuryong from enemies."

I nod. I vaguely remember reading about this myth in one of Mom's books. "But what are these dragons guarding?"

"Exactly."

Marc takes off down the hall while searching on his tablet at the same time. I scamper after him, cringing as I pass through the obstacle course.

"There really isn't much information on it since everything in North Korea is so hush-hush. But if the Council believes the orb is in the Kumgangsan region, and this cave is there, too, it seems too coincidental to ignore."

We enter his room. It looks about the same as the last time I was here. Piles of books stacked against the walls, and artifacts that he discovered on archaefology trips with his parents crowding his bookshelves. I pause at his bulletin board, staring at all the pictures of the two of us together. I finger the edge of a strip of photos we took in the photo booth in Sinchon.

Me kissing Marc while holding bunny fingers behind his head. The two of us cross-eyed. Tongues sticking out. Pouting lips.

I look so happy in every picture. Probably because I thought I was free.

"Here's the book I was looking for," Marc says, pulling me away from my memories. "This explains the myth."

He sets the book on his desk and the tablet on a tilt next to it. According to the website, Kuryong Falls is located not far from a popular hotel called Kumgangsan Hotel. The book doesn't explain much about the ancient myth except how nine dragons guard the waterfall.

"So we're going to assume the myth of the Nine Dragons is true."

"Dragons are dangerous," Marc says.

"Tell me about it," I mutter.

"Promise not to wander off or enter any portals without me."

I don't like the thought of him coming on this trip. I nearly lost him once, and I certainly won't do it again. Still, I'm not sure I can succeed without his help.

One hurdle at a time, I tell myself. To Marc, I just smile and squeeze his hand.

CHAPTER 12

The next few days, Michelle, Lily, and I plan the Dano mask party until I'm sick of the whole thing. The school board has approved our endeavor as long as we have our parents' permission and sign a butt-load of waivers. It makes me wish we could find a wealthy donor to supply all the medical funding and pretend we did it all. But that would lead to suspicion. We have to appear to be purely a humanitarian effort not only to the North Korean government, but also to Kud.

Between school, planning this event, and Tae Kwon Do lessons, Marc and I haven't seen each other except between classes. It hasn't helped that every day after school he's over at Jung's house learning secret Guardian stuff.

"So when are you going to tell me what you've been doing with Jung?" I ask Marc one day between classes.

"Can't." He grimaces. "I've been sworn to secrecy."

"You can't be serious," I say, stopping midstride and blocking the flow of traffic. "I've told you everything that has happened to me."

"It's extreme. I know." His brow wrinkles. "Hey, it's not that big of a deal. Come here." He pulls me against the wall and then whispers into my ear, "They're teaching me an ancient form of fighting. It's supposed to be able to combat immortals in our world."

I think about how Grandfather and Komo tried to fight Haemosu. Maybe they'd have had a chance if he hadn't brought his wild boars. I swallow those bloodstained memories and trail my finger over Marc's palm.

"I don't like the thought of you fighting immortals," I say. "They may not be as powerful in our world, but they've been around practically forever and have learned too many tricks along the way."

"Don't worry about me." He kisses my forehead. "It's you we should be worried about. This training is good. From now on, I'm not going to be a burden to you, but someone who can help you. Next time Kud shows up, I'll be ready."

I watch him saunter back to class, so confident and hopeful. A mix of emotions jumbles inside of me. I'm glad he's found something that makes him happy, but at the same time I hate it. I hate the Guardians of Shinshi for taking my boyfriend from me. I hate the idea of him facing Kud.

"Nothing good can come of this," I mutter.

Friday after school, I wait outside the infamous elevator at Yonsei University for Marc to show up, leaning against the wall and smacking on my bubble gum. Grandfather wants us to meet to work out the details of our trip.

Marc strides in through the door, his hair disheveled as usual, but there's a confidence in his gait, and I wonder if that's due in part to what he's doing with the Guardians. As part of the plan, I don't acknowledge his presence but blow out a long bubble instead, focusing on the blur of letters in the book I'm supposedly reading. Marc pushes the elevator button, and the two of us slip inside.

The doors grind shut, and Marc opens the compartment and presses his ring into the slot.

"Do you think all this cloak-and-dagger business really tricks Kud?" I say.

Marc shrugs. "I don't know, but it's worth trying to keep what we're doing a secret."

As the elevator shudders down the shaft, he reaches over and squeezes my hand. "I'm glad we're in this together," he says.

"You might be changing your mind in a few days," I say.

Even though it's my second time entering the Guardians of Shinshi's secret headquarters, it still gives me goose bumps. Jung greets us just like he did on my first visit. We slip through the front doors, and even though the whole Council isn't there, the candles still flicker in their holds.

Marc directs me across the main room where the Council meeting had been to another passageway. It twists around until we come to a series of marble steps that lead us into another room. This one is so different, I wonder if we've stepped into another dimension.

The wall in front of us must be a giant computer screen. It's full of data and charts that someone sitting before it is typing in. The wall to the right is tacked full of more charts and graphs and a row of computers, while the wall to the left is a map of Korea at the bottom with pushpins stuck in it at different locations. Above that is another rough outline of a map, of a place I've never seen before.

As we step inside, the person at the computer spins around in his chair. I gape in surprise as I recognize Kumar, Marc's best friend from school. His dark hair is combed back neatly, and his olive complexion almost looks darker in the mix of light from the computer screen and the oil lamps tucked into the walls.

He flashes his typical wide grin at me. "Surprised to see me?"

I try to speak, but I have no words.

Kumar claps his hands and rubs them together. "I hope I get an extra bonus point for that."

"But you're not—" I start, then close my eyes and shake my head. "You're not a part of all this, are you?"

"The Council recruited him," Grandfather says, coming in from behind us. "When he gained Dartmouth's and Harvard's interest, he also gained ours."

"You can't get him involved in all of this!" I say. "He's got his whole life ahead of him."

"He does not have to do this for his whole life," Grandfather says. "But we have much to offer him and he us, especially his research on multiple dimensions."

"Don't be mad, Jae," Kumar says. "I just joined ranks a month ago. I couldn't resist. When Marc's dad came to me with the proposition that these theories I was studying on multiple dimensions were in fact true, and he had a way to allow me to study them, I couldn't say no."

"What about Lily? Does she know?"

"No." Kumar looks down at his hands. "They say it's better if she doesn't."

I couldn't argue with that.

"We should get to business," Grandfather says. "Kumar, do you have the region map and itinerary ready?"

"Yes!" Kumar starts rummaging through a stack of papers on the long desk beside him. He hands each of us a folder. Inside, I find a one-page summary of our trip, a map of the trailhead that leads to Kuryong Falls, and the legend of the Nine Dragons.

"Excellent," Grandfather says as he scans over the documents. "You must read through this carefully and memorize it as best you can. These documents cannot be brought outside of this headquarters."

The complete organization of everything is daunting. I sit at the table and review the pages.

"Did you have something similar to this when we went to Busan?" I ask. When both Marc and Grandfather nod, I feel a rush of anger. "Why didn't you tell me about all this stuff then? I was already involved with Haemosu."

"They made me swear not to tell you," Marc says.

"Our methods call for the least amount of involvement possible," Grandfather says. "It was purely for your safety."

"How do I know you're not keeping other secrets from me?" I say.

"Jae Hwa," Grandfather huffs, sounding exasperated. "You will have to trust that I only want the best for you. You wanted to do this mission when I did not. If you want to back out, I have no problem with that. But if that is the case, we will have to find another way of dealing with Kud."

The room grows silent except for the hum of the computers. Kumar suddenly becomes interested in his haphazard stack of papers, and Marc pretends to read through the report.

"Fine," I say. "Let's continue. Explain how we'll get the orb."

Grandfather nods at Kumar. "As you know, the five of us will go in under the guise of delivering medical supplies. Michelle is the only one with limited knowledge of the full reasons for the trip, and by the way, I'm against her coming."

"She knows too much not to come," I say.

"Perhaps." Grandfather sighs and shakes his head. "Then there's Kang-dae. He couldn't make it today, but I will make sure he is briefed.

"Once there, I will make arrangements for us to hike to Kuryong Falls. If we find the orb, we will then journey to the royal tomb of King Kongmin and enter the Spirit World through it to return the orb to the Heavenly Chest."

"So we will need to take the *samjoko* amulet," Marc says.

"Indeed," Grandfather says. "It is a risk bringing the sacred amulet into a restricted area, but it is the only way for us to enter the Spirit World. Do you remember how to use it, Jae Hwa?"

I nod, remembering how I took a boat out to the island where King Munmu's tomb was buried under the water. I had fit the amulet onto a golden plate that opened a portal to the Spirit World. Legend has it that all the royal tombs are portals to the Spirit World.

"Very good," Grandfather continues. "Hopefully we will not encounter any issues along the way. But if we do, you will have both Marc and Kang-dae as your Guardians."

"You will also need this." Kumar hands Grandfather a small box. At Grandfather's raised eyebrows, Kumar explains, "It's a bug scrambler. All the hotel rooms near the North Korean border are bugged with listening devices. If you need to have a private conversation, you'll want to use this."

"Nice," Marc says, studying the device and slapping Kumar on the back. "You're smarter than I thought."

Kumar shrugs as if it's no big deal. "Just looking out for you guys. Having unrestricted funds makes everything a little easier."

"What are these two maps?" I ask Kumar, moving to the left wall. I trail my finger from each of the pinpoints on the map of Korea, trying to figure what is so important about these locations.

"Those pinpoints are where the Guardians have found portals to the Spirit World," Kumar says. "Or at least we think they're portals. Actually, you'd probably know more about that kind of stuff since you've actually been there. And I have not."

He grins and jams his hands into his pockets. I can see from the look in his eyes that he is loving this new job. He's swimming in his element here.

I point to the map above Korea. "And this map?"

"That's my rough sketch of the Spirit World," Kumar says. "Again, this is purely based on hearsay. I've interviewed your grandfather and Marc, since they went there not long ago. It would be pretty cool to hear about your experiences."

I run my fingers over the map, studying Kumar's sketches and remembering the flying trip Palk took me on. "It's a lot bigger than this," I tell Kumar. His eyes widen. "When we get back from North Korea, I'll sit down with you."

"Really?" Kumar says. "That would be great. Really great."

Once we finish studying, Grandfather has us put our papers into a stone basin by the door. He takes a match, lights it, and tosses it onto the papers. I watch as the plans go up in flames, hoping our mission won't follow the same fate.

CHAPTER 13

"This is going to be the best event *ever*," Michelle announces as the taxi stops at gate eight of Namdaemun Market.

This past week, with worrying about and planning for our trip, I hardly got any sleep. I have to admit I was looking forward to a Saturday-morning sleep-in. I resist groaning and promise myself a coffee at the first coffee shop sighting. Last night Marc and I stayed up late again, spending hours reading old Korean myths and wondering which ones were actually reality rather than fantasy. When I finally collapsed onto my *yo*, I slept restlessly, worried that Kud or some other mythological creature would creep into my room and stab me in my sleep.

Even as I stand here in the bright daylight, I still can't quite shake my horrifying dreams. I try to focus on the quaintness of the market to shut off the images floating in my head. Dad explained to me once that long ago, all the markets of Seoul were stationed outside of the four gates of the walled city. This made it easy to trade with outsiders. Of course, those ancient walls have long ago crumbled, replaced by huge concrete buildings that are multiple stories high and packed to the brim with shops.

"I'm glad someone's feeling confident," Lily says, her forehead puckered as she goes over her list for the hundredth time. "There's so much to do and not enough time."

"It will be great," I say with false brightness, and I squeeze her arm. "If anyone can pull this event off, it's you and Michelle."

We scoot out of the taxi. It's the perfect spring day, with a cool breeze sweeping down from the northern mountains. The shopkeepers are still stripping tarps off their tables and unrolling awnings. Lily was insistent we arrive right at nine o'clock so we'd avoid the crowds and get through all of our shopping before lunch.

Ducking past a delivery truck, we stroll down the narrow lane. I eye the shadowed alleyways for creatures lurking about. Lily and Michelle's laughter pulls me back to earth, and I cling to the sound, forcing myself to smile. To pretend.

Socks, shoes, shirts, dried squid, and jewelry are all piled high on the tables we pass by. Little shops are tucked inside concrete walls, but their colorful awnings and tables heaped with goods give them character, and each shop has its own personality. We pass one with every T-shirt imaginable, and another with stacks of pots, pans, and kitchen utensils. The air is a mix of gasoline, *kimchi*, and fried food.

"It's crazy, the random things you find here," I say.

"A shopper's paradise," Michelle announces, strapping her purse over her shoulder. "You never know what glorious treasures we'll find."

I laugh. "Uh-oh," I tell Lily. "See that look in her eyes? We might never leave this place."

Lily reads her phone. "The lantern shop is located one block down, shop number one forty-five," she says.

As we wander, Michelle stops and lingers at every other table. We'll never make it to the lantern shop at this pace. It doesn't help when Lily finds a coat on sale that she proclaims she adores. While she pays for it, Michelle and I wait outside of the shop, rummaging through their winter sale items.

"So how are you doing?" Michelle asks as she picks up a hat and tries it on. "Any more stalkers?"

I think a moment and realize there hasn't been, which is kind of weird, but good at the same time. When Haemosu was alive, he and his cronies seemed to show up everywhere, all the time.

"No." I tug the ends of my spring jacket. "Everything has been oddly calm."

"Well, that's good," Michelle says.

"Maybe." For some reason, I doubt Kud liked the idea of me slipping through his fingers. He doesn't strike me as one who accepts defeat. Unease curls through me. He must be up to something. The problem is, I don't know him well enough to know what that is.

"Because I've got to admit"—Michelle moves to the rack of scarves—"that whole mirror episode has changed how I think about everything. Two of Marc's Council dudes even came to talk to me. They asked me a bunch of questions."

My head jerks up at this. I resist the urge to grab her arm and demand for her to tell me everything that happened. Marc must have told them Michelle knew. How could he do that? I could strangle him for getting her wrapped up in his secret Council.

"What kind of questions did they ask?"

"Nothing much. Mainly the details of what happened. But they did give me the name of a therapist I can talk to if I feel worried about anything." She digs through her pocket and produces a smooth, cream-colored card with a name and a phone number on it. "Have you talked to a therapist yet? It might help. You seem stressed out."

"That's not going to solve my problems." I glance over at Lily to make sure she isn't overhearing our conversation. She's still at the counter paying for her coat. "Dad wants me to go to a special school where they have a full-time counseling staff and can treat me if I have any more 'episodes,' as he likes to call them." I focus on the design on a nearby beret. "He's already talked to the admissions counselor."

"When did this all happen?" Michelle's eyes practically bug out.

"Two nights ago." I rub my temples, trying to avoid the headache coming on. "I need coffee."

"You need to let me help you out. What can I do?" She sets the scarf down and plants her fists on her hips, practically glaring at me. "That mirror freak show was horror at its finest, but we can find a way through this."

"What was horror at its finest?" Lily asks from behind me.

I literally jump, not expecting her. My brain spins, trying to think of a clever recovery. "Michelle's last date," I say, and then bite back a laugh at Michelle's glaring eyes.

"You had a date?" Lily gasps. "And didn't tell me?"

"I didn't have a date," Michelle snaps, rolling her eyes. "Jae is making up nonsense."

"Well," I say, taking Lily's arm. "We need to brainstorm new possibilities for her. She hasn't dated anyone since Charlie."

"Excellent!" Lily grins. "This sounds positively evil. Come on, I see a rice paper store up ahead. We can brainstorm and stock up on paper at the same time."

As we scurry up the concrete steps of the shop, a cool sensation slithers over me. I glance around, but I don't notice anything. If Marc were here, he'd be able to tell me right away if something from the Spirit World was nearby.

Shrugging off the sensation, I open the glass door and step inside the shop. The air smells of fresh-cut paper and wood shavings. Massive sheets of rice paper are stacked one on top of the other along the tables. Rolls of colored paper climb the walls all the way to the ceiling.

Lily sighs in ecstasy. "How am I supposed to decide on styles? There's like every color in the universe here."

I skim my fingers over the paper, loving its soft, bumpy texture. Then, as I pass the window, my eyes scan the crowded street. I dig my nails into my palms, hating how completely paranoid I've become.

I let out a quick breath as my gaze falls on Kang-dae, sipping coffee and leaning against a concrete wall on the other side of the street. A slow grin crosses his face as our eyes meet. He nods once and lifts his coffee cup as if in a toast.

My fists clench at my sides. Is he spying on me? The Council better not have sent him to babysit. It's bad enough my boyfriend has to be my Guardian. I definitely don't need two. Why won't anyone believe that I can take care of myself? I hate this lack of privacy.

"I'll be right back," I call over my shoulder at Michelle and Lily. "Going across the street."

When I reach Kang-dae, he just smirks and takes another sip of his coffee.

"Trying to blow my cover?" he asks.

"You're spying on me, admit it," I say.

"Spying is a relative term. I'd prefer to call it ensuring your safety. There are plenty of creatures around here that wouldn't mind tearing you to shreds after they find out what you're up to."

"I don't need anyone *ensuring my safety*. I can take care of myself."

His eyebrows lift slightly as he smirks. "So I've heard."

"Besides." An edge of annoyance cuts at my nerves. "Marc is my Guardian. I don't need another."

"Feisty, aren't we? Jung is teaching him the art of the sword."

I open my mouth, then shut it. Marc didn't tell me he was training today, too. The realization hits me. Kang-dae knows more about Marc's whereabouts than I do. Not that Marc and I tell each other *everything*, but still, ever since Marc was inducted into the Guardians of Shinshi, he has had this other life—a secret life—that he hasn't been telling me about.

"I take it your boyfriend didn't tell you about the lessons," Kang-dae says.

I turn my head away, not liking the way his eyes study me, trying to read my thoughts. Or maybe I do like it, which is all the more disturbing. I speed-dial Marc and press my phone to my ear. It rings and rings until I get his "May the force be with you" message, and I disconnect the call.

Annoyed, I text him: Where r u?

"I doubt he'll have his phone on," Kang-dae says. "It's forbidden during training."

"You seem to know all about this training."

"I completed the tests last week," Kang-dae says, arms crossed. "Broke the record for quickest to pass."

Show off.

Maybe this is why Marc doesn't like Kang-dae. There seems to be some grudge between the two of them. It's hard to know, since Marc won't talk about it.

"Listen," I say, "you don't need to babysit me. Tell the Council I can take care of myself. No more stalking."

"They weren't joking when they said you were stubborn."

I frown, not liking the idea of other people talking about me.

"I'll leave you to it, then." Kang-dae slips on his sunglasses. "Cheers."

Jamming my hands into my jean jacket, I take off across the street, already bustling with shoppers and scooters stacked with goods, weaving in and out of the swelling crowds.

When I reach the stoop of the rice paper store, the air shifts as if a heat wave has washed over me. I turn and inspect the street, shading my eyes against the morning glare, but Kang-dae has disappeared. Then, out of the corner of my eye, I catch a glimpse of what looks like a lion standing on top of a tall building.

The lion creature nods once to me. The sun glints off his body, making him look like he's burning with fire. The single horn and fangs come into focus. Even though I know he'd do almost anything—has done almost everything—to protect me, I still shudder at his fierceness.

"Haechi," I whisper.

Careful, little one, he says in my mind.

He's the protector of Seoul, and knowing he's near, my muscles relax. Until I realize he wouldn't be here unless he had a reason to be. Maybe Kang-dae is right. My eyes sweep the market once again, wondering which creatures are watching me.

And why.

CHAPTER 14

The silverware clicks against china and mixes with soothing classical music. Our table borders the window, giving me the perfect view of Seoul spread below like a patchwork quilt. The Hyatt brunch is one of my favorite things. We usually come only for special holidays, but Grandfather insisted this was the place we should meet. The waiter arrives and passes Dad his coffee, Grandfather his green tea, and me my tall orange juice.

Dad's got on a pair of khaki pants and a white button-down shirt underneath a black jacket, a little more relaxed than his usual business suit. This is the first time since we went golfing that I've seen him without a tie. Grandfather, on the other hand, is wearing his usual Korean-style jacket with a black stand-up collar, buttoned all the way up. It's form fitting and shows off his muscular frame.

"So," Dad begins the conversation. "What is the occasion for such an extravagant breakfast?"

I'm assuming he's referring to the fact that I'm not wearing my usual jeans and T-shirt, rather than to the food. Today

I want Dad to see how serious I am, so I chose a short brown embroidered jacket over a white shirt and tight brown pants. I'm wearing a long dangle necklace that Michelle bought me for my birthday.

"I have a humanitarian opportunity for Jae Hwa to take part in," Grandfather says. "With your permission, of course."

Dad leisurely sips his coffee, but I see the muscles in his neck stiffen. "I'm listening."

"My school has found a way for us to deliver medicine to TB patients," I say, and then hold my breath, listening to how ridiculous this whole idea now sounds. He's never going to allow me to go into the most dangerous place on the planet. "Can you imagine how that will stand out on a college transcript? Michelle says it's a first-class ticket to Ivy League."

"Tuberculosis?" Dad says. "Isn't that contagious? I don't feel comfortable with you doing something like this."

"We'd just be delivering the supplies," I say. "Not interacting with patients. It's more of a gesture of goodwill between North and South Korea. It's all been approved by the school and both the South and North Korean authorities."

"North Korea?" Dad's eyes widen, and he sets down his coffee cup with a clatter. "Are you saying you would go to North Korea for this? Absolutely not."

"It is an excellent opportunity for Jae Hwa," Grandfather says. "We do not know how long the window will remain open for us to enter the country."

"I didn't think any foreigner was allowed into North Korea." Dad scowls. "Besides, she has an American passport. You know how they feel about Americans."

"Dad," I say, gripping the edge of the table. "Grandfather has already applied for the visas, and they've been approved."

Dad scowls at Grandfather. "You did this behind my back?"

"It's a very short trip." I lean forward to get Dad's focus back on me. "It will only be for one night and two days. We are going into the Diamond Mountains tourist area. It's perfectly safe there."

Okay, that may have been a slight exaggeration.

"You mean Kumgangsan? Didn't a lady get shot there for walking on the beach?" Dad says. "Yeah, that sounds *real* safe."

"Things are different now," Grandfather says. "The North Koreans need money and our medicine. There have been no issues in the area for over two years. She would be under my protection. I promise to keep her safe."

Dad dumps a packet of sugar into his coffee and swirls his spoon through it. He rubs his forehead and then says, "My answer is no. I can't let her go."

I stand too quickly and knock my chair backward. It's hard to focus because I can see our whole plan unraveling before my eyes. I want to tell Dad that if I don't do something, Kud is going to kill everyone I love. If nothing else, this trip buys us more time. And if Kud is watching, he'll think I'm following his instructions.

"Don't look at me like that," Dad says. "You know I couldn't bear it if something were to happen to you."

I nod, pressing my lips together, and pick up my chair. "I'm going to the buffet to find something to eat."

Before I go, though, I pull out my folder with all the photos Kumar printed off for us. They're pictures of the TB patients.

Each patient's medicine is different and specialized depending on that patient's needs. I toss the folder in front of Dad, and storm off to the buffet.

I'm not sure how long I stand by the buffet, but soon Grandfather comes beside me and pats me on the shoulder. I flinch at his touch.

"Never give up hope," Grandfather says. "We must always cling to it even in our darkest hours."

I stare at my plate, seeing it has only a slice of cheese and a piece of sushi on it. I've lost all appetite. Grandfather heads over to dish soup into a bowl while I shuffle back to the table. Deep down, I can't blame Dad. If things were reversed and he announced a business trip to North Korea, I'd throw a fit. I swallow my disappointment and plop into my chair across from Dad.

Sitting on my plate is an origami of a paper frog made from one of the coffee napkins. I lightly touch it with my fingers and look up at Dad. He gives me a sad smile and reaches over and squeezes my hand.

"You really think this is safe?" he asks. I nod, afraid my voice will expose the truth. "I'm glad you're thinking about your future. This is a huge step in the right direction. I'm just not sure if a humanitarian trip is the right solution."

"You know that poster in your office? The one that says, 'Don't let your dreams be dreams'? This, Dad, is one of my dreams. To make a difference in the world. To not sit by and wait for someone else to take risks while I sit back on a cushy couch, and to not watch others suffer when I have the power to help them."

He stares at me with his dark-brown eyes as if he's in pain. "The frog is a symbol of safe travels," he says, gripping my hand in his. "When you go to North Korea, carry it with you and come home quickly to me."

"Thank you." Gingerly, I scoop the frog into my palm. I bite my lip, the tears welling up in the corners of my eyes. "I'll never forget this."

CHAPTER 15

Tuesday after school on the afternoon of the Dano Festival, I hurry to the gym to meet Michelle and Lily. As I rush inside, my heart sinks. The place is a mess. The three-foot paper lanterns that were supposed to be hung are scattered about on the floor. The tables we ordered brought in are MIA. Boxes, overflowing with the strings of flowers that Michelle, Lily, and I strung last weekend, are tossed in a heap in the corner.

And the worst part? Not one volunteer in sight.

"You can't be serious." I drop my backpack and sag against the wall. "We'll never be ready."

"Need some help?" a deep voice says behind me.

I turn to face the volunteer, already formulating a list of things to do—until I see who it is.

It's Kang-dae, standing there in his black leather jacket, long hair half covering his dark eyes and that strong jaw cracked in a half smirk.

"What are you doing here?" I ask. "How did you get on campus?"

"I told the guard I was with you." He gives the room a quick glance. "Not as in dating, of course. Just helping with this party you're apparently putting together to raise medical funds."

"Oh." I glance around, hoping for someone to show up, while clutching my fists, furious no one had. *Where are Michelle and Lily?*

"Appears you need a little help," he says.

I follow his gaze to the paper flower piles, the trash scattered about the gym, and the easels heaped by the bleachers where the pictures of North Korean kids are supposed to be displayed. I can only imagine the panicked look I must be wearing.

"I could put you to work." I plant my hands on my hips and pretend to size him up. "You man enough?"

"I hadn't pegged you for a party organizer," Kang-dae says. "But I'd hate to disappoint someone of your lineage."

I scowl. He has no idea how mentioning my lineage disturbs me. "I can put on a party if I need to. But since you're here, you can go find some humans to hang these ridiculous lanterns."

He laughs, shakes his head, and with a salute, marches off. The moment he leaves, I text Michelle and Lily, asking them where they are. Next I call the maintenance office about the tables and dump the first box of flowers onto the gym floor. By the time I have flowers stretched out in long roped lines across the gym floor, Kang-dae saunters through the gym doors, a parade of soccer players following in his wake.

"Will these suffice for the humans you were asking for?" Kang-dae asks.

I've no idea how he managed to wrangle the soccer team to help hang decorations, but who am I to complain? I show them the ladders and hand them fishing line. Meanwhile, a group of *ajusshi* come in with the tables. After I direct where to set them up, I drag the ropes of flowers to the tables and start taping them to their fronts.

"Care for help?" Kang-dae asks.

I glance at my watch. Four o'clock. I have three hours to finish decorating and somehow slip into my dress. I'd call Marc, but he's at his training until 7:00 p.m. He won't even be at the party on time.

I hand Kang-dae a rope end. "Hold this," I say, and stalk to the other side of the table, where I tape down my portion of the rope.

"Quite the operation you've undertaken," Kang-dae says, lazily watching as I wrestle with the rest of the string before we move onto the next table. "Do you think this whole clandestine endeavor will work?"

"I hope so." I stand back to assess my work. The flower strand is skewed and two of the loops are off-center. "Let's hope it works better than my decorating."

"Agreed. But if it were me, I'd just lie my way into North Korea. Why mess around with all of this nonsense?"

"Because it has to look believable. We can't just go traipsing into North Korea without a reason. There is no way the government would allow a bunch of teens into the country. Plus, what would our parents say? You know it would be all over the news."

"If you say so." He sprawls out on a bleacher, crossing his arms. "So how long have you and Marc been dating?"

It feels like we've been together forever, but as I think about it, I realize it's only been about four months. Then I blush as I remember our first kiss. It was right after he'd saved me when Haemosu pulled me into the Spirit World through my locker.

"Not long," I say, trying to fluff a flower I'd accidentally stepped on. "He's been really supportive through all of this. I don't know if I could've made it without him."

"Oh, I'm sure you could. You're tougher than you think. You should give yourself more credit."

I focus on the flower, not sure what to think about Kang-dae's look or why he's complimenting me. We work for the next few minutes in silence, putting the final touches on the flowers and then piling the flower arrangements onto the tables. The soccer team hauls in ladders and yells directions to each other.

Kang-dae and I are tacking the photos onto the easels when Michelle and Lily rush in, each holding a long white cake box.

"Girl," Michelle says, out of breath. "I'm over-the-world sorry. The vendor called and we had *issues*. Lily and I had to taxi it to the other side of eternity to find another bakery that had fresh *kongtteok*."

"Those rice cakes better taste good." I peek inside the box, discovering round cakes of steamed rice sprinkled with beans and smelling of honey. My stomach growls at the sight. "Don't worry, though, I saved plenty of work for you."

"So." Michelle scoots closer to Kang-dae. "Who's your friend?"

"Kang-dae, meet Michelle and Lily," I say. "He's a friend from Yonsei University. While the two of you were touring Seoul, he came to my rescue."

Michelle is all smiles and she bats her eyelashes. Even Lily looks a little overwhelmed by Kang-dae's striking looks as she sets the boxes on the table.

"You could drag that background against the wall and set it up behind the donation table," I tell him.

"Your wish is my command," Kang-dae says. He flashes my friends a smile and then heads across the gym.

"My, my," Michelle says. "Where did you pick that specimen up?"

"Does Marc know about him?" Lily asks.

"He's actually a friend of Marc's." I smile over this, because Marc actually hates Kang-dae.

"Does he have a girlfriend?" Michelle asks as she uncovers the cakes.

"He's a college boy," Lily says. "I'd stay clear."

Michelle grins. "I know."

"I really don't know much about him," I say. "But I do know we've got a party to get on."

Astonishingly, by seven o'clock, the room is set up. Techno music plays over the system, and the air smells a mix of sweet from the rice cakes and savory from the sesame-seed sauce for the *kimbap*. A table in the corner is stacked with lanterns that people can buy later and write their wishes on. At dark, we'll light the lanterns and release them into the air. I already know what will be on mine.

We've strung the pillars in the lobby with tiny white lights to greet partyers as they come in, as well as looped lights along the bleachers. A disco ball, which the soccer team somehow managed to hang along with the colored lanterns, spins from the ceiling. It spits sparkles across the walls, making me feel a little light-headed. The background is set up behind the lantern table, asking for medical funds, while the easels are strategically placed about the gym.

I stop and stare at one of the pictures on the easel in front of me. It's a girl, her hands clasped together. Streaks of dirt are smeared over her cheeks and forehead. Wisps of black hair have been pulled out of her ponytail. But it's her eyes that make my breath catch. They stare at me, empty and hungry. I'm not sure if it's hunger for food or a hunger for life, and that thought twists at my heart.

Even though the forefront of this mission is to find the White Tiger orb, my heart warms knowing that even if we fail at that task, we're still providing relief and hope to many North Koreans.

"Jae Hwa," Lily says, traveling up to me in her blue gown. Her top is tight, with spaghetti straps, while the chiffon skirt swings freely around her knees. She's curled her long blond hair into perfect ringlets. "You haven't changed yet? People are arriving. You'd better hurry."

"You look gorgeous," I tell her. "Kumar is going to have a heart attack when he sees you."

"I sure hope so." She smiles slyly. "He's supposed to be here by now. He was going to give Marc a ride."

My heart sinks, knowing he's being dragged into this insane world I'm a part of. I almost spit out everything, but I bite my tongue instead. Now isn't the time.

"Marc said they'd be here around seven thirty, so you'll have to wait a bit."

"At least Michelle is having a good time."

I follow Lily's gaze. Michelle is standing by the punch bowl with Kang-dae, lightly touching the sleeve of his navy button-down shirt. She whispers something into his ear. He laughs, throwing back his head as if what she said was the funniest thing ever. Which it could possibly be. Michelle's not only smart and gorgeous, but she can put the charm on when she wants to.

Still, a stab cuts through me. Which is ridiculous. I shouldn't feel jealous that he'd rather talk to her than me. I should be thrilled. My best friend finally found somebody to help her recover from her jerk of an ex-boyfriend back in Ohio.

"I'll be back in two seconds and help you cut those cakes," I promise Lily.

Snatching up my backpack and dress, I dart down the steps into the basement of the gym. I don't want to be caught changing in the main bathroom when everyone is arriving, so I head to the girls' locker room instead. After swinging the door open, I grope along the wall until my hand scrapes across the light switch.

The bulbs blink, a skittering noise, as if resisting the electricity. The light settles over the lockers and worn benches in an uneven, yellowish glow. I toss my pack onto the first bench. I strip down to my bra and panties, eyeing the shower and wishing I could rinse off. But there isn't time, so I resort to slipping on my black dress. It hugs my body, and I have to stretch to zip up the back. The one strap over my right shoulder is all twisted. I am trying to adjust it when the faucet squeaks in the adjoining bathroom. Then a rush of running water echoes over the tiles.

My skin chills. Did someone else come into the changing rooms after me? I peer around the corner to where the sinks are, but no one's there. Before Haemosu messed with my brain, I would've shrugged the noises off. But those days are over.

My heart speeds up as I pad barefoot to the sink area. A row of five sinks with identical mirrors stretches before me. The bathroom stalls are all propped open, empty. The sound of rushing water has vanished, replaced with a steady *plink, plink, plink*. Water drips from the sink directly in front of me. I clamp my hand over the cold, clammy handle to turn off the faucet. It doesn't budge. It's as if it's been welded into place.

The plinking sound rises around me, reverberating until it's deafening. Instinctively, I push my hands over my ears.

My gaze slides up to the mirror. A face that's not mine stares back at me. I scream and stagger backward, desperate to escape, but my eyes are paralyzed by the face that floats out of the mirror and becomes a whole body, wispy as a ghost.

It's a *gwishin*. My temples pound. She's wearing a floor-length white *hanbok*, and her long black hair blows as if she's trapped in a wind tunnel. Her lips move, but all I can hear is the pounding of the water. She reaches out to me, her gnarly fingers grasping, almost clawing.

My back presses against the concrete wall. I should run or yell or *something*, but I'm immobilized. A small part of my brain reminds me how I promised myself I'd never let fear immobilize me again.

The faucet squeaks and water gushes from all the spigots, full blast.

"Danger surrounds you"—the *gwishin*'s voice finally breaks through the madness.

Water spills out of the sinks, tumbling in waterfalls onto the floor.

"Trust no one," she continues.

I'm standing ankle deep in water. "Leave," I say. "Now."

"Death wants you." She's reaching out both hands. "Come with me instead. Join us."

Terror spears through my chest. It empowers me enough to wrench myself away from whatever power she holds over me. I swipe my arm at her face, but swing only through chilled air. She cackles and vanishes.

The noise plummets into silence.

Somehow I'm standing by the sink again, hands hugging my sides, my chest heaving. The sink is dry. Not a drop of water on the floor. I chance to look back into the mirror and see Kang-dae strolling through the bathroom door. I jump and scream.

"Whoa!" he says. "I came to check on you. Heard some screaming. Everything all right?"

"God," I yell, running shaking hands over my face. "You scared the life out of me. What are you doing in here? I could've been naked!"

He holds his hands into the air. "Calm it down. You know the Council wouldn't be too pleased if I let anything unpleasant happen to their most prized girl."

"Like you could do something about it." I let out a long breath, feeling idiotic for acting like a fool in front of him. I push my hair back and press it into place.

"Come here." He wraps me in his arms. "You're still shaking."

It's true. That *gwishin* freaked me out, but it was more than that. I always had some kind of supernatural power when I fought Haemosu in the Spirit World. But here I felt useless. It brought back all the memories of being at Komo's house when Haemosu kidnapped her, and I was powerless, bolted to the wall by my bracelet.

A twinge of guilt sweeps over me as Kang-dae rests his chin on my head. He smells of cologne, spicy. Suddenly the comforting hug feels more intimate than friendly. I pull back, untangling myself from him. What would Marc think if he saw Kang-dae holding me like that?

I draw in a deep breath to pull myself together. It was only a hug, I tell myself, and I'd been attacked by a *gwishin*. It's nothing more than that.

"There," he says. His hands linger on my arms and his eyes on my lips. "Better?"

"You should leave," I say, adjusting my crooked dress. "I'll be fine. I think I was attacked by a *gwishin*."

He frowns and looks about the bathroom. "The fact you were attacked by a *gwishin* means I will definitely be staying. You're decent enough, and you're going to tell me exactly what happened."

I knead my forehead, trying to ease the piercing headache I now have. Maybe he's right. Keeping secrets has never helped me before. But I've always shared this kind of stuff just with Marc and Grandfather, and I find myself hesitant to talk to anyone else.

Back in the locker room area, I shrug into my heels and stuff my jeans and tee into my backpack. I explain what I saw as I brush out my hair, leaving it to hang long and straight. Every once in a while, I glance over at Kang-dae, but his face is unreadable.

"Sounds like a classic *gwishin* sighting," he says dryly.

"You make it sound like it's not such a big deal." I swipe on lipstick, avoiding the way my hands still shake or how close the mirrors are to me in the adjoining bathroom.

"Oh, it is rather a big deal," he says as he follows me out of the bathroom, his hand on the small of my back protectively. Before we head back into the lobby, he holds me back and glances around. "We're good."

"So what would you do if a ghost or creature jumped out at us?" I ask skeptically.

"I can't see them like your boyfriend." I don't like the way he talks about Marc, but I continue to walk alongside him. "I have power over them, though. They obey my commands."

"Really? Why?"

"Why can Marc see beings from the Spirit World?" He shrugs. "I don't know."

I press my lips together, deciding not to spill Marc's secret. That when he rescued me from Haemosu, he was touched and forever changed. It's my fault Marc is bound to the Spirit World.

A whispering sound slips through the hallway. We both pause, bodies tense. Kang-dae's perfect features contort in a frown, and he grips the railing of the stairs so tightly, the veins in his hand bulge.

"I'd rather not seek trouble," I say, and hook his arm in mine, dragging him along until we're back upstairs in the gym surrounded by my schoolmates. Usually, being in thick crowds comforts me, but after the incident with Kud's assassin, I don't put anything past him.

"After I help Lily cut the cakes, I'm in charge of selling lanterns," I tell Kang-dae. "Do you mind helping me, or do you have to be somewhere?"

"Tonight you have my devoted service. Especially in that dress." He grins, and I hit him on the shoulder.

"I wore it for Marc," I say. Then, to prove my point, I pull out my phone and call him. There's no answer. I start to panic until I check my texts and find one from Marc that tells me he's running later than he thought he would. I watch couples dance under the disco ball and sigh, wishing he was here.

"Why don't you find Michelle?" I say. "She seemed to like hanging out with you earlier. Plus, she doesn't have a boyfriend."

"You reject a guy so delicately," he says.

The rest of the evening moves by in a blur. Kang-dae actually proves useful, and by the time it gets dark, we've sold all the lanterns. When there's a pause in the line, we talk about the trip and places we might find the orb.

"Interesting. So Palk also thinks there is an orb in the Diamond Mountains?" Kang-dae rubs the stubble of hair on his chin. "You know there are rumors that nine dragons guard Kuryong Falls. There's no way we could get inside."

"How do you know that?"

He shrugs. "I make it my business to know."

"Palk seemed to think the dragons would help me."

"Really?" Kang-dae's eyes light up. He lightly touches my arm. "What would we do without you? The Council is lucky to have you working with them."

"I'm not someone to be used." I grab the last lantern and a marker. I set it aside for later. "And don't forget I'm not on the Council or one of the Guardians. I don't have to abide by their rules."

"Of course. And you shouldn't have to."

Michelle and Lily's cakes have vanished, and everyone's had their fill of dancing by the time Michelle announces it's time to take our lanterns outside to light them. I text Marc again, asking where he is. Finally, my phone dings. Marc.

Sorry. Ran into some trouble. Will be later than I thought.

My chest squeezes with worry. Trouble? Do u need me 2 come?

No. Everything is ok now. Kumar 2.

I let out a long breath, shaking my head. I always seem to think the worst of everything these days. I decide not to mention the *gwishin* showing up. He'll find out eventually, but right now he's got enough to worry about with helping plan this whole North Korean trip.

"What are you going to wish for?" Kang-dae asks as he strolls up to me.

I tap my marker on the lantern. At the beginning of the night, it seemed so simple. Find the orb. But after watching Lily's slideshow depicting the North Koreans in need, I realize there is so much to wish for.

To keep my family safe, to protect Marc, to heal Komo, and now to help those in need. Before, I'd always wanted to be normal, but tonight I don't want to be normal. I want to be powerful enough to stop all this pain and suffering. My thoughts turn to the Spirit World and the feeling of power I had there with every step I took.

I stare at the picture behind me of the little girl, lying on a mat in a barren concrete house. I don't know her name, but I want to. Nearly everyone is exiting the gym to head outside to the soccer field, except Kang-dae, so I scribble my wish onto the lantern.

To be powerful enough to stop the evil.

As Kang-dae and I carry our lanterns outside, he points to mine.

"Interesting wish," he says.

My cheeks warm as I realize he saw my wish. "What did you wish for?" I say.

"You don't want to know."

I pause at the top of the gym steps. Below on the soccer field, all the kids are spread out, lighting their lanterns and releasing their wishes into the sky, a canvas of colors.

"Actually I do," I say. "You saw mine; it's only fair I know yours."

He laughs and hurries down the steps out to the field. By the time I reach him, he's already prepping to light it. I dive to grab the lantern, but he holds it high out of my reach.

"Are you planning on standing like that the rest of the night?" I ask, laughing.

His lips twitch. "I suppose you've got a point."

He fakes left and moves right, but my reflexes are too fast. I block his way and snatch for the lantern. One word is scrawled across the rice paper's surface. My heart skitters as I see it.

Jae

I don't know if I'm flattered, angry, or scared. The lantern flutters from my fingers to the turf. Kang-dae silently picks it up and stares at my name.

"Now you know why you weren't supposed to read it?" he asks, and comes closer to me. Dangerously close. His breath practically whispers against my forehead.

I look away, and that's when I see Marc. Standing at the edge of the field, his expression unreadable in the night shadows.

I've done nothing wrong, yet as we stare at each other from across the distance, it's as if I've betrayed him.

When I race to him, I stop short of throwing my arms around his neck like I usually do, unsure of that look in his eyes. He doesn't wrap me in his arms either. Instead, I stand there, cold and awkwardly scraping my heels along the crack in the sidewalk while he focuses on the field of students.

"You and Kang-dae have become pretty good friends." Marc's voice is wary.

"It's not like that," I say, even though I know it kind of is. Especially now that I know Kang-dae's wish. I glance over at Kang-dae and see him lighting both our lanterns. They lift into the sky. But it's all just for fun, isn't it? It isn't like these wishes actually come true.

"A *gwishin* came for me in the bathroom. Kang-dae showed up and scared it off."

For a moment, the wall of anger in his face cracks, and worry fills his eyes. "Are you okay? I shouldn't have left you alone. I knew it was a bad idea."

"I'm fine. Somehow, I was able to pull away from it," I say. "Kang-dae was there to help."

"How convenient." His jaw clenches. "I know Kang-dae is a Guardian, but I still don't like him."

"Don't be jealous. He's cocky as all get-out, but you know you're the only guy for me. If it wasn't for him, who knows what would've happened in the bathroom?"

"I didn't realize I was so easily replaced."

"It's not like that and you know it. Stop being this way."

"We had a good reason for being late." Marc twists his ring around his finger. "We were attacked by a group of *dokkaebi*."

"What?"

"Yeah." He shrugs. "It wasn't so bad. They just like to cause trouble. Flattened our tires at a stoplight and then ran off. We tried to chase them down, but they disappeared."

"You should've called me."

"You're right, but I wanted you to enjoy your night. Not get phone calls about mythological creatures."

"It doesn't work that way. We are a team. Your problems and mine, and vice versa."

"A team?" He shakes his head. "And is Kang-dae on this team?"

"That's not fair."

"I saw how he was looking at you. How he *always* looks at you." Marc runs his hands through his hair. "Jae, I just wanted to give you a night off. One of these days it's all going to go to hell. I don't want you to be around when that happens."

The thing is, he knows I don't want him involved with the Guardians of Shinshi, and I know he doesn't want me to go on this mission.

And that's how it ends. Both of us angry, with nothing else to say to each other. He leaves, and I catch a ride home with Michelle. As we drive through the streets of Yonhi-Dong, I realize Kang-dae went home without saying good-bye. Not that I expected him to. I'm mad at him, too. If he'd just left me be, none of this would've happened.

CHAPTER 16

My suitcase, resting against the plastic chairs lining the bus terminal, looks like a beat-up, dull, and unsparkly version of Michelle's, which is practically twice the size of mine. I check my pouch one more time to make sure I have my temporary passport, which is what I'll use to enter North Korea. Regular American passports are strictly prohibited.

Dad pats my shoulder. "I'm proud of you for taking on this project. It will help so many people."

I nod, not ready to look him in the face. I can't tell him the truth, or he'd flip out. He was against everything with Haemosu. I can't blame him, because for so long, he had accused Haraboji of inventing Haemosu's existence as an explanation for my other aunt's disappearance. But if I hadn't listened to Grandfather and Komo, I know I would've been one of the kidnapped souls myself.

Grandfather comes up to our group and waves us together. A man trails behind him, lugging a compact suitcase and wearing khaki pants and a dark-brown shirt. A crisp white name tag is stitched into his navy-colored Windbreaker.

Park Chu-won is written in Korean across it.

His dark hair is neatly combed to the side, and there's an easy, carefree grin stretched over his face. From the man's slight build and relaxed shoulders, I'd bet he's never been trapped in a room with mythical creatures before. I rub my wrist, hoping Grandfather knows what he's doing by bringing a clueless tour guide with us.

Or maybe I'm completely paranoid and this trip will be smooth as a bamboo shoot.

Marc, Michelle, Kang-dae, and I move toward him while Marc's parents and my dad crowd around us. Michelle's mom is pacing by the line of plastic seats, yelling at someone in Japanese, then switching to Korean and then back again.

"Your mom okay?" I ask Michelle.

"I don't want to get into it." Michelle crosses her arms and looks away with a shake of her head.

The only person who doesn't have family here is Kang-dae.

"Welcome," Grandfather says. "This is our guide, Chu-won. He'll review the procedures with you one final time before we leave."

"I am very excited to be your guide this weekend," Chu-won says, grinning and making the wrinkles edging out from his smiling eyes even more pronounced. "I will be traveling with you to the clinic and escorting you to the presentation ceremony. I also serve as the clinic's mechanic and fix their equipment when I make my yearly visit. They will be pleased to see me twice this year. Now if you'll bear with me as I review all the policies." He takes out a clipboard and starts reading through it. "No laptops, cell phones, cameras with 160 millimeters, or binoculars with 10x zoom. Oh, and definitely no video cameras."

Kang-dae makes a disgruntled noise and mutters under his breath, "Is there anything we *are* allowed to bring?"

"I feel like I'm going on detox," mutters Michelle. "I've only been parted with my phone for five minutes, and I'm already going into withdrawal."

"I have all of your reentry permits already," Chu-won continues. Then he hands each of us a small booklet with our passport information in it and two other cards. "This you will keep as your temporary passport. You also have your debit card to use in the tourist zone. This will pay for any of your needs. The final card will be your embarkation card. Put all three of those in this plastic sheath, and make sure you wear it at all times when in the tourist zone."

"What if we lose this?" I ask.

"Don't." Chu-won's smile drops into a frown.

"Uncanny how quickly our happy tour guide can turn on us," Marc jokes into my ear.

The twinkle in Marc's eyes sends a flicker of optimism through me. Maybe he's not mad anymore. Maybe we can get back to the way things used to be. But then my eyes fall on Kang-dae leaning against one of the plastic terminal chairs, methodically rubbing the stubble on his chin as if in deep thought. With Kang-dae on the trip, I doubt anything will be normal.

The whole process is a bit daunting. I arrange my cards in the exact way Chu-won tells us to. Once my plastic pouch passes our guide's approval, I hang it over my head, the strap already scratching against the skin on the back of my neck. Next we are each given a tag for our bags. Dad helps secure mine, pulling apart the plastic and then sticking the ends together so they line up perfectly.

Ms. Myong, Michelle's mom, joins us; her black leather boots that stretch up her thin legs practically make music as she moves. From her sleek navy rain jacket to a slicked-back ponytail, she has the air of someone who gets what she wants. She flashes me a polite, distant smile and tugs on Michelle's arm.

"What?" Michelle mumbles under her breath. "I need to pay attention."

I've never actually held a conversation longer than two minutes with Ms. Myong. As a traveling journalist, she's rarely at home, and I always get the distinct feeling that she believes I'm not to the standard her daughter should be hanging out with.

"Just take the damn pictures," Ms. Myong whispers, and then passes Michelle a tiny black box that settles easily in her palm. "It's hardly complicated."

Michelle lifts her eyebrows as if daring her mom to change her mind. They stare at each other for a half second before Michelle tucks what I'm guessing is a camera into her pocket.

"Time to say your good-byes," Chu-won announces to our group. "In order to make it to the border on time, we must follow a strict schedule."

"I guess this is it," Dad says. A pained look crosses his face. He unbuttons his black suit jacket, only to button it again, but now the buttons are off by one. "Follow the rules. Do not go into unsupervised places. They shoot people who do, remember that."

"Don't worry, Dad," I say, fixing his buttons so they are even. "I'll be fine. I'll bring you back a souvenir or something."

He takes both my hands in his and clasps them, squeezing once. "Yes. A souvenir. That would be nice."

He kisses my forehead and lets go. As I step away, grasping my suitcase handle tight, the closeness of him fades and I feel a sense of loss.

I clamber onto the bus with the others and deposit my suitcase on the top rack. The back of the bus is filled with boxes of medicine that we're delivering. Hopefully that will keep the border officials from giving us any reason not to gain entry into North Korea.

When I slide into one of the window seats, Michelle plops down next to me, twiddling the black box between her fingers, staring at the seat back. Marc and Kang-dae climb into the seats behind us.

Outside, our parents crowd along the curb and wave us off as we pull out of the bus station. Michelle's mom is back on her phone, her red lips moving a mile a minute. She's not even looking at the bus.

Dad doesn't wave. His hands remain in his pants pockets. His face looks lost, and his shoulders are slightly stooped. I press my palm against the glass, remembering how tightly he'd held my hand only minutes ago. Just as the bus turns the curb, I see him wipe the back of his hand against the corner of his eye.

I bite my lips, falling back against my hard vinyl seat. Is Dad crying? No, he doesn't cry. At Mom's funeral, he might have. I can't remember. I was too lost in my own grief to notice the world around me, then. This must have been my imagination.

"You okay?" Michelle asks.

"Yeah, but I'm not sure if my dad is. I don't know what he'd do if he lost me."

"Don't be ridiculous," she says, squeezing my shoulder. "North Korea doesn't want to start a war by hurting a bunch of kids delivering medical supplies."

"I heard what your mom said," I say, studying Michelle's face. "That's got a long-range lens, doesn't it?"

Michelle bites the inside of her lip and shrugs. "*Umma* thinks she has it all figured out."

"So you're not going to take the pictures?"

"I'm going on this trip to help bring medicine." Michelle lifts her chin. "Not start a war. This is my trip, and I'm going to do what I think needs to be done."

I think about Michelle's words as I stare out my window, watching the rice fields spread out before me. She's talking about a physical war while I'm trying to stop a spiritual one. Perhaps we are more alike than I thought.

We drive through smaller towns, but soon it becomes fairly rural. The landscape grows more forested, and we pass massive camouflaged concrete structures.

"What are those for?" I ask our guide.

"They're positioned so that if things fall apart between North and South Korea, they can push the two barriers into the road. They're made to interlock, so it's a quick roadblock if the North decides to send down its troops."

It never ceases to amaze me how the two countries could be separated so completely. The farther we drive, the more I feel as if we're entering a war zone. Barbed wire is strung around fields, and warning signs remind us to turn back. Yet at the same time, there are beautiful farms and sprawling houses that are so different from anything I've seen in Seoul.

"We are entering the DMZ, which stands for the demilitarized zone. It's the strip of land between the North and South and under heavy military rule. People get bonuses for living in the DMZ," Chu-won explains. "The South wants to show off how prosperous they are to the North."

After we go through a checkpoint, our bus pulls into the parking lot of the Goseong Observatory. When I step out of the bus, the air smells like ocean, full of brine and whispers of wide-open spaces. Grandfather takes off to talk to some officials about our medical supplies. The guards will take the supplies from here and then meet us in Kumgangsan, where the supplies will be transferred back to us after they've been checked.

Chu-won has us take out our suitcases and waves us to the main entrance of a white concrete building. "Refresh yourselves at the observatory until we are ready to go through customs," he says.

In the distance, I can make out the East Sea and two little islands. Coils of barbed wire string from the sea to as far inland as I can make out. Tanks, old aircraft, and military trucks are parked and roped off for viewing.

"What an unusual place," Michelle says. "We're standing in a war zone, but this feels more like a tourist area."

"Shall we walk around?" Kang-dae asks.

"I say we shall," Michelle says with a big smile.

We head into the lobby, which is full of vendors selling food, hats, and sunglasses. Michelle's right, the atmosphere reminds me more of a tourist attraction than a military zone. There's even a museum here. The room smells of dried fish and *kimchi*, and my stomach rumbles. Michelle nudges me when the guys go buy some drinks. "If Kang-dae wasn't all hotness, I'd wonder which century he belonged in."

"That's probably because he's one of the psychotic Guardians obsessed with protecting me," I say sourly.

"They are both part of the group?" Michelle asks.

"Unfortunately, they think I can't handle things myself." I shrug. "Whatever. It's fine. I wanted Marc to come, but Kang-dae—" I decide not to finish that thought because it reminds me too much of Kang-dae's hot breath against my forehead, and I can already feel that stab of guilt.

"At least they're nice to look at," Michelle says. "I'm thinking of making a move on Kang-dae."

I don't want to go there. "I'm going to buy some *kimbap*. You?"

Michelle joins me, and soon we join the guys and head upstairs to the observation deck. The entire observatory is oddly barren, with only a few families looking through the binoculars and an elderly couple taking pictures. Evidently it was built for big crowds that never came. Outside the overbearing gates, construction trucks and supplies are parked in random places on the roadside, forgotten. They were probably brought in hopes of a reunification. But the place has an air of desertion, like it's been forgotten and left behind.

From up top, we have a perfect view of the coast where swift, unending currents roll onto the sand. The brown beaches merge into rolling hills that grow into staggering jagged peaks. The first thing I'm surprised about is how brown and dry the land looks, a sharp contrast to the area we just passed through. The entire landscape is free of trees except for the area we'll be heading toward.

"Looks pretty desolate," Marc says as he takes in the scene through the scope. "Most of the trees in North Korea were cut down to provide heating during the winters."

"We've got a walking encyclopedia in our midst," Kang-dae mutters next to me.

"Which isn't a bad thing. I like knowing what's going on." I cross my arms and step away from him.

"A keeper, then?" He lifts his eyebrows mockingly.

That comment isn't even worth acknowledging. I'm adjusting the tag strapped around my neck when I notice him pull out a phone from his pocket. He starts texting on it.

"You do remember Chu-won said not to bring cell phones." I give Kang-dae a pointed look.

He smirks and shakes his head. "I'll be keeping it until they wrench it away from me."

Marc's head whips around, his eyes wide, searching the porch.

I step closer to him. "Something wrong?"

"Did you hear that?" he asks. I don't like how wild his eyes are right now, as if he's seen a *gwishin* himself. "Like chains breaking, dragging—it's getting louder."

My heart stutters as he takes off to the stairs. I run after him, calling his name to stop, but he doesn't. He tumbles down the steps, muttering something about wishing for a sword.

"What's going on?" Michelle says, following us with Kang-dae at her heels.

I have no idea, which sends my pulse into overdrive.

When Marc hits the main level of the observatory, he squeezes between groups of people until he's in the center of the courtyard, swiveling in a circle. I'm out of breath when I reach him, but it's not because I'm tired or winded. It's because of that look in Marc's eyes. It means danger is near. It means he senses something he shouldn't.

"What's wrong?" I ask.

"It appears we've got company," Kang-dae says as he and Michelle catch up to us.

"Yes," Marc says vaguely. "They're at every exit."

"Who is at every exit?" Michelle asks, her voice shaking.

"*Dalgyal gwishin*, I think," Marc says. "I just wish I knew why."

I glance at Kang-dae. His eyes gleam dark, and his jaw is rigid as if he is holding back anger. The *dalgyal gwishin* are supposed to be the freakiest of all the ghosts. They have no eyes, mouth, nose, or even arms. No physical features. And according to legend, if you see them, you will die.

"What do we do?" I ask. "Can we fight our way out?"

"The real question is, what do they want?" Kang-dae rubs his chin. "And how do they know of our plans here? Did you tell the *gwishin* anything in the bathroom?" I shake my head. "The fact that it touched you means it must have read your mind. Fear breaks down your barriers and allows them to read your thoughts."

"Perfect," Marc says. "Now we have the Underworld to deal with."

"There must be a back door or an emergency exit around here," Michelle offers.

Then their forms appear as if floating out of a mist. The bodies are chalky white, long floating gowns flowing in a nonexistent breeze. Their faces are blank and smooth on top of formless bodies. I bite back a scream.

"I can see them," Michelle whispers, and grabs on to my arm. "That isn't a good thing, is it?"

"Not especially," Kang-dae says.

"If you see them, it means you are going to die," Marc says.

"That's a comforting thought." Michelle frowns and crosses her arms. "What if I'm not ready to die?"

I study the few shoppers and shopkeepers going about their own business. We get a couple of odd glances, but no one even notices the *gwishin* gathering along the perimeter of the courtyard.

"And it appears by everyone else's reaction that the *gwishin* are here only for us," I say.

"Look!" Michelle points to the far back corner. "I see a back exit."

The four of us travel to where Michelle pointed, trying to be inconspicuous. Marc's footsteps quicken and his back tenses. As we pass a cleaning cart tucked into a dark corner, Marc snatches the broom.

"Touch pathetic, don't you think?" Kang-dae laughs as Marc grips the handle. "As if that will stop them."

"Never underestimate the power of the broom," Marc says.

He slams open the heavy door, and we rush after him into the long, narrow corridor. I throw a glance over my shoulder. The *gwishin* remain stoic, not moving from their posts.

"Do you think they're just going to stand there, and not follow us?" I say.

"No," both Kang-dae and Marc say.

Marc freezes so abruptly I bump into him. Kang-dae slides up next to Marc, while I peer around to spot an animal about the size of a large dog blocking our path. Its fur is shaggy and caked with mud. Small ears pop from its head, and its beady eyes are as red as fire.

"It's a blood weasel," Kang-dae whispers. "Dreadful personalities."

"We are just passing through," Marc tells the weasel. "We wish to go our own way."

"No, no, no." Michelle whimpers. She scurries to the door and yanks on its handle. Her face reddens from the strain. It doesn't budge. "We're locked in."

"Lovely," Kang-dae says.

"We know your errand." Its voice slurs out the words in Korean. "Our great King Daebyeol of the Underworld is most interested in what you wish to acquire. Give us the girl, and no harm will come to you."

I slide between Marc and Kang-dae. "Your way is not ours. Leave us."

"Scat," Kang-dae says.

The weasel chokes, or perhaps it's laughing, I'm not sure. Saliva drools from its mouth, and it shakes its body, flinging off chunks of dirt. But as the dirt splatters over the walls, I realize it's actually blood, caked on the creature. The blood on the walls liquefies and begins to ooze down to the floor into puddles. I gape as the puddles bubble and dark forms rise from their depths, twisting and contorting until they create at least twenty weasels flanking the first one. They snarl and growl, their red eyes flashing hungrily.

"So you see," the first weasel slurs, "we do not jest. Hand her over."

"That broom of yours may come in handy, after all," Kang-dae says.

Marc twirls the broomstick in his hands. "No joke."

"Stand behind me, Michelle." I crouch in preparation.

"Yeah, right." Michelle sidles next to me and holds out her fists. "I might not have all the moves, but if I'm going down, it will be kicking and punching."

With a sneer, the leader hunches down and springs at us. I see nothing except the whites ringing its red eyes and those sharp claws stretching out to me. I whip into a roundhouse, smacking its jaw with a snap.

Beside me, Marc and Kang-dae meet the other weasels as they attack. We are all fighting for our lives. Marc blocks one assault with his broom, knocking the creature away. He spins and thwarts another by twisting the broom and jabbing it down the creature's throat.

Kang-dae moves faster than I imagined, chopping the side of his hand down on the neck of one, while side-kicking another.

Michelle screams behind me. A weasel has her pants leg in its mouth, ripping it apart, a desperateness in its eyes as if it is hungry for her flesh. She boxes its ears, but the creature appears unfazed. I backflip, my feet kicking the beast as I make my descent. Squealing, it flies through the air, smacking against the far wall and crumpling onto the ground.

There isn't time to celebrate because two more weasels are sneering and snapping at my feet. One jumps at me. I strike it away and spin into a roundhouse, kicking the other one. Another weasel seems to leap out of thin air and tumbles on top of me. The impact sends me to the ground. I wrap my arms around its snarling jaws. It smells rank, and I gag. The creature wriggles and writhes in my arms. I groan under its pull, but I know if I let go, those teeth will sink into me.

With a snarl, another weasel lashes out a clawed paw, grazing my forehead in an ugly swipe.

"Their bite is poisonous," Kang-dae shouts from farther down the corridor, fighting off two weasels of his own. "It will kill you!"

The air is full of Michelle's screaming and the foul stench of hell itself. Sweat drips off my forehead, and my muscles shudder as I wrestle the beast across the floor. I glance up to see another weasel, its massive bulk bounding across the hallway, eyes boring straight into mine. It's the leader. His jaws widen. I can see every jagged yellow tooth in his mouth.

Panic seizes me. Marc and Kang-dae are both surrounded. I'm on my own. With a shout to propel me, I leap to my feet, still holding the wild beast, and throw it with every ounce of strength within me at the oncoming weasel leader. With a shriek, the smaller creature crashes into its leader, sending them both sprawling to the ground in a tangle of limbs. I rush toward them, twisting in a flip over their bodies so I make a surprise landing on their other side. My foot kicks the leader with a hard front blow. He drops silently to the ground, vanishing in a cloud of dust.

The moment the leader's body fades into oblivion, the other weasels cry out in agony. They run in circles as if chasing their tails before flip-flopping across the concrete floor, tortured. Then, like their master, they too disappear, leaving us in a startling silence.

CHAPTER 17

Gasping for air, I swipe the sweat off my forehead. My hand comes away full of blood. It must have been from when the creature ripped its nasty claw across my forehead. Marc, shoulders hunched as he draws in big breaths, looks over at me.

"You okay?" he asks.

I nod. "Where do you learn those moves?"

"Training paid off." He gives a lopsided grin.

A figure I hadn't seen before moves out of the shadows at the far end of the corridor, footsteps silent against the concrete. At first, I think it's another *gwishin*, but as the figure steps into the weak corridor light, I see it's a girl about my age. She's wearing a long *hanbok*, deathly white and whispering about her like puffy clouds shifting across morning skies. Her black hair is twisted into a long braid that falls over her shoulder and lands at her waist, a contrast to her white dress.

She purses her pale lips and nods once. "He won't be happy."

"Who?" I ask, stepping closer to her, but she lifts her hand and a jagged spear appears in her grip. I stop midstride.

"The master of the Underworld," she says. Her dark eyes assess us with a puzzled look. "He shall also be interested in the company you keep."

"Who are you?" I ask.

"We are not so different, you and I." She gives a ghost of a smile. "I am sure we shall meet again."

She pounds the hilt of her spear against the concrete floor, and white dust shoots into the air, blasting around her. As it falls, her body merges into the dust particles, evaporating.

"That was weird," I tell Marc.

He sags against the wall. "That was weird? I would have picked the ghosts or the weasels that formed out of blood."

"Good point," I say, wanting to collapse from the sheer impossibleness of what just happened, but Michelle is calling my name.

"Who was that girl?"

"Don't know," Marc says. "But she works with the god of the Underworld. My guess is it was Princess Bari. The girl from the myth I read to you at my house."

"Jae!" Michelle says.

"What's wrong?" I stumble to where Michelle is leaning over Kang-dae, terrified something has happened to them. "Tell me you're okay."

"He was bitten," Michelle says, revealing a jagged open wound.

Skin has been ripped off his arm as if the weasel had sunk its teeth into him and torn away the layers of flesh. Sweat beads on Kang-dae's forehead. Blood pools out on the tiles and cement, and his wound is oozing yellow pus, stinking like sewage. With shaky fingers, he withdraws his phone and punches a button.

"Ambulance," he gasps into the phone, then pushes his GPS locator before dragging out a painful moan and closing his eyes.

"Okay, I'm not mad that you kept your phone anymore," I say, holding Kang-dae's head in my lap. "You're going to be okay. Help will come soon."

Michelle rips a strip off the bottom of her shirt and wraps it around his arm. Then she races to the end of the corridor and throws open the doors, so Marc and I can carry Kang-dae outside to wait for the ambulance. A pair of guards at the entrance to the parking lot eye us.

"Please!" Michelle calls out to them in Korean. "Help us!"

"It's going to be all right," I keep telling Kang-dae as he moans on the pavement, but I can't hide the terror in my voice. Hadn't Kang-dae said their bite was lethal?

We don't have to wait long before an ambulance whizzes to us, tires screeching.

"That was fast," Michelle says.

Two paramedics leap out the back doors, scoop Kang-dae up, and deposit him on a stretcher. I draw Michelle in close, wrapping my arm around her as we watch. Tears trickle down her face, and I can't stop the dread filling me that this is a bad omen for our mission.

"He's been bitten," Marc tells the paramedic in Korean. "We think it's infected."

"We've got it from here," one of them tells us in Korean.

The other stops short and inspects my forehead. He unzips his pouch and swipes my forehead with a cool cloth. Ripping open a bandage, he slaps it on my forehead, saying, "Check for infection in two hours."

Gingerly, I touch the slippery rubber of the bandage, amazed at how efficient these paramedics are. They load Kang-dae into the back of the ambulance, slam the back doors shut, and take off, sirens blaring. The three of us stand in on the service parking lot, gazing after the truck.

One of the guards runs to us and asks if everything is okay.

"One of our friends got hurt," Marc explains. "But they're taking him to the hospital."

The solider calls in the incident over his walkie-talkie, and before returning to his post, tells us to fill out an accident report in the office.

"The paramedics left so quickly." Michelle stares at the road the ambulance drove down. "I should've gone with him."

"I can't believe this happened," I say.

"The bite—it's poisonous." Michelle bites her lips. "Will he be okay?"

"Probably not," Marc says. He tosses the broom aside and rubs his jaw, now blooming a bright red. "We should find your grandfather. He won't like what we have to say."

"There's no way I'm going back in that cursed hallway," Michelle says.

So we head around the building, catching the eye of a guard and a glare from a gardener. When we head back into the main observation area, Grandfather is standing near the doors, a frown filling his face.

"Where have you been? What happened to your forehead?" Grandfather barks. I open my mouth to tell him, but all my words seem to get stuck in my throat. "Come," he says, waving his hand as if batting away a fly. "We are set and must not lose a moment."

The three of us follow him to the building, where we join a special line labeled "Foreigner."

"Where is Kang-dae?" Grandfather asks, his whole face red with frustration.

"He's on his way to the hospital," I say.

"We ran into some trouble," Marc says.

"Some?" Michelle opens her mouth, horrified. Tears edge the corners of her eyes. "That is the understatement of the century."

"What?" Grandfather says. "Why did no one come find me? How did this happen?"

"We tried to escape through a back corridor," I say. "But we were trapped."

"Tricked, more like it," Marc says.

After we explain all the details of the fight, he runs his hands over his face, muttering. Finally, he waves us to the booth. "We cannot wait. We will have to go without him. I will call the hospital before we leave and get details. Once we cross the border, we will have no contact with South Korea. You can tell me about what happened on the bus."

Hearing that we'll actually be leaving without Kang-dae worries me. I felt so much more in control with both him and Marc at my side fighting off those weasels. I couldn't have survived on my own. Not in this world.

When I reach the booth, the attendant studies my permit and temporary passport. He stamps it with a South Korean exit stamp. Once we've all gone through unscathed, we head out of the building into a wide parking lot.

I glance uneasily at the guards ringing the area. Standing so close to the barbed wire and towers slows down my steps, but somehow I shuffle my way to board another bus. Michelle can't stop crying, and I pull her in tight after settling into a seat.

"You think he'll live?" she asks.

"Absolutely," I say. "Kang-dae is tough. And there's still time to back out from this trip. You don't have to come."

"No." She pulls out a notepad and taps her pencil on the blank paper. "I'm in this with you. I couldn't live with myself if I didn't take this chance to help deliver the medicine. I'll always feel like I didn't follow through on something big. I think I've been given this opportunity for a reason."

Grandfather boards the bus and lightly touches my hand, reassuring me in a soft voice that Kang-dae is in good hands. "I have made arrangements for him should he recover and wish to join us."

After riding for fifteen or so minutes, we arrive at the North Korean checkpoint. The bus door opens, and a North Korean guard enters. He struts down the aisle wearing an olive uniform, crisp and tight. His square-billed hat shadows his face, but I can still see the firmness in his jaw. Silver buttons trail down the center of his jacket, and his collar bears two yellow bars. I can't help but feel intimidated.

"Hand over your bag," the guard tells Michelle in Korean. His accent is thicker, sharper perhaps. I almost don't understand him.

Michelle's hand shakes as she passes him her handbag. He rummages through it, grunts, and shoves it back at her before giving each seat one more look and leaving. I glance over at her notebook, the once-white pages filled with notes. It's probably a good thing the guard didn't ask for that.

My muscles loosen when the bus's ignition starts, and we begin rumbling down a winding road that follows the coast.

"We will deliver the supplies first," Grandfather explains. "Then tonight they will have a ceremony to thank us."

"I think I'll skip the ceremony," I say, thinking how much I hate being in the spotlight.

"It is a necessary procedure we must follow," Grandfather says. "It will be more for the newspapers and publicity than anything."

Chu-won pulls out a map and shows us our course. "We will travel up north, just outside the tourist region, to drop off the supplies and then return to the tourist area of Kumgangsan."

"That's where Nine Dragon Falls is located," Grandfather says.

As Grandfather and Chu-won discuss the medicine drop-off in greater detail, we pass a small village, hugging one of the hillsides. The houses look like clones of each other, constructed of concrete blocks and sagging tin roofs with no greenery in sight. I hope our medicine will reach someone from that village.

The farther we drive, the rougher the road becomes. The whole region reminds me of Colorado, with its brown countryside and mountains in the distance, yet even more barren, as if it had been stripped of all life, leaving behind death and despair in its wake. It's a stark reminder of Haemosu's lands. I wonder how much the Spirit World and ours are connected. I shiver at the thought.

"We just barely escaped the Underworld god's cronies," Marc says, leaning over the aisle to whisper to Michelle and me. "I don't know if Kang-dae will make it."

I nod. "If you and Kang-dae hadn't been there—" I don't finish my sentence. There isn't a need to.

"Why did they want you?" Michelle says. "I don't understand."

Marc gives me the look that says I shouldn't tell her. I shrug, saying, "Who knows?"

But the truth pricks at my mind like a cut that won't heal.

They either think I have the orb or believe I know where it is. Which means that won't be their last attempt to try to take me and kill my friends. They'll be back. And stronger next time.

I stare out the window, watching the ocean slide in and out of the barbed wire lining the beach as if on patrol. All the walls, barbed wire, and guards here make my skin itch. An irresistible urge to run, far and fast, shoots through my veins. To be free of the chains that this place is already wrapping around me.

If anything goes wrong, there won't be any quick escapes.

CHAPTER 18

Our bus comes to a stop at a concrete building on the side of the road. Nothing else is in sight beyond endless brown grass and rutted dirt roads. The building's whitewashed walls and bare windows blend in perfectly with the barrenness of the countryside. Just ahead, a group of workers are pushing a wheelbarrow full of rocks. Every few feet they stop, pick out some rocks from the cart, and then set them into the dirt. They must be building a road.

A soldier marches onto our bus with an old Kalashnikov resting lightly in his arms. He barks in harsh, sharp Korean to exit the bus. Chu-won explains that we need to transfer to a four-wheel drive vehicle. "This bus could not survive the roads we will take," he says. "Outside of the tourist zone, you will see the truth of how these people live."

We clamber out of the bus, and the soldier points with his gun to a battered SUV that we'll take from here. The fenders sag and the hubcaps are rusted. I wonder if it will break down before we even make it to the clinic. From the lack of cars I've seen on the roads, I figure it's one of their best to offer.

The air is cooler here, as well as dry, and disturbingly lacking in any scent. It's as if the deficiency of vegetation precipitates a vacuum of emptiness.

Two soldiers are transferring our boxes of medicine from a military truck into the SUV. The supplies must have passed inspection.

"What about our bags?" Michelle asks.

"The bus will remain here to take you to the hotel," Chu-won says. "Your bags will be safe until we return."

Safe? I eye the soldier standing by the door to the building. His visor hangs just above his eyes, which stare out unblinking and emotionless. He stands so still that his brown uniform maintains its crisp folds. Beside me, Marc doesn't give the soldiers a glance. He's staring off at a warped wooden telephone pole. I don't like how his muscles are tensed or how his eyes narrow.

"What's wrong?" I ask.

"Nothing." Marc grabs my arm and pulls me toward the SUV.

"You're looking at a dilapidated telephone pole like it's going to attack us. Don't tell me nothing's wrong."

"We need to move," Marc tells Grandfather.

With a nod, Grandfather hurries us all into the back of the SUV, while Chu-won slides into the driver's seat. The soldier with the gun sits in the front passenger seat.

"He's coming with us?" Michelle asks.

The soldier settles his gun on his lap. "You will call me Sergeant Han. I will be your keeper."

None of us utters a word as the SUV revs up and takes off down the road apparently being cut this very moment by the group of workers. We rumble past them. One of the men lifts his eyes and studies us as we pass, our dust kicking into the air around him. He seems undisturbed by the cloud as he holds his rock, staring after us.

It's a good hour of rough, bumpy riding until we come over a rise, and there's the Dongdaewon Clinic before us. I don't know what I expected, but this sure isn't it. The building reminds me more of a long shed that would belong behind a barn in the United States than an actual clinic. Like most of the buildings in the countryside, it's whitewashed with a flat tiled roof. The surrounding terrain is hard and barren, like the spirit lands of Haemosu and Kud. I shudder.

"Oh, look at those pretty bushes!" Michelle points at the few scraggly ones that line the front of the clinic, alone in the vast, desolate countryside. "It's a nice touch."

"Those are not bushes," Chu-won says. "They are trees."

We scramble out of the truck. My limbs ache from being jostled about, but my worries are quickly forgotten when I see a man wearing a doctor's coat exit the building. He's got a full head of dark hair, and he's all smiles and bowing as he hastens toward us. Grandfather bows low to greet him.

"Annyeong haseyo," the man says, trying to bow even lower than Grandfather to show respect. Then he switches to English. "I am Dr. Jong. We are honored you have chosen to visit our clinic."

"As are we," Grandfather says, and then introduces each member of our group.

"Come." Dr. Jong smiles, and I can tell from his bright eyes that we're the biggest excitement they've had in a long time. "Please see our work."

"Remember," Grandfather tells the three of us, "do not enter any room with a patient with tuberculosis. It is too risky."

"Sir?" Marc grabs Grandfather's arm and pulls him back. "I need to speak to you."

Grandfather frowns. "What is the problem?"

I move over to Grandfather and Marc while Michelle engages Dr. Jong in a conversation about the medicine and the patients.

"I think we should leave," Marc says. When Grandfather looks at him questioningly, he just lets out a long breath and says, "I can't explain it, but this place has a bad vibe."

"Of course, it has a bad vibe," I say, rolling my eyes. "We're in a totalitarian country at a clinic for people dying of tuberculosis."

"We will be careful." Grandfather pats Marc's shoulder. "Come, let us help our keeper unload the supplies."

I hurry to join Michelle and Dr. Jong. He's explaining how far they've come in their medical practices here in North Korea. "Recently I was asked to assist with a surgery on a young girl at Mount Taesong Combined Hospital. She'll never walk again, but she's alive."

A pained look crosses Michelle's face. "I wish I could meet this girl."

We step through the crumbling doorframe of the clinic's entrance. There's a distinct smell of burning grass. Once I slip off my boots, the warmth trickles up from the floor, and I realize they use traditional *ondol* heating here. The smell must be coming from the furnace at one end of the clinic.

We enter a long corridor with rows of rooms on both sides. The walls are bare except for trails of yellow watermarks and grime. Dr. Jong leads us to their main room, where they have a computer dating back to the early nineties and chipped cabinets to store their equipment. Two ladies stand and bow deeply as we enter. We bow back as Chu-won rushes in behind us, holding a small box.

He opens it, pulls out a cylindrical object, and bends down to begin work. "This is the part you have been waiting for!"

The women chatter excitedly.

"We have waited nearly a year for this to arrive," Dr. Jong tells Michelle and me. "We are deeply grateful you have come."

"I want to meet the patients," Michelle says. She's fingering the small black camera, and I wait for her to pull it out and snap some pictures. She doesn't.

Dr. Jong's forehead wrinkles. "If you wish. I was not aware you were allowed to be so close to those infected with TB."

"It's fine," Michelle says, waving her hand dismissively, and marches down the hallway. "I want to speak to them."

I know I should stop her, but there's a look in Michelle's eyes and a set to her jaw that I've never seen before. Michelle has always been determined, and when she's on a mission, nothing stops her. I shake my head, but follow them down to the first door on the right.

It's a tiny room barely fitting the four *yos* laid out on the floor. On each mat is a patient. Three are sitting up while one is very still, lying down, eyes closed. They all have white hospital gowns on, but from the sharp edges of the folds, I can tell they only put these on just now, for us. Beneath the gowns I see their drab brown clothes.

They flash us weak smiles with gray or missing teeth and bow their heads. There's barely enough room for Dr. Jong and Michelle to stand in the middle of the room, so I hang back in the doorway. Michelle sits down comfortably on one of the *yos* and begins speaking to the patients in Korean. She falters somewhat with her words, and I'm sure her accent is hard for them to understand, but there's no doubt that she's in her element. Despite the fact that these people are probably highly contagious, she doesn't hold back. She leans in close and pats the one woman on the hand.

Still, something nags at me, and I struggle to focus on their conversation. There's a presence in this room, this whole clinic actually, that presses down on me. Why did I disregard Marc's warning? He's almost always right.

The nape of my neck tingles. I reach back and rub against the sensation. Now, thinking about Marc, I realize I haven't seen either him or Grandfather in the last few minutes. It couldn't have taken that long to unload.

"I'm going to check on the supplies," I tell Michelle, and then head back down the corridor.

After I slip on my boots, I turn right to exit the main door but come to a screeching halt, letting out a strangled cry. A massive, snakelike head thrusts through the doorway. It opens its wide jaws, revealing razor teeth and putrid yellow ooze. It roars so loud the sound vibrates through my skull and tears through my body. The force of the wind from the creature's breath sends me flying, and my back slams against the wall.

A giant tongue lashes out at me. I take off down the corridor in a full sprint. I pass by the room where Michelle is laughing with the patients. My only hope is that I can distract this creature and lead it somewhere outside, far away from her and the patients. I glance over my shoulder, and sure enough, the creature is snaking its way down the hallway. Its bitter red eyes are focused only on me.

At the end of the hall is a small, clear plastic window. I kick my foot through the plastic surface, tearing it away from the window, and then dive headfirst outside. I tuck myself into a ball and roll out of the dive across the dead grass.

Out in the open, I have a better chance of maneuvering around the creature. As it pours its long body out of the exit I created, shrinking to the window's size and then growing larger and larger before my eyes, I realize what this is: an *imoogi*, a wannabe dragon trying to earn its right to dragon status. But even worse—its midnight color and slender form, with a hood that stretches out from either side of its head like a cobra, reveals this one to be a dark *imoogi*, one that absorbs the soul energy of its victims to gain strength.

I scan the area for a weapon and spot a shovel resting against the wall next to the *ondol* furnace. I fling open its door and scoop up a heap of burning grass and sticks. I toss them at the *imoogi*. The creature howls in rage and whips its long body, slamming its tail into me. I fly through the air and land hard, sprawling on the unforgiving ground.

Groaning, I somehow manage to get to my knees. The *imoogi* roars again, and I wonder how everyone in the clinic cannot see or hear what's going on. Where's Marc? Where's Grandfather? The clinic is settled alone in the valley; not a tree or house is in sight for miles. Still, the *imoogi* must have enough power to cloak not only its form, but also its sounds from those around us.

The *imoogi* rises into the air, soaring above without wings. Then it turns and plunges straight down at me. Its hood opens wide on either side like a cobra preparing to strike, revealing long, sharp spikes, and its fiery eyes focus on me, hungry and full of desire.

CHAPTER 19

I leap to my feet and cartwheel down the hill just as the *imoogi*'s jaws swoop across where I once knelt. I spin away and race toward the shovel. I'm not sure how good a shovel will do in this situation, but just the thought of holding it makes me feel better somehow. The moment my hands wrap around the handle, I feel a blast of heat against my back. *Crap.* I forgot about their ability to breathe fire.

Snatching up the shovel, I try to escape to the other side of the clinic. Waves of heat singe my back. As I careen around the corner, dread fills me. There in the courtyard next to the SUV is our supposed keeper, lying on the ground with his chest gaping open and his gun still clutched in his hand. Grandfather and Marc are each holding a hoe and a pitchfork aimed at two other *imoogi.*

I rush to join them. "What's happening?" I scream.

"Took you long enough to find us," Marc says.

"I had no idea! They must be able to keep us from seeing and hearing each other."

"We have managed to weaken their power," Grandfather says. "They are not able to conceal themselves like they were."

"How did you do that?" I point my shovel in the direction of the incoming *imoogi.*

"The only way to overcome an *imoogi* is to weaken it by slowly wearing it down," Grandfather explains. "It must feed to gain strength, so we must not allow that to happen."

"These *imoogi* aren't too pleased we've interrupted their soul-sucking business," Marc says as the one that was chasing me slides across the ground, decimating the poor bushes that gave this place its only glimpse of beauty.

"Obviously," I snap. "What do we do? We can't just leave them here to continue to hurt these patients."

"The only way to defeat an *imoogi*"—Grandfather spins and thrusts his hoe into the tail of a gray *imoogi* that was sneaking up on him—"is to outlast them. As long as they do not consume any souls or feed off these people, we have a chance."

"I take it our 'keeper' didn't help out too much," I say.

"Not especially." Marc lifts his pitchfork and stabs the black *imoogi* in the neck.

The creature rears back, screaming. I race around to the other side of it and plunge my shovel into its scaly body. More of a mix between a lizard and a snake, its skin isn't as shiny or as beautiful as a dragon's.

Just then Michelle comes running out of the clinic with Dr. Jong. They both scream in terror. I can't blame them. Seeing three giant monsters larger than the clinic's roof is enough to make anyone have a heart attack.

"Go inside," I yell at them. "Get back with Chu-won, and don't let them touch you!"

As if sensing what I've just said, the midnight *imoogi* cocks its head and curls around to see who I'm talking to.

I break into a full sprint, tossing my shovel at the *imoogi*'s body. But the shovel just flicks off the creature as if I've thrown a stick at it. Michelle pushes Dr. Jong back inside, but they neglect to shut the door. The creature lunges for the entrance. I pump my arms and then leap into the air, kicking out so that my foot smacks the *imoogi* in the side of the face and causing it to smash into the side of the clinic. The concrete around the doorframe crumbles under the *imoogi*'s weight.

As I fall back to the ground, I pick up the shovel and grab on to the *imoogi*'s hood, straddling its neck. The creature whips its head back and forth, but I cling tight, determined it will never touch Michelle or any of these patients again.

I'm floundering up and down, back and forth as the *imoogi* flips its head in all directions, trying to fling me free. My neck pops, and my arm screams out in protest.

"Don't let go!" Marc says, running to attack the *imoogi* I'm riding as if in an evil rodeo. "Give it time to weaken."

Sensing Marc's attack, the *imoogi* shifts and wrenches violently into the air. The creature roars in taunting triumph as it soars higher and higher. My stomach dives in terror: I remember how, earlier, this *imoogi* spun upside down.

I groan, straining to hold on, but panic seizes me as I watch my grip on the *imoogi*'s hood slip, inch by inch. I scramble across the creature's skin, digging the heels of my boots into its scales and spikes for traction. Sweat trails down my face, and my hair, once tucked neatly into a braid down my back, has loosened and now swings wildly around my face.

The other two *imoogi* swoop in for an attack, snapping at me, eyes burning with desperation to consume my soul. Fire sparks through the sky, and I duck into the folds of the hood as flames burst around me.

When the midnight-blue *imoogi* swoops in with jaws open wide, I wait, holding my breath against its foul breath. Then, with a battle cry, I drive the shovel into the center of its tongue and rip it in half. The blue *imoogi* rears back; a curdling scream scuttles across the barren land. It writhes through the air until it lands with a crash on the ground. From the corner of my eye, I watch the creature diminish in size as Grandfather and Marc race to stab it with their makeshift weapons.

But there isn't time to celebrate, because the gray *imoogi* is attacking again, its jaw gnashing and furnace-red eyes focused on my chest.

I crouch low and then spring up off the edge of a spike. I lift my shovel high, and with perfect aim, I plunge its end into the onyx *imoogi*'s eye as deep as I can ram it.

But I'm too late.

The gray *imoogi* flicks out its tongue. Its slimy, gritty surface curls around my neck, and I'm jerked back.

It's strangling me.

I can't breathe!

Just then the two dragons butt heads, and the black one sinks its teeth into the gray one, releasing me from its hold.

I fall.

I stretch out my arms and my nails scrape over my *imoogi*'s onyx-colored scales. If only I could hold on to something, but its surface is too slick. I slide down its body and free-fall. I'm stretched out, clinging at nothing, watching the two *imoogi* above rip each other to shreds. When I hit the ground, stars swirl through my vision and a buzzing sound fills my ears. Pain shoots across my back and down my legs.

The sky rains blood, spattering across my face.

CHAPTER 20

I blink my eyes open. I'm lying on a *yo* in the clinic, and a noise rumbles through my ears as if I'm riding a screeching train out of a tunnel. The last thing I remember is watching the *imoogi* fall, crashing at my feet, smaller than horses, and then seeing Grandfather and Marc emerge from a fog with their farm tools to cut off the heads.

"Jae Hwa," Grandfather says, drawing me to the present. He's holding my hand. His is rough and strong. The wrinkles around his eyes seem deeper than I remember. A bandage runs along his hairline. "Yes, there you are, my strong one."

I lick my lips. Michelle leans close and presses a cup to my mouth. I take a sip.

"Is she okay?" Marc peers over Michelle's shoulder; his hair is full of hay and grass. Streaks of dirt cover his face, and his once-clean gray shirt is slashed as if a claw caught a hold and sliced it. "Can you move? Can you hear me? How about your hands? Can you use them?"

"Shut up already!" Michelle says and pushes Marc away. "Asking her fifty million questions isn't helping."

"That was a great risk you took," Grandfather says. "Riding the *imoogi* as you did. But you must remember, this is not the Spirit World where you heal or can control it as you wish."

Everything hurts too much to even nod, but he's painfully right. People begin speaking around me, and then Michelle starts arguing with Grandfather how I shouldn't be moved. Meanwhile, Dr. Jong keeps bowing and thanking us. I'm sure they'll never forget our visit.

In the middle of the chaos, Marc slides to the floor beside my *yo*. He brushes at my hair and then kisses my bandaged palm.

"I could say I was right about how we shouldn't have come," he says. "But then I would've missed out on watching how amazing you were. Your grandfather and I couldn't have defeated them without your help."

I try to smile. "You weren't so bad yourself."

"You think you're up for traveling to the hotel?"

I strain to sit, groaning from the action, because every bone and muscle in my body aches. Marc lifts me into his arms and carries me out of the clinic. I gape at the sight before us. All of the patients, as well as Dr. Jong and the nurses, have created two long lines ending at our SUV. As we pass, they bow low. Some have tears in their eyes.

"We are overwhelmed, but eternally grateful." Dr. Jong's hands shake as he grabs mine. "You have saved us from the darkness that eats away at our souls. Now we know why we suffered so. And we thank you for the medicine. We will never be able to repay you for this."

A tear escapes and falls down my cheek. The power of Kud is so much deeper and darker than I even thought possible. His lands are desolate, evil is free to scour the countryside as it wishes, and no one is here to hold the monsters in check.

I push my hand to Marc's chest. "Let me try walking."

He sets me down. Pain shoots along my back and legs, but I can stand. I grip Marc's muscular arm and bow back to Dr. Jong.

"No," I say in Korean. "The honor is mine."

Then, leaning on Marc for support, I hobble my way to the SUV where Grandfather and Michelle are waiting. Chu-won is sitting at the steering wheel, mopping his forehead with a handkerchief.

"Hurry!" Chu-won calls out the open window. "I do not think we should stay here for another moment."

As we drive away, jostling over the rough dirt road, I gaze out the back window at the patients and staff until they vanish from sight. Our truck dips down into a valley. My heart feels as if it's being pressed down by a mound of rocks. This trip was supposed to make me feel like I was making a difference. Instead, it only made me realize how great a task we've taken on.

"Someday I want to go back," Michelle says. "And change their world."

CHAPTER 21

When we drive up to the Kumgangsan Hotel, my muscles relax. Its modern white curved design, with a single tower that runs up about fifteen stories high, gives the building an artistic flair. The brochure Chu-won handed us said our hotel is supposed to have a performance hall, a gymnasium, a buffet restaurant, and a sky lounge. It's shockingly different from the world we just left. This tourist zone is a facade over the realities of North Korea.

When we step out of the bus, Grandfather bows to the attendant who helps us with our meager luggage.

"Do you notice anything out of the ordinary?" I whisper to Marc as we follow the attendant inside the hotel.

Marc gives the parking lot a quick perusal and shakes his head. "Nothing yet."

The lobby is as large as our school gym, decked out with planters, vinyl chairs, and a mirrored ceiling over the reception desk. The air smells musty and stale, but the tile floors shine so clearly, I can almost see my reflection in them. Soothing bamboo flute music plays through the room.

The attendant escorts us to our rooms. Michelle and I will be sharing one room, Grandfather and Chu-won a second, and Marc, who was supposed to room with Kang-dae, is in a third. Maybe it's best Marc and Kang-dae didn't room together. They don't ever seem to get along unless they are busy fighting a common enemy.

"Take a quick break," Chu-won tells us. "We will meet in the lobby at three o'clock for our hike to Kuryong Falls. It's a brisk three-hour round-trip, so make sure you're prepared. I must speak with the authorities about the accident with the guard."

"How are you going to explain the soldier's death?" Marc asks.

Chu-won takes out his handkerchief again and dabs his forehead. "I have not come up with a good enough lie yet, but I am working on it."

"One hour?" Michelle asks. "But we just got here."

"After what just happened at the clinic," Grandfather says, "I am worried one hour is too long to wait."

I eye Michelle and bite my lips. We never told her about our plan to hike to Kuryong Falls and scout the area for signs of the orb. After what happened at the clinic and watching that *imoogi* nearly bite her head off, there's no way I'm putting her back into danger. But how can I get her to stay without her feeling as if she's missing out?

Marc comes over to me and rubs my arms. "You ready for this? No one will think less of you if you decide not to go."

I stare at his chest. Going to the falls could mean danger and more injuries. Or worse. My heart thumps, thinking how inadequate I would've been fighting the weasels or the *imoogi* alone.

Plus, I'm in so much pain that I can barely walk. It doesn't help that we are weaker without Kang-dae. I don't think I could kick anything without falling to the ground in agony.

No, I think to myself. *I'm not ready. At all.*

"We must review the mission in my room before we go," Grandfather whispers to Marc and me. "Especially now that Kang-dae isn't here."

"I'll just drop this off and change for the hike," I tell Grandfather.

Following Michelle, I lug my suitcase down the hall. Her fingers shake a little as she fits the key into the small lock in the keyhole.

"What is this?" she says. "The dark ages?"

"Here." I take the key from her fingers, slide it inside the lock, and twist. The door clicks open. "We're spoiled back in Seoul."

The room is simple but clean. White walls and matching linoleum flooring with two single beds. I abandon my suitcase on the floor, while Michelle shuts the door behind us. I sag onto the bed, which feels like a rock slab rather than a mattress. After two different attempts, I finally manage to shift my body just the right way to even lie down. I pop some more ibuprofen, deciding not to mention I'm pretty sure my back is completely screwed up.

Michelle falls backward onto the other bed, groaning. "I can't stand the thought of doing anything other than sleeping. After what happened back there at the observatory and then at the clinic . . . I don't know how much more of that kind of stuff I can deal with. Does that make me a wimp?"

"No, it makes you smart." *Way smarter than me.*

"Besides, I feel like I've used up all my energy facing those creatures. A three-hour hike seems horrifying. Why even bother with the sightseeing trip?"

"Yeah." I shift so my head is propped up on a pillow. "It does. Especially Grandfather's version of a hike. Knowing him, he'll want to jog the whole thing just to get in some exercise. But there's a chance that there might be a clue at the falls to help us find something."

I'm trying to be as vague as possible, not only for Michelle's sake, but also because Grandfather warned us that the rooms were bugged. We don't need to give them any reason to kick us out of the country.

"Seems like a lot of work just to look for something that probably doesn't exist," she says.

"I hope Kang-dae is okay," I say, trying to change the subject.

"Yeah, me too."

We lie there, and all I can think about is Kang-dae injured, maybe dying. If I fail at finding this orb, or if Michelle's right and it doesn't exist, then Kang-dae will have risked his life for nothing.

"I wish I had a phone or a way to call the hospital," I say.

Michelle rolls onto her side, playing with the edge of the yellowed pillowcase. "I know. Me too."

I manage to slide off my bed, my spine prickling with pain. I seek out the faucet and splash water over my face, hoping the coolness will soothe me. Then I remember the *gwishin* from the school bathroom, and how Kud reached through the mirror at the hospital to grab me. I turn the water off and pull off my pillowcase, using it to cover the mirror.

Better.

"Damn, girl," Michelle says. "That Kud guy really messed with your head."

I stare at the covered mirror. "Let's not talk about him, 'kay?"

"Sure." Michelle shrugs and tosses her boots against the wall, but from her puckered forehead and how she keeps nibbling at her pinky, I know her mind is whirling. She's too smart. It's only a matter of time before she figures out the truth about this whole mission and gets involved. And I can't have her involved.

"You don't have to come," I say. "We're just going on a hike to see a waterfall. You should stay and get some rest." I hobble across the room to grab my day pack and stuff it with snacks and water. "I'll be back from the hike in no time."

She stares at me skeptically, but then sighs. "It does sound so tempting. Maybe I will. I've been working on this idea I got when I saw all of those pictures that Lily put up at the Dano Festival."

She pulls out her notebook and starts flipping through it.

"Really?" I ask. "Tell me about it."

"This is just a start, but sometime in the future I want to set up something bigger than just this trip. If we could get more people involved, we could make a bigger difference. These clinics shouldn't have to wait a whole year just to get one part so their computers will work again. If we teamed up with other schools, we could provide enough medicine, food, and warmth for anyone who needed it."

"You plan it and I'll help," I say, relieved she's staying behind. "It sounds awesome."

I wave good-bye and slip out before she changes her mind. It's a miracle she's still alive considering everything that's happened today.

Marc is already in the hallway, leaning against the flowered wall. His arms are crossed, and his hair half hangs over his eyes. I start toward him, aching to sink into his arms, but Grandfather opens his door at the other end of the hall and motions for the two of us.

Once we're in his room, Grandfather presses his finger to his lips, telling us to be quiet. Then he takes out Kumar's debugger device and places it on the table.

"This will give us five minutes where we can talk freely before the authorities suspect anything." Grandfather taps his pencil on the table, his brows furrowed as if he's searching for an answer that won't come. "We have good news. Kang-dae is well. I have to return to the border and escort him across since he's a minor."

"This is wonderful." I take a deep breath of relief, but when I look over at Marc, he's shaking his head and scowling as if this is terrible news. "Don't act that way. He's one of your fellow Guardians. Aren't you supposed to have a bond or something?"

"Enough!" Grandfather frowns, his eyes narrowed. "We must focus. Normally I would say wait for my return, but after everything that has happened today, I am concerned we are not only being watched, but time is limited before our secret mission becomes not so secret."

“If it hasn’t already,” Marc mutters, flopping into the nearest chair.

“Indeed.” Grandfather unrolls a map showing the falls and the path. “I need you to scout out the falls. See if there is anything out of the ordinary. Without Kang-dae, and with your condition, Jae Hwa, I am concerned about the two of you undertaking this mission by yourselves. Regrettably, we will need to refrain from attempting to collect the object until tomorrow. I cannot allow you to risk your lives.”

He points to the area he wants us to scout out.

“Look for anything unusual,” he continues. “Symbols of dragons or codes written in Chinese, since that was the language of Korea during the time the object was last seen.

“And one other thing.” Grandfather digs through his pack and pulls out a leather pouch attached to a cord. “If for some reason you find the orb and have to take it, you should put it in here. Avoid touching it if at all possible. We do not understand its full potential.”

The leather is soft in my hand as I slip it over my head. “Why shouldn’t I touch it?”

“The orbs are powerful objects,” he says. “They were not created for humans. Power of that kind is not to be taken lightly.”

“Sounds simple enough,” I say.

“Let us hope this is true,” Grandfather says. “Whatever you do, wait for me before you engage in acquiring the object. It is far too dangerous to walk anywhere with it without proper supervision.”

Chu-won hires a driver to take Marc and me to the Onjeonggak rest area. There we get out and start our trek. For the first time in days, Marc and I are alone. He takes my hand, and even though it hurts to walk, a smile creeps across my face. I hadn't realized how much I was craving this.

The narrow path is canopied with overhanging trees. We skirt around rocks and fallen branches. I breathe in the fresh air, full of pine and bark, and I'm amazed at the sharp contrast this tourist area is compared to where most North Koreans live. After a little over an hour of brisk hiking, I hear the rush of falling water, and I know we can't be far from the falls. The woods close around us, and a thick mist from the waterfall trickles along the path as if joining us in our journey.

"I've been acting ridiculously immature about the whole Kang-dae thing," Marc finally says. "What he did back there at the observatory proved how wrong I was about him."

"Kang-dae has that effect on people," I say. "Making everyone hate him. But I'm glad he's okay and coming back."

Marc's face almost smiles, and I know we've crossed a barrier and somehow we're closer because of it. A concrete bridge carries us over a dry riverbed where a thick mist curls through the rocks. After passing through a small tunnel, the sound of roaring water shatters the silence of the forest. The path bends around and the tree line breaks, revealing Kuryong Falls.

"It's lovely," I whisper.

The water plummets as if waves are rushing down, frothing until it races over the edge and dives forever into a storm at the bottom. Swirls of whites, blues, and grays push into each other. I love the power and energy it all creates. I take a deep breath of the pine air and feel a sudden urge to move closer to the water. My blood pumps faster, and the muscles in my back loosen, almost as if the pain is receding. It's a familiar sensation, and at first I can't place it.

"What is it?" Marc asks.

"There's something in the air that feels familiar," I say. "Do you notice anything?"

"Yes." Marc's gaze narrows to the falls and then to the pond beneath it. "Yes, I do. Let's go up to the pavilion. Maybe we can get a better view."

Up in the Nine Dragons Pavilion, we have a breathtaking view of the falls, which sit between two sharp mountain peaks. Its beauty almost makes me forget the needles of pain in my back. It's one of the tallest waterfalls I've ever seen. Water sprays up, creating momentary crystals before tumbling into the foaming pond. The area has a rugged, worn feel, as if it's seen and endured too much.

"They say that a trip to Nine Dragon Falls is a trip your heart always remembers," Marc says.

Whispering sounds swirl around me. Spinning on my heels, I notice the paintings of dragons on the pagoda. The painting shifts, and a dragon's eye blinks. Another's tail twitches.

I grab Marc's arm. "Did you see that?" I point to the dragon painting. "It moved. I'm sure of it."

Or maybe it didn't. I hold my breath, waiting for something to happen. But nothing does. It's hard to know if I'm completely losing it or somehow incredibly in tune with the Spirit World.

Marc's forehead scrunches up in concentration. "There's something strange about this place. I'm just not sure what it is."

He takes off down the steps back onto the path. I race after him until he stops before a massive stone wall with Chinese writing on it.

"What does it say?" I ask, struggling to read each of the characters.

"It's about the pool and the dragons that guard it."

"What pool? I don't see any."

"I suppose it's above the waterfall. There's also something here that talks about the Seonyeo—they're angels—that bathe in the pool at the top of the waterfall. Wait. Look here." He points to the left side of the stone's lettering.

"I don't see anything."

"There's another message on this wall," he explains. "It's shimmery, and it moves almost like a dragon itself. It says, 'We guard the entrance for all eternity.'"

"What does *that* mean?" I ask.

"That something guards the entrance for all eternity."

I hit him. Hard.

"I don't know. I'm just reading it." He laughs. "Hey, I'm only sixteen. Give me a couple more years, and I'll know everything."

I roll my eyes, then leave the wall and wander down to the water's edge. It roars against my ears, and the spray splashes against my cheeks, cold as winter ice. A mist has curled down from the mountains, shrouding the valley in white and gray shadows.

Then the water buckles, and a form pushes against the water's surface, rising out of the foam. A *gwishin*. Her white dress whips below her legless body. Long black hair flies with the wind, yet still covers her face. She must be a *mool gwishin*, always connected to water. Maybe even the same one who found me in the bathroom.

She reaches out, calling for me. "Princess. Come to our lands where you belong."

Once again I'm immobilized. My legs grow numb as she pulls me closer to the water's edge. My fear crystallizes into ice, and I stare as her fingers touch mine. A chill courses through me, and then I fall, the air pushing against me until I hit the sharp water, needles spiking through my flesh.

CHAPTER 22

Water crashes around me, shockingly cold. My body sinks below the surface, and I'm drawn into the surging waters, round and round. I crash into rocks, helpless in the waves. Farther I sink. Below me is an endless darkness, and I know I'm being pulled into some sort of hell.

Until I see them. The dragons. Their sleek bodies slice the water. Fire erupts around me until everything is a shocking red. I'm released from the *gwishin*'s hold, and as her fingers slip away, the heat licks warmth back into my body. My back tingles, and I'm able to bend and twist again. I kick my legs, and my lungs scream for oxygen.

A dragon swoops underneath me. *Hold tight*, it says in my mind. I latch on to his back and we take off, flying beneath the surge of water above us. It takes only moments, but each half second becomes eternity as my body craves air. A rock wall comes into view, and then, just beneath where the waterfall crashes into the pond, I spot a crevice in the rock. My lungs scream for air as my dragon aims for that narrow hole. I'm not sure if it's my imagination, but it appears to crack open just enough to allow us inside.

Red spots fill my vision, and my grip on the dragon loosens. We rise until we're cannonballing out of the water, so fast, so swiftly, I nearly tumble off.

The dragon slides onto a rocky surface, slick from the water. I fall off his back and onto the cold stone floor, gasping for air, choking on water, and completely unsure what just happened. Through my oxygen-deprived haze, voices speak around me. Not out loud, but in my mind.

What have you brought? a voice says.

A human, another says. *The mool gwishin had its hold on it.*

You should've let it drown.

But look, the first dragon, who I think is my rescuer, says, *it has the silvern sheen. There's something different about this one.*

As my vision loses the red spots, I blink away the haze and drag my hair out of my face. I'm in some sort of cave. The stone walls are dark and natural, with no carvings that I can see. In fact, the cavern is completely barren except for the large group of dragons slinking out of their hiding places, observing me with their blue eyes.

Is it immortal? a large-eyed one asks.

No, it is mortal. This I am sure of, the thin red dragon says. *Look, its heart beats and blood flows.*

Such a strange creature. The black one flicks his tail as if contemplating me. *Never have we seen such a one, half mortal, half immortal.*

I grit my teeth, choking on water that I must have swallowed. "Palk sent me," I tell them, hoping his name will catch their interest.

Palk, is it? Beady Eyes says. *Ha. No one speaks to Palk. Especially a mere mortal like you.*

Yet how does a mere mortal know of Palk? the red one asks.

"I'm searching for the White Tiger orb, and there were rumors you were its keepers. I want to return it to the Heavenly Chest."

Risky, the green dragon says. *Very risky.*

Terrible idea, says another.

Impulsive, Beady Eyes says.

Impetuous, the large black one says.

We have kept the orb a secret for a thousand years. Why change now?

"We believe Kud wants the orb and is very close to finding it," I explain. "We're afraid if he gets his hands on it, he may use it to seek the other orbs."

Silly child.

Silly thing.

Yes, definitely a mortal.

I stand, wobbly at first, but I realize the pain in my back has vanished. "You must be the Nine Dragons who guard the falls. Please let me in."

I do not like this.

Very bad idea indeed, Beady Eyes agrees. *We should kill her.*

But this one is different. She has spoken of the Heavenly Chest.

That worries me even more, the black one says. *Send her back to the water's clutches.*

Be gone! the blue dragon says, and with a flick of its massive tail, hurls me back into the water.

I gasp as the icy current sucks me beneath the water like a hungry lion, eager to eat me whole. Flailing, I fight the current, but it drags me deeper and deeper. The water rushes around me. I can't determine which is up or down.

Until I see her below me. A cloud of white. Outstretched arms reaching to mine. She's singing this time, and a crooked smile rips her face like a scar. I kick at the water to rise away from the *gwishin*, but her voice coils around my body until my every nerve numbs under her spell.

And I fall.

Down toward her.

My insides are screaming. My heart is pounding. My lungs are bursting.

Strong arms grip my shoulders, and a hand stretches out to the *gwishin*. She screeches in agony and falls away.

I'm ripped to the surface. As my head breaks the water's surface, I gasp for air once again. My arms hang at my side, but I allow myself to be dragged and hauled onto dry land.

I choke on the water and throw up. Kang-dae has his arms wrapped protectively around me as if guarding me with his life. Then I watch as Marc rises out of the water and splashes to shore. He was trying to save me, too. My heart crashes against my chest.

"Jae!" He races to me and cups his hands around my face. "You're okay. You're alive."

I reach to him, but Kang-dae holds me back, almost possessively. "You can let go now, Kang-dae," I say.

"Yes, of course," Kang-dae says, parting strands of hair out of my face and tucking them behind my ears. "After seeing you nearly drowned, I'm slightly paranoid some other creature will take you."

Marc pulls me to his side. I shiver against his warm body.

"As soon as you fell in," Marc explains "we both dove in. We've been looking for you for maybe ten minutes. I thought we'd lost you."

"I thought you were at the border." I look over at Kang-dae in shock. "Haraboji went to pick you up."

He grins. "The paramedics bound my wound and gave me some medicine. I hated knowing I'd failed the Guardians, so I took the next bus across the border. I thought you might need me."

"Someone needs to tell Master Lee," Marc says. "He's going to be worried when he doesn't find you there."

"It's fine." Kang-dae waves his hand and shrugs. "I left him a note."

I grab Kang-dae's hand. "I'm so glad you're okay. We've been worried, but I guess you're tougher than I gave you credit for. Nothing can stop you, not even weasels from the Underworld."

"Well-spoken," Kang-dae says. "Words I'll remember."

I wipe the water out of my eyes and wring out my hair, wondering how I'm going to tell them I've failed with the dragons. I eye the water, itching to dive back in and search for that underwater cave, but I'm too worried about the *gwishin* and even the disagreeable dragons.

"What did you do down there?" Marc asks Kang-dae. "You said something to that *gwishin*, didn't you?"

"The *gwishin* was dragging Jae into the Underworld." Kang-dae shrugs. "I think I intervened at just the right moment."

"He can control supernatural creatures," I say.

"Interesting." Marc's grip tightens around my body. "You never mentioned that before. I didn't know humans could have power over immortals."

"Give him a break," I say. "He's saved my life twice. That's enough to make me happy."

Kang-dae bows to me, his eyebrows rising and eyes twinkling.

"I got inside the dragon's cave," I blurt.

"What?" they both say.

"Yeah." I rub my eyes, trying to process what actually happened. "A dragon rescued me from the *gwishin* when she pulled me in the first time. He took me to their cave, just in time. I nearly ran out of air. I explained why I was here and asked for their help. They didn't want to give me the orb and kicked me out. Literally."

Marc whistles, while Kang-dae's eyes narrow.

"So all this work coming here was for nothing," I say.

"This isn't nothing," Marc says. "You've discovered that these dragons are real. That the legends are more than just stories being told. This is a huge discovery. We need to think this over and not jump to conclusions. Besides, your grandfather said we're only here to check the area out."

"They wouldn't listen to me," I say. "Between the dragons and the *gwishin*, there's no way I can get in there."

"Unless there's another way in," Marc says, rubbing the back of his neck. "It's hard to decipher what the words actually say, but the engraved messages seem to hint at more than one entrance."

"Let me see it," Kang-dae says.

We trudge back up to the pavilion, and as we do, my back and legs prickle with the memory of the pain from fighting the *imoogi*. I grind my teeth. Marc shows Kang-dae the inscription.

"Yes, you may be right." Kang-dae rubs his chin. "I think it's referring to a back door."

Marc and I stare at Kang-dae. "You do?" I ask.

"That's cool, man." Marc crosses his arms. "But that still doesn't help. We've no clue where this back door might be."

Kang-dae ignores Marc and spins on his heels to march down the shoreline, his eyes scanning the forest as if searching for something.

Marc moves to follow Kang-dae, but I pull on his sleeve, holding him back. I squint through the mist to where the path spits out into the falls area, realizing for the first time that there have been no other hikers since we got here.

"Do you find it strange that there are no other tourists here?" I ask.

Marc's body tightens, his legs bent as if ready to spring at the slightest movement. He must feel that pressing urgency that is tugging at my chest. The mist has gathered over the water. It begins to stretch and pull until the water froths up in a whirlwind. I grab hold of Marc.

"Something is happening," I whisper. "Something not good."

Then, out of the water rise the dragons. One by one they emerge as mountains of fire into the mist. First their eyes, then snouts, blasting out steamy air. Next stretch up their necks. Higher and higher they rise until they form a wall, formidable beasts of ancient days.

Their power ebbs off them in scorching waves, and my skin soaks it up as if hungry. Back in the cave, they were merely mischievous creatures, but here at the water's edge, their blue eyes have turned lava red and focus on Kang-dae inspecting the rock face's edge. My heart slams into the pit of my stomach as their graceful necks rear back, pythons prepping to strike.

I take off running toward Kang-dae. I must be screaming his name, because he glances at me and then at the dragons. His eyes widen.

The black one in the center rears back. I cartwheel and then leap into the air right in front of Kang-dae, kicking against the tail that was aimed to hurtle into Kang-dae. The dragon misses its mark and shakes its head, eyes burning.

A blast of fire erupts from each of the nine dragons in succession, inferno balls spewing toward Kang-dae and me.

As I drop to the ground, I lift my hands, drawing the water to me and holding it up. The water forms a wall, barricading the dragons' fire from hitting Kang-dae and myself.

"You will not hurt him," I cry out. The wind blows and whips my hair against my cheeks.

The silly thing, the black dragon says, recognizing me. *We should have killed her.*

"What wrong have we done to you?" I ask the dragons. "For you to treat us this way?"

The one you guard is not wanted, the dragons say in unison. *We stand against him.*

"You will have to come through me first," I say. But the truth is I don't want a fight. These dragons are on Palk's side, even if they are temperamental.

You will not pass, they speak as one.

Kang-dae wisely scampers away, and the dragons sink back into the water until all that's left is mist and the hint of sulfur tingling my nostrils. I rush to Kang-dae where he is sitting on a rock at the edge of the forest.

"You okay?" I ask.

"Yeah, I guess so. Thanks to you." His shirt lies in tatters, and his face is chalk white.

"Still alive, I see," Marc says, sauntering toward us. There's a tone of disappointment in his voice.

"Yes, well," Kang-dae nods to me. "That was a close one. You came to my rescue, though, Jae Hwa. I won't forget that."

"Payback." I hit him on the shoulder. "Now we're even."

"So any clue where this secret entrance might be?" Marc asks, his brows furrowed. "Otherwise I think we should head back."

"Before those demon dragons attacked me, I think I spotted it. Follow me."

"We should hurry," Marc says. "It won't be long before the dragons see us and guess what we are planning next."

Kang-dae leads us back into the forest, carefully avoiding the water and the dragons. I scan the area for the dragons or *gwishin* or even *dokkaebi*, known to like remote places, but I detect nothing. The air smells fresh and moist, and the only sounds are the whistling of the wind through the trees and our bodies brushing against the plants as we hike.

We break away from the path and trudge through the forest until we come back to the rock wall on the back side of the waterfall. Just like the pavilion, this wall is engraved with Chinese characters.

My fingers itch for my bow. If I had that, I'd feel safer. There are too many strange creatures out here to be wandering around with no weapon, but there's no way North Korean security would've allowed it.

Kang-dae points to the writing on the wall. "What do you think?" he asks Marc.

Marc's face scrunches up in concentration. He eases up to the rock and starts muttering softly.

"What does it say?" I ask.

"Like the one out front, this rock has a hidden language beneath the red symbols," Marc says. "The hidden words say, 'For the mortal with an immortal heart.'"

"Why does everything have to be so cryptic?"

"I believe it means if you're mortal, but strong of heart," Marc says, "you can go inside."

"Right," Kang-dae says. "But a mere mortal couldn't read this. So actually it's a trick offer."

I run my hands over the red inscription, but I'm unable to see the one Marc has read except that the letters appear to almost shimmer. Is it a good or bad sign that I can see hints of the Spirit World language? I think about how the dragons were arguing about what I am in their cave. What had they meant?

My worries are forgotten when I spot a jagged crevice that splits the rock face open just wide enough for a human to squeeze through. "Do you think this is an entrance?" I ask, pushing away the vines to get to the crack.

"Maybe," Marc says. "Let's check it out."

We both move to enter, but Kang-dae hangs back. "I'll stay and keep guard. Between those blasted weasels and wretched dragons, I believe I've had enough for one day."

"Of course." I study him as he glances around furtively. There's something about him that's off, but I can't quite put my finger on it. "We'll check it out and be back soon."

I have to wedge myself through the crack while Marc slides in sideways, nearly getting caught twice. Finally, I stumble through an opening where I'm assaulted by stale, damp air. The pale stream of sunlight does little to illuminate the place. Marc pulls two flashlights from his backpack, which we snap on. It appears we've entered a tunnel, slick with water and moss. It rounds up ahead and then stretches on for an eternity.

"What do you think?" I ask Marc.

"I think your grandfather said we shouldn't do anything on our own. We shouldn't rush into this."

"We can't stop now. I think we're onto something here. And my back is feeling better," I lie. "You were right. We don't know when some creature from the Spirit World will try to stop us. Besides, there's something about this place that feels almost magical. It's the same feeling I get when I enter Haemosu's world. I think this is the right place."

A surge of power seeps into my pores like ice water flooding my veins. If only it would sharpen my vision, too.

"All right," Marc says grimly. "Let's make sure we stay close together."

We begin our shuffle down the tunnel, and I hope the dragons haven't sensed our presence yet. My back muscles begin to loosen with each step I take. A groaning sound echoes through the tunnel. I freeze and listen, waiting.

"Did you hear that?" I whisper to Marc, clutching his arm.

"We should turn back." He jerks his chin ahead, his eyes wide.

"Yeah. Maybe this wasn't such a good idea."

The noise ricochets through the passageway, sounding like stones rubbing against one another. Dark shadows flitter across the beam of my flashlight. I whip my light to follow them, but they've vanished. I steel my nerves, telling myself I'm mentally strong enough to face anything after dealing with Haemosu. I'm not sure if this tunnel is playing tricks on my eyes or if something really is stalking us.

Slowly, we turn around. Above, something moves, skittering across the ceiling. I swing my flashlight to follow the sound. The dark shape freezes, as if hoping it won't be seen, but as my light engulfs its form, my heart skids to a halt. It reminds me of a gorilla, but the skin is a shiny black shell, like a cockroach.

The head cocks sideways, stretching to gaze down at us. Neon-like eyes glow in my flashlight's beam. It opens its jaw, revealing sharp teeth and slime drooling from a flicking tongue. A horrible screech erupts from its mouth and cuts through the tunnel. I scream, and Marc grabs my wrist and drags me down the tunnel, back the way we came. I stagger through the heaving darkness until we collide into a wall. My hands swipe over the rough stone surface, desperate for a crack or opening.

"This wall wasn't here before, was it?" I ask, flashing my light around.

"Nope." Marc yanks me again, pulling me toward him this time, as the creature on the ceiling leaps down and crashes into the space where I just stood. We dash off deeper into the tunnel, listening to the angry cry of the creature scuffling behind us. I let go of Marc's hands and pump my arms, willing my body to go faster through this endless tunnel.

The skittering sound magnifies, growing louder. There are more of them, I realize. Lots more. Chasing, hunting, stalking us. The floor grows rugged, scattered with boulders and stalagmites that seem to almost have claws themselves. I stumble and trip. My pants tear, and my skin slickens with blood.

Something swipes at my back, snagging my shirt. I dive ahead faster, not caring about the sound of my shirt tearing, and bite back a scream. And that's when I find Marc's flashlight, lying abandoned on the ground. I snatch it up, panning the light across the stone walls. Something shudders to my right. I whip the light in the direction of the sound. A creature disappears into a fissure, which seals before my eyes.

"Marc!" I scream.

Everything has vanished. Marc. The creatures. The tunnel lies empty.

CHAPTER 23

My heart thumps.

My throat dries up.

"Marc!" I yell, and stagger in a circle, straining against the gloom and swallowing back the terror of losing Marc.

Are they at this very moment ripping him to shreds?

I hurtle to the wall, clawing at its surface, hoping to somehow find him. It's useless. The wall is smooth; all signs of a crack have faded. I swipe the area around me with my flashlight and realize that the passageway turns. It wasn't that way before. I'm sure we ran straight. What is happening? It's as if this place is alive, with walls that have eyes and ears.

The rumbling vibrates the tunnels again. Like a falling gate, a wall begins to drop from the ceiling. If I don't move, I'll be trapped between two partitions, a prisoner in this place.

Bursting into a sprint, I dive through the small crack between the plummeting wall and the ground. I land hard, rolling across the ground just as the divider lands with a boom onto the path, pelting me with a spray of dust and pebbles.

"Marc!" I scream again, hoping somehow he will hear me.

But I'm left with nothing but grinding walls and deathly shadows.

I swing my flashlight around, trying to determine which way to run. I bite my lip in an attempt to stay calm and break into a sprint in the only way left to go. Before me, walls slide into the passageway I'm running through, closing me in.

Somehow I squeeze through one opening before another wall slams shut behind me, but as I push my legs to run faster, I know there's no way I'll be able to sprint fast enough to get through all of the closing walls. It's only a matter of time before I'm trapped in here forever.

The path before me wavers, and I lurch, dizziness washing over me. A barrier appears before my eyes. I'm blocked in. A chill slithers up my spine. The dragons must know I'm here. Or maybe this is the magic set in place to protect the orb.

My only consolation is that the gorilla-bug creatures have disappeared. But that's not really a consolation at all. They could be gnawing away at Marc's body for lunch. Marc might be in pain right now. I shove the back of my hand into my mouth to stifle a cry.

But falling to pieces isn't going to solve anything. I think about what Komo would want me to do in this situation.

Listen and wait.

Closing my eyes, I quiet myself, straining my ears intently until I can hear my heart thumping against my rib cage faster than a hummingbird's. The groaning sound fades. Water drips from somewhere in the distance. And then I hear it. Pounding footsteps in a rhythmic *thump, thump, thump.*

My eyes pop open. This isn't the sound of two feet running, but four. Something is coming for me. And fast.

The wall to my left groans and rumbles, drawing back inch by inch. I click off my flashlight and scuffle backward until my back presses against the cold, clammy wall.

I wait, shivering, until the divider stops moving, buried into the labyrinth of walls. I hold my flashlight before me as a weapon. Maybe I can switch it on and blind whatever hunts me.

Something shuffles over the rocks about twenty yards away. Unable to wait any longer, I snap on my flashlight and shine it in the direction of the noise. The beam catches a black form, and orange eyes glint in the light. It's a pale and hairless beast, smoke spitting from piglike nostrils. It paws at the ground and bolts into the air, barreling toward me. Tossing aside my flashlight, I charge toward the beast at full sprint.

Right before we meet, I leap into the air and smack my foot into the creature's snout, flipping backward and landing on the other side of the tunnel.

A growl cuts the silence, and in the rolling light of the flashlight, I spot massive front teeth jutting out of the creature's mouth while saliva flings across the tunnel. I smack it hard, but the creature only tosses its head and swings around to face me with an earsplitting roar, foam spewing from its jaws. It attacks again. I leap, double-kick, and spin away, landing in a crouch back on the ground.

I don't think I can beat this creature.

My head is spinning trying to decide which way to go next when the massive black form bounds across the space between us. I fake left, grab the flashlight, and race to the stone wall. I use the momentum of my run to kick off the wall and roll through the air and over the beast. The moment my feet touch the ground, I'm sprinting again. I have no idea where I'm going, but hopefully I can get away.

My arms are pumping. I careen around a bend, smashing myself into a wall. The beast's breath is hot against my neck. Another wall rises before me. Instead of retreating, I bolt to it, running up the wall and propelling myself into a backward flip, kicking at the beast's snout once again. It growls in anger. I land and kick its rear before it even turns.

The beast flies through the air, crashing against the wall. I shift back and forth on the balls of my feet, my fists at the ready in front of my chest. Still, the creature remains motionless. I stagger over to its body and shine my light into the beast's beady orange eyes. It whimpers.

I've defeated it, but that hasn't changed my situation. A quick scan tells me I'm still trapped in a section of the tunnel, just now I'm trapped with a stinking, wretched beast.

"Where's Marc?" I demand from the creature. "What have you done with him?"

I don't expect it to respond, but I kick it when it doesn't answer. The creature blinks once and then wheezes a final breath. The orange fades from its eyes, replaced with endless dark pools.

I step back.

The tunnel groans and trembles once again, resisting and yet stretching all at the same time. The wall to my left shivers, and the stone peels back to reveal a massive double door. The Nine Dragons and Kuryong Falls are engraved on each arched door. A silver knocker with the face of a tiger in its center glints in my shadow.

I tread toward the doors tentatively. My boots click on the stone floor. The air changes, as if a window somewhere has opened, allowing for a soft breeze to explore this stench-filled warren. The noise from the walls and the beast and even the pounding of my heart have washed away. All that's left is myself, the door, and the decision I'm about to make.

CHAPTER 24

My fingers touch the knocker, and the doors swing open into a wide room. The walls are lined with vibrant-green vines, twisting and tangling around each other in a solid mass. In the center of the room rests a golden pedestal in the shape of a lotus flower. A white glow emanates from its core, so bright against the darkness of the tunnels that I have to shield my eyes from its radiance.

I tread inside, my arms at my sides, but every muscle is tense, ready to react to an attack. This glow must be from the White Tiger orb. The coloring reminds me of the image that was shown to me in the Guardians of Shinshi's secret chambers. A mist spills off the pedestal and trails down to the floor, so as I grow closer, it almost appears as if I'm walking on clouds.

Warnings buzz through my mind to check the room for traps or guards, but I can't stop my feet from stepping closer and closer to the orb. I'm utterly drawn to its power.

Something shifts inside the room, and I drag my eyes away from the glow. To do so tears at my insides. But when I do, I see them. The nine dragons, lined up in a perfect row. Waiting. Staring at me with eyes that make me feel as if I'm drowning in depthless pools of water.

Foolish child.

Insolent.

"Where's Marc?" I ask. "What have you done with him?"

Safe for the time being.

"He hasn't done you wrong," I say. "Release him."

Such demands! You do not know the power you are dealing with.

I take a step closer to the orb, watching their faces for a reaction. "You're right," I tell them. "I don't. But I do know that because one of the other orbs was in the wrong hands, my ancestors were captured and held prisoners for over a thousand years. I can't let that happen again. I can't risk it."

Risky. Yes, that is what you are. Risky.

"That's exactly the opposite of what I'm saying. Palk agreed with me when I told him my plan." I clench my fist as I take another step toward the pedestal. As I draw closer to the orb, heat radiates from it. A mist snakes over to where I stand and curls up my legs. I feel the pulse of the dragons' power.

The dragons are speaking once again, but I can't be bothered by their prattle because the orb is so beautiful, so perfect. Now that my eyes have adjusted to the shift in light, I can see how it rests as a giant egg nestled inside the golden flower.

"So you're just going to let me take the orb?" I ask the dragons. This seems too easy.

You defeated the curse.

"The curse?"

The dragons speak in unison as if reciting an old tale:

To those who tread between the worlds,
Their hands to grasp the power of the orb.
To the one who can span,
The worlds of spirit and of man.
The power to find both riches and loss,
Will be given to the one who can reach across.

"Worlds of spirit and of man?"

This sacred hall rests between the Spirit World and the human world. Those who are from either cannot enter. Only those with a connection to both.

The black dragon snaps his wings. *Every lock comes with a key. We had not expected the key to find the lock.*

"I can't keep track of what you think I am. Childish, risky, a key."

The black dragon growls from deep within its throat. I decide to change the subject.

"So that is why Marc was able to enter? Because he has links to both worlds, like I do?"

Yes. But his connection was not strong enough to find a way out.

Yet beware!

I jump at the intensity of their words.

The orb is powerful. The weak of heart cannot bear the burden.

I nod, understanding. The last time I touched an orb, I allowed it to suck all the life out of me, to transfer it to Komo. They are powerful objects and not something to take lightly.

The bearer becomes the keeper of the orb, until willingly giving it to another. And yet, to let it go will tear at the threads of a soul.

I think back to when I gave up Haemosu's orb and how easy that had been. This can't be very different. In reverence, I walk up the steps that lead to the top of the flower. I reach my hand out to grab it, but my fingers freeze halfway. Licking my dry lips, I shove my doubts aside and grasp the orb between both hands.

A burning sensation cuts into my palms and trails through my entire body. But I don't let go. In fact, I clutch the orb tighter.

"Please," I whisper to it. "I need you to stay safe with me so I can return you to where you belong."

A beam of silver flashes out of the orb and bursts above me. It illuminates the room, drenching my body in sparkling silver rain. I look back down at the orb cupped in my palms: my arms and then my entire body are flooded with the most soothing warmth. The orb begins to spin until it feels as if I'm twirling around with it. The world twists and pulls until I'm sucked into a vortex. A ringing clamors through my ears until it suddenly washes away, leaving only silence.

I'm standing in what appears to be a grove. Tendrils of vines cluster about me smelling like fresh-cut grass. Mist curls at my feet and trails up tree trunks, weaving through the branches. Below the vines, grass glistens like emeralds beneath my feet, and through the tree boughs stars twinkle within an abyss of darkness. It's as if this grove is suspended in space.

A growl from the bushes attracts my attention, but instead of running away, I step closer. The leaves draw back of their own accord, bringing me face-to-face with the White Tiger. I draw in a deep breath, my body chilling as his glacial-blue eyes assess me.

Standing there, I hang my head, knowing I fall short of the caliber of warrior who should be facing the White Tiger. He's twice as tall as any tiger I've seen in a zoo, and his skin glows brighter than the moon on a cloudless night.

"Who are you to speak to me?" the tiger asks.

I open my mouth, but I'm in such awe, nothing comes out. I rub my hands against my sides and try again. "I am Jae Hwa, bearer of the Blue Dragon bow. I saved my family from Haemosu's curse."

The tiger cocks his head to the side and then shakes it. "You stand before me, yet you know nothing of the Korea of your ancestors. You know not what my people have suffered: the pain of loved ones ripped from your arms, of watching your city crumble at your feet until nothing, *nothing* is left standing. To have your language, even your name, stripped from you. You are nothing but a child."

A *child*? I swallow hard at his words. An angry pressure builds up against my chest. "You're right. I'm nothing. But while others fled, I stood up to the monster of Haemosu, and now once again I must protect my family. My *komo* is lost and I must find her. And Kud, who seeks your orb, has threatened my family if I don't bring it to him."

The White Tiger roars. I stumble backward and fall to my knees.

"How dare you seek me and speak the dark lord's name?"

"Wait!" I scream over the howling winds, and I hold up my hands. "Palk tasked me to return the orb to the Heavenly Chest before Kud finds it. This is why I came."

The winds still, and he begins to tread in a circle round me. "Perhaps you believe you have felt pain and loss, but you have not. Yet." He stops and stares at me, and as he does, it's hard to breathe, as if I'm drowning in icy water. "But you will suffer. You will know true pain."

I clutch at the glistening grass to gain my bearings. "What do you mean?"

"It will be hard. Maybe impossible. But I will be there with you. Even in death."

Confused, I open my mouth to argue, but it's too late. My body yanks backward through time and space. The wind rushes through my ears, and stars gather around me.

And then I'm back in the cave, collapsed on the floor, the orb clutched in my palm. I lift my head; it still pounds like I'd smashed it into the ground. Meanwhile, the orb shrinks smaller and smaller until it's no bigger than a half-dollar.

I gasp in awe. What just happened? Did I ruin it somehow?

The orb has found you sufficient. You are now its keeper.

Wrapping my fingers around the stone, I look up at the nine dragons. "Thank you. I promise to return it to the Heavenly Chest." But then the words of the White Tiger tumble through my mind, and all I can focus on are his last words. *Even in death.*

They bow their heads and I bow back. Yet I sense their frustration is still there. They must be irritated that this small, risky intruder now holds the prized treasure that they've been guarding for a thousand years.

"Please," I say. "Can you show me the way out?"

No. This is your task, not ours. And now, with the orb passing into another's hands, our mission is complete. Our time here is finished.

They vanish in a funneling swirl of colors and a breath of wind, leaving a strange void as if they had been an essential part of this sacred room. I peek at the orb in my hand, so oddly small compared to its original size. I rub my fingers over it, smooth and warm, and clench it tight in my palm, hoping it will find me a way out of this cavernous maze.

I retrace my steps. I don't know what to do or where to go, but I need to find Marc. Suddenly I remember Haraboji's words about not touching the orb. But it hardly seems dangerous. And it's supposed to seek out whatever those who hold it wish for. All I can think about is Marc and if he's okay.

I lift the white stone and whisper Marc's name into it. A flash of light swirls through the core of the orb. It vibrates ever so slightly in my palm and then nothing. I keep staring at the stone, waiting. Nothing happens.

Right. Maybe the Council had the legend all wrong. Knowing my luck, I probably just sent some horrible creature to search for and kill Marc. I take off through the double doors, using the orb to light my way, and head down the corridor at a slight jog. The beast I fought earlier is nowhere to be found, and I wonder if that too was a part of the orb's protection.

The tunnel appears to have opened up ahead of me in a wide yawn.

"Marc!" I yell as I run. My voice skitters off the walls, making it sound as if a hundred of me are calling.

After I've run for what seems like forever, I spy a light in the distance. I race to it, only to find my flashlight on the ground. Had I really dropped it this far away? I shrug, pick it up, and take off again. I'm not sure how long I run, but suddenly I get this urge to stop, as if something is tugging at my insides, telling me Marc is close.

Pivoting in a circle, I don't see him anywhere. The stone walls run forever on either side, and I've no clue where the crevice we first entered through could be. These walls have moved so many times I wonder if I'll ever reach the outside world again.

The light from the orb shifts until it creates a beam shining on the rock wall to my right. Is the orb showing me the way? Even if I'm not supposed to touch the stone, it hasn't hurt me yet. Besides, what would it matter if Marc and I were going to die lost in this maze anyway?

It's then I spy a small crevice, and through the new opening, another tunnel stretches before me. I step through it and take off running until that same urge compels me to stop and readjust my course. I lose track of how many times I do this, but all the while, I keep calling out Marc's name, hoping I'm getting closer rather than lost in this madness of a maze.

"Jae!" Marc's voice finally responds to one of my calls.

I freeze, wanting to cry, wanting to scream.

"Marc!" I focus on where his voice came from and sprint in that direction until I find him lying on the ground, bound in a strange type of rope.

"Jae," Marc says. "Thank God you're alive."

"I found the orb, and it helped me find you." I slip the orb into the pouch Grandfather gave me and start tearing away at his awful bindings. The ropes are sticky and slimy. "What is all this stuff? It's repulsive. What happened to you? You just disappeared."

"Those bug things hauled me here and bound me up in this weblike stuff." He screws up his face.

Once he's free, we cling to each other. All I can think about is how solid and sure he feels with his arms wrapped around me.

"Jae," he whispers. "I thought I'd never see you again."

"This place is well guarded." I laugh, but it comes out more like a shaky squawk. I pull him closer, wishing I could protect him from all of this. Yet at the same time, I think about the dragons' words. How only those who have a connection to both the Spirit World and the human world may enter. Maybe whatever Haemosu did to Marc had a greater effect on him than we ever realized.

"Look," I say, finally breaking apart.

I open the pouch and the orb glows bright, illuminating our faces. It's just the two of us, cocooned in a shimmery whiteness, warmth pulsing as the air before an electric storm. I can't speak, afraid of shattering this sacred moment.

"You found it." He breathes out a long breath. "I wanted to believe it was here, but I didn't know if it would really happen." He closes my hand around the orb. "Be careful."

"It helped me find you," I say.

"So the White Tiger orb actually seeks." There's a twinkle in his eyes. I kiss him on the mouth, then his forehead and then his nose. If we weren't in this horrid, creepy place, I don't know if I would've stopped kissing him.

We backtrack down the corridor. I try to listen to the "feeling" inside of me to know which way to go. My body tingles as if an electric shock from touching the orb still trickles through my bloodstream. Finally, we find the crevice again. I pause at the crack where we entered this insane tunnel in the first place. I press my palms against either side of the opening, the coldness of the rock cooling my skin.

Deep inside my heart, I know that when I step back outside, everything will be different, and I hope I can be strong enough to handle whatever we face.

When we finally squeeze our way back outside, the light of the day blinds me. Whites and blues and a rushing noise overwhelm me. I stagger and cover my eyes, trying to control the dizziness whirling around me.

Marc grabs my arm. "You okay? You look—"

"Yeah. I think." I blink against the world to pull it back into focus. I press my hands to my face and check my body. "What's wrong with how I look?"

"Your skin is glowing." He brushes my cheek with his knuckles.

"You are back already?" Kang-dae says, spotting us and jumping off the rock he was standing on. "I was hoping you'd discover something."

"What do you mean already? We were gone a while," I say. "Maybe an hour."

Marc and I look at our watches.

"My watch isn't working anymore," he says.

"Mine either," I say. "That's weird."

"What happened?" Kang-dae asks, his eyes nearly wild with eagerness. He grips my arms with such intensity, I worry he's going to pull them out of their sockets. "Did you find it?"

"Find what?" I tease, ripping myself free of his grip before taking off down the path.

Marc chuckles as Kang-dae catches up to me.

"You know what I'm talking about," he says.

"Do I?" I grin as his face practically emits steam. "Fine. Yes, I did."

"Let me see it."

"Not now." I glance around as we cross the bridge and pass a group of security guards. "This isn't the place to be talking about it."

"I saw it," Marc says, strolling along with us, a big grin on his face.

"Did you, now?" Kang-dae says. "Well, this means war."

I laugh along with them, but there's something in Kang-dae's tone that sends a whisper of worry curling through me. I think he actually meant what he said.

CHAPTER 25

"Where's Grandfather?" I demand from Chu-won when we return to the hotel. "He should be back by now."

We found Chu-won and Michelle lounging in the lobby, sipping mango juice. It seems crazy to see them so relaxed and normal after the insanity we just endured, but at the same time, the scene before me calms me down. This is what I want for Michelle, to lead a normal life. My legs shake, weak as jelly. I collapse next to Michelle and take a sip of the juice she offers me.

"Did you have a nice sightseeing trip?" she asks.

I literally spit out a stream of juice. My face burns as I snatch a napkin to mop up the mess.

She lifts her eyebrows and sets her juice down. "It was a sightseeing trip, right? You better not be lying to me again."

"It was great," Marc interjects for me. "The falls were gorgeous."

"Your grandfather has yet to return," Chu-won says with a shrug. "Maybe he had some trouble with the officials. The last I heard was for us to meet him at the show tonight."

Marc, Kang-dae, and I glance uneasily at each other. I'm not used to being away from my phone for this long and out of communication with everyone.

"I don't like it," I say. "Let's head over to the Kumgangsan Culture Center early. I'll feel better when I see him."

"As you wish," Chu-won says. "We can leave whenever you are ready."

"Excellent," Marc says. "We'll get cleaned up and meet you back here in about fifteen minutes?"

After a short, lukewarm shower, I slip on a black skirt and a navy silk top, trying my best to look somewhat dressed up. I don't take the orb's pouch off, even in the shower, and I find myself clutching at the strings as if it might suddenly fall off or something.

As I brush the tangles out of my hair, I stare out the window. I have the perfect view of a town in the distance. The brown houses stand under the wash of the sunset as if forgotten by loved ones and weathered by harsh winters. A few citizens, small black forms that meld into the gray of their surroundings, stagger down the empty roads back to their homes. There are so few cars here that the roads are mainly used for bikers and walkers. It's as if I've stepped back a hundred years.

Guilt tugs at my chest, knowing I'll be sleeping in a warm, soft bed tonight, but the townspeople will never have that chance. It's hard to really see the details of the town since we couldn't bring any long-lens cameras into the country, but I can guess this is a typical North Korean town.

I send a prayer for them, hoping someday I'll be able to come back and bring more medicine. My thoughts turn to Mom, and though she's been gone for four years, it's as if her spirit lingers, telling me that being here is the right choice and delivering this medicine is a small step in the right direction. I know there isn't a single South Korean who wouldn't rush through the borders and offer their blankets to these people. But sometimes walls of pain take a lifetime to break.

If only I could be there when they crumble.

Michelle rushes through the door, pulling me away from my musing.

"Tonight is going to be amazing," she says. "They've got this fantastic acrobatic show."

We head out the hotel lobby, past two guards, to where our small group gathers. Marc's hair is still wet, slicked back. Kang-dae hovers by my side as if ready to pounce on anything that could hurt me. I shift uncomfortably as the two guys flank me, but I can't blame them for being overprotective after today.

I listen numbly as Chu-won explains that we're taking the bus to watch the acrobatic show, and while we're there, we'll get to present a document to a North Korean government official that explains in detail the medicine we donated. It's more of a formal presentation, but it's good for the press on both sides. Normally I'd be nervous about being on stage and meeting government officials, but I'm so exhausted after everything that has happened that I feel like I'm just dragging my body from place to place. The only thing keeping me alert is my worry for Grandfather.

"Afterward, we've been invited to a buffet dinner back at the hotel with the other tourists," Chu-won finishes.

I'm pretty sure I'll be snoring by then.

"For your safety, you must stay close to us," Kang-dae whispers into my ear as we march out to our bus.

"Don't be ridiculous," I say. "I'm perfectly fine. Besides, who knows I have the orb?"

"The entire Spirit World," he mutters grimly.

"Don't be ridiculous," I say.

Kang-dae doesn't respond. Instead, he clamps his mouth shut, his jaw rigid.

As we step onto the bus, his words haunt me. What if he's right? The plan was that if we found the orb, we'd try to get permission to visit the royal tombs of King Kongmin, a known sacred location, and we'd use the *samjoko* amulet to enter. I guess secretly I hoped Palk would send someone to come take me into the Spirit World. But hours have passed and no one has shown us the way, so I assume we're on our own.

As we load onto the bus with a group of Chinese tourists to head to the acrobatic show, a lump of anxiety settles inside my stomach.

"I don't know about you," Marc whispers as we slide onto our seats, "but I've got a bad feeling about all of this."

"After everything that has happened," Michelle says, "I want to follow this whole mission through to the end. We've come this far. How can we stop now?"

I nod at Michelle's words, but even still the hair at the nape of my neck pricks up. Maybe Kang-dae and Marc are right, but I refuse to verbally agree with them. I know it's selfish and dangerous, but like Michelle, I want to present the medicine to the group. I want to be there when it's handed off. Memories of those rows of brown houses, absent of color or joy, the patients' smiles as they greeted us from their *yos*, and the wide brown eyes of the girl from the poster at the lantern festival still haunt me.

"It wouldn't make any difference if I was sitting in the hotel room or going to the show," I say. "If Kud wanted me, he'd find me anywhere. Besides, nothing has happened yet. Let's not panic."

Marc rubs the back of his neck. I grab his hand to reassure him, but he won't look at me, and I know he's annoyed at me for getting involved. His jaw works as it does when he's upset.

"I have to do what I think is right," I say.

When he doesn't answer, I pull my hand away and slide closer to the window, swallowing back my own annoyance. The trees still hold their buds here, the land on the cusp of spring. I take in the mountains slicing the sky with their sharp edges. They seem so free of all the worries that I have bottled up, and I long for that feeling again. Deep down, I worry I'm making a mistake in undertaking this mission.

What if I'm not strong enough? What if I'm wrong?

I press my hand against my chest. The warmth from the White Tiger orb pulses against me.

Depending on me to keep it safe. To bring it to the right destination.

The bus jerks to a stop, and we shuffle off. I can't stop glancing around at all the tourists on the bus, worried one of them might be a threat, but no one gives me even the slightest glance.

Across the parking lot, I spot Grandfather, his back straight as a rod, his hair cut to perfection. His blue button-down shirt whips with the wind.

I run to him, causing a few soldiers to start and step closer. But I don't care, because he's safe. That's what matters. I bow awkwardly. This is one of those moments when a hug feels more appropriate, but completely inappropriate here in front of all these people and soldiers.

"Kang-dae is here," I say in a rush of words. "He showed up at the falls not long after we arrived."

"Yes, so I was told. Made the trip for nothing. All is well?" Grandfather rubs my cheek gently, his troubled eyes assessing me. "I hope you did not do anything risky."

"I got the object," I whisper, barely able to contain my excitement.

His eyes widen, and he takes my hand. "Truly?"

I nod. His lips press together, and he grips my hand as if he doesn't want to let go. His eyes scan the parking lot. "No problems?" he asks.

I shrug and attempt a smile. "Not that we couldn't handle. I think we're safe. For now."

"This is good news," he says, looking back at me intently. "Unfortunately, I do not have such good news. I have been trying to negotiate with the authorities to let us access King Kongmin's tomb, but with no luck. We must find another alternative."

"That's okay," I say. "We'll figure something out."

Grandfather's eyes move down to my neck and narrow. I look down, realizing I'm gripping the pouch with the orb protectively. I turn away, not liking Grandfather's piercing gaze, as if he can read my thoughts. Despite all my faults, I hope I can see this journey through to the end. I have to put my faith in that.

Chu-won rushes over to us, waving his arms as if the building is about to explode. It turns out that he's here to tell us the ceremony is about to start.

"Do you notice anything strange?" I ask Marc as we cross the parking lot and veer inside the domed, tan-colored building.

"No," he says. He stops outside the door and studies the area. "Nothing."

"Excellent," Grandfather says. "Let us hope everyone stays safe until morning."

Yet, even after Grandfather and Chu-won head inside, Marc lingers at the doorway.

"If all is well, why so worried?" Kang-dae asks, a smirk creeping across his lips.

"Because he's completely paranoid." I yank on Marc's arm. "Come on, I don't want to make a scene walking in late."

"There's something not right here," Marc says. "I can feel it."

"Ah. Is this your new power emerging?" Kang-dae hits Marc on the shoulder. "Jedi intuition?"

Marc scowls at Kang-dae.

"Knock it off," I say, "or I'll knock some sense into the two of you."

I push Kang-dae through the door before they decide it's best to fight this out. Inside, an attendant meets us and directs us down a hallway. She explains how we'll come to the stage to present our gift, and there the director of the tuberculosis clinics, Gwangsoo Han, will accept it.

Michelle hooks her arm through mine and squeezes me. "This was the best idea ever," she says. "I'm so glad we did this."

I nod in agreement, my chest tight with excitement. So far, this whole mission has been a success. I wonder if I'd ever have done this if I hadn't had to get the orb. Would I have continued on with my own life, not thinking about a whole country only thirty miles from where I lived? People die from TB every night, while I live in comfort.

All the kids in NHS flash through my mind, eager to make a change in the world. I've spent most of my life thinking only of my own troubles, and not just here in Seoul. After Mom died, I wallowed in my own misery. I'm hardly the person to be standing on that stage passing out the medicine. But here I am.

We follow the attendant through a narrow door and down a fluorescent-lit corridor. The pale light yellows our skin and washes out the colors of our clothes. Our boots click on the linoleum, breaking the silence of the corridors. Beside me, Marc's tension grows. His body is stiff and his jaw tight.

"I don't think I'll ever look at long creepy corridors the same again," Michelle mumbles, and she sidles next to Kang-dae, hooking her arm with his.

"What?" Kang-dae says dryly. "Now I'm your bodyguard? When will the demands end?"

We enter another door that takes us to a backstage area. I shake hands with the show director and nod respectfully to some of the performers.

They whisper and glance our way from the corners of the room. Their makeup looks overdone in the backstage area without the lights to fade it. Outside, the audience chatters in hushed whispers. There's a sense of foreboding as we wait, and I can't shake the urge to run.

Every sound becomes amplified. A ladder squeaks as it's dragged. A girl dressed in a full *hanbok* giggles. The director's clipboard clatters onto the wooden floor. I want to press my hands over my ears, but Marc is already doing his nervous tics. He's rubbing and tapping his chin, and he can't seem to stop looking over his shoulder and staring at everyone and everything. If I freak out, he's going to cancel the whole thing.

Fortunately, Michelle breaks the crippling silence by going over to one of the actors and introducing herself. I stand frozen, afraid that if I move, the serenity will be broken. Kang-dae and Marc flank me. It's becoming stifling, this constant shadowing. At least Kang-dae appears relaxed, lounging just behind me against the wall, a sly grin spread over his face.

"Why are you grinning?" I ask. "This isn't funny."

"If you saw it from my perspective," he says, "you'd find it funny. It's always about perspective, Princess."

"Don't call me that."

"It annoys you, doesn't it? You must be in denial."

I dig my nails into my palms. I'm going to lose it between these two Guardians.

Finally, the director, dressed in all black with neatly combed hair, comes over to where we wait and directs us to follow him. I'm about to pass through the wings of the stage when I see a strange-looking bird sitting in the rafters above. It's the oddest creature. A beak like a rooster, yet at the same time it almost looks like a swallow. The odd part is its neck, long and writhing like a snake.

I freeze as it focuses on me. It blinks, sending my heart diving into my chest.

"You okay?" Marc asks, resting his hand on my arm.

I jerk my arm away and force myself back to the present. I refuse to let some magical beast control my life. Somehow I drag myself onto the stage with Marc and Kang-dae at either side. I manage to stand tall next to Michelle.

"Something wrong?" Kang-dae asks.

"Which direction?" Marc asks me from the other side.

Figures. Marc doesn't need me to say anything. He knows me well enough to identify that something is wrong. I ignore them both, clenching my fists. Nothing will ruin this moment for me.

I'm determined.

Grandfather hands Dr. Han a paper that details the medical supplies we have with us. Michelle then goes to the mic and explains what we've brought.

"The students at Seoul Foreign have raised all the money to pay for these supplies," she explains fluently in Korean. "And we're hoping this is something we can do in future years."

The crowd claps politely. The nurses and doctors who have come to collect the supplies are also on the stage, and each of them comes over, bows, and thanks us. I return their bows, and my heart fills. Our group poses for pictures, and we step off the stage back into the audience, where they have saved seats for us.

As I sit, I search for that strange bird, examining the ceiling. It's gone. If I hadn't gone through everything I've experienced, I would've thought it was just me imagining things. But I know better. It was real. I should tell Marc and Grandfather about it, but I'm sick of mythological creatures running my life. For once I want to sit here and enjoy this beautiful performance.

The question is, whose side is that bird on, Palk's or Kud's?

"Wasn't that amazing?" Michelle asks, leaning over Kang-dae to talk to me.

"It was," I tell her. "I'm so glad we did this. Let's do it again next year."

If I have another year.

"I started drafting up the plans while you guys were hiking," she says.

The acrobatic show begins. I can hardly concentrate on the daring flips, the swirls of colors from the acrobats' costumes, or the beams of lasers flashing like lightning across the stage. Now that the ceremony is over, all I can focus on are the possibilities of tomorrow and worrying about how we're going to get into the Spirit World. Then there's the question of whether to even give the orb up, and how to deal with Kud once he finds out that I've tricked him.

Komo's face comes to mind. Using this orb would give me the best chance of finding her. If I give this orb up, who knows if I'll ever find her lost soul?

Marc sits on one side, stiff as a board, while Kang-dae sits on my other side, slouched and relaxed.

At the end of the show, when the performers are bowing to the audience, I see the bird once again. My mouth dries up and my skin chills. With a twist of its long neck, it spreads out its wings, spanning at least ten feet. It swoops above, soaring along the arched dome. Then it sails across the stage, curving around until it faces the audience. Its purple eyes focus on me as if it's the tip of an arrow and I'm its mark. Soaring, the bird barrels toward me.

I open my mouth to shout, but no sound comes out, just a croak. No one even glances up at the dark shadow plunging above them. Except for Marc and Kang-dae. They both leap to their feet. Marc shoves me behind him, while Kang-dae withdraws a stick that with a flick of his wrist doubles in size. A sharp blade projects from the end.

"Fly, little one, fly!" the bird screeches out across the audience. "Before it is too late."

Kang-dae swipes at the air as it draws closer, but before the bird comes within reaching distance, it vanishes. Swearing, Kang-dae hits his bat on the chair in front of us.

The audience gasps, turning to focus on us. Kang-dae slips his strange stick away, so quickly I almost think I imagine it. Marc holds up his hands as if in surrender.

"Our apologies," Marc says in Korean. "Please forgive our disturbance."

I sink into my seat, grabbing hold of the armrests. The vision of the creature's piercing purple eyes lingers. It was warning me. But of what?

CHAPTER 26

When we arrive back at the hotel, I drag myself into a lobby that's quieter than a morgue. The two soldiers who have been standing at the entrance all day move in and wrap a chain around the door, then secure it with a padlock.

"Did you just see that?" Michelle grabs my elbow and jerks her head toward the door. "They locked us inside!"

"They lock all the public buildings, especially if there are people inside. It's for your safety." Chu-won purses his lips and shakes his head. "At least, that's what they tell us."

"Let's just hope there isn't a fire or something," Michelle says.

"You look tired," Kang-dae tells me.

I shrug. I'm alive and I have the orb. That's all that matters.

Grandfather rests his hand on my shoulder. "I will go make preparations and persuade all I can. Why not go to the terrace and get some juice before dinner?"

"Perhaps something stronger," Kang-dae mutters.

"The hotel gift shop is about to close," Michelle says, her eyes panicked. "If we're leaving first thing in the morning, I've got to pick up some souvenirs before we leave."

"Crap," I say. "I need to get something for Dad, too."

I find a set of North Korean stamps and ginseng tea, pay for my purchases, and sag against the wall to wait for Michelle.

"You should take a break," Marc says. "Head up to the balcony and get some food."

"I can't leave Michelle alone," I say.

"I'll keep an eye on her for you," Marc says.

"That's sweet of you," I say.

"Don't worry." Kang-dae steps up. "I'll keep her safe. Where can I take you?"

Marc shoots him a dark look, while I roll my eyes. "I can take care of myself, but thanks," I tell them. "You two are way too protective. I'm going to drop this stuff off at my room, and I'll meet you both on the balcony."

"You shouldn't go alone." Kang-dae lifts his eyebrows and waves a finger at me as if I'm being naughty.

I blow them a two-finger kiss and head upstairs. After I drop my stuff off, I find Kang-dae loitering outside the elevator.

"You stalking me?" I ask.

"Does that turn you on? If so, then yes."

"No. Not at all."

Kang-dae raises his eyebrows and presses the Up button. "You look as if you could use a stiff drink."

"I don't drink," I say. "I like to stay in control."

He chuckles. "I should've known."

"Why are you so determined to egg Marc on?" I ask Kang-dae as we ride up the elevator to the bar on the roof.

"It's addictive."

When we step out of the elevator, a sharp breeze whips around us, chilling me to the bone. It's cooler up on the fifteenth floor than I had expected. I wrap my arms around myself as we secure a seat near the edge of the hotel. The terrace is strung with tiny white lights, and tea candles glow from each table. It's very romantic, and a sudden rush of guilt cuts through me that I'm up here with Kang-dae instead of Marc. Maybe I shouldn't have agreed to come up with Kang-dae, but I needed a break from everything, especially Marc's stifling urge to protect me. Of course, even that thought spins a strand of guilt around my chest. He's stifling me because he's afraid of losing me. Again.

I suppose if I had had to watch him die like he had to watch me, I'd feel the way he does.

A waiter rushes to our table. I order a glass of juice while Kang-dae orders wine.

"Juice?" Kang-dae asks after the waiter leaves.

I push the napkin shaped as a swan away, avoiding his penetrating gaze. "What I drink isn't your concern."

"Perhaps."

There's that smug look on his face again. He leans back in his chair and flips his fork to a perfect beat on the gray tablecloth. I shift in my seat at his relentless gaze.

"So how does it feel," Kang-dae asks, "to be the keeper of such a powerful artifact?"

His words propel a shiver down my spine. I don't want to talk about it, especially not now. "It's not really a big deal. Hopefully I'll be able to get rid of it soon anyway."

Maybe.

"So sacrificial." Kang-dae's voice envelops me as if rich chocolate. "If it were me, I'd use it for my own reasons."

"No, you wouldn't." I cock my head to the side. "Or maybe you would. You're so egotistical."

He laughs and lightly touches my hand. "I'd be tempted to search for buried treasure. Or a hidden tomb. Or find my true love. If you could seek anything, what would you look for?"

I study his face. Has he guessed that this is a question I've been secretly thinking about ever since Kud mentioned using the White Tiger orb to find Komo?

"Buried treasure doesn't sound so bad," I say, trying to stay focused. But Kang-dae's presence is overwhelming right now. Or maybe it's the combination of surviving the day and now sitting here in candlelight with the north winds whispering around us.

"I think we'd make a good match, Jae Hwa. We have a lot in common. We could help each other."

The waiter sets our drinks before us and skitters away. Kang-dae takes the corkscrew and begins to caress the wine bottle.

"Do you know what makes this wine so special?" he asks. When I stare at him like I don't care, he continues. "This is snake wine. Once the wine bottle is filled, a live snake is put inside."

"You're kidding, right?"

"Definitely not." He wraps his hand around the top, prepping to pop the cork. "Watch carefully. If the head of the snake is at the top of the bottle, it means good luck."

“That’s repulsive.”

He pops off the cork, and I can’t help but be curious and peer inside. Sure enough, a head rises out of the top of the wine bottle, bloated eyes and wide jaw. So gross.

“Great.” I stare back at Kang-dae, refusing to appear intimidated by his stupid snake. “We’ve got good luck in store for us.”

Kang-dae pours himself a glass and lifts it into the air. “To us.”

I study the scales floating about in his wine and resist grimacing. “Us?”

“Don’t tell me you didn’t think we were good there at the falls? We were the perfect team.”

I lift my glass and clink against his. “Thanks for rescuing me today.”

“Twice now.”

Kang-dae drags his chair next to mine and wraps his arm over the back of my seat. Heat radiates from him, a relief from the cool air. I shiver again, and he takes off his leather jacket and drapes it on my shoulders. His face leans in close, and his hands linger on my shoulders.

“So are you going to show it to me?” he asks.

His spicy cologne fills the air. I could sit and listen to his voice all night. His fingers push my hair out of my face. Then they trail from my cheek down my neck. He tugs on the string that holds the pouch.

“This it?” He smiles.

It can’t hurt to show it to him. I reach to untie the strings when a screech erupts in the stillness. Through the night air, that same bird from the performance spirals from the darkening sky toward us like a bolt of lightning. Streaks of light sparkle fireworks in its wake. It dives and opens its strange mouth. A stream of light bursts from it, blinding. Debilitating. Every muscle in my body is enveloped in complete numbness.

Beside me, Kang-dae yells, covering his face, and yet at the same time reaching across me to protect me.

He drags me to the ground. I tumble over him. My glass topples, shattering. Juice drenches me. Kang-dae gropes for his stick. His hand moves sluggishly. I drag myself away from him and stagger to standing. I take my fork and wait as the bird swoops back for another round, my vision swimming with sparkles and feathers and violet eyes.

"Fly, Princess," it screams at me. "Fly with the winds."

The fork falters in my hand. Is this bird trying to save me? If so, then why? Those words sound so familiar. Then they come back like a stampeding horse. That is what Haechi once told me back in Seoul when Haemosu was chasing me.

I swivel to face Kang-dae, gripping the edge of the table, knuckles white.

"Do something, Jae!" Kang-dae yells. "He'll kill us both! You need to kill it!"

The bird screeches again, a battle cry, as flames rain down over Kang-dae.

"Stop!" I scream and slip the orb from its hiding place. I lift it into the air. Silvery light washes the terrace, wavering as the stars glistening over the ocean. "Leave him alone."

The bird screeches and swerves away, vanishing into the void.

"Kang-dae!" I rush to him and grab his shoulders. "Are you okay?"

Kang-dae's body twists and shimmers beneath my hands. He screams in agony. Whatever that bird showered on him is killing him. I draw him into my arms. Guilt stabs me. If only I hadn't hesitated. I couldn't even throw a stupid fork to protect him.

But then his body shifts in my arms, twisting and enlarging. Surprised, I let go and watch in horror as his body lifts into the air, higher, until in an explosion of shattering darkness, he stands again before me.

A black-clothed form with a shrouded hood, the ends ragged, stretching out into thin snakes of material manifesting from the void.

Writhing. Twisting. Hungrily seeking.

I stagger backward. My mouth dries up. My words are ripped from me.

"You saved me," the clothed figure says. "Once with the dragons, and now with the *Bonghwang*. You are brave indeed. You have exceeded my greatest expectations. But even better, you have found the White Tiger seeker orb. Tucked within a realm that neither mortals nor immortals could touch, it rested for a thousand years. Until you came. You who are neither mortal nor immortal. Truly one of a kind."

"Kang-dae?" My voice shakes.

"That is the form you seem to prefer," he says in a deep voice. "Regrettably, I have been revealed, thanks to that foolish bird."

"Kud." I choke out his name.

I'm a complete fool.

"Yes. So you recognize me after all?"

I spot a crooked grin struggling on his face and recognize a slight resemblance. Why hadn't I seen it before?

"Leave me alone."

"You were not thinking that moments ago."

My face turns heated, shamed at how close I let him come to me. I back up farther.

"We have a connection, the two of us," Kud says.

My heart stops at the possibility. "You're wrong."

"Join me or give me the orb." Kud's voice turns sour. "And you can go back to your pathetic life."

My hand clenches the orb, still tucked inside my palm. The power of it pulses against my skin as if fire.

"Never," I say. "It will be returned to the Heavenly Chest."

"You followed my instructions perfectly." He steps closer. His tentacles writhe at my feet, sliding up my bare legs. "I enticed you to take this quest to find the orb at the Council. Even when the king of the Underworld tried to thwart me, you defeated his weasels and Princess Bari. I returned to my land barely in time to heal my wounds. Then I showed you the back door, and you once again took the bait. You were my only hope for obtaining this orb. Excellent work."

His words sicken me. They are truth, and I'm ashamed as I face it.

I spin and make a break for the elevator, but his tentacles cinch tight around my ankles. I fall to the ground, barely catching myself, but the orb tumbles out of my grip, rolling across the concrete floor. I look for the waiter, but his head is resting on the counter. I pray he's sleeping and not dead.

Kud looms over me. His eyes focus on the orb, just out of my reach. I slap the ground, grasping for the orb before he can reach it, but he lifts my body upright using his robe's tentacles. They snake tightly around me until my arms are bound. I'm practically a mummy, everything tucked in except for my neck. He leans in close as if taking in my scent. I gag. His breath reeks like death.

"Yes. It is mine now," he says, and swoops to pick it up.

The orb flames bright as a shooting star. He screams in pain, cursing, and it tumbles to the ground. With his unscathed hand, he grips his searing red palm. A sizzling sound and the stench of burnt flesh fill the air.

"What curse have you put on this, witch?" he snarls.

"The dragons bound the orb to me. I'm its keeper now until I give it away. Only I can hold it."

"What is this?" Kud spins in ferocious anger, lifting his fists and shaking them. He opens his mouth, and the terrace erupts into a windstorm. Chairs and tables fly across the roof and fall away. The lightbulbs shatter in their sockets and are scattered across the ground. My hair flies around me, but I stay upright, still bound.

The elevator doors slide open, and Marc races out. He's pushed back by the gusts and is pressed against the elevator shaft's wall. His eyes are wide.

"You can't win," I yell at Kud over his storm. "I am the orb's keeper until I return it to the Heavenly Chest."

Just speaking those words, a strength builds inside me, because I know they are true. The storm stops. Kud turns his attention to me. "Until death do you part."

"No!" Marc yells and darts to me. "Don't touch her!"

Kud holds up a hand and Marc freezes, unable to move.

"What have you done to Kang-dae?" Marc says.

Kud starts laughing, a deep, devious, guttural sound. "I am Kang-dae," Kud says. "The perfect disguise, don't you agree?"

"I don't believe it," Marc says. But at the same time, I see the understanding wash across Marc's features. "You murderous demon."

"Yes, indeed," Kud says.

My heart breaks into a million pieces. How wrong I'd been. I stare into Marc's eyes and beg his forgiveness. How many times did he warn me he had a bad feeling about Kang-dae? But there isn't a flick of anger in Marc's gaze as he stares back at me. Only that lock of his jaw to show his determination to stop this madness. This is what I love about him. He understands me like no one else can.

"You can kill me," I tell Kud, "but the orb will follow me into death. It is forever bound to me."

"Unless you release your hold," Kud adds.

"I'll never do it." I lift my chin. "Nothing will persuade me."

"Nothing?" Kud's lips twitch, and his gaze leaves my face and focuses on Marc.

"No," I choke, realizing Kud's new intent. "Don't."

"You have been such a nuisance," Kud tells Marc and struts to him. "She was almost mine. She let me touch her. If that blasted bird hadn't shown up, her lips would have kissed mine."

Marc's face turns ashen and his head jerks back as if he's been slapped. My heart tears in half, and I gasp out a sob.

"Don't believe him, Marc," I say. "You're the one I want to be with."

Kud laughs, his voice shattering the pain that hovers over us. It's as if he's plunged a knife into my soul. I've caused more hurt to Marc than I could possibly imagine.

Marc stares at me, his brow furrowed, his wavy hair hanging over his eyes. I want to run my hands through it. Tell him I'm his and he's mine. That it's always been this, even in my stupidity. But more than anything I want to erase the doubt.

"If I had more time," Kud says, ignoring me, "she would've been mine. Maybe she still will be. She's saved my life twice now, and she brought me the orb. A worthy companion, don't you think?"

Marc grits his teeth. His usually calm green eyes are full of fire.

"It would give me such pleasure to have you watch her become mine," Kud says. "That would be more painful than death, wouldn't it?"

I stare at the orb, willing its powers to come to me. It skitters once and then stills. I close my eyes and focus all my concentration on the object, speaking to it in my mind. Begging for it to hear me.

A glow seeps from it and grows, wider and larger. The power from the orb infiltrates my skin, my bones, my soul. It's as if a portion of the Spirit World has spilled out of the orb and drenched me. There before me is the White Tiger. Its pale-blue eyes sparkle with white fire, and its skin glows brighter than a star. The jaws widen and its roar envelops me, filling me.

I rip free from my bonds and sprint toward Kud. I leap, practically sailing on air, and double-kick him. He falls back, stunned. With a sweep of his arm, he flings a gale force that smashes into my chest, propelling me across the terrace until my back hits the railing. His talons ripple across the ground to snatch hold of me once again.

Reaching out my palm, I call to the orb, sucking a stream of power into my hand. As it touches my skin, it explodes into a ball of white fire, sizzling. I untangle from Kud's grip, spin around, and fling the ball at him. It smacks into his chest, and he bursts into silvery flames. It engulfs his cape, all the way down to his tentacles. The flames lick my ankles where his talons once gripped me, but it's as if my body is immune to their burn. I cartwheel across the terrace and leap into a snap-kick, striking him in the face. He staggers and groans. But as I spin around to face him again, my heart seizes. A red pulse throbs over his heart.

The Red Phoenix orb.

Kud has grown to twice his size. A writhing cloud of shadows.

"If you will not see things my way," he says, "perhaps you need motivation."

Kud stretches out his gnarled hand. Red electricity streams from his palm and hits Marc on the arm. Marc cries out in pain. I race to him, but he's already on the ground, passed out, by the time I reach him. Black swirls tangle into a knot on his wrist. The electrical sparks sink into his skin, forming the symbol of a black snake.

I cradle Marc in my arms and glower at Kud. "What have you done to him?"

"I placed poison in his arm. Slowly, it will work its way to his heart." Kud draws his cloak around him. "You must choose between saving his life or saving the orb. But what I really want is you. Never have I witnessed a fighter of your ability. You would be my greatest prize."

I spit on him. "I am no one's prize."

"If you do not bring me the orb in three days, he will die. And I will keep killing your loved ones until you do as I ask."

"This is an impossible choice," I say, bewildered. "I don't even know how to find you."

He smirks. "Then choose me now, and you can save your loved ones and rule the world with me."

"Never."

"Stupid girl." He laughs and then disappears into the thick of the night.

I clutch Marc's body to mine, hating Kud for ruining everything. But mostly hating myself for my stupidity.

For once I have no tears.

Only vengeance.

CHAPTER 27

I wrap Marc's arm over my shoulder. He groans from the movement, and his eyes flutter. I hobble us into the elevator and push the button, waiting for eternity until the doors reopen and we're on our floor. By the time we reach my room, Marc is panting, and I'm struggling to keep him upright. After today, my energy has been sucked away, and I can barely stumble to the bed. I untangle him from my arms and lay him gently into the bed. Silently, I send a million curses to the North Korean government for not allowing cell phones. I need to talk to Grandfather.

"I'll be back in a second," I say as I adjust the two flat pillows for Marc. "Grandfather will know what to do."

Marc closes his eyes. "I'm fine. Just need to rest."

I hold his hand with the mark on it and trail my fingers over the design. The skin still feels warm to my fingertips. I press my lips to his palm and gently press his hand to my chest.

It's hard to leave his side seeing him so pale and weak. It takes me way too long to find Grandfather, but in the end, I find him at the most logical place. The buffet dinner. My head won't stop spinning. Right now I can't think logically at all. I can barely see straight, I'm so furious.

Angry at Kang-dae for tricking me. Angry at myself for being so gullible. Angry we all fell right into his scheming scam. Angry that Marc is the victim of my idiocy.

By the time I find Grandfather eating at the buffet table, I'm so worked up I can hardly form a complete sentence.

"Haraboji." I bend down and grab his arm. "You need to come with me right now."

Grandfather doesn't question me. The two of us fly out of the ballroom. As we make our way back to Marc, I tell Grandfather the entire story. He remains silent, but his face grows harder with each step we take. By the time we enter my room, I've already thought of a million horrifying things that could've happened to Marc while I was gone.

Grandfather rushes to Marc's side and studies his hand. Then he presses his palm to Marc's forehead. I hover over Grandfather's shoulder, clenching and unclenching my fists, anxious to do something to fix this disaster.

"Kud gave us three days," I say. "If I don't give him the orb in that time or join him, Marc will die, and he'll choose someone else to kill. He won't stop until I do what he asks of me."

Grandfather sighs. "Sounds just like I imagine Kud."

"There must be a way around this." I pace the room, my head spinning.

Grandfather rubs his forehead. "We've been through this before with Komo. There isn't a way."

"There must be some healer or something that can counteract this curse."

"We need to get him home to his parents," Grandfather says. "They will know what's best. Keep all of this a secret for now. I don't know what consequences this will bring."

I think about Marc's mom, her kind green eyes that are mirror images of Marc's. There's no way she'll ever look at me in the same way. I'm responsible for this happening to her son.

The door swings open, and Michelle and Chu-won run into the room.

"What's going on?" Michelle asks. "What happened to Marc?"

I sit on the bed and grab Marc's hand with the tattoo. "We had some trouble on the roof."

"Trouble?" Michelle looks around. "Where's Kang-dae? Is he all right?"

I swallow. Sure he's all right. Laughing hysterically back at his palace right now. "He got called away. He won't be joining us anymore."

"Marc is very ill," Grandfather tells Chu-won. "Make the preparations. We leave for Seoul at first light."

Chu-won nods, wide-eyed, but doesn't question Grandfather.

"I should pack Marc's stuff," I tell Michelle. "Will you watch him?"

Her eyes narrow. "What happened? Did he get into a fight?"

I nod, but I can't say anything else. Grandfather thinks it's best to keep this secret, but how will that help Michelle? I don't even know what to tell her. Instead, I kiss Marc's forehead and leave the room.

Outside Marc and Kang-dae's room, I stare at the door for some time. I can't stand the thought of knowing that this was once Kang-dae's room. Licking my lips, I quietly turn the doorknob, expecting some type of danger. But once inside, the room is quiet, designed similar to Michelle's and mine.

Marc's bag is set against the wall. Clothes spill out from its top as if someone's gone through it in a hurry. I wonder if that was Marc or Kang-dae. I start stuffing the clothes back inside; Marc's scent lingers on them. His blue sweatshirt is the last to go into the bag, but I find myself clutching it, pressing it against my cheek.

I quickly scan the room, curious about Kang-dae's stuff. If I remember correctly, he had a backpack and a suitcase. But there is nothing here, as if it all vanished when he left.

That night I wish I were alone with Marc, so we could figure out all of this together. But Michelle is persistent, unwilling to leave or let what happened to Marc slide away. I squeeze into the bed next to Marc. There isn't much room, but I'm glad. It's good to have him close. As if the closer we are, the less chance that Kud can split us apart.

Marc sits up and takes a sip of the seaweed soup Michelle ordered for him.

"So spill. What really happened to Kang-dae?" she asks.

I hug my knees against my chest. "I don't want to talk about it. In fact, I think we should ban his name altogether. He doesn't even deserve to have a name."

"Don't be that way," Michelle says. "What happened to you agreeing to tell me everything? Listen, I was there when Kud first showed up. I deserve to know."

Actually, I don't tell her everything. I don't tell anybody everything. It's not that I don't trust them. But the people I love who get involved always, every single freaking time, get hurt. I don't know how much more I can handle.

"Kang-dae was Kud in disguise," Marc finally tells her.

Michelle's eyes widen, then she shakes her head. "I can't believe that. He stood there and fought with us in that corridor when we were attacked by those horrid weasels. You must be mistaken. Like how do we know that Kud doesn't have Kang-dae captive and was pretending to be him?"

"He fooled us all," Marc says. "But it makes sense now, thinking about how Bari thought the god of the Underworld would be interested in the company we kept. I wish I could say I'm surprised, but I never felt right about him. Should've listened to my instincts."

"Don't say that," I say. "None of us saw it. Even the Council of Shinshi didn't see that coming. He was named a Guardian. I should have listened to the dragons. *They* knew. And there I was, defending him at the waterfall."

"Dragons?" Michelle asks.

"Long story," both Marc and I say simultaneously.

Marc shrugs and slurps at his soup.

"Hey," I laugh. "What's up with the slurping?"

"You only live once." Marc tries to give me that grin, but the effort must be too much. He passes me the bowl and sags against the pillow.

"We're going to figure out a way to help him." Michelle folds the blanket over Marc and smooths down the bedspread until every wrinkle is gone. "There must be someone who can find a cure. I don't know how much more I can handle of this."

"Yeah," I say. "I know."

That night I curl up next to Marc. Outside the air is eerily quiet and calm. I'm so used to the sounds of Seoul buzzing in the background. Here the silence presses against me. I can hear Kud's laugh, echoing through my head, and feel his silver eyes boring into mine.

I think back to every moment Kang-dae and I were together. Every word we shared. Every touch. My skin crawls, and I grip the covers closer around Marc and myself, burrowing my face into his neck.

Marc's breathing grows more even than before, and it soothes me. I want to believe some of the pain is gone and tomorrow we'll find some answers.

"I'm so sorry," I whisper into his ear, trailing my finger across his jaw, memorizing his silhouette. "I'm going to make this right. He can't have you. I won't let him."

CHAPTER 28

We travel home from North Korea in complete silence. Even Michelle, usually a chatterbox, is oddly quiet. "I want to help get Marc home safely," I tell Grandfather once we reach Seoul Station. I know they think I can't do anything to help Marc, but if our places were switched, I know he would never leave my side.

Grandfather frowns. "You might not like his parents' reaction. His mother will be upset. You should leave before they arrive."

"Jae," Michelle says, tugging on my arm. "You should stay out of this. It will only make things worse."

Her words stop me cold because she's right. If I had listened to myself long ago and kept Marc out of this mess, he'd be safe right now.

I set down my bag and sit next to Marc on the bench. Despite the warm spring air, he's shivering, his arms clutching his body. His face is paler than ever, and his eyes are blank and glassy.

I take his clammy hand in mine and press it to my cheek. When I lay my head on his shoulder, his body trembles beneath me. My heart shatters. There must be something we can do.

Grandfather leans down and pats me on the knee. "Maybe his mother will know some medicines that will slow down the process and give us more time to find a way to save him."

I bite my lips until I taste blood. I can't stand any of this. I can't stand not knowing what to do. Every choice has become a millstone, and I don't want to make any more choices again. I take in Marc's tattoo and the thin vine winding its way up his arm. The poison is making its way to his heart. I suck in a deep breath.

Somehow, I manage a nod and stand. Marc's hand slips from mine. He cranes his neck back to look up at me, and a shaky smile breaks loose.

"Don't worry, Fighter Girl," he says. "I'll be fine. I'm sure I just need time for my body to adjust. I'm feeling a heck of a lot better than last night."

I press my lips together and clench the handle of my suitcase until my knuckles whiten. I refuse to cry. I won't. I must save all my energy and strength because something must be done. I don't know what yet, but I can feel that energy building inside of me, screaming to come out.

"Want me to come over and help you make a plan?" Michelle says, worry filling her eyes.

"No." I bow to Grandfather and give Michelle a hug. "I need to take care of some things."

"Remember," Grandfather says, his eyebrows rising as he gives me a knowing nod, "the Council meets tonight to determine which portal we should use to enter the Spirit World to return the object."

I nod, not looking him in the eye. I know where the closest Spirit World location is. My archery center. But the words are lodged in my throat. I've avoided telling Grandfather, knowing that if I return the orb I lose the chance of using it to seek Komo. Now with everything that has happened with Marc and Kud, I'm even more resolved not to part with the orb. Not yet. Not until I know what the right choice is.

"Be careful," Grandfather says.

"Don't worry," I say as I drag my suitcase behind me. "Nothing is going to get in my way tonight."

Halfway across the terminal lobby, I spot Dad running toward me, his jacket flapping haphazardly around him.

"Back so early!" Dad exclaims. "Is everything all right? I haven't slept a wink since you've been gone."

"I'm fine." I fiddle with the handle of my suitcase. "We got everything done earlier than expected and came back."

He wraps his arms around me. "When your grandfather called, I was surprised, but all that matters is that you're safe." He looks over my shoulder at Marc slumped on the bench. "Heard Marc got sick while you were there." Dad puts his hand on the side of my face. "How are you feeling?"

"Tired," I say.

"I have meetings scheduled late tonight, but I am free later this afternoon for lunch. How about I drop you off at home and we can meet at Gwanghwamun?"

"Sounds great." I muster up a smile.

"Wait!" Michelle yells after us. "I'm coming with you. We can plan our strategy before you go to lunch." I open my mouth to say no when she adds, "And you're not going to stop me."

How can I say no to that kind of determination? Besides, if anyone can solve a problem, Michelle can.

"Two and a half more days," I mumble to Michelle after Dad drops us off. "That's all the time I have left before Kud steals Marc's life away. I can't bear the thought. Especially knowing that Kud's back in his hellhole of a palace cackling away."

"Listen." Michelle takes my hand as we head up in the elevator to my apartment. "You aren't a quitter. I know you. This isn't the time to give up. This is the time to fight back."

I roll my eyes. "Girl, he's a god. As in an all-powerful god of darkness. I don't think little me is any match for him."

"Maybe you're right." She leans against the elevator wall. "Maybe you should just let Marc die without a fight."

"You really know how to get your way, don't you?"

"Always." She grins. "How about we do a brainstorming session? You know I love those. Plus, I've got a really wild, crazy idea."

"Right now the wilder the better." As I press my finger to the scanner to unlock the apartment, I can't help but be glad she's here with me. After everything that's happened, I would've hated coming home to an empty apartment. We toss our bags onto the floor.

"What are you thinking?" Michelle asks.

"A million things." I sigh. "There must be a way to stop Kud. Stop his insane idea of killing Marc. This is a no-win situation."

"Well, let's start thinking of a million ways to stop Kud," Michelle says.

"Just don't tell Lily about any of this, 'kay? She will freak."

The image of Kumar working on his computer at the Guardians of Shinshi's secret headquarters squeezes my chest. I can only hope that Lily won't be affected by any of this.

I take out an old project poster and scrounge through my desk for a Sharpie. Michelle stares for a moment at the sheet covering my mirror. She raises her eyebrows. I shrug and tape the poster to the wall, scribbling across the top: *WAYS TO STOP KUD.*

Michelle starts her search on the Internet while I drag out Mom's box of old books. "There's bound to be something in here that can help us," I mutter.

"Semiwon is supposed to have healing waters that bring peace and tranquility to a soul," Michelle says after a few moments.

"Where's that?"

"Just outside of Seoul."

I write it down anyway, then continue heaving out the boxes of Mom's books I had crammed into the corner. Within minutes I'm practically buried in them.

I'm flipping through an interesting article on Korean ghosts when Michelle yells, "Oh!"

My heart dives into a near heart attack, and I leap to her side as she's reading her tablet. But she's only looking at a quaint brick inn with gardens in the mountains. She passes the tablet to me, and I read the article.

Local Mystic

Can decipher and assist with paranormal activity. Located in Heungjeong-li 303, Bongpyeong-myeon, Pyeongchang-gun, Gangwon-do. Phone: 343-34343.

"It's a hoax." I pass the tablet back. "She would laugh us out the door."

Michelle lifts her eyebrows and pulls out her cell phone. "I thought you'd do *anything* for Marc."

"We don't have time to run off on random tangents," I say. "Going there would take a whole afternoon or more. Marc doesn't have that kind of time to lose."

Michelle stares at me. "You're glowing."

"What?" Can she see a silvern sheen, too? I thought only Marc could see that kind of supernatural thing.

"Your shirt." Michelle reaches over and yanks on the cord wrapped around my neck. "Do you have a glow-in-the dark necklace on or something?"

Realization strikes me. I could slap myself for my stupidity. The orb. It's a seeker orb. It searches for what you want, like when it helped me find Marc in the cave.

"I'll be right back." I snatch the tablet from her and scurry into the bathroom. Once the door is closed and locked, I pull out the orb and whisper against its snowy-white surface, "Is this where Marc can find healing?"

Michelle pounds against the door. "You promised you wouldn't keep any more secrets from me," she says.

Ignoring her, I watch as the orb pulses to life with a quick flicker, as if it's speaking to me. I sigh and lean against the door.

Maybe this mystic is the one. Then again, I could be seriously delusional. I jerk open the door. Michelle's arms are crossed, and she's glaring at me.

I hold up the White Tiger orb. "This is a seeker orb," I say. "And I think it's telling us that this mystic can help Marc."

Michelle and I part ways: she heads down into the subway station, I round the corner at a fast clip to meet Dad. I try to focus on the gentle breeze crossing my face, smelling of cherry blossoms and the promises spring loves to bring. The fountains are spraying toward the endless blue sky. The statue of King Sejong looms over a full eight lanes of traffic.

Straight ahead, Gwanghwamun Palace stands impressively, massive gates, tall walls, and crimson-flagged guards surrounding it. I pause, the memories of Haemosu's palace tumbling back. With them comes the remembered pain and terror of not knowing how I'd survive. I reach instinctively for the orb dangling around my neck. The need to touch it and be reassured by its power is nearly overwhelming.

I stop and glance around. Shoppers and businessmen and businesswomen bustle past. Tall buildings rise high above, glittering in the spring sunshine. Cherry blossoms cascade from the trees and coat the sidewalk. A Seoul tour bus screeches to a halt, spitting out a handful of tourists.

And that's when my heart grows cold. A *dokkaebi* emerges from the bus along with the rest of the tourists. His monstrous bulk can barely squeeze through the bus's doorway. He has to duck due to his sharp horns. Then he clomps onto the street, his red body naked except for a dirt-infested loincloth. He blinks in the daylight and swings his club as if ready to smash someone on the head. His eyes find mine and he grins.

I spin around, but his reeking form magically appears before me.

"Well, well, pretty girl," he says. "You broughts me a pretty little treasure, yes?"

"I'm still angry from the last time we met." I glower, pretending my heart isn't pounding in my chest. "Move out of my way."

"I know not what you speaks of."

I'm frowning with annoyance as the *dokkaebi* mimics my steps, when I notice the shadows around the building are also moving. The gargoyles and statues twist, blinking eyes. A black thing—half wolf, half dragon—stalks down an alley, eyes intent on mine. A swarm of lizards skitter round the corner, blinking against the brightness of the afternoon.

Following my gaze, the *dokkaebi* says, "Yes, they wants pretty treasure, but I's gets it first. Pretty girl owes me."

My pulse pounds against my temples. Things are getting out of hand. My phone rings. This is definitely not the time to answer.

"I owe you nothing," I say. "Should I call Haechi? He won't be pleased."

The *dokkaebi* snarls, but one of the pedestrians comes up to me. It's my dad.

"Jae Hwa? Who are you talking to?"

I swallow and lift my chin, glancing between the grinning *dokkaebi* and my frowning dad.

"Hey," I say, afraid to say anything in front of the *dokkaebi*. From the corner of my eye, I can see the other creatures sliding out of their hiding places, growing closer. My mind flies, trying to come up with a solution.

"You're on time," I continue, trying to keep my voice upbeat. I step backward, away from the *dokkaebi*. "I'm starved. You?"

Dad hesitates, his eyes darting about, and I watch his grip tighten on his briefcase. "Are you feeling okay? You're scaring me."

"I'm fine," I say.

"I'm fine, fine, fine," the *dokkaebi* mimics from behind me.

I wince, listening to the *dokkaebi*'s sick cackle over my shoulder. I'm so tempted to smack him in the jaw, but instead, I smile at Dad, pretending I can't hear the trickster.

"I'm practicing the speech that I'm going to present to the school in two days explaining our trip," I say as we enter the restaurant.

"Trip!" The *dokkaebi*'s voice ripples with excitement as he follows us into the restaurant. "Yes, trip, trip, trip. Trip is where pretty girl finds treasure. Give me treasure, pretty girl."

"That's great," Dad says. His voice sounds forced, and his forehead is puckered up. "You'll have to practice it on me. I want to hear all about your trip."

My hands shake as I check my phone. There's a missed call from Grandfather.

"Jae Hwa." Grandfather's accent comes across thick in his message. "I wanted to check on you. Your father says the two of you are having lunch. This is good. We need to talk about the fate of the orb. It must be returned to the Heavenly Chest tonight. As long as it is out in the open, it and you are in grave danger. I will be expecting you at the Council meeting at headquarters tonight. Kumar is calculating which portal is closest to enter.

"And remember my earlier warning, *do not touch it*. I know it helped you fight Kud, but we do not completely understand its power."

I lower the phone and slip it back into my jacket pocket. We're seated quickly, thanks to Dad's reservation. The white tablecloth is tight and crisp, and the square rice paper lantern on the table creates a calm atmosphere. Scanning the room for exits, I take in the jagged chrome beams set sporadically around the room and the sleek slate flooring. When I focus back on Dad, I realize he's scrutinizing me intensely. I must look like a disheveled wreck. When was the last time I showered or ate a proper meal?

"It's good to see you back in South Korea," Dad says. "I don't function well with sleep deprivation."

I pull out my gift for Dad from my minibackpack. "As promised."

Dad smiles and unwraps my package. "Ah!" He pulls out the ginseng. "My favorite. And stamps for my collection. Your *umma* would have loved these. Did you know we started our collection on our honeymoon?"

"No, I didn't."

"We went to Kauai, Hawaii." Dad stares at the stamps, but I get the impression his mind is far from here.

I can't remember the last time Dad talked about Mom like this. I've been waiting for the moment where we can talk about her without one of us being angry or hurt, but now that it's here, my words are all jumbled in my throat.

Just as I'm letting myself relax, the *dokkaebi* clomps up to our table. I'm surprised the entire restaurant doesn't hear his stomping or cringe at his reeking smell. I focus on ignoring it because I've no idea what to do or what this *dokkaebi* is capable of doing.

"No, no, no, pretty girl. I's not likes this. You must give it to meeee. Now!"

The *dokkaebi* smashes his club onto the table. The porcelain plates fly, airborne. My teacup topples to the ground, shattering. Both Dad and I leap out of our chairs.

"What was that?" Dad asks, wide-eyed. "Did you do that?"

"No," I say, but then, not wanting to explain the *dokkaebi* or give his obnoxiousness any credit, I say, "Yes, actually, it was me. Master Kim says we need to practice a new move where if done correctly, even a teacup wouldn't move." I flash Dad a shaky grin.

"Teacup wouldn't move, teacup wouldn't move," the *dokkaebi* mimics. Slobber drips from his mouth and puddles on the tablecloth.

Everyone in the restaurant is staring at us. Dad loosens his tie and tilts his head to crack his neck back into place.

"What's going on, Jae?" Dad tosses his napkin on the table. "You can't do this in public."

I take a deep breath as two servers rush over and reset the table back to perfection, even replacing the silverware.

I apologize profusely while Dad slips them extra *won* to cover the damage.

Then my nightmare grows. More creatures appear, crawling out of the woodwork, literally, sliding in under the doorways and trailing through windows. I rub my palm over my eyes, wondering if I'm completely losing it. Dad's giving me a rundown of his workday, and the noise in the room is deafening. I want to clamp my hands over my ears and drown it all out. But I refuse. I won't let them intimidate me.

The food arrives, but there's no way I can eat my pasta. I slap my napkin down in frustration and plaster on a smile for Dad.

"I'll be right back," I say. "Restroom."

I waltz to the back of the restaurant. I can feel hundreds of eyes trained on my back. At the bathroom door, I snap my fingers, and the creatures follow me. A light classical music is playing in the bathroom. Scented candles are lit along the sink counter, and hand towels are set out in perfect white stacks.

I'm starting to love the irony of my life. Perfection mixed with insanity.

The creatures crash through the door, clambering over each other. Snarling. Growling. I've no idea what half of these creatures are, but I know that I have a few brief seconds before they attack me, ripping my body into pieces. I may have conquered Kud's assassin, but I'm hardly a match for the dozens that surround me.

I know I shouldn't be messing around with the orb, but desperate times call for desperate actions. I slip it out of the pouch. It's hot to the touch. The glow is such a bright contrast to the dim lighting that even I'm nearly blinded.

The creatures leap through the air, diving for the orb. I whirl into a wheelhouse-kick, scattering creatures into heaps onto the floor. Still, there are nearly fifty of them. How long can I last?

Heat seeps from the orb into my palm. My heart quickens, stronger, as if I could run a marathon. My vision sharpens. I can make out each individual creature's breath, each nostril bulging, even the individual hairs on their skin.

"Stop!" I command, holding my arm out as if to hold them back. "Don't come any closer."

The creatures shrivel back, mouths gaping wide. Slowly, they creep into the corners, cowering.

I glance at myself in the mirror and almost drop the stone in shock. A silvery glow washes over me until my leggings, boots, and shirt are practically sparkling. My hair whips around me in some unseen wind. I look so beautiful, I hardly recognize myself. It's as if the orb has taken every part of me and made it complete and perfect.

I no longer feel insignificant and small, but strong and fierce. My black hair is radiant, my skin glows. Energy rages through me as if I've gulped down a million cappuccinos.

Below me, the creatures tremble at my feet, and it becomes clear. I can do anything. Be anything. I could kill them all with one swoop of my arm. But something stops me. A part of me that knows that wouldn't be right. *The balance can't be upset.* I frown at this thought. Did I think that, or is it the orb speaking to me?

"Leave," I say, pleased at how my voice sounds like music. "Do not seek me again, or there will be consequences."

They squeal and skitter away, ants before a giant. Images run through my mind: blazing them with a shattering light, crushing their brains with a clench of my fist, renaming them so they don't remember who or what they were.

I slip the orb back into its pouch. My hand shakes a little as I do, and a part of me wants to rip it back out and hold it longer, taking in more of its power. The other part of me is shocked I would even consider these things.

My reflection stares back at me from the mirror. A silvery glow lingers on my skin before it finally fades. Sadness tugs at me as I watch my features return to normal. I press my hands to my cheeks. Perhaps this is what Marc was talking about.

I splash water on my face and stare hard at my reflection, gripping the sides of the sink. I think about Grandfather insisting that I need to return the orb to the Heavenly Chest. But I can't. Kud said that if I handed over the orb, Marc would be free. But that look in Kud's eyes haunts me. He won't let Marc free. Ever. The only thing keeping Marc alive is that I haven't given Kud the orb yet. I have two days to find a cure or think of a way to outwit Kud, and I plan on using every second I can.

Besides, with the orb's help, I might be able to find Komo.

As I stroll back into the restaurant, no one even looks my way. Conversations continue without a hint of what just happened a few feet away in the bathroom.

Somehow I get through the meal with Dad. I tell him about my trip, focusing only on the positives, and try not to think about the White Tiger orb dangling from my neck.

"Everything was perfect." The lie flies out with ease. It's sad how good I've become at lying to Dad because I can't tell him anything. "The medicine will make a huge difference, I think."

"I'm glad." But Dad looks anything but glad. He sets his fork down and threads his fingers between each other, his elbows on the table. "You're seeing those creatures again," Dad says a low whisper. "But you are too scared to tell me."

He lifts his eyebrows as if to challenge me to deny it. I press my lips together and look away.

"You know I care about you, Jae Hwa," Dad says. "There are two ways to solve this. You start seeing a therapist and taking the medication she recommends. Or we transfer you to a special school where they can help you recover."

"I don't think either of those are necessary, Dad." I want to tell him he's being ridiculous, but that actually isn't true. He's taking my issues seriously. But his diagnosis is wrong.

"I'm giving you a choice, Jae," Dad says. "It's one or the other."

He has no idea how much more serious my choices have become. I groan inwardly. "I'll see a therapist," I mutter.

"Good." Dad swirls his pasta around his plate, staring at it. "I'm glad we got that out in the open."

Then Dad talks about his clients and his next project, which will be held at the World Cup Stadium. I promise him I'll attend. He promises me he won't work so much. I wonder how many lies we can stack up in one lunch date. Will I ever be able to tell him the truth and have him believe me?

Maybe it's better this way. Safer this way.

Every once in a while, I glance around me to see if any more creatures have shown up, but nothing does. Whatever I did worked. One thing I do know, I'm not the same girl who walked into this restaurant.

This both thrills and terrifies me.

CHAPTER 29

Somehow Michelle has wrangled Marc into coming on our little excursion of insanity.

My body rocks back and forth, following the sway of the subway. The sound of the train nearly lulls me to sleep as I lean in close to Marc. "Are you sure your parents won't flip out if they find out you're gone?" I ask.

"Mom went to the college to do some research on my illness," Marc explains, "and Dad is prepping for the meeting."

I sigh. "Which I'm supposed to be attending in four hours. Grandfather is going to be ticked."

"You should tell him we're on our way to find a cure," Michelle says.

"Not until I feel more confident," I explain. "I want to come back with answers, not a list of crazy ideas."

"This isn't a crazy idea." Michelle sticks out her lower lip.

"You're right," I say. "It's a smart, proactive one."

"You seem better this afternoon," Michelle tells Marc. "Not so pale and shaky."

“Thanks. I think.” He gives us a lopsided grin. “My mom set me up with one of her concoctions.”

“Do your parents have any idea how to stop this curse?” I ask, and then wish I hadn’t said anything at all. I keep thinking if I don’t acknowledge what has happened, it will magically disappear. I reach for Marc’s hand.

“They haven’t a clue,” Marc says, leaning against the window and closing his eyes. “They’re reading everything they can get their hands on.”

The subway screeches to a halt at Gangbyeon Station, and we hop off. Marc zips up his leather jacket as we truck up the concrete stairs. Stepping outside, it almost feels as if we’re still in Seoul even though we’re on the outskirts, since the buildings still tower above us and the streets bustle with activity. Michelle hails a taxi and we push inside, giving our driver directions.

The taxi veers onto the highway, and soon we’ve left the city behind, sailing into the mountains. After thirty minutes of driving through the winding mountain roads, we pull onto a smaller, rougher road that leads us into a thick forested area. A sign is planted on a wooden post: Herbnara Farm. Through the evergreens I spot a large creek to our left, raging full of frothy whitecaps.

“This is a popular place with tourists,” the driver says.

“Really?” I ask, gazing out the car window. “It looks pretty deserted.”

“You sure this is the right place?” Marc says.

Usually, Marc is the one who’s got his eyes peeled, but not today. His shoulders droop and his eyes are downcast. This trip might be too much for him. I take in a deep breath, wondering if bringing him will turn into disaster.

"It's the only idea we have," Michelle says.

I peek at the orb. It's still glowing. I have to believe we are on the right track and the orb isn't lying to us, because Michelle's right. This is our only option. My stomach sinks.

The road soon spits us into a large gravel parking lot with two mountains looming up on either side of us. I step out of the car, feet crunching on gravel. The air smells of basil, rosemary, and lilac all swirling together. Gardens and greenhouses fill most of the valley. A large lodge with peaked roofs and gables is tucked against the side of the creek, with smaller cabins trailing up the mountainside.

"Isn't this quaint?" Michelle says.

"I guess so," I admit, eyeing the area. Everything is too perfect, too normal, too happy. I want to scream. To tell the world it should be in mourning and nothing can continue as it has because my world is falling apart.

Beside me, Marc shivers. I pull him closer to me, looping my arm with his, glancing around furtively. "Do you see anything out of the usual? Are you okay to walk? Are you too cold?"

He kisses my temple. A slight chuckle escapes his lips against my skin. "Now who's being protective?" he says.

We amble down the cobblestone path to the largest house. It looks like something that should be tucked against the Austrian Alps with its sloped roof, ornate door, and cute flower boxes adorning each window. The door to the main house creaks as we open it. It's a gift shop of sorts—dolls, candles, cards, jars of herbs, and jams. I frown. This is not what I expected. A quick check tells me the orb is glowing, but now I'm not so sure. Maybe it just glows all the time, and I hadn't noticed it before. Maybe it only glows at certain times of the day.

"We came all this way for nothing," I say as Michelle strolls up to the plump lady at the counter. "This is not the place for a mystic healer."

"We are looking for Madame Shin," Michelle says. "Do you know where we can find her?"

The plump lady's eyes widen. She tucks the strands of her hair behind her ear and smooths her red jacket over crisp khaki pants. "Come," she says after a few moments of assessing us. "She's in her greenhouse."

We head back outside, where the lady rattles off directions and points to the farthest greenhouse.

"This is starting to seem like a dead end," Marc says. We pass a sign that reads "Emotion and Energy" with a picture of doll-like girl crying, and Marc nods his head at it, saying with raised eyebrows, "This is supposed to make me feel better?"

"I'm not going to let Kud kill you," I say as we travel down the winding path. "I'll do whatever I need to to stop it from happening."

"That's an even worse idea," Marc says. "The most important thing for you to do is stay safe."

"You two are so depressing," Michelle says. "Let's see what this lady has to say."

As I step inside the greenhouse, the smells of herbs and dirt assail my senses. Roots climb the walls and trail to the ceiling, where bundles of herbs are drying. The aisles are so narrow, I'm afraid I'll knock over one of the plants or ceramic pots. In the back, sitting on a small stool, is a woman wearing a cream-colored linen top and brown pants, the perfect working outfit. Her gray hair is pulled up in a loose bun secured with a chopstick. She hums as she trims the plant set before her. As I skirt around the plants, I can't help but think there's something a little off about this lady.

"Excuse me," Michelle says in Korean. "Are you Madame Shin?"

The lady looks up, her eyebrows knitting together, and frowns when her eyes land on Marc. "What evil do you bring to this place?"

The three of us glance at each other. I inch closer to Marc.

"Great," Marc says. "Now *I'm* the evil one."

"We're from Seoul and we have kind of a strange question." Michelle looks to me for help.

"We were wondering if you knew anything about—" I pause, eyeing her carefully, wondering if she'll think I'm crazy. "Supernatural creatures."

"Perhaps." She turns and digs through a bucket behind her, whipping out a necklace. Dangling on the end is a bronze circle, the middle cut out in the shape of a square, with Chinese symbols on it. Marc cries out, bending over and holding his arm as if in pain. The orb in my chest burns through the pouch.

Whatever she's holding is causing havoc. I reach to snatch it out of her hand and fling it to the far corner, but she grabs my wrist. Her grip is surprisingly strong for someone her age.

"Put that thing away!" I demand. "You're hurting him. We came here for your help, but obviously we were wrong to try."

As she releases her grasp, I let go, narrowing my gaze as I watch her slide the necklace over her neck and tuck it under the folds of her shirt. Marc exhales, and the orb cools off on my chest.

"This is highly irregular," the lady says.

"What is that?" I point to the necklace now hidden.

"Looked like an old coin bearing symbols of the five elements," Marc says, slowly righting himself.

"Well, he's smart like his girlfriend and evil to boot," the lady says. "Not good. Not a good combination."

"Listen, lady," Michelle says. "You've got him pegged wrong. He's not evil like you're saying."

"So you aren't just some gardener," I say. "That's apparent. First, I need to know whose side you're on."

"Not his." The lady jerks her head, strands of hair flinging out of her bun, toward Marc.

"I think you're confused." I decide to dive in and tell her the bare minimum of what happened. Her bushy eyebrows spike in interest as I explain about Kud, and she sits straighter when I tell her about the tattoo Kud put on Marc. When I nod to Marc, he pulls up his sleeve to show her the tattoo on his wrist, eying her warily. The old woman rises to her feet, clucking that tongue of hers, and shuffles closer, but not too close, to Marc.

"Kud is not one you should get mixed up with," she says. "Terrible temper, he has. Take off your shirt, boy."

He hesitates, and then with a roll of his eyes, pulls off his shirt. He's lean, with ripples of muscle along his stomach and chest. Normally I'd be focused on how hot he looks, but all I can think about now is how the tattoo has traveled halfway up his arm. I shiver as I study its black twists and coils. They almost seem to move as I study them.

Tentatively, she touches his arm. I hear a sizzling sound, and she cries out, leaping back.

"Evil! Evil work," she says, clutching her hand, then backs off, searching through her rows of plants.

"Did his tattoo just burn you?" Michelle asks.

The lady wraps a leaf around her finger. "That it did. Kud and I don't get along. No, not at all."

"You know Kud?" I ask, not able to stop myself from gaping.

"Indeed. The worst enemies we've been, for a very long time."

"That's great," I say, then shake my head at my bluntness. "I mean, this proves we're on the same side. Please. You have to help us. How can we stop the tattoo from reaching his heart?"

"Oh, you can't, my dear girl," the lady says. "No, no. Your boy will be dead, and Kud won't care. He'll be too busy searching for a fresh victim. The question is why he even bothered letting him live. He rarely worries himself with mortals. This boy doesn't look all that significant."

I bite back a cutting remark. "I might have something he wants."

"Well, there you have it. The only way to stop him from being so vindictive is to give him what he wants." The lady scrutinizes me with her beady eyes. "What is it exactly that you have that would interest an immortal?"

I lick my lips. My fingers itch to pull out the orb and show her, but what if she's lying? What if she's one of Kud's creepy servants? Or perhaps she has an agenda of her own.

"Ah." The lady shuffles closer, squinting. "She has the glow. Yes, I see it. So you aren't completely mortal, are you?"

“Leave her out of this,” Michelle says, sliding between the two of us. “We just need you to give us a potion or a wrap or one of those concoctions of yours to help Marc.”

“Half mortal, half immortal, eh?” The lady taps two fingers against her lips. “Never have I seen the likes of this before. But I’ve heard rumors. Of course, that was hundreds of years ago.”

Michelle rolls her eyes and slams her purse onto the table. “Listen, lady. You need to take us more seriously. No more funny games.”

“Games?” The woman glares at Michelle and harrumphs under her breath.

“I think she is being serious,” I say.

“What does this half-immortal, half-mortal thing mean for Jae?” Marc comes to life, pushing off the wall. “Will she be okay? Does this mean she won’t die?”

“This isn’t about me,” I tell the woman. “This is about Marc. There must be *something* you can do to help him.”

The lady hobbles to her worktable and starts cutting off herbs and flowers, tossing them into a bowl. She mutters under her breath, and I catch snatches of words. “It’s possible. Could be. Disturbance. He’ll use her. He needs her.”

Then her eyes widen, and she stares at me with piercing brown eyes. “Yes, you do have something. Something he wants so desperately. So desperately.”

I nod.

“What is it?” She leaves her bowl and scurries to stand before me. “You have one of the six, don’t you?”

"What's she talking about?" Michelle asks, moving closer to me and drawing me away from the lady. "Don't get so close to Jae. You're making me nervous."

"If I did, would it be enough?" I ask. "To fight Kud?"

The lady cackles, clapping her hands. She nearly breaks into a jig.

"I think we should leave," Michelle says. "I bet she's high on one of her drugs."

Marc folds his arms over his chest, and his jaw tightens as he focuses on me. "You're not going to fight him. I won't allow you."

Michelle glances between the two of us. "So what's this about?"

"You can't tell me what to do," I tell Marc, ignoring Michelle.

"There are other options," he says. "This is not one of them."

"How do you think I feel?" I snap. "Here you are about to die, and you expect me to just watch you shrivel away?"

"Enough!" The woman raises her palms into the air. She picks up a bowl and spoon, passing them to Marc. "This will give you strength and perhaps a few extra hours. It will slow the poison if luck finds you."

"What is that?" I ask, snatching the bowl from Marc and inspecting the mush. It appears harmless enough: pink petals mixed with what smells of rosemary and olive oil. "How do I know you're not trying to poison him, too?"

"It's but a few herbs mixed with a Seocheon flower," she says with a lazy shrug, but I don't miss that dark twinkle in her eyes, and I don't like any of it.

"Don't eat this, Marc," I say. "I don't trust anyone who can't be up front about who they are and what they're about."

“The Seocheon flower?” Marc taps the spoon against his palm, scrutinizing the hag. “Such a plant really exists? I’ve read about it in the myths. Who are you, really?”

“So many questions for such undeserving,” the woman chuckles. “I have dabbled with flowers from time to time to suit my purposes. Even won a special contest or two.”

“Samshin,” Marc says. “That’s your name, isn’t it? The goddess of life. You won the flower bloom contest against the Yongway’s daughter.”

“Ah yes. Those were the days.” The woman utters a distressed sigh, rips the bowl from my hands, and shoves it back into Marc’s. “Until I was cast out in shame by the master who put that mark on you. Eat.”

Then Samshin ambles to the shelf behind her herbs and starts rummaging through them.

“Here’s to nothing.” Marc scoops up the herb slop mixture and, with a shrug, shovels it into his mouth. He grimaces and swallows. “Blech.”

“Well, if you die,” I say, unable to mask my annoyance, “don’t say I didn’t warn you.”

“Hello. That’s it?” Michelle stomps over to Samshin. “A few more hours? If luck finds us? What a waste of a day. Come on. We’re leaving.”

As we leave, the lady seizes my arm. I startle. Her face is so close, I can make out each crevice and mole on her skin. “How strong are you?” she whispers in my ear.

“I defeated Haemosu.”

“Well, well. That is something.” She studies me intently, as if reading my thoughts. “But Kud is stronger. Far stronger. Still, it would please me greatly to see him writhe in agony, put in his proper place."

Then Samshin presses something hard and cold into my hand. As she pulls away, I inspect the object. It's a hollow sphere created by twisted platinum strands dangling from a chain.

"I know the object you bear." Her breath smells of garlic. "Favored, you are."

I unravel the chain, so the sphere suspends from my fingers. "Um, thanks." I can't hide the questioning tone at the edge of my words. Why is she giving me gifts?

"I know what you carry, so let's stop pretending. The orb fits inside the sphere. The necklace was created for such. Go on. Try."

With tentative fingers, I withdraw the orb hidden within Grandfather's pouch and undo the latch of the sphere. Samshin is right. The orb slips into its folds so easily they were obviously made for each other. I snap the sphere closed, mesmerized even now by the orb's shimmer, a Milky Way of brilliance in my palm.

"There. Now put it on, and don't be giving that little treasure away anytime soon. You'll need it. Haemosu was child's play compared to what you're dealing with. These things I know." She moves away, muttering again and shaking her head. "Yes, I know."

I watch Marc and Michelle head down the path, thinking about Madame Shin's words. She's right, of course. Haemosu was nothing compared to Kud.

"With your little token, the right weapon, years of training, maybe you could put that brat into his place." She taps her fingers over her mouth, deep in thought. "But probably not. No, probably not."

"You don't think I have a chance, do you?" Panic tumbles through me, and I grip both her arms, too tightly I'm sure, but I don't care because she knows more than she's telling me. I'm sure of it.

"The power runs strong through you," she says. "But it won't be enough. No, indeed. Not enough. You have to make the choice."

"I don't understand."

"Immortality or mortality, my dear girl. Yes, that is it. The choice. But are you willing to pay the price?"

"So I lose him either way," I say, dropping my hands.

"I was right about you. I always am." She pats my hand. "You are smart, that you are."

I want to collapse at these words. If there isn't any hope, then why continue? If I sacrifice myself, I can still have him from afar, but is that enough? To wander eternity without him? Without feeling his lips brush mine or his warm arms holding me tight?

It will have to be, because this is my curse. I won't have him suffer the consequences of it.

For once, he doesn't get a say.

CHAPTER 30

We ride in silence the entire taxi ride back. I snuggle closer to Marc, breathing in his smell, memorizing his profile. Even still, the taxi's lulling movement does nothing for my battered nerves. Outside, the rice fields roll by, endless lime-green oceans. Samshin's words rattle through my brain. Could I really just choose? How is that possible?

I press my hand to my chest where the orb hangs beneath my shirt.

Neither choice is a good one. If I choose mortality, I won't be strong enough to fight Kud. If I choose immortality, I might win, but then I'd be separated from my family and friends, stuck living in Haemosu's lands. Or, according to Palk, my lands.

"I can't let Kud do this to you," I tell Marc.

He kisses the top of my head. "Nothing can separate us. We'll figure something out."

I will, I vow. I should feel guilt for keeping Samshin's revelation a secret, but I don't. I rest my head on his chest, his heartbeat strong against my skin. My determination melds into iron.

When the taxi drops us off at the subway station on the outskirts of Seoul, my feet drag me to the ticket booth. Each of us will have to take a different line to head home, and I don't like the thought of leaving Marc. Besides, I've gotten five messages from Grandfather panicking about my whereabouts and a bunch of texts from Dad. I'm just not ready to face anyone right now.

Michelle is chatting on her phone with Lily and then hangs up suddenly. "A bunch of kids from school are meeting up at a club in Gangnam in about an hour. What do you say we go? We need a little cheering up after everything that has happened."

"We don't need cheering up," I say, scowling. "We need a cure. Besides, we don't even have fake IDs."

"Tara's boyfriend is the bouncer tonight," she says, waving her hand as if it's no biggie. "We're good."

"We're supposed to meet my grandfather," I tell Marc. "They're waiting for us."

Marc checks his phone and then pockets it as if, just like me, he doesn't want to deal with the messages. "You know," he says to Michelle, pursing his lips, "that might not be a bad idea."

"You can't be serious," I say. "You want to waste a whole night drinking and dancing when we could be finding solutions? Besides, that herb lady didn't give you those herbs to buy you more time to get drunk."

"We spent the whole afternoon finding out that there are no solutions," Marc says. His jaw is tight, and I catch anger mixed with pain in his eyes. "I've got two nights tops before this poison makes it way to my heart. I'll be damned if I don't enjoy my last moments and have some fun."

Michelle lifts her eyebrows and grins. "Marc's finally living a little."

I want to physically hurt her for throwing out this possibility. It's an idiotic plan. But that look in Marc's eyes tells me he's determined to do this.

"Fine." I cross my arms. "I'll go, but only to keep an eye on you."

Marc chuckles, and I scowl even more, but he seems better. Maybe Samshin wasn't a complete flake. I clench my fists as we step onto the train bound for Gangnam, deciding nothing good will come of this.

Darkness has settled over the city when we scramble up the stairs of the subway and find ourselves spit into mobs of people. Shop signs blare neon, vendors have set up tables of goods everywhere, and as we shove our way through the crowd, I spot a guitar player and a juggler.

Bright lights scream the name of the club: Trance. Michelle hooks arms with me and drags me to the entrance. The bouncer is a heavyweight with a buzz cut and two earrings in his left ear. Tattoos crawl up both arms, highlighting the cut of his muscles.

Michelle whispers something into his ear, he nods once, and she tows me inside with her. I glance over my shoulder to make sure Marc is following, but he hasn't moved. Instead, he's got his back to us, scanning the crowd. I'm about to ask him if he's changed his mind when he spins on his heels and waves for us to continue.

It takes a moment for my eyes to adjust. Except for the neon laser beams cutting across the room and flashes of light illuminating random walls and the stage, the room is darker than pitch. Techno music blares from speakers. Even though the night is young, crowds of people are already shoving their way to the dance floor.

Michelle yells something that sounds like, "Let's get a drink."

There is no way to respond, so instead, I clutch an end of her jacket so we won't get separated and shuffle after her. At the bar, Marc and Michelle each order a drink. I muster up the nerve to text Haraboji and Dad. They're both going to be beyond ticked.

The next hour goes by in a pounding blur. Grandfather tries to call, but I can't hear a word he says. He finally answers my text saying the Council is "very disappointed" in both Marc and me. A quick glance over at Marc tells me he's beyond caring. Between the throbbing music, flashing lights, and Grandfather's messages, I acquire a headache to match the music. After much prodding, Michelle finally manages to drag me out to the dance floor.

"You coming?" I ask Marc.

He shakes his head no and takes another swig. I bite my lips, hating the look of hopelessness filling his eyes.

"Drinking isn't going to solve any of your problems," I yell over the music.

"Right now," Marc says, "I don't care."

"If you were in my shoes right now, what would you do?"

"I don't want to talk about it, all right?"

"Fine," I say, and stomp off to dance with Michelle. Even while I'm with her, I keep one eye on Marc. I've never seen him act this way, and it scares me. He's never been one to lose hope.

The crowd presses around me, sweat flinging from bodies. The air reeks of body odor and alcohol. Then, during one of the flashes of darkness caused by the strobe lights, I lose track of Michelle. Panic rushes through me. I start pushing, searching for her. She can't have gotten far.

One of the guys I push shoves me back, and I find myself tumbling backward, lost in a sea of bodies, arms flailing and blocking my vision. I try calling Michelle's name, but the drum of music drowns my voice. It takes forever to maneuver myself back to the bar. When I arrive, Marc's chair is empty.

Numbly, I run my fingers over the empty seat, scanning the club for signs of either of my friends.

"You sitting here?" a guy asks, a girl hanging on his arm.

I'm on the edge of panic. I shake my head and take off down one of the dark corridors. The music throbs in time with my heartbeat. I duck in and out of groups, focusing on the light of the pulsing beams to guide my next step. The bathroom comes into view, and I storm through the doors. A group of girls hover together by the squat toilets, smoking in secret.

But Michelle isn't here either, so I run back out, down another corridor, passing by room after room. All I find are groups lounging on couches near game boards and couples pressed together in the shadows.

Soon, I find myself back out by the dance floor, but on the other end of it. I've come full circle. I notice a staircase to my right that I hadn't seen before. My eyes follow it up, and I see there's a second floor to this club. It's worth trying.

I shove two dancers aside and squeeze my way up the stairs. It's quieter up here, and tables are scattered about with small lanterns emitting a blue glow. I'm about to run forward, but then I freeze.

Marc is sitting at a table against the far wall, tipping back his chair like he does. Across from him on the long couch is Michelle, head tipped back in a laugh, her drink spilling over her shirt. But that isn't what has turned my heart to ice.

Kang-dae is there, his arm wrapped around Michelle. He's staring at her as if completely riveted. With his thumb, he trails the length of her jaw and then moves to her lips. Her mouth opens in either shock or fascination, I'm not sure which, but she drops her glass.

It bounces over the aluminum flooring, breaking the shock of the moment. I jerk back as if waking from a dream and march over to the table.

I slap Kang-dae across the face.

"Get your arm off her," I bark.

Slowly, he removes his arm, but he hardly looks angered. If anything, an amused expression crosses his face as he rubs his cheek. "Touchy, aren't we?" Kang-dae says.

"What is wrong with you, Jae?" Michelle asks. "It's Kang-dae. He was just explaining to us that Kud used him to get to us. It was all a trick."

"A trick." *Good one*, I think as I glare at Kang-dae.

"Kud captured him," Michelle explains, "but Kang-dae escaped and now he's back and safe with us."

"How convenient," I say.

"This is just what I was saying," Marc says, his words slurring.

"Jae Hwa," Kang-dae says. "You really know how to put a damper on a good time."

"Thank you," I say, "I'll take that as a compliment."

I grab Michelle's arm and pull her up, but Kang-dae wraps his arm around her waist.

"Don't be so eager to leave, my love," he tells Michelle.

She rips her arm from my grip and smiles at Kang-dae. My stomach twists in horror, and I let my hold fall away. He somehow has her under his spell.

"Don't touch her," I tell Kang-dae. "Whatever you wish to talk to me about is between the two of us. You don't need to bring my friends into this."

"It's a pity we aren't working together," Kang-dae says, stretching out his legs and running his fingers around the rim of his glass. "We'd make a great team, you know."

"Um. Let's see." I pretend to think about it. "No. We wouldn't."

"He says he wants to talk to us," Marc interjects and then lifts his eyebrows meaningfully at me. Is Marc trying to tell me something? "We should at least listen to what he has to say."

"Yes, a proposition, if you will." Kang-dae motions to the seat next to him, indicating for me to sit.

I grind my teeth together but stalk over and sit on the seat's edge, not trusting him for a millisecond.

"There, isn't that better?" He grins, but I can't take my eyes off his hand rubbing Michelle's knee. "Jealous?"

I cock my head to the side. "If you don't stop touching her, our conversation is over."

He lifts both hands into the air as if to surrender. Then he digs through his jacket pocket and withdraws a slip of paper. It shimmers in the blue glow.

"What is that?" Marc leans forward.

"It's a map to my house, if you will," Kang-dae says to me. "You can still save him. Hand over the orb and your boyfriend lives."

I glance over at Michelle. She gazes at Kang-dae, oblivious to our conversation either from some spell he's put on her or from the drink.

"How do I know I can trust you?" I ask. "Besides, what will stop you from doing something else horrible once I hand over the one object you want?"

He says nothing, but his eyes harden, so I know I'm close to the truth.

"I'll pass on your offer," I say.

"I thought you'd squander this opportunity," Kang-dae says, and then slides the map to me. "That is why I created this for you. In case you change your mind."

I pick up the map. It tingles beneath my fingers, and I can feel it aching to speak its contents to me. My fingers hesitate only briefly before I begin ripping the map into halves, quarters, eighths.

Kang-dae's mouth draws into a straight line. Cupping the scraps of paper, I toss them over my head, not letting my eyes leave Kang-dae's.

"A touch pathetic, don't you think?" Kang-dae says. "You are nothing compared to me. You cannot withstand my power or wrath."

"Leave us," I say, gripping the edge of the table.

"Until next time." Kang-dae rises, still holding Michelle. With a gallant swoop he leans down and kisses her hand. She giggles, and then he strides away.

I let out a long, relieved breath and lean my head against the back of the chair. The music of the club isn't as loud up here, but I rub my temples, trying to ease the battering headache I have.

"I can't believe he has to leave already," Michelle says, interrupting my worries.

"We should go," I say, eyeing her bloodshot eyes. Beside me, Marc is oddly quiet.

We head to the stairs, but as we begin heading down, Marc says, "I'll meet you at the entrance. I forgot something."

Michelle leans against me, practically passing out, so I don't argue, but I don't like the thought of us separating again. By the time Michelle and I reach the exit, he's caught up, looking pale once more and panting as if he'd run ten miles.

"You okay?" I ask as we step outside, breathing in cool air.

"Yeah." A smile creeps over his face. "Surprisingly so."

CHAPTER 31

I retreat to the archery center the next morning, needing the sensation of my arrows breaking free from my bow and flying across the distance. I'm desperate to watch them sink into their target, for the mark to hit center. The hike up the gravel road helps my head to clear.

Even as I'm escaping the city, I can't resist calling Marc. He doesn't answer. Figures. His mom probably put me on the banned list after we skipped town yesterday and he returned home half-drunk.

I send him a text: Practicing w my bow. Want 2 meet 2night?

My heart aches knowing I am so useless. Why couldn't I have been stronger and actually done something last night? All I did was tear up that freaking map. *Way to go, Jae.*

Samshin's words echo through me like treason. I can't defeat Kud, she said. His powers far exceed mine. I'm just a mortal, inexperienced and clueless. He's been around for a few thousand years, playing these games. What am I even thinking?

By the time I reach the main building of the archery center, I've already fixed Kud's face into the target in my mind's eye. There has to be a way to fix this mess. There's no way I'm handing him that orb or allowing Marc to die. I'm going to fight this.

I pick up my bow and wave at Master Ahn.

As I'm heading back up the hill, I see the spot where I stepped through last time. I pause and stare at the place between the trees. Had that just been a fluke last time or had Palk orchestrated it? Or is it really a place where the Spirit World and ours connect?

When I called Grandfather last night and explained the situation, he told me the plan. We are to leave today at noon to take a trip to the southern coast to return the orb. He'd flip if he found out I knew of a portal right here in Seoul. My conscience battles between entering the Spirit World and seeking Palk to return the orb to the Heavenly Chest or keeping it to find Komo and help Marc. I tap my bow against my thigh.

Marc has made it clear he thinks I should return the orb, but thinking about him only sends a stab through my heart. I rub my forehead and scuff at the stone road.

In the end, I head to the top of the hill. I'm sweating, so I shrug off my jacket and toss it at the edge of the pagoda. The cool morning air buffets my back. It doesn't take me long to unpack my bow and tie my *goong dae* to my waist. The bow's wooden frame is solid, reassuring, in my grip. Like we belong together.

I stride to the line for target practice. Squinting against the sunlight, I pinpoint the target, 120 meters away. It's far, but already the adrenaline has started rushing through me. The not knowing. The wonder of hitting something so far away, nearly impossible yet attainable.

I notch my arrow, pull back, lift, aim. The wind whispers against my ear. The buzz of the city below rushes across my face, alive and free.

I release. The string twangs, and I hear the gust of the arrow cutting the air. I purse my lips, waiting. And then it hits. Just slightly off the bull's-eye. A smile cracks the corner of my mouth. It's a good shot.

Someone starts clapping behind me. I spin, fear squeezing my heart, and whip another arrow out. But it's Marc, sitting on the concrete wall next to the pagoda, his back resting against one of the wooden pillars. He gives me a lazy grin, his dimple showing. My heart melts into a river that never wants to end.

I lower my bow and race to him. I've barely set it down when I'm practically tackling him.

"What are you doing here?" I ask. "Are you feeling better? How did you know I'd be here?"

"Whoa, girl." He lifts his hands into the air. "Easy now."

But when I step back and assess him, I see he isn't as well as I'd first thought. His skin is still pale, and beads of sweat line his forehead.

"You're here, though." I take his hands in mine, squeezing them. Too tight, but I don't care.

"Dad brought me. I begged."

The wind kicks up, and the clouds shroud the sun. I shiver against the breath of cold wind, feeling as if Death itself is laughing at me.

"How much time do you have?" I ask.

"It's more like how much strength do I have left. My dad's hanging out below, waiting. And your grandfather's down there, too. Said he's here to pick you up for the Council meeting."

"Figures he'd find me." I sit next to him and shrug back into my jacket. "Do they have any idea how we can fix all of this?"

"No." He shakes his head. "My parents are working on it, though. Don't worry. We'll get through this. And about last night . . . I just lost it. This whole situation just sucks."

"You seem better today." I decide not to mention that this is his last full day.

"This morning my parents came up with a list of possible ideas for a cure. They're pretty determined."

"That's great." I stare at him, drinking in his green eyes and wild hair, even the air that hovers around him. He's as perfect as anyone could possibly be.

"I should go. My parents are taking me to see a specialist today. He thinks he can help me." He stands and wobbles. I catch hold of him. He bats my support away. "I'm good. Sometimes I get dizzy. My vision is a little blurry."

"Just give me a second." I could kick myself. I sound so stiff and awkward. It's as if we barely know each other. I hate myself for it because I can't seem to break through this impossible barrier that Kud created between us. I grab my bow, slip it back into its case, and strap the case to my back, and then we start back to the center.

As we tread down the hill, I hear voices farther down the road, around the bend. There's no mistaking Grandfather's voice. My heart quickens, and instinctively I reach for the orb. If

Grandfather sees me, he's going to make me go with him to meet the Council of Shinshi. I latch on to Marc and shove him into the forest.

"What are you doing?" Marc chuckles. "That's just my dad and your grandfather."

I glance around and spot the ruins not far from where we're standing. An idea forms in my head.

"Would you do me a favor?" I ask, grabbing Marc's arm so he won't go back onto the path. "You know, since you're dying and you won't be able to do anything for me in the future."

I mean my words to be playful, but they come out serious instead. Marc jams his hands in his pockets and groans. So I reach up and kiss him, dragging my fingers through his hair. Then I whisper, "Just say yes."

"How can I say no to that?"

I take his chilled hand in mine and drag him over to the ruins. The wavering light twists and bends as if calling us to enter.

"Just hold on tight," I say.

After the disaster of the last few days—months, really—I need time alone with Marc. Because if everything falls apart, I want the precious few moments that we have to be special.

He shakes his head as if to tell me this is a bad idea. But I keep pulling, and then the world is being pushed and squeezed all at the same time. We're in a vortex, a blanket of stars cloaking us. There are so many doors, but I feel the pull of one in particular. The carvings along its surface glow golden in the midnight as if beckoning to me.

I reach out to open it and then see the *samjoko* symbol etched on its surface. The amulet opened this door for me once before, but that isn't necessary anymore. I press my palm on the imprint, and the door swings open.

The two of us soar through the door as if we are flying. Then we tumble into this new world. My world. The thought sends a ripple of fear through me.

I shake away all doubts as I take in my surroundings. This is the only way for the two of us to gain time, I tell myself. I can tell we're near the palace. In the distance is a series of sloping roofs, dark and faded against a dull-gray sky. I bite my lip. Today I can't go there. The painful memories linger, too fresh.

Turning, I see the ocean in the distance and a pagoda resting on top of a cliff above it.

"How did you do that?" Marc asks, gazing back at the wavering lines where the portal opens.

"The portal?" I shrug. "Apparently I'm in charge of this place until Palk can find someone else."

"Full access, huh?"

I laugh. "Something like that."

"Are you going to take me on a tour? Or am I a prisoner?"

I cringe at the word prisoner. Too much of a reminder of the past, but he's grinning at me and looking less pale by the second. "You know, this place might be good for you, after all. You're looking better."

"You're not so bad yourself."

A smile creeps across my face. "Come on."

I take off running, the ground bursting into green beneath my feet. My heart leaps in my chest. The air is sweet and invigorating. Marc's running beside me, the wind cutting against his hair. He grins as we head across the field, and I know the power of this place is surging through him, too.

"Race you to the beach," he says and takes off.

"Oh no you don't," I yell after him.

My feet pound the ground. We sprint through tall sea grass and over sand dunes, our heels sinking deep into the hot sand. Just as Marc reaches the top of the last dune, I tackle him. We tumble together down the dune. Our limbs tangle, and when we land, sand coats us. I laugh, only to start choking on a mouthful of sand.

Marc catches me spitting and drooling like a baby. He bursts out laughing. "Serves you right, Fighter Girl."

I try to glare, but it probably only makes me look even more comical. We lie on our backs, the sky above hovering in a gray and dull void.

"If you could have the perfect sky, what would it be?" I ask Marc.

"Icy blue. With wispy white clouds."

I close my eyes and envision it. When I open them again, the sky looks exactly like I imagined. I grin. This is kind of fun.

Marc sits up. "How did you do that?"

"What else?" I look around. "Should I change the beach? The water?"

"You're freaking me out."

"Just think of it like a dream." But then my heart slams against my ribs. Hadn't Haemosu said something similar to me before? *The land of the wonderful dream.*

Am I somehow becoming like Haemosu? Had it all started this way with him?

"What's wrong?" Marc's staring hard at me, and his hand cups my chin. "I can't figure you out."

"Me either." I scoot closer to him. "I just know that I'm about to lose you and I want our last moments together to be the best ones. When we're back at home, you can barely walk. Here, it's as if Kud never existed. As if the mark he left on you doesn't exist."

"We can't stay here forever. We belong to only one world."

"I want to make this special," I say. "Lasting."

I press my finger to his lips. I don't want to talk about any of this. It's beyond depressing, and I can't deal with it.

Instead, I pull him up and slip off my boots and jacket. Then I run into the ocean. I kick up water, splashing Marc. He scoops up a handful and douses me.

Seeing I'm now completely soaked, I dive into the water. It rushes over me, the perfect temperature. Marc dives in next and grabs me from behind. He pulls me close as if to throw me over his head. But instead, he stops and draws me closer. I wrap my legs around him and run my hands through his hair. He kisses my neck, his lips hot against my skin.

The water laps around us, and suddenly I'm lost in his touch. His mouth moves up my neck, inch by inch, until he finds my lips. Then we're kissing as if it will be our last. Maybe it is. I hold on to him tight. Tears threaten to burst from me. I can't let them. I refuse to ruin this moment. This place has become a million possibilities, and here it's just the two of us, our breaths matching in even beats.

I'm not sure how long we are out in the water, clinging to each other, touching each other, never wanting the moment to end, but eventually we slosh our way to shore.

We grab our clothes, and I squeeze the water from my hair.

"We should probably head back," he says. "It's already getting dark."

"That's just this land's time. The two worlds are on different time zones."

I'm gazing out into the water, watching the sun squeeze below the horizon, when I notice something sparkling along thc water. Curious, I step toward it. "What is that?" I squint at the horizon.

"No clue," Marc says.

Then I hear a voice, calling out to me from the lights. "Jae Hwa! Jae Hwa!"

My breath catches. I know that voice.

I race deeper into the water, stumbling against the drag of the current. "Komo!" I scream. "I'm here!"

The golden light moves closer until it's nearly hovering over me. I crane my neck back to see it.

"Komo?" I whisper this time.

"Jae Hwa," a voice says within the golden light. "Finally. I've been looking for you for too long."

"Komo!" I spin in a circle, wondering how to reach her.

"Use the White Tiger orb. What you seek is here in your lands. The orb will lead you to what your heart desires."

"What are you talking about?"

"Good-bye, Jae Hwa. Be strong of heart. You will need it for the journey before you. I must move on. My time on earth is finished. We will meet again in the heavens."

The golden light shimmers and slowly vanishes into the darkening sky.

"No!" I splash after the light until I can't run anymore. Then I plunge into the water and start swimming. Stroke after stroke, I cut through the waves until I'm far from the shore. But it's useless. She's gone.

CHAPTER 32

Marc calls to me from the beach, startling me back to reality. I swim back with slow, hesitant strokes. When I finally wade out of the water, my heart is tearing in half. Tears trickle down my face, but I wipe them away. I must stay strong. For Marc. For all those who will be affected if Kud manages to get this orb.

"What just happened?" Marc asks.

"That was Komo. She's gone." I sink into the sand. Marc drops next to me, and the two of us watch the sun set. The stars are released from their sleep and now glitter in the sky.

"They say love is life itself," Marc says and takes my hand. "I'd rather this end in death than to have never known you."

I have no words for the emotions swirling through me. I lean my head on his shoulder and withdraw the White Tiger orb from its holder, thinking about Komo's words. "She said this would lead me to my heart's desire."

Brilliant, blinding light shatters the darkness, and we both cover our eyes. Soon the light seems to stretch out, and I uncover my eyes. But the light doesn't lead us anywhere, and I can't feel any particular tug inside me. I drop my hand in disappointment.

"Look!" Marc says, pointing behind me.

Once I stand, I can make out how the beam of light forms a silvery trail from my palm all the way to the cliff. Marc whistles in amazement, and we follow the light. Once we reach the base of the rock, I spot a narrow staircase carved into the cliff, leading to the pagoda sitting on the top.

Marc gives me a mischievous grin. "I'm dying to know what your heart's desire is."

I roll my eyes and give a half laugh. "You and me both."

We climb up stairs as smooth as silk, probably eroded from the winds and waves. Even still, I hesitate at the first curve, thinking about Kang-dae. What if this is actually a trick?

I run my palms over the wave-washed stone walls as I tread up. The stairs twist and turn inside the cliff. At times it's so shadowy I can barely see my way. But when we reach the top, the view is breathtaking. A plump moon has risen and illuminates the land. The ocean sprawls out forever in an endless midnight blue.

The pagoda itself is dilapidated. "I just don't understand how Haemosu could let his place fall apart like this," I say.

"Maybe there just hasn't been anyone to take care of it since he died," Marc says.

"Thank God he's dead."

I touch the wooden beam in front of me and colors, once faded, spread bright and fresh across its surface like spilled paint. I jerk my hand away.

"Do that again," Marc says. "That was pretty awesome."

I start touching everything. The tattered curtains, the torches, the walls, the shattered shutters, the fallen beams. I laugh, amazed at the transformation once I'm finished. It's just too incredible to believe.

The pagoda, I realize, is actually a bedroom that overlooks the sea. A large bed is set in the center with gauzy white curtains that flutter in the breeze. A bench rests in one corner and a nightstand in another.

"So this is your heart's desire?" Marc grins. "A bedroom? Nice."

"Tempting." I scan the area. "There must be something we're not seeing."

"I'm crushed."

"I'm sure."

Then I spot it. A chest pressed against the far wall. It's with painstaking slowness that I finally make my way to it. I unlatch the hook and pull open the lid. It squeaks in resistance. When I look inside, I gasp.

Marc's shadow hovers behind me, and for a moment, I worry he'll suddenly transform into Kud and I'll realize I've been tricked all over again. But no, it's only Marc.

"Can I have a second?" I ask.

"I'll be outside on the porch," he says. Guilt pulls at me, and I wonder if I'll be able to truly trust anyone ever again.

There are two objects inside the chest: a journal and a cloth bundle. The journal is leather bound and soft in my hands. A thin cord coils around it to keep it closed. I unwrap the cord and let the pages fall open. My other aunt's name, Sun, is written in the upper left corner on the inside of the journal. So this is the journal that Komo was looking for all these years. She had said she'd hoped it would help her save her sister. And here I am holding it, too late.

I start reading. It begins with her meeting a guy at school, just like Komo had said that Haemosu had met Sun. Then he gilds her. But according to this journal, Sun remains enthralled with him. I guess she didn't have anyone to show her the truth like I did. I continue reading:

School was hard today, and Father's rules are impossible to abide by. I needed to get away, so I entered through the secret entrance in the tunnels that Haemosu showed me. There were many doors, and at first it was confusing. He warned me to avoid the door with the snakes. But my dearest love appeared and showed me a clue. I must always seek the door with the symbol of the three-legged crow, the samjoko. *Now I have a private place, a beautiful room overlooking the sea, to escape from school and from Father. Haemosu says I must keep it our little secret.*

"Everything okay?" Marc asks, peering back into the room.

"It's my aunt's journal." My stomach twists as I think about her words. She was completely blind to Haemosu's true self, and she paid the price. "Not the one in the hospital, my other aunt. The one Haemosu kidnapped. Her name was Sun."

Marc steps closer. "You think this will help you?"

"I don't know." I move to the bed and motion for Marc to sit next to me. "I think this was her place. The whole journal is about how much she loved him. Listen to this:

I can't decide if I'm dreaming or awake, but today I have decided never to go back to my old life. I have everything I could possibly want here with Haemosu.

"So she was in love with Haemosu."

"At least in love with the idea of an escape," I say. "And the worst part is, this was her last entry. He must have killed her right after this." I gently caress the cover, wishing I could have known my other aunt. "There's something else in the chest."

I retrieve the bundle and set it on my lap, staring at the soft gray cotton. Then I unpeel the ends, revealing two swords and a bunch of leather straps connected together. The swords' hilts match, a bird etched on each, each eye gleaming purple from the stone lodged inside it. The blades glint sharp silver in the candlelight.

"Wait. That's the *Bonghwang*," Marc says, snapping his fingers. "It was once the royal emblem of the rulers of Korea. That's the same bird that showed up at the theater. I thought it was trying to attack you, but maybe it was trying to warn you about Kud."

I pick up the swords, one in each hand. As I hold their cold metal handles, a snap of electricity flutters through me. Similar to the power I feel when I hold my dragon bow.

"I wonder how she got these," I say, setting them down and trying to untangle the leather straps. "And why she had them."

"Maybe your grandfather. You know him and his weapon obsession." Marc takes the bindings and untangles them. Then he straps them to my back and shows me how the swords are sheathed inside.

"How did you know how to do that?" I ask.

"Jung's classes." He traces the *Bonghwang*'s image with his finger. "There is the possibility the *Bonghwang* itself might have given these to Sun. Perhaps the creature was trying to help her."

"There must be something in this journal that Komo wanted me to look at. A clue or something."

I set the swords aside, flop backward on the bed, and groan.

"It'll come to you." Marc leans on his side next to me. "It always does."

"By then it'll be too late."

"In that case, you'd better kiss me."

His lips are warm and soft. He runs his hand over my cheek.

"I don't want you to ever leave me," I whisper.

He looks away.

I tug on his shirt. "I want to see how far it has traveled."

This is the second day since Kud marked him, and tonight will be his last night. My only hope is that whatever Samshin gave him will give him a few more hours tomorrow night. Marc shrugs the shirt over his shoulders and head, revealing those lean muscles.

"All that working out," I say, trying to avoid the reality of the mercury-colored tattoo that has snaked all the way up his arm to his shoulder.

"I've got to keep up with you, Fighter Girl."

"I want to kill him," I blurt out.

"Yeah, I noticed that last night, even as a half-drunk jerk."

"I still do."

"No, Jae." Marc's eyes are wide now. "No, you don't. You need to return your orb to the Heavenly Chest and not worry about anything else. That's what you're supposed to do."

"If I could just get close enough to him in the Spirit World where I'm stronger, I'd attack." I stare up at the white curtains, waving in the sea breeze. "If I could find a way to reach him."

"Don't forget that he's stronger in the Spirit World, too. Besides, how do you plan on finding him?"

"There's a split in the Spirit World. Kud created the rift, so that North and South Korea are divided in both our world and the Spirit World. I'd have to figure out which of the ancient tombs would lead me to his lands. Probably only the ones in North Korea. I could use the *samjoko* amulet to enter and find him. Then I could use the orb to kill him."

"I don't like it," Marc says. "You're walking right into his plan. Again. You're basically just handing him the orb, in his lands, where he's even more powerful. You need to give Palk the orb."

"The only way to save you is to kill Kud."

"You're not strong enough to kill him, and you know that." Marc stands and starts pacing. "It's a complete suicide mission. If anyone should be doing this mission, it's me. I'm already doomed to die."

Frowning at how right he is, I unstrap the swords from my back. Komo said that this, the swords and journal, would bring me my heart's desire, but she was wrong. This hasn't helped me at all.

"How about a little sword-fighting lesson before we head back?" Marc's smiling again, spinning a sword in his hand. It's like he's in his element holding it.

"I'd like that."

He shows me the overhand back-cut move, as well as how to sweep and jab. I try not to get distracted as his arms wrap around me, or by the way his muscles flex as he slices the air with the swords.

"I'm impressed," I say. "You're really good."

After we finish practicing, I hand him the swords. "I want you to have them. They're not much, but maybe they can help you when he comes to try to take you. Plus, you're trained in sword fighting, unlike me."

"They're your aunt's. I can't take them."

"Please. For me?"

"You know I hate it when you do that." Marc glares at me but takes the swords. The pressure in my chest lessens, but only for a few seconds. Who am I kidding? There's no chance in this world that he can fight off a god.

CHAPTER 33

I don't want to leave the Spirit World. As much as I hate to admit it, it's become my private escape. Yet even as I think that, I'm reminded of Sun and how she came to the Spirit World to escape her old life—only to be murdered by Haemosu. Perhaps I'm not so different from her after all. I can't hide away here forever and live in an alternate reality.

The weird part is stepping back onto the road outside of the archery center. The air smells different; dew lingers on the ground, and the morning is fresh. I can hear the distant city. It's as if time held still for us.

Marc checks his watch. "It stopped working again." He slips on the leather straps and then slides the swords inside.

I scrutinize him. "Your dad will ask questions."

"Yup. Wish me luck."

As we start trudging down the hill, my body tenses up, knowing I need to face Grandfather. When I spot Marc's dad's car, my chest twists.

"I'll see you tomorrow at school, right?" I ask, lingering in the shadows of the tree line.

"Sure." Marc stares over the top of my head, refusing to look at me.

I step closer to him, taking both his hands. "We're going to find a solution to this. I know we will."

"Don't do anything stupid."

"What makes you say that?" I grin, then reach up on tiptoes and kiss him.

We hike into the parking lot, holding hands. Grandfather's arms are crossed, and his face is drawn and pale. I expect him to be full of angry energy, but he is oddly still.

"I have been trying to get in touch with you," he says, and then his voice chokes. He presses his lips together and looks away. "Your *komo*. I got a call from the hospital. She is gone."

I know this already, and yet hearing the words from Grandfather sends another wave of grief through me. Maybe it's that I've always separated the Spirit World from this world. Coming back and feeling the reality of her death squeezing at my insides makes it all so final. I clamp my palms over my eyes, shoving back the threatening tears. Marc wraps his arm around me.

"Are you going to tell him you saw her?" Marc whispers into my ear.

I shake my head. I'm not ready to tell anyone anything. I need more time to think this all over and decide what to do.

Marc's dad gets out of the car and calls Marc over. "We don't have much time," Dr. Grayson says. "The specialist is waiting."

Marc kisses me on the forehead and then eases himself into the car, his face scrunching. I wonder how much he is hurting from the tattoo.

Grandfather comes over to me then and wraps his arm over my shoulders, drawing me to him. We stand there, watching Marc's car back up and drive away, crunching on gravel. Fear washes over me, and I almost race after the car to make Marc promise me he'll never leave me like Mom and Komo did. But that's silly and impossible, so I just hug my arms over my chest. My only consolation is Kud won't bother him since he's already been marked.

At least until tomorrow.

"I talked to the Council," Grandfather says. "They've agreed to put off the decision until after Komo's burial."

"When will that be?" I ask, my voice barely a whisper.

"In two days." Grandfather turns me toward the car. "Your father is already at the hospital waiting for you."

When we get to the hospital, they've already taken Komo's body away to be prepared for the viewing tomorrow night. I don't tell Grandfather this, but I don't want to see her dead body, pale and cold. I want to remember her alive, full of spunk and power. That's who she was. As we ride up the escalator from the parking garage beneath the hospital, I focus on the memory of her voice calling out to me over the ocean. She seemed happy and ready to move on. I cling to that thought.

As we step into the lobby, I spot someone who stands out from the rest of the crowd. It's the spirit girl who confronted us after the weasels attacked. Bari.

Ghostlike, she glides along, her white iridescent *hanbok* a sharp contrast to her long black hair. She holds a rope of white lilies. Trailing behind her are the translucent souls of young and old, clutching on to the rope. Their expressions remain unmoved as they shuffle along in shimmering light.

I freeze at the top of the escalator, watching them, and then I rush and grab Bari's arm. She turns on me, her dark eyes narrow and pale lips open slightly. She thrusts her spear between us, and I jerk back from its sharp tip and engraved hilt.

"What do you think you are doing?" she asks.

"I just . . ." My throat tightens. "Did you take my *komo* to the heavens?"

"Is she dead?" Bari lifts her eyebrows. At my nod, she says, "Then yes. But something is wrong with you."

"Jae Hwa," Grandfather says from behind me. He grabs my shoulders and turns me around. "Who are you talking to?"

"Have you started fading from his sight yet?" Bari asks from over my shoulder. "That's how I first realized what was happening to me."

"I don't understand what you're talking about," I say, pushing away from Grandfather to face Bari. "What happened to you?"

"Jae Hwa." Grandfather's voice is terse. "What is going on?"

"I used to be human," Bari says wistfully. "It's not that bad. After a while. It's the fading that's hardest."

"What?" I ask. "You and I have nothing in common."

"Once you accept your fate, it gets easier." Then she glides away, and I hear her mutter, "Poor soul. She doesn't even know."

I watch Bari leave, my mouth gaping. Grandfather shakes me, and I focus back on him. His eyebrows are knit together and a vein is popping up on his forehead.

"Something is going on that you are not telling me." He lets go of my shoulders. "We are on the brink of something huge, Jae Hwa. For Korea. For the world. And you are in the dead center of it. I hope you know what you are doing."

"I don't."

"Good," he says. I stare at him incredulously. He lets out a long breath and rubs his chest, saying, "A wise person knows their weaknesses."

"Bari thinks I'm becoming immortal."

"But you are not yet." He steers me forward. "Remember, the future is in your hands."

I want to believe Haraboji, but Bari is right. I don't understand what's happening, and I definitely don't like this idea that my fate is already determined.

We find Dad in the lobby, sitting on a bench by the tall glass windows. His body is folded over, hands clasped in front of him.

"Dad!" I run to him.

He lifts his head at my voice and stands, holding his arms out to me. Tears are streaming down his red face.

"She was younger than me," Dad says. "Too young."

I nod against his chest as pain slices through me. All this time we were hoping she could be saved. Grandfather comes toward us and rests his hands on Dad's shoulders. We stand that way, silent and still, remembering her.

I lift my head, wiping away my tears and sniffing. "She's in a better place now," I say. "She's happy."

Dad shakes his head, not really believing me, but Grandfather's watery eyes focus on mine. I can't tell if he thinks I'm just saying that or if he suspects something. But right now I don't care. All I care about is that we are there together.

"She helped me understand how important family is," I say. "And that there are ways around impossible situations. She'd want us to stay close and depend on each other."

Both Grandfather and Dad nod. For the first time I can remember, we all agree.

CHAPTER 34

Sunlight creeps through my windows. I rub my eyes and jerk up, panic pounding at my temples. I study my room, inspecting every detail. The sounds and smells from the city waft in through my open window—*kimchi* mixed with honking taxis. My English essay lies scattered across my floor, strewn about by the wind. Clothes litter my dresser and pile up around the floor of my wardrobe. My wall bears the dents and scars of too many punches and arrow nicks.

Tossing aside my blanket, I stand on my *yo*, curling my toes into the mat. My hands prep, my knees bend. I never sleep with an open window. Not since my *dokkaebi* encounter.

Something was here. I know it. Feel it.

Then I remember the orb. I grope for it, digging under my tee until my fingers wrap around the stone's warm surface. Letting go a sigh of relief, I sink back onto my *yo*. The orb radiates in my palm, glittering brighter than snow. Its heat soothes my nerves, but I quickly let it go. Between Grandfather's warnings not to touch it and the effect it had on me in the restaurant, I don't trust it.

After I give the room a quick check to make sure no one is there, I shrug into a pair of khakis and a T-shirt. My phone reads 7:30 a.m. Then I notice a text from Marc that he sent around five thirty this morning.

Hey Fighter Girl! See u at school. I want my last day 2 b normal.

Then another text at 7:25 a.m. Whatever happens, remember I love you.

That one must have been what woke me up. I text back: I love u 2.

There's no way I'll make it to school on time. I scramble about on my hands and knees picking up my English papers and stuff them into my backpack, hoping I've collected them all.

I shut the window, slamming it with a definite thud. Once the lock slides into place, I stand still, trying to remember everything I did last night. No matter how hard I think, I can't for the life of me remember opening the window.

After I sling my backpack over my shoulder, that unsettled sensation nips at me. I wish I could figure out what is bothering me, but everything appears to be its usual disaster. I turn to leave, when my eye catches the poster I'd made listing ways to stop Kud. My heart stops for a beat and then takes off racing. I don't know why I hadn't seen it right away. Probably because I'd been looking for a creature, not words. But they're there, in big bold Chinese characters.

The victory is mine.

The words I'd written on the poster, *WAYS TO STOP KUD*, have been slashed out with a black marker.

Damn it. He was here. I tighten my grip on my backpack, imagining him watching me while I slept. My eye finds my bow resting against the wall. If only there was a way to take it to school without being sent straight to the principal's office. I can totally imagine Dr. Baker's expression if I were to get caught.

I drag my fingers along the bow's smooth surface and then tuck it into the bottom of my wardrobe. There's no way I'm going to risk it getting confiscated, even if I'd feel better armed.

"Wow. Don't you look high-class," I tell Michelle between first and second period. "I must have missed the memo." She's wearing a black blazer and pencil skirt. She applies a swipe of lipstick and smacks her lips once before she slams the locker closed.

"There's no way I'm getting in front of the school body looking like a hobo."

"I wouldn't have pegged you for a hobo," I laugh. "If I didn't know better, I'd have guessed you were presenting for a Fortune 500 company, not our high school student body." I glance down at my ankle-high boots, casual tan pants, and turquoise crewneck shirt. "Me, on the other hand? Definitely hobo material."

"Don't be silly. You're like Lara Croft meets Buffy the Vampire Slayer."

"Thanks," I say. "I think. By the way, have you seen Marc? This morning he texted me saying he'd see me later, but he hasn't responded to any of my texts since."

"Really?" Michelle adjusts her books and stares at me, pursing her lips. "That doesn't sound like him. Still, I can't blame the guy for sleeping in. Things haven't exactly been peachy."

"He said he'd see me at school." I recheck my texts just to make sure.

"Well, there you go. He'll be here. And as long as he shows up for our presentation today during the pep rally, it doesn't matter how many classes he misses."

I grab her arm. "You don't think anything happened to him, do you?"

"Girl." She rolls her eyes. "Something already happened to him. He's having a tough time. Give him a break. If I only had a few days to live, I sure wouldn't spend it in school."

"I'm not upset with him." I let her go. "Just worried."

"I know. I am, too." Michelle gives me her puppy-face look. I figure now is not the time to tell her how much I hate that look. "We'll figure this out. I know it."

I cross my arms, unable to speak, as she strolls away to class, blowing me a kiss. Anger stirs inside my chest.

Marc is dying. And I have no way to stop it.

Students pack the gym until the bleachers are overflowing and kids jam the doorways, squeezing in from the lobby. Music blasts from the speakers as the cheerleaders dance—pom-poms flying, smiles plastered across their faces. The soccer team runs out next as each of their names are called. The crowd goes wild. They're projected to win the APAC tournament this year.

I stand in the corner, arms crossed, body numb. I got another text from Marc about fifteen minutes ago. Meet u at the gym for the presentation. There is something cryptic about it. I frown at the words, wondering why he keeps sending me texts, but not answering my questions.

I tap my foot, casting glances every half second at the door. Marc still isn't here, and all I can do is worry and text and call. Still, he doesn't answer. I don't like it. Something is wrong. He's never ignored my calls, except when he was training, but there's no way he's training today.

"Still no sign of Marc?" Michelle says. I shake my head as she hands me a card. "Maybe he wasn't feeling up to it," she says. "Read the card and smile every time it says smile."

"You're telling me when to smile now?"

"Trust me on this one. You need to be told when to smile. Otherwise you look ticked off all the time."

"That's because I am."

"You're impossible."

"Which is why you love me."

"True." She grins, then takes off across the gym to the mic.

I realize they must have called our names, so I scramble after her.

"Together we make a difference." Michelle begins her speech with our motto. "Together we change lives."

Then she recaps what we did to raise funds for medicine and explains how successful we were. She stands back as a slideshow comes up on the big screen. When did she have time to make this? She must have created it in the middle of the night. I swear Michelle doesn't sleep.

Once the slideshow is over, they call Marc's name. I feel my insides freeze. I wait, expecting him to break through the crowd. Or maybe Kud will show up and make a huge scene and kill us all.

Nothing happens. Except for the fact that everyone's staring at me.

I shake my head and step to the mic. I read the card. "We raised enough *won* to purchase fifty multi-drug-resistant TB medical kits." SMILE. "Each kit is designed for individual patients, so they will be able to get the medicine they need." SMILE.

My heart warms knowing that if nothing else, we've made a difference in people's lives. That a child will breathe easier. That a man's life will be saved. I have to cling to those thoughts, otherwise I might break down in tears in front of the entire school. Which would be horrifying.

I wish Mom or Komo were here right now. I know they'd be proud.

Once our presentation is over, the audience is oddly subdued. At first, no one claps, then a few start, and then the entire gym is roaring with shouts. Michelle and I smile at each other, and my heart is full. I don't ever want to forget this feeling.

The dismissal bell rings, and there's still no sighting or word from Marc. I even hunt down Kumar.

"I haven't seen him since last night," Kumar says.

I don't like how Kumar won't look at me but focuses on his tablet instead. "You saw him last night? I thought you were working until late."

"Yeah, he stopped by the headquarters to check something out."

I don't know why, but I feel like there's something he's not telling me, and nothing is adding up right. That worries me.

I pull out my phone and text Marc: Where r u?

Kumar's tablet peeps with a message. My heart stops for a half second before I rip the tablet from Kumar's hands. Sure enough, my text to Marc has popped up at the top of the screen.

"Give that back!" Kumar says as he reaches for the tablet, but I twist away. All of my recent texts to Marc are on the screen. I'd been talking to Kumar this whole time.

"How could you?" I yell, shoving the tablet into Kumar's stomach. He grunts. "You lied to me. Did Marc tell you to do this?"

Kumar grimaces and nods before hanging his head.

"What has he done?" I clutch Kumar's shirt. "Where is he?"

"Girl," Michelle says. "You need to chill out. He's probably resting. Right, Kumar?"

Kumar shrugs. I race outside into the courtyard. Behind me, Michelle calls out my name. I stop, biting my lip, and racking my brain for a reason why Marc would ask Kumar to do this. Cherry blossoms tumble onto my hair and shoulders, scattering across the cobblestone walkway. The air fills with the sweetness of blossoms and azaleas. I love this courtyard. I wish I could sit here on one of these benches with Marc and enjoy the moment.

"Where are you going?" Michelle asks.

"To his house. Maybe he'll be there. I have this horrible feeling something is wrong."

"Let me come with you."

"No." I think about last night and how Kud entered my room. He's prowling, waiting, and I am not about to risk another friend in all of this. "If you want to help me, you need to stay out of this. It's too risky."

"Don't be that way," Michelle says, frowning. "Are you still upset that I was hanging out with Kang-dae the other night?"

"Don't you remember what I said?" I ask. "That wasn't Kang-dae. It was Kud in disguise."

"Why can't you just be happy for me? I finally find someone who is interested in me, and you turn it back into your craziness."

I stare at her, lost for words. I never once thought she wouldn't believe me. I snatch her phone out of her hand and scroll through it. My heart skydives. She's been texting Kang-dae.

"So this is who you've been texting with all day?" I shove the phone with its stream of texts back into her hand.

"You're jealous, aren't you?" She presses her sparkly pink lips together and practically glares at me.

"Uh, *no*. I'm worried."

"Do me a favor," she says, adjusting her bag over her shoulder. "You worry about Marc. I'll worry about myself."

"Please." I grab her arms. It takes all my strength not to shake her. "Promise me you won't see him or talk to him again. I'm begging you."

I'm torn. Should I stay with her or go find Marc? I don't like the thought of her possibly meeting up with Kud, but at the same time, Marc is the one who is dying. She's perfectly healthy.

She pulls away from me and presses her skirt straight. "I don't know, Jae."

"Fine," I finally concede. "At least promise me you won't see Kang-dae until we talk about it. He's not who you think he is. You have to know I want you to be happy."

She shrugs and nods once. It doesn't really satisfy me, but I don't know what else to do.

"I'll text if I hear anything," I say, and then take off down the courtyard, my feet feeling as if they're dragging through snow.

CHAPTER 35

I knock lightly on Marc's door, holding my breath. It swings open. Marc's mom stands in front of me, eyes red, face white as ash.

"Is Marc okay?" I blurt out, dropping my backpack onto the floor with a thud.

Her lips quiver. She remains silent. My head whirls. I duck around her and run up the stairs. It's rude, but I can't stop the panic that's threatening to block the air from my lungs.

At the top of the stairs, I freeze. The living room is crowded with people. I search the faces, trying to figure out what's going on. Then I recognize some of them, even though they are mostly hidden beneath their hoods. They're the Council of Shinshi members. I search the group until my eyes land on Grandfather.

"What are you doing here?" I demand. "What's going on?"

Grandfather rubs his hand over his face. "Marc is gone."

"What do you mean he's gone?" My voice practically screeches. I'm finding it hard to breathe. "He still has until tonight. We still had time."

"No, not gone like that, my child," Grandfather says. "He broke into the headquarters last night and took the *samjoko* amulet."

"What?" I ask. "Why would he do that?"

"We think he left for the North Korean border this morning," Marc's dad says. "His North Korean visa is gone."

"I hacked into his computer," Jung says. "Looks like he's reentering North Korea with a fake visa as a tourist."

"But how—" I rub my forehead. If anyone could pull off something as insane as this, Marc could. I bet he got Kumar to help him with this crazy scheme. I want to pull my hair out. "Why would he do this?"

"And there is this." Grandfather hands me a folded piece of rice paper. It's soft to the tôuch as I open it. My hands shake as I recognize the handwriting.

Jae,

Don't be mad. I have less than ten hours left. I can't sit here and do nothing. For good luck, I've taken the gift you gave me last night. I've never believed in luck, or fate for that matter. Which is why I must do this. You know, that whole destiny-is-in-your-hands thing. I love you.

Forever yours,

Marc

"He's gone to find Kud," I say, letting the note fall to the floor.

"Yes," Grandfather says. "That is what we believe."

"We need to do something," I say. "We need to go after him."

"It is too late," one of the Council members says. "We are sure he has long passed the border. It is three o'clock."

"No," I say. "There must be something we can do."

No one will look at me. They all believe Marc is already dead.

Un-freaking-believable.

Marc's mom passes us carrying a stack of candles and enters Marc's room. Wordlessly, she starts setting candles around the room and lighting them. I snatch up Marc's note and pad over to the door, but I can't enter. Instead, I listen as she says a prayer for every candle she lights.

Where are you, Marc? What have you done?

A lump forms in my throat as I look around his room. Books tumble over his desk, posters of various languages are tacked to the walls. Where most guys would have a row of trophies, he's got his own collection of artifacts from just about every culture lining the top of his bookshelf.

My feet drag as I cross the threshold. His mother doesn't even glance my way, intent on her pleas to God. My fingers trail over a picture tacked to the bulletin board. Marc and me on top of Seorakson. His arm is slung around my shoulders, and my head is thrown back, laughing. He's punching the air in victory because we conquered the mountain.

The moment after that is imprinted in my memory. He swung me in a circle and drew me into his arms, whispering that after everything we'd been through, nothing could stop us. He kissed my forehead, my lips, and promised his love for eternity.

A sob escapes my chest. I jam my fist into my mouth and pretend the tears haven't escaped once again. Because I'm strong. I must stay strong. It's not over yet.

I crumple his note in my fist and press it to my chest. The White Tiger orb radiates warm and powerful against me.

It's not over yet, Kud. Not even close.

I turn and watch Marc's mom meticulously light more candles. The scent of candle wax and smoke fills the room, along with a soft glow. And with it, hope. I move to her and hold out my hand.

"Let me help you," I say, my words choked and aching with pain.

She almost smiles. "Every prayer will help."

She passes me a box of matches, and soon the room is full of lit candles, our prayers, and hope reaching for the heavens. And my heart.

Like a sledgehammer, it comes to me. I know what I must do.

I unpin the picture of Marc and me on the mountaintop, jamming it in my pocket. Spinning on my heels, I march into the living room. The Council and the Guardians are in an uproar, arguing and yelling like a pack of lions.

I try to push through them, but the head of the Council, Mr. Han, grabs me. "Don't lose sight of what you need to do, Jae Hwa."

"What are you talking about?" I shrug out of his grip.

"The orb," he says. "We must return the orb. In fact, now would be the perfect time."

Just those words alone—*the orb*—have shut the Council into complete silence. I bristle over the word *we* because I highly doubt he is planning on entering the Spirit World to have a little chat with Palk.

"I'm not returning it yet." I straighten my shoulders.

There are gasps and frowns. I should feel guilty, but I don't. Only desperate and angry and on the brink of complete despair.

"Marc needs my help," I say. "I'm going to find him and free him of Kud's curse."

"How do you plan to do that?" Jung asks.

"That's impossible," Marc's dad says. "Unless you give Kud the orb, which means you'll be doing exactly what he wants you to do. Walking straight into his trap."

"I do not approve of this," Ms. Byun says. "It is against what we as the Guardians believe in. We cannot allow it."

I search Grandfather's eyes, needing his approval, but he says nothing, crossing his arms and frowning. I used to think that he was just cranky all of the time, but now I know that look. He's thinking.

"If I return it to the Heavenly Chest, not only am I condemning Marc to death, I also sentence my own family," I say and push through the group. "I'm going whether you approve or not."

"No!" A Guardian named Young leaps across the room, kicks me in the side, and grabs the chain around my neck.

I choke as the chain pulls against my throat, then Young yanks it over my head. It slips through his fingers, and the latch holding the orb inside pops open. The orb tumbles across the hardwood floor, looking like a Ping-Pong-sized pearl. Seeing it lying there, I hardly recognize it. It looks so different, and I'm not sure why. The Council members around me mutter and step away from it.

The need to pick it up and hold it overpowers me. I reach, but Young grasps it first. A blinding light sears from his hand. It fills the room, hungry to consume every inch of shadow. Young screams in pain, dropping the orb as if it were a ball of fire. He collapses to his knees, clutching his palm. Everyone in the room now covers their eyes except me.

I step forward and, taking the orb and chain, drape it back over my neck. Once it's tucked safely beneath my shirt, the room shifts back to normal. If Young weren't rocking back and forth on the floor, moaning, it would've been hard to imagine that anything had happened.

"You should see a doctor about that," I say.

"The White Tiger has chosen her," someone behind me says in an awed whisper.

"We must return it to the Heavenly Chest," Mr. Han says.

"Wielding such a powerful object is dangerous," Grandfather finally says. "It is not meant for mortals. Jae Hwa, I do not know what this will bring, but it is not natural. I cannot risk losing you."

Marc's dad says, "What if the orb can lead her to Marc?"

"And then what?" Grandfather snaps. "Marc still dies tonight."

"Then I must defeat Kud," I say.

"That is impossible," Mr. Han says. "He's immortal."

Marc's mom slips into the room, her head high, eyes resolute. She's carrying a small wooden box. It's carved with strange markings that I don't recognize.

"I found these in an ancient tomb in Norway." She opens the box. Inside are three bronze arrow tips. "Legend says they were infused with the power to weaken an opponent."

"Bronze tips?" I ask.

"Faith can overcome the impossible," she says, and tips them into my hand. They clang against each other, cool as ice against my skin. "I have faith in you."

"Do not go." Grandfather's eyes bore into mine.

As we study each other, I know I'm about to cross a bridge that will separate us. And once I do, there will be no turning back. The image of Marc's tattoo and his pale face fills my mind. I can't stand the thought of living without him.

"I have to," I say. "I'm sorry."

"Grab her!" Mr. Han commands.

Someone grabs me from behind in a vise grip. I twist to set my attacker off guard and then bend, so his kick swings through the air above me. Spinning, I kick, punch, and jam my elbow hard into my attacker, so he grunts and falls to the ground. Standing with my fists before me, I see my attacker is Jung. According to Marc, he's got the best martial arts skills of them all.

I don't have time for a full-out fight. I'm not sure how long it will take me to reach Kud's lands or even how I'll get there. So I pull out the orb. Its glow blazes in a fiery white, blinding everyone. Guilt at using the orb against the people who've tried to help me rips through my insides, but I can't allow myself to care. Not if I want to save Marc.

I grab my backpack and race out the door.

CHAPTER 36

I sprint down the stairs, not bothering to wait for the elevator. I forgo the subway and opt for a taxi. At this time of day, traffic is manageable. I bark out directions to the driver and then sink my head into my hands. I've never felt so alone. Marc has left, Komo is dead, Michelle is wrapped up in Kang-dae, and the Council is against me, even Grandfather.

Am I making the right decision? Marc was idiotic to just walk into Kud's hands. But hadn't I done the very same thing with Haemosu? Regardless, I can't give up on Marc, not when there is the bleakest amount of hope.

Back in my apartment, I write Dad a note saying I'm going to hang out at Marc's tonight. Then I find my bow. Before leaving, though, I open my bow case and run my hand over its smooth surface. A light tingling shoots up my arm, and with it, a spark of hope.

I take out one of the arrows and secure the bronze tip that Marc's mom gave me. It doesn't fit perfectly, but with a little pressing, I finally notch it in. I twist the arrow, letting the beam of sunlight glint against the tip. I pocket the other two for good luck. I find Princess Yuhwa's pin locked away in my bottom drawer and add it to my good-luck collection. Then I spot the three origami animals Dad made for me, taped in a neat row at the top of my laptop screen along with Marc's drawing of Bora Bora. I peel them off and slip them into the pocket of my jacket, pressing my hand against the outside of the pocket and closing my eyes.

How will Dad feel if I never come back? I'm doing this because I have to keep him safe, but he'll never know or even understand that.

Whatever happens, I must destroy Kud.

After strapping the bow case to my back and sliding on my boots, I grab a water bottle and granola bar. I'm about to leave when I hear a pounding at the door. I freeze, wondering who it could be.

The door kicks open, slamming against the wall, and light floods the room. I stumble backward, shutting my eyes and fumbling with the zipper of my bow case.

"There is no need for weapons," a deep, rumbling voice says.

My heart catches in my throat. It's Haechi. His half-lion, half-dragon form looms large in the doorway, too large to fit. He growls low. I step back. I don't care if he says he's my protector, he still scares the heck out of me.

"You bring trouble everywhere you go, little one," he says.

I decide not to argue that one. Even standing at the other end of the apartment, I hear a crashing at the front door, as if a huge monster is trying to get in. It's a solid metal door, but based on those sounds, it won't last long.

"Run," Haechi says. "I will give you a few moments."

He swivels and pads toward the front door. I hurry after his massive form, determined not to leave him alone to fight whatever is on the other side.

"For once, do not be stubborn!" Haechi says. "Flee!"

His urgency—or is it fear?—sends me spinning on my heels toward my bedroom, but as I do, a boom cuts the air and the floor shakes. Glancing over my shoulder, I watch the front door break and fly across the couch. I stumble into my bedroom, the front door smashing to the floor at my heels, milliseconds from hitting me. A massive creature hulks in the doorway. Blacker than night.

Strange neon-orange symbols fill its entire form, moving as if ever changing. Its tongue licks out, snakelike, and yet it has hands with gleaming claws, scratching across the ground. Its white eyes jut out and erupt with blinding fire. Haechi dives at the creature, and the two roll across the floor, snarling and biting. I hesitate and reach for the orb. But Haechi, as if sensing my intention, snaps his head my way, a chunk of the monster's skin dangling from his mouth.

"It's a trap," Haechi says. "Run!"

Then I see the symbols skitter over the monster's skin and clatter to the floor. Like a thousand orange bugs, they scamper across the floor toward me. I rip out the orb, its light flashing brighter than the sun. But the scorpion-like bugs don't even hesitate.

They must be blind, intent on the hunt by smell.

Sliding open my window, I leap onto the balcony and toss the rope attached to the railing over the edge. Ever since I sneaked out of the apartment this way several months ago, I've taken measures to always be ready with an emergency rope in place.

I clip myself into the harness and literally throw myself over the ledge. But not fast enough. As I plummet to the ground, cringing at the snap I'll feel once the rope cinches tight, I feel one of those strange creatures skittering over my pants. It seeks my skin. I kick at it with my boot, knowing its bite must be lethal.

The rope jerks me up, but I'm already unsnapping my harness, allowing myself to fall the rest of the way to the ground. The scorpion thing clings to me and chews at my pants, frantic for a taste of my skin. Above, I see hundreds of the orange bugs, skittering down the side of the building.

Hunting.

My heart hammers in my chest. I'll have nightmares for the rest of my life if I survive this.

I pull one of the bronze arrowheads from my pocket and stab the side of the bug. It sizzles and vanishes. I wonder if Marc's mom really did find an enchanted tip.

I take off in a sprint, tucking the tip back into my pocket as I run and shrugging the bow case on tighter. I've no idea where I'm going, but I head toward the subway, hoping to outrun the freak-worthy bugs.

I need to be around people, lots and lots of people. It's the safest bet. While I jog, I'm continually glancing over my shoulder, desperate to keep my distance from the bugs, yet they are gaining on me. Their bodies clatter across the pavement behind me sounding like pounding rain. I practically fall down the subway's concrete steps, desperate to get on a train. Once on the platform, I race toward a train prepping to leave, pumping my arms and squeezing through the sliding doors before they shut.

The bugs pour down the steps and onto the platform as our train begins to move. I press my hands to the glass windows, urging the train to move faster. I grit my teeth, imagining how the bugs could latch on to our train and follow me everywhere.

But once they hit the platform, they swarm in circles, perhaps searching for my scent and unable to find it. I let out a long breath and sag into the train's seat while trying to think of a way to get into North Korea. But my mind comes up blank. Why didn't I pay more attention or keep Kud's stupid map?

If I enter the Spirit World through Haemosu's lands, I cannot pass the Great Divide. Kud made sure of that. I need to physically enter North Korea in order to do this, which is a half day of travel and proper visas.

I get off the train at Myeong-Dong and step into the streets. Couples are strolling, holding hands, laughing. Groups of college students stand around, chatting. I'm still for a moment, drinking in the sight. My heart aches until I don't think I can stand it anymore. I pull out the picture of Marc and me standing on the mountain cliff. Remembering his lips against mine, soft and yet hungry for more. With his arms wrapped around me, we were one and strong and unshakable.

But now he's gone off and done this, and he's never felt so far away. Every other time I've had him close to me, knowing he would know what to do. But now I'm just fleeing, and I don't know how to find him.

The orb heats against my chest. It's trying to tell me something, I realize. I duck into a dark alley, glancing around. I'm such an idiot. It isn't called a seeker orb for nothing. Could it seek Marc for me? I slip the orb out, and its silvery glow engulfs the alley. Heat pulses through my palm and rushes through my entire body. I stare into it, waiting for it to tell me something. But it only radiates light. Then I remember the cliffs in the Spirit World with Marc and how the light led me to the pagoda and chest on top of the cliff.

I look up and spot a stream of light trailing down the alley, away from the bustle of the shops and the people. I track the light, slowly at first, but then I break into a light jog. The alley spits me out onto one of the massive streets, with cars jammed in traffic. The sidewalk here is fairly empty, so I continue my jog, hoping I don't attract any attention.

Soon I gain my bearings. I'm not far from Komo's house. I run until I'm standing in front of the gate to her house. I stare at the boarded-up windows, the glass never repaired from Haemosu's attack, and I'm pulled back to the last time I was here—when Haemosu broke in with his boars and injured Grandfather, immobilized me, and kidnapped Komo. I had refused to come back since then, the memories too sharp, too painful.

I take a deep breath and push open the gate. A breeze kicks up around me, rustling the dying trees in her yard, sending fallen leaves skittering. It seizes the gate, slamming it shut. I startle, but as I glance around, I decide it is nothing more than the wind. The silvery light leads up Komo's steps. The door is locked, but I know the combination to open it. Once inside, I close the door, locking it and pressing my back against its solidness. Not that it would help if I'm still being followed by the bugs. My eyes find the window that Haemosu smashed through. I shiver, trying to shake off that memory. The light falls onto the mat in the middle of the floor. The trap door. The door that leads to the tunnel. The tunnel that supposedly leads to North Korea.

The memories crash over me as rushing waves.

Beneath the trap door is Komo's secret tunnel. At the end stands an iron gate that blocks off the rest of the passageway. I remember shining my flashlight through the bars into a gaping blackness.

"Where does that go?" I had asked Komo.

"North Korea," she'd said. "You do not want to go there. Trust me."

That was then. This is now. Because the place she warned me against, the place I don't want to seek, is where I must go. Then I remember Sun's journal, and everything falls into place like a sledgehammer. It's almost as if Komo knew I would come here to save Marc. He is my heart's desire, and yet the only way to find him is to enter these secret tunnels. The very same ones that Sun once entered to find Haemosu.

But Sun never returned.

After I toss the mat away, I scamper down the ladder into the tunnel. I don't bother with a flashlight once I'm below. I've got the orb to provide enough light. I take off running, the path familiar after all the times that I'd met Komo down here in her secret room, where we once trained together. When I come to the locked gate I pause, eyeing the lock, then give it a good shake.

I unstrap my backpack and fit Princess Yuhwa's pin into the lock, hoping it will unsnap. Evidently this lock isn't magical in any shape or form, because the pin does nothing. Crap.

I race back to Komo's house, scrounging the kitchen drawers for some type of key, but there's nothing. Finally, I resort to the hammer I find jammed in the back of a drawer. Back in the tunnel, I slam the hammer on the lock, thrusting with all my force. It bends with each blow, and I'm sweating and cursing at the lock all the while until it shatters.

I toss the hammer aside and tug at the gate. Its aged hinges resist, but it scrapes open enough for me to squeeze through. There's something different about this side of the gate. I'm not sure what I'm sensing—maybe it's just the feel of a place that's been long unused.

I check my watch. It's already five. I only have two hours left at most if the countdown started from the moment Marc was imprinted. There's no way I'm going to make it. I can only hope Samshin's herbs gave Marc a few extra hours. I pull out the orb, warm and soothing, to light my way, and dart down the passageway. The border of North Korea has to be at least thirty miles away. *This is ridiculous*, I think, my feet pounding on the rocky path. There's no way I can run this, but I keep running because I don't know what else to do.

The orb illuminates my trail. I'm panting and my sides burn. My heart feels a million pounds right now, so heavy that I'm not sure how much longer I can run.

The walls narrow until I have to slow my sprint to squeeze through sections. Their rock surfaces cut my skin. I step around giant boulders and duck as the ceiling grows lower and lower. This passageway reminds me of the one in the Diamond Mountains in North Korea, almost alive, sinking sharp stalactite teeth into me.

My breath is sharp and raspy. I can't decide if I'm out of breath or if it's claustrophobia creeping over my skin. Soon the ceiling hangs so low that I resort to crawling through the rubble on my hands and knees. Rocks slice my palms and tear through my pants.

And then the path disappears completely, and I come face-to-face with a solid wall of rock.

I pause, fear of failure drowning me. All I can think about is how I'm practically buried beneath the earth, helpless while Marc is dying. Then the orb shines into a small crack before me. I'd have to go in on my belly, but I'm not sure if I'm thin enough to squeeze through. I peer into the small space. The floor and ceiling in this section are flat, like two pancakes hugging together. I look behind me, racking my brain for another way.

There is no other way. There are no other options.

I unstrap my bow case and backpack before flattening myself on the ground. I hook my backpack to my ankle and start crawling on my belly, dragging my case along beside me, slapping the cold rocky floor to strain my body forward.

Images of the ceiling collapsing on me crowd my mind. My bow gets stuck twice, and I have to yank and twist to get it free. There's no way I'm leaving my bow in the depths of this cave. Panic keeps taunting me, and the air is thin from lack of oxygen.

When I crawl out of the space, I find myself in a large cavern. I brush the dust off and strap on my case and backpack. Doors of different sizes line the walls on either side. Each has a different symbol imprinted on it. I spot a *samjoko* symbol like the one Sun sketched into her journal on one of the doors.

The pull of the Spirit World tugs at me from each door. It's that same draw I experienced outside of the archery facility.

But the light from the orb spears ahead, straight across a narrow, natural bridge, slick and wet from the condensation dripping from above. It's not really a bridge, more like the tip of a rock that happens to stretch to the other side. The sides fall down into an endless nothingness. I can't even see the floor.

On the other side of the chasm stands the strangest of all the doors, round with fiery-red Chinese symbols in its center and snakes twisting around its edges.

This is it, I realize. All I have to do is cross this bridge. It's simple.

As long as I don't slip and plummet to my death.

CHAPTER 37

I drop to my hands and knees, dizzy, and push myself along the bridge, which looks more like a balance beam than anything. I squeeze the rock between my legs and grip what I can of the sides. My body slips easily along, and that worries me. A wrong move or a tilt too far left or right would send my body flying below. My backpack and bow combined throw off my balance. It pains me, but I know I need to get rid of my pack.

Shimmying backward, I scramble back onto the rocky shelf where I began and toss away my backpack. Without its extra weight, I already feel lighter. I hope I don't come to regret leaving it behind.

Sucking in a gulp of stale air, I plant myself back on the bridge. The going is slow and painful. Halfway across, my pants catch a tip of rock sticking out. It snags before I realize what's happening, and I teeter. My bow throws me off-balance, and I'm slipping over the edge. Frantically, I grasp the rock, my legs dangling below me over nothingness. My arms burn as I try to pull myself back up on the bridge. I grunt, straining, and slowly, I inch my way back up until I lie belly flat on the moist bridge, heart pumping. It takes me forever to move again. I must. It's the only way to survive.

When I finally slap my hands on the rock shelf on the other side, I practically hug the ground, so grateful to have made it. I only hope I can open the round door. I really don't want to think about going back the way I've come.

Slowly, I stand, and as I reach for the door, it's almost as if the whole rock shelf pulses with a thrumming beat. A thin wisp of smoke trails out from the keyhole and curls around me.

"Who seeks the forgotten?" it whispers into my ear. "Who treads darkness's halls?"

"I, Lee Jae Hwa, seek the presence of Kud." My voice is nothing more than a breathless gasp.

"Yesssss," the smoke hisses. "So you do. So you shall."

The entire door spins, clicking as it does. Right two notches, left three, a full circle, and then it stops. The bronze knocker, which is a face with a mouth frozen wide open in a scream, sinks inward. As it does, the door groans as if full of agony. There is nothing to do but step inside. Yet instead of touching a hard rock path, my foot finds nothing, and I fall.

I scream, my heart jammed into my throat. I grope for something, but there is nothing but stars and endless space. I must be in the place outside time, I realize. The void between worlds. I plunge, my hair flying, and clutch my bow tight, determined not to lose it. A panicked sensation fills me as I fall endlessly. Did I make the wrong choice? I'm about to give up hope when the orb shoots a beam of light toward a red door, shimmering like fire in the distance.

I focus on the door and put all my energy into reaching toward it until my fingers scrape its surface. The moment I touch it, it disappears and I'm tumbling onto a hard, rocky surface, not much different from the one I left. My head smashes against a rock, and I feel faint.

When I finally open my eyes, a red haze fills my vision. Two round holes that remind me of eye sockets gape at me.

I'm lying in a pile of bones.

My eyes widen, and I feel the scream rising up within me, shoving its way up my throat until it echoes through the hall like a clap of thunder. I scramble to my feet, shaking off the bits and shards clinging to me. I clamber out of the pile to the center of what I realize is a passageway. This one has smooth rounded walls with strange crimson symbols as tall as myself carved into their surface. I move closer to one and realize fire burns within the etchings. I shudder as the evil of this place seeps into my skin all the way to my bones, until they physically ache.

My throat burns. I wonder if the air within these passageways is poisonous.

The corridor looms before me in shifting red waves, like heat waves rising off the pavement on a hot day. I take deep breaths to calm myself as I unzip my bow and tie my *goong dae* to my waist. Then I place the two bronze tips onto arrows and notch one into my bow before striding down the corridor, following the orb's beam of light.

The bones make the hike cumbersome, and at times I have to clamber over them, gritting my teeth at the thought of stepping on other victims' remains so carelessly. With every step, my anger burns stronger. My fingers itch to shoot my arrow through Kud's heart.

Shadows begin to swirl around me. They sting my ankles, trailing their way up my calves beneath my pants. Terrified, I press my hands over my ankles, hoping to stop the pain.

I pick up my pace, stumbling and crashing like a wild animal, hoping to outmaneuver the wisps of burning smoke. Soon the orb draws me into a new tunnel, this one filled with water. The walls are smooth as alabaster with arched ceilings. Candles are scattered about, floating on the water's surface. I hesitate for a moment, unsure whether the water is safe, when I hear a sudden, high-pitched scream.

My heart constricts, and I rush heedlessly through the ankle-deep water. The water burns my skin and tears at my flesh. I'm screaming until I stumble into a wider area, where I crumple to the floor in agony. The water must have been acid. I can't even open my eyes to check on my injuries while my consciousness wavers. But within a few moments I recover, revived from the Spirit World's power, I suppose. I manage to stand and stagger closer to the two massive pillars reaching far above. Candelabras stretch out on either side, flanking me like soldiers. The scent of candle wax hangs in the air.

Droplets of fire rain down around me. Something plops onto my shoulder and sizzles. My eyes widen as I realize my jacket is on fire. I swat at my shoulder and spin in a circle, trying to wrap my mind around what is happening. That's when I gaze above, into the arched ceiling. It's carved just like the walls of the first tunnel, with more fiery symbols, and it casts down bits of sparks every once in a while like rain droplets.

A scream shatters the stillness again, and I race to the source of the sound. I skid to a halt at the top of a stairway, nearly tumbling down.

The room below reminds me of an ancient cathedral. Pillars span the open area, and arches roll one after the next along the sides, leading all the way to a platform at the far end of the chamber. Between each pillar, fire pits burn, casting up forklike crimson flames. On top of the platform sits a massive throne made of twisted metal rods roped around each other to resemble hundreds of snakes.

Two clawlike bones rooted at the base of the throne curl above it to form almost a circle. Yet the ends never meet, instead displaying sharp tips at the top.

And there sits Kud, arms draped over snake-head armrests, their tongues flicking out alive and hungry. He's dressed in his black robe, his draping hood shadowing his face. The tendrils of his robe slither out, ravenous eels along the base of the platform, always moving.

My eyes follow one particular tentacle that is taut and stretched out all the way to one of the thick stone pillars. The tentacle is wrapped around a body like a cocoon. My heart seizes as I recognize those wide brown eyes and the hair pinned back with butterfly clips.

Michelle.

I pull my bowstring taut and let my arrow fly. Before I even check to see if it's hit its mark, I break into a sprint, screaming, "No!"

I'm not even halfway across the open floor when panels in the wall burst open, and out bound five gigantic hounds aimed straight toward me. I stagger to a stop, backtracking as they bark, blood drooling from their jaws.

The Bulgae.

Or so the legends have named the dark god's lapdogs.

They don't attack instantaneously, even though their eyes practically bulge from their sockets and their necks strain to devour me. Some unseen leash is keeping them in check.

"So good of you to visit me, Princess." Kud's voice oozes across the hall as he plucks my arrow out of the armrest snake's eye. "I was worried that you would never pay me a visit. Yet here you are. How timely."

"Let Michelle go," I say, aiming at him once again with my bow. "She is not a part of this."

He laughs, a mirthless gurgle. My hate for him freezes me; it's even deeper than anger.

"You amuse me, Princess. Perhaps you are jealous? You should be." He stands and his robe shifts, a swirling darkness. "She is beautiful and so full of life."

A tentacle loosens from Michelle's lips. "Jae," she says. "You were right. I shouldn't have listened to him. I didn't realize—" A sob catches in her throat.

"You don't need to apologize for anything," I say.

I let my arrow fly. It hits with perfect aim, sinking into where Kud's heart must be, but he lifts his arm as if batting away a fly. The arrow clatters to the floor.

"Do not bother with such trinkets. Unlike Haemosu, I do not have a heart. I am purely spirit. I exist on the darkness this land provides."

Michelle whimpers and tears stream down her cheeks from panicked eyes. I should never have let her get involved. This is all my fault.

As if reading my thoughts, Kud says, "Insurance policy, as you humans like to phrase it. Two are more useful than one."

"Where is Marc?" I demand.

"Somewhere." He laughs again, as if this is a game that he's been anxious to play for some time. I attempt to mask the dread that I'm sure is filling my face. How can I stop this monster?

"Hand over the orb and all will be as you wish."

"I won't negotiate with Michelle bound and held hostage," I say. "You must let her go and return her to Seoul."

Kud's form grows, expanding before my eyes. His hood falls back enough that I can see his gaping mouth. A piercing growl emanates from him, and the sickle lying by his throne sails to his fingertips. He pounds the ground with its hilt. The floor shudders, and the hounds howl in response, shaking their heads. Sweaty blood slobber flings across the stone floor.

"Who do you think you are?" he asks. "Your games were once fun, but I know every secret you bear. Do not forget your place, human. I never take no as an answer, and you have tried my patience too long."

In horror, I watch his sickle spin in his palm and lift above his head. Fumbling, I grasp for my orb, which somehow has hidden itself back beneath my shirt. I clamp my fingers around it. An explosion of light bursts from the orb, and like a bolt of lightning, it hits the sickle.

The tentacles release Michelle from the pillar and shove her forward, so she meets the tip of the sickle and it cuts into her chest. Her scream pierces the air, shattering my soul.

She latches hold of the sickle and rips it out of the tentacle's grasp. Then she spins around and plunges it into the hound beside her. The dog shrieks and collapses to the floor before evaporating to dust.

"No!" Kud rages. "How dare you destroy one of my beloved creatures?"

Michelle leans over the sickle, gasping, and glares at Kud. "Go to hell where you all belong."

The tentacles flock her, grasping for the sickle. She tries to fight for it but collapses to the floor. I'm at Michelle's side, dragging her slumped body into my arms. I see nothing but darkness around me. My whole focus is Michelle, the orb illuminating her perfect face. It's ashen now. Her lips tremble and her eyes widen with fear. She gasps, as if breathing is too difficult to bear.

Blood gushes from the wound in her chest. My hands flutter over her body, my mind reeling.

"You were my best friend," she whispers. "I'm glad you told me your secret."

I shake my head, damned tears streaming down my face. "I'm going to save you. Just hold on for a little longer."

"Don't give him what he wants," she gasps. Her eyes bulge. "You have to destroy him."

"Please. No. Don't go!"

"The swords." Her voice is thinner than air. I press my ear to her lips. "He fears them."

Her body shudders, and her grip tightens on my arm. And then she lets me go, and her body sags against the floor. Her glassy eyes stare into the darkness, and I know she's gone.

CHAPTER 38

"It seems you must learn the hard way," Kud says.

He hovers not far away, as if eager to watch Michelle take her last breath. Her body lifts from the ground and swirls in a circle. I latch on to her, wrenching her body to me. The pull is too strong. Her arm slips from my fingers. Screams fill the hall. They're mine, as the pain hurtles through me in wave after wave. Higher and higher she lifts, and then she's gone, vanishing into thin air.

I drop to the ground, sobs racking my body. She didn't deserve to die. She didn't deserve to meet evil and confront it alone. My hand scrapes across something hard on the floor. It's Michelle's butterfly clip, sparkling in the orb's light. I clasp it in my palm and press it to my chest.

"How could you?" I grit my teeth. "She was innocent."

"Hand over the orb."

"Never."

"It appears you will also be the one to watch him die," Kud says, his voice booming loud as if talking to someone else.

With dread, I scan the room, trying to figure out who he's talking to. That's when a burst of fire rises from the floor, creating a wall barring me from the other side of the room. The shadows hovering in the corners are now illuminated in shades of red, flickering over a long row of bodies chained to the wall. All are skeletons except one that appears to still be rotting.

And Marc.

I didn't think the pain tearing at my insides could get any worse. Marc's tangled hair hangs over his eyes, and a jagged cut runs along his jawline, blood trailing down his neck. Without his shirt on, I can see the tattoo clearly, now almost radiating from his skin. The inky vine is an inch from his heart. Though his mouth is bound, I can read the pain mixed with anger flashing through his green eyes.

I shake my head. "No, no, no." My words come out anguished, pain-ridden, and desperate. But I can't just watch Kud gloat. I think back to the time I golfed with Dad and how he said all that mattered was what was inside of us. But here in this place, facing Kud, those words feel petty, childish, useless. How could anything inside me overcome this?

"What will be your choice?" Kud asks. "I will not stop with the deaths until you give me what is mine."

"Never."

I grasp the orb. Its power surges through me, spreading from my palms through my arms, and awakening every nerve in my body. My skin twists and pulls. I don't even wait for the full transformation. I sprint toward Kud, and as I do, my body bursts into the form of a white tiger. My paws eat up the ground in seconds and I'm leaping, claws outstretched, toward this demon. My roar fills the room.

Kud dives away with his mouth open in surprise. I fall on him, snapping at his neck, ripping at his cloak. Darkness slips around my body, and despite the brightness of my fur, I'm drowning in an endless nothing. His tentacles wrap around me, choking my neck, twisting around my paws. I snarl and flip in resistance, but here in this endless darkness, I can't find him. Kud's cords pull and tear at me everywhere.

That's when I see it: the Red Phoenix. It flies at me, claws outstretched. I roar, but with the bonds strapping me down, I can't leap in attack. The phoenix dives at me, eyes dripping blood, and its claws rip across my mane and down my back. That pain in my back from my fall off the *imoogi* pricks at the base of my spine, and inch by inch it returns, burning like fire and creeping its way up my back, immobilizing me. I flick my head and clamp down on a tentacle, ripping it in half, refusing to allow the agony to stop me.

But I can't hold on any longer. The phoenix had known exactly where to attack me. That hadn't been an accident.

Soon I'm unable to move. I'm falling again until my head smashes onto the ground. When I open my eyes, I'm lying in a pool of blood. I groan as I survey the giant gash down both sides of my face, down my neck and back. Yet even with the blood streaming down my body, the rest of my skin sparkles like snow on a bright day.

The bloodhounds grovel at my feet, their muzzles pressed to the ground, whimpering from the blinding light of the orb dangling from my chest. A sharp guttural growl erupts from Kud, and he almost smiles.

"Look at you lying there, hopeless. You and your White Tiger orb are nothing compared to me," he says. "Even with an icon of such power, you are powerless. Hand it over. You don't deserve it."

A shot of light breaks from the orb across the expanse of the chamber to the throne. The orb must be trying to tell me something. A hint of steel glints from the tangle of the black iron throne. *What could that be?*

Kud spins around to follow the light's trail. Before he can react, I whip out my bow, and despite my bloody hands, I unleash another arrow into the spot highlighted by the beam.

"Stop!" Kud yells out.

He flings a finger at me. The tentacles swarm my body, like a nest of snakes. Burning, strangling as they twine their way up my body. Even still, Kud's not fast enough, because my arrow has pierced the iron. An explosion of color erupts from the throne. Smoke billows into the air, and with a resounding clatter, two swords tumble to the floor. The swords I gave to Marc.

The hounds resume their barking, teeth bared. The tentacles snarl around my waist, my stomach. I can't feel my legs any longer. I'm sure if the tentacles weren't so tightly woven around me, my legs would buckle from the numbness.

I twist so that I'm facing Marc now. Fear claws my stomach. Choosing not to free myself from the tentacles is a risk. The darkness is so thick I can practically taste it, bitter and burning. I aim, worrying that I'll miss, which makes my fingers twitch.

But there isn't time for hesitation. The tentacles squeeze around my chest, clawing for the orb.

I draw back on the string and release my arrow. I send out a prayer as it flies across what feels like forever. The tentacles crush my ribs, and pain shoots through my rib cage as if someone had stabbed me. The sound of my ribs cracking mixes with the snarl of the hounds. My bow drops from my hand as I reach for the orb, doubling over in agony.

This can't be happening.

Breathing is next to impossible, and my vision blurs. The orb pulses in my palm, warm and reassuring. I strike it to the tentacle wrapped around my chest, and with a sizzle, the orb burns my bonds. Smoke curls around me. With a swoosh, the tentacled cords tumble away from my body and snake back toward Kud.

I crumble to the ground, my vision swimming. I press my palms to the floor, trying to focus on Marc. But when I search for where he was hanging, I see he's no longer there. Panic ricochets through me.

I look up just as Kud raises his sickle above me, the tip glistening.

"Hand it over," he says, in a booming voice.

"The dragons said the orb would stay with me even into death."

Then I spot Marc racing across the hall, a sword in each hand. With a cry, he charges, lifting both swords, aiming for Kud.

CHAPTER 39

Kud spins. His sickle clashes against the swords. Fire sparks around them. Undaunted, Marc pushes back with one sword while driving the other into Kud's belly. Kud screeches in agony but twists his sickle until its tip points at Marc's chest.

I want to tell Marc to stop. That he will get killed fighting Kud, an immortal. But I am in awe of Marc's fighting skills. I had no idea he was so good.

Marc shoves against Kud's weapon and stabs another blow into Kud's form. Again, Kud reacts in pain, hissing. There must be something magical about these swords. Somehow I stand, trying to think of what I can do to help.

I clutch the orb once again. The power of it rushes through me, almost overwhelming. My body tingles, and my ribs push back into place. At the same time, it's too hot. Searing pain courses through my mind, and my head throbs so hard, I let the orb fall back against my chest so I can press my hands to the sides of my head.

This must be what Samshin warned me about. Drawing too much power from the orb would eventually kill me. Without immortality, the orb is more than I can bear. But how do I make that choice to become immortal? She never explained that.

Marc screams. Kud's hounds have surrounded him, biting at his ankles, and he falters, sweat beading on his forehead. He's beyond deathly pale, more like ghostly. I focus the orb's power through me to shove the hounds away.

With a desperate cry, Marc hurls the swords through the air. I watch as they spin toward me like shooting stars. I reach out for them, crying out from the pain in my ribs. Their magic sends them sliding into my hands. I swoop them before me in a side-cut, feeling the power of their blades.

"Let him go," I say.

"With every treasure comes a cost," Kud says. "He will die, and then your father will be next."

I charge at him, screaming at the top of my lungs. I twist both swords in the overhand, back-cut move. He lunges at me, but I parry with a twist of my wrist. His sickle suddenly erupts into a fiery blaze, and I'm startled enough that my movements falter. How do I defeat such a weapon?

Darkness surrounds me, so that I see nothing other than Kud's sickle streaking toward me and my own two swords blocking the cut. I spin and dive, breathless as I barely miss each blow that Kud hammers into me.

I move just fast enough to cross-block a massive blow that sends me to my knees. The sickle presses down on me. I push my swords against it, groaning against his power. Something slides and curls around my ankles and up my legs once again. My stomach turns as I realize his tentacles are at work.

A hound dives through the darkness and sinks its teeth into my shoulder. I cry out in pain as my left arm goes numb. One sword clatters to the ground, and I know I'm defenseless against Kud. For all my weapons, I am a mere mortal. I'm sure Kud will thrust his sickle through my heart, but he turns and looms over Marc. I watch in horror as the sickle bears down on Marc, perfectly aimed at his chest.

"No!" I scream, holding my hands up, dropping the other sword. "I will negotiate!"

The sickle halts, the tip cutting Marc's skin. Blood trickles out of the wound. Marc staggers backward, panting. The poison must be too much for him. I'm desperate to run to him and pull him into my arms, but that won't save him. Kud's hood shifts until it faces me.

"Negotiate, you said?" He cocks his head.

I glare. "Yes."

"I am not so keen on negotiation. This had better be interesting. You still have a number of family members that could become instrumental in persuading you to hand over your little trinket."

"Let him go and I accept your proposition."

"Remind me of which proposition you refer to."

"I will join you."

"Jae!" Marc says, breathlessly. "Don't do it. He'll just kill us anyway."

"How pathetic," Kud says. "Only after complete desperation do you agree to my proposal. Besides, why should I trust you? You have gained some notoriety for slaying immortals."

"Accept my proposal, or I will use the power of this orb," I say. "Too much will kill me. If that happens, you will never get this orb or its power."

"Haven't you grown clever?" Kud presses the sickle tip deeper into Marc's skin.

"So your answer is no," I say and grab the orb.

"I didn't say that."

"Your actions do," I snap.

Slowly, Kud pulls away his sickle. "How do I know you won't run off and change your mind?"

"As long as you don't touch my family members or friends, the agreement is on."

Kud pounds the end of his sickle on the floor. "I like this."

The ground cracks from the impact. The tentacles from his robe swirl about him until a long rice paper roll, a traditional brush, and an ink bottle flutter before me. Words blaze in fire over the paper. I read it carefully. It's a contract.

> I ______ (Princess Jae Hwa of Haemosu's realm) do agree to enter Kud's service. In turn I ______ (Kud, master of the realm of darkness) agree not to kill or kidnap any of Jae Hwa's relatives or friends.

"There is no time limit here," I point out. "I want out after a year."

"Pff," Kud snorts. "A year? Hardly. You are mine forever. Letting this idiot free is no small gift. Are not your friends and family worth your life?"

My hand shakes as I grab the brush pen. *This is the right thing to do*, I tell myself. But still, it feels wrong. So very, very wrong.

"Don't do this, Jae!" Marc screams. "I'm begging you. If you love me, you won't do this."

"I love you, too," I say. "That's why I have to do it."

"There's got to be another way," Marc says. "Tell her, Kud. Give her another option. This isn't an option."

"We went over my conditions already," Kud says. "This is ridiculous."

"I won't be the one responsible for your death," I tell Marc. "I have to live with the guilt of knowing Michelle died because I wasn't strong enough to stop her from getting involved. Her death is on me. I can't have yours be, too."

"What about your dad?" Marc says. "And grandfather?"

"You will be dead to them," Kud says. "But they will be alive to you. They must not know you live."

I drop the brush. "They will think I've died?"

"This is my way."

"That is hardly a fair deal," Marc says, eyeing the swords, but then he sags to the ground, releasing a frustrated growl as if that final stand against Kud was too much for him.

I eye the paper, imagining Dad, alone on the couch, waiting up for me. And me never coming home. Grandfather will finally break the news to Dad that I'm dead. I think of his golf balls, motivational posters, and origami creatures. My throat burns as I try to hold back my tears. I don't know if either of them will recover. My death alone might kill them.

"I won't sign this unless you promise I can visit my family and Marc," I say. "Every week."

"You will have every finery I can offer in my world. But your family will be off-limits to you. I may offer rewards for good behavior from time to time."

I press my hands over my eyes. What should I do? Who is faced with this kind of decision?

"I grow weary of your ways, Princess! Decide now."

I search my brain for an answer. I look to the orb for guidance, but it doesn't shine its light. I'm alone in this. This is the only way to keep Marc and my family safe without handing over the orb to Kud. Kud may think he has power over me, but I will never let him. I promise myself that.

"I'm sorry, Marc." My tears finally break free. "Sometimes losing is the only way. The only power we have."

I pick up the brush, dip it into the ink, and sign my name.

EPILOGUE

The wind cuts across my cheeks, cold despite this spring day, as I stand on the bald summit of Seorakson Mountain. It's a narrow crag, but wide enough for a few hikers to stand and see the view of endless mountains, swooping in jagged summits one after the next all the way into North Korea. A mist weaves through the dagger-spiked peaks. I breathe it all in.

I hear him hiking up the path, rocks tumbling in his wake. My body tenses, and I pray he's come alone. But I have nothing to worry about. It's only Marc climbing up the last rope that will lead him to me. I check my watch, already feeling the minutes ticking away.

Once he's scrambled up, he pauses, his eyes taking me in. I search his face for a sign of how he feels about us. His eyes are guarded, wary. Fear clamps my heart. Does he still love me? I follow his gaze to my tight black pants and black turtleneck top. My hair is braided down my back to keep it out of my face. I wonder if he even recognizes me.

"I miss you," he says.

He misses me.

I almost smile, but then I remember. He should forget my existence. Michelle's death still tortures me, and I wallow in it because I deserve nothing but misery. The distance between Marc and me might be a few feet, but it feels like an eternity. We are worlds apart.

"I miss you, too." I swallow the ache in my throat.

"Are you okay?" he asks.

No, I'm not. "Yes, I'm getting used to it."

He looks away, focusing on the mist curling at our feet. "You've never been a good liar. I'm surprised Kud allowed this. Good behavior?"

"Yeah." I grimace. "Something like that. How are my dad and Haraboji?"

"Your funeral is next week." He lets out a long breath. "I think your grandfather suspects something."

I close my eyes, hating how I'm bringing them both so much pain. It's almost too much to bear, and the weight of it all presses down on me.

"Hold my hand." I reach for him. His hesitation stabs me. Yet through the strain and uncertainty, our hands find each other's. His warmth against my cold.

"I'm going to find a way to get you out of there," Marc says.

"No, you're not." My fingertips find his face, and I trail the scar along his jawbone. "You're going to stay alive. If things go well, we can meet again."

But I know the truth. He must move on. Find a new girl. Because for his safety, I must be dead to him now. I check my stopwatch.

"Fifteen seconds." I can't hide the panic in my voice.

"I love you," he whispers into my ear.

His lips find mine, and for a moment, our worlds collide. I clutch his jacket with both hands, clinging to our every second.

Then I feel Kud's pull. I'm ripped from Marc's arms, and a tunnel of stars and emptiness swirls around me, yanking me back into Kud's lands. The last image I have of Marc is the pain carved on his face, the hardness of his jaw, and the spark in his green eyes. Our moment has vanished, leaving me once again alone with only the darkness for company.

My arms never stop reaching for him.

GLOSSARY

ajusshi—man older than you

annyeong haseyo—hello (formal)

annyeong kyeseyo—goodbye

Black Turtle—guardian of the north and of rain

Blue Dragon—guardian of the west and of the clouds

Bonghwang—mythological bird with the beak of a rooster, face of a swallow, forehead of a fowl, neck of a snake, breast of a goose, back of a tortoise, hindquarters of a stag, and tail of a fish

Bulgae—Kud's bloodhounds

Chollima—winged horse

dak-gangjeong—sweet-and-sour fried chicken

dalgyal gwishin—a ghost with a featureless egg-like head

Dano Festival—holiday that falls on the fifth day of the fifth month of the lunar Korean calendar

dobok—Tae Kwon Do uniform

dojang—training center for Tae Kwon Do

dokkaebi—gremlin, trickster

Eereumee muhyehyo?—What's your name?

goong dae—quiver for arrows

Guardians of Shinshi—an ancient sect of warriors dedicated to protecting Korea

Gwanghwamun—downtown Seoul

gwishin—a ghost

Haechi—legendary creature resembling a lion; a fire-eating dog; guardian against disaster and prejudice

Haemosu—demigod of the sun

hanbok—traditional Korean dress

haraboji—grandfather

imoogi—half-dragon that must wait a thousand years to become a real dragon; some are good while others are evil

kalbi—grilled beef or pork

kimbap—Korean dish of steamed white rice and other ingredients rolled in sheets of dried seaweed and served in bite-sized slices

kimchi—spicy pickled cabbage; the national dish of Korea

King Daebyeol—ruler of the Underworld

komo—aunt on the father's side

Kud—god of darkness

kumiho—fox-tailed female shape-shifter

Kukkiwon—the world headquarters for Tae Kwon Do

Kumgangsan—the Diamond Mountains; a tourist region in North Korea where Kuryong Falls is located

Kuryong—Nine Dragons

mool gwishin—ghost of one who was drowned by water

odaeng—fish skewers

ondol—under-floor heating system

Oryonggeo—Haemosu's chariot, drawn by five dragons

pagoda—temple or sacred building, typically a many-tiered tower

Palk—sun god and founder of the realm of light

Red Phoenix—guardian of the south and of fire

Princess Yuhwa—demigoddess of the willow trees

samjoko—three-legged crow; symbol of power and of the sun

Samshin—goddess of life and childbirth

Seijak—begin

Tiger of Shinshi—protector of the Golden Thread that ties and binds the Korean people throughout time

umma—mom

White Tiger—Guardian of the west and of the winds

won—the basic monetary unit of North Korea and South Korea

yo—Korean mattress that easily rolls up

Yonsei University—one of the most prestigious universities in Korea

ACKNOWLEDGMENTS

To God, for holding my hand through this entire journey.

Thanks to the teachers, librarians, booksellers, and readers across the world who have supported the Gilded series. It is through you that Jae Hwa's story unfolds.

I would like to thank Sally and Nick Corben for their help and support for all things related to Gilded's world.

A big shout-out to my second-grade teammates at Keene's Crossing Elementary: Diana Hammond, Jessica Reimann, Amanda Lewis, Becky Wesolowski, Angela Connell, Linnell Koffarnus, Becki Evans, Lisette Andreani, and our amazing media specialist, Jennifer Drone. Not only do you make awesome shirts, but you're the most supportive group anyone could dream of.

To Sara Schmidt for her Skype chats concerning TB clinics in North Korea. Your firsthand accounts were invaluable to the North Korea scenes. You're a true friend—even oceans and continents can't break us apart.

To Cliff Nielsen, who nailed another gorgeous cover. Your talent blows my mind.

I keep pinching myself that the Gilded series landed in such a supportive and wonderful publishing team with Skyscape. They are rock stars, and I know readers would never discover *Silvern* without them: Courtney Miller, Timoney Korbar, Erick Pullen, Andrew Keyser, Deborah Bass, Kyra Freestar, and Katrina Damkoehler.

No journey is complete without writing friends. Big hugs to Beth Revis for your unwavering support and answering those five million questions. Amy Christine Parker, I have a feeling our escapades are just beginning. And Vivi Barnes, I love our get-togethers! To the MiG Writers and OneFours for being my sounding board and go-to peeps.

Silvern wouldn't have made it to my editor's desk without the critiquing superpowers of Debbie Ridpath Ohi, Andrea Mack, Kate Fall, Casey McCormick, Emily Lloyd-Jones, and Larissa Hardesty. I'm so lucky to have you guys!

To my agent, Jeff Ourvan, who is always an e-mail away (even when he's out on those secret missions), thanks for all those emergency reads, keeping my sanity, and guiding my career.

Thanks to my fantastic editor, Miriam Juskowicz, for always asking the right questions and making my writing deeper and richer. You brought my words to life, and I will never forget that.

This whole publication process has shown me what an amazing family I am a part of. I am appreciative of Mom, Dad, David, and Julianne, and thankful you are with me along each step of the way. I love you guys!

The dragons are for you, Caleb, and the dueling swords are for you, Luke. I love you both so much, and I can't wait to watch the story of your lives unfold.

And lastly, but most importantly, to the guy I'm still wildly in love with—Doug. Let's never stop creating new adventures.

ABOUT THE AUTHOR

©Liga Photography

Christina Farley was born and raised in upstate New York. As a child, she loved to explore, which later inspired her to jump on a plane and travel the world. She taught at international schools in Asia for ten years, eight of which were in the mysterious and beautiful city of Seoul, Korea, that became the setting of the Gilded series. Currently she lives in Clermont, Florida, with her husband and two sons—that is until the travel itch whisks her off to a new unknown.